VEIL OF TIME

I had anticipated finding Uastis, but she had grown more astute with the years, the sum of my whole lifetime . . . She had twice my years, but she looked, as I had suspected she would, far older. Her face was, as ever, covered with a veil of heavy white silk. Yet her arms and throat were bare, and the long talons of her hands were enamelled the color of dying fire.

I could say no word. I had sworn to slay her when I discovered her, but I was helpless. Her voice was young and fresh and beautiful:

"I was rid of your father by means of my hate. You also I may kill. Unless you consent to serve me."

I could speak. I said, "If you wanted my service, you should have kept me by you."

"You were his curse on me," she said.

"And I am still!" And my hand shot out and snatched the veil from her face.

I jumped backwards with my eyes starting from their sockets. It was not a woman's face at all, but the head of a white lynx. . . .

QUEST FOR THE WHITE WITCH

by

Tanith Lee

DAW BOOKS, INC.
DONALD A. WOLLHEIM, PUBLISHER

1301 Avenue of the Americas
New York, N.Y. 10019

Cover art by Gino D'Achille.

FIRST PRINTING, FEBRUARY 1978

1 2 3 4 5 6 7 8 9

PRINTED IN U.S.A.

Contents

Prologue

Previously*, I have recounted how I spent my youth among the tribal krarls of the Red Dagkta. How I was named Tuvek and believed myself the son of Ettook, the krarl's chief, and his out-tribe wife, Tathra. How I was tattooed in the Boys Rite, when the tattoos did not remain on my skin I must fight grown men to prove myself—which skirmish I won and to spare, earning thereby the enmity of the krarl's stinking seer, Seel. Neither did Ettook much like me, though he told me to pick a gift from his treasure chest. I chose a silver lynx mask, because it was workmanship of the old cities—his prize. I became a warrior of the krarl, unequalled and fighting-mad, yet I was dissatisfied with my life, not knowing why. My flesh had a strange knack of healing. No wound festered; I even survived the bite of a venomous snake.

When I was nineteen, the krarls were at a Spring Gathering when we were attacked by city-men and their cannon. These cities lay over the mountains, ancient, corrupt and decayed. The folk there went masked, man or woman—only our females hid their faces in the shireen—and supposed themselves descended from a god-race, superior to humanity. They captured many of our men in their raid, and bore them off to be slaves.

I alone dared follow, with rescue and loot in mind. However, near the raiders' camp, a strange force seemed to take possession of me. I found I could speak the city tongue. More, the raiders mistook me for another, a man they feared and named Vazkor. It was easy to free their captives and slaughter the city-men in their alarm. Among their pavilions I

* *Vazkor, Son of Vazkor* by Tanith Lee

discovered a gold-haired city girl whom I greatly fancied, and carried home with me to the krarl. Here, I interrupted my own Death Rites—to the dejection of Seel and Ettook.

I came to love my city girl, Demizdor, and she to love me, despite her contempt for my tribal origins. Soon I wed her. She was much superior to my krarl wives, Chula and the rest.

I had neglected my mother, Tathra, who alone, formerly, I had cared for. She was heavy with Ettook's child, and presently bore the thing and died of it. On the night of Tathra's death, Kotta, the krarl healer, told me this: That I was not, after all, the son of Tathra and Ettook, but of a white-haired city woman—she whose silver lynx mask Ettook had taken. This woman had given birth about the time that Tathra had, But Tathra's child died. The tent being empty, the city woman had substituted for the dead baby her unwanted one: myself. This story I credited when Kotta told me the white woman claimed to have killed her husband, a sorcerer and city king, by name Vazkor.

In a turmoil of grief and arrogance, I meant to slay Ettook. But another peculiar power came to me, and I struck him down with a white lightning that burst from my brain. However, I could not control this phenomenon, which overwhelmed me too. When I recovered my senses, I was helplessly bound and about to be executed by the krarl, Demizdor, too, when they were done raping her. It was Sihharn Night, when reputedly ghosts walked. But the ghostly riders who entered the krarl were Demizdor's city kin. She, they saved. Me, they also took. Believing me the son of the hated Vazkor, they would make a spectacle of me in their city of Eshkorek.

Vazkor had been creating for himself an empire, which crumbled at his death, bringing war and ruin to the cities. Uastis had been his wife, an albino sorceress, believed by some to be a reincarnated goddess of the old Lost Race. She had murdered Vazkor, escaping herself. These then: my father and my mother.

Now the cities existed in poverty-ridden luxuriousness, tended by a dark ugly slave-people. The lords of Eshkorek were hot for second-hand vengeance on Vazkor, through me. But I healed fantastically of the grim wounds they gave me, without even a scar, and was taken under the dubious protection of Prince Erran. To the amazement of all, I instinctively understood and could speak and read the language of the cities. I concluded this was due to my magician father's blood in me. I was treated well enough, and, despite despising them, came to enjoy the things of Eshkorek, their books and music, their arts for battle and for the bed. My ancestry seemed to surface in me. I was no longer the tribal savage, but what they called me, Vazkor, son of Vazkor. But Demizdor had begun to hate me again, for her treatment by the braves, and because her proud kin regarded me as a barbarian and this shamed her.

At her instigation, one of her princely lovers let loose on me a demented horse. Its madness came from poison he had given it, but, astonished, I found myself able to heal the animal. In my rage, though, I killed Demizdor's prince. I was instantly imprisoned and promised a grisly death. However, Demizdor, relenting, enabled me to get away via an underground route which led from the city and beyond the mountains. Her plots had cured my love, yet I asked her to accompany me, for her own safety. She refused.

The tunnel opened into a vast subterranean concourse built by the Lost Race. Perversely, in view of its magnificance, they had named it SAVRA LFORN—Worm's Way. Here I saw frescoes of this magician people performing miracles—walking on water, in sky flight, and so on. Many were albino, like Uastis, some were very dark, as my father had been, as I was. One other fact became clear. The Lost neither ate nor drank, nor did they need to relieve themselves—the wretched latrines were plainly for their human slaves.

Emerging above ground, pursuit followed me. The chase was led by Demizdor's kin, Zrenn and Orek. I killed most of their soldiers. One I slew by means of the white lightning Ettook had perished from—and, as then, I was debilitated by its use. I sought refuse in a krarl of the black people, by the sea, and discovered I could master their language, too. I assumed I had inherited all these powers from my father.

Peyuan, the krarl's chief, spoke to me of my mother, for she had come among his folk after leaving Ettook's krarl. His words confused me. Though he had only seen her masked—I had met none who had seen her face—he told me she was beautiful, charismatic, yet a gentle friend who had saved his life. I inwardly rejected his version. Peyuan advised me to seek refuge from the city-men on a small island, invisible from the shore. This I did, accompanied by Peyuan's daughter, Hwenit. She was the healer-witch of the krarl, and went with me in order to make jealous her half-brother, whom she loved, scorning his scruples against incest.

On the island, Hwenit, who was cunning, schooled me usefully in my own psychic abilities. Yet she made a fire-magic by night to witch her brother. The fire was spotted by enemies, and soon Zrenn and Orek ambushed me, having been rowed to the island in a stolen boat by their dark slave. In the ensuing fight, Hwenit was viciously stabbed by Zrenn. But I mesmerized this bastard, using my powers, and killed him. Orek chose suicide, having told me Demizdor had hanged herself. I was burdened by this onerous news, but the dark slave galvanized me into action. He had formerly seen me strike the man dead with the white light—now the slave, Long-Eye, reckoned me a sorcerer-god. He expected I would heal Hwenit, who was near death. I had healed the horse in Eshkorek, and a child in the black krarl, but I was unsure. Still resolved to try, and indeed, I saved Hwenit and she lived.

Stunned at the magnitude of my 'sorcery', I faltered. I had reached a hiatus in my life. Earlier, I had sworn a secret oath to Vazkor that I would avenge his death on Uastis, the white witch. I too had a score to settle—my desertion, the king's birthright she had deprived me of. Now, I resolved to seek the bitch. In a moment of prescience, I ascertained I must travel east, then southward, across the sea.

Long-Eye, electing me his new master, took me to Zrenn's stolen boat, and we put out on to the morning ocean.

What follows is the second portion of my narrative. . . .

BOOK ONE

Part I

Great Ocean

1

The boat Zrenn had chosen to steal was a skiff, very similar to Qwef's craft, but capable of sail. The slave had stepped the mast and unfurled the coarse-woven square, rigging it to catch the ragged morning wind that came slanting from the mainland far behind. He told me after, for he was unusually talkative to me, how his people sailed back and forth over a wide blue river in the course of trading. They understood ships and boats in the same way they understood gods—a hereditary oblique wisdom, passed from father to boy. This blue river lay a million miles distant west and north; he had sculled there in his childhood before the slave levy fell due and he, along with countless others, was taken to black Ezlann, later bartered to So-Ess and finally absorbed, via a raid, into Eshkorek Arnor.

Long-Eye was four years my senior and looked old enough to have sired one twice my age. He said the girls of his people were nubile at nine or ten; many had borne babies at the age of eleven; even among the tribes, this would have been considered forward. Not surprisngly, the poor wenches were used up before they reached twenty, wizened hags at twenty-five, and dead most often a couple of years later. The men fared not much better. An elder of forty was unusual and greatly revered. Their hair and the hair of their women commenced turning gray about the twentieth year. I saw some evidence of this, for, as Long-Eye's pate began to blossom into blue-black stubble, badger gray tufts sprouted along the ridge of his skull. Oddly, his face remained bald. I had occasion to envy that, as the thick growth of beard continued to push, itching, through my own jaw and upper lip.

Long-Eye raised the sail to catch the wind, put it to rest,

and took up the oars when the wind failed. At night we drifted, but by various sailors' tricks he kept abreast of the skiff's inclination and the mood of the sea. We must head east before south, his old map had told him. We baited lines with dead Zrenn's provender, and caught fish. There was even a fire-box in the boat on which to grill them, and two clay water bottles Long-Eye had replenished at the island spring.

I had lost my discomfort at the size of the ocean; yet the curious phenomena of the sea did not leave me untouched. The height of the sky, the large clouds at its edges, looking close enough to put your hand on; the light of a fine day penetrating liquid like glass; the shine of fish burning with their own cold fire in the darkness; the sea laced with phosphorous, the oars catching it, turned to silver.

Looking over my shoulder at this wild venturing of mine, I try to recall what I must have felt, having abandoned myself with such fatalistic, grim optimism to the unknown. I think my life had moved too swiftly for me, and I had not caught up. That would account, perhaps, for my complaisance and the curious, uneasy sense of waiting that lurked beneath it.

Five days went swimming by. The climate was deceptively, as I might have noted, threateningly mild. The sea went down under the skiff, blue-green and clear, into a shadowy weed-forest, peopled by fish.

Toward the end of that fifth day, just as the innocent sky was folding itself into a scarlet sunset, something loomed up on the sea's eastern edge, a bar of red-lighted cliff stretching north to south, and out of sight.

The wind had been dying, though the sea was heavy as syrup. Long-Eye unstepped the mast, and sculled. We reached the cliff wall as the last embers went out in the west. A rough escarpment led up from the sea; the base of the wall was clogged with the green hair of Hwenit's sea maidens: They must have enjoyed much love on the barren ridges. We hauled the boat aground for the night, and found birds visited there—one to its regret, since it provided dinner.

An oddity, that wall of rock, breaking the ocean end to end, as it seemed, yet only a mile or so wide. I climbed the bastion at moonrise and looked out to the east, beyond the barrier, at new miles of white-painted water and that other great ocean of stars. Perhaps a continent had sunk here, leaving only the tops of its highest mountains, transmuted ignominiously to cliff. I had been childishly expecting to reach new land every day, and thought this marvel to be the outpost of it.

At sunup, after a breakfast of eggs—two other potential birds that had lost out at a chance of life—we slid the boat back in the water. I took the oars, the god feeling in need of exercise; Long-Eye acted as lookout. Presently he located a curious hollow tunnel that passed through the cliffs to the open sea.

The sky was like the inside of a glazed pot. Little fine hairs of pale blue cirrus were all that disturbed its enamel perfection. The storm did not come that day but on the next.

The ocean, credited here and there with being female, has a woman's wiles and ways. She wants you to love her, but she wants your guts into the bargain. Man's weight and dominion of ships she bears with a honey groan, but soon she means to swallow you whole into the hungry, salty womb. At her most benign, she is promising a scourge.

That day of transcendent quiet ended with another crimson, copper sunset. Fish leaped from the swells, ruby plated along their backs, their wings spread as if they would fly up to the red clouds. Black night, with no wind, followed; next, a silver dawn, and still as metal. By midmorning every hair on my body was electric.

"What is it?" I said to Long-Eye.

"It has been too calm. A storm, perhaps."

I glanced around like an idiot, the way a man will, looking for something he wishes for but knows is not there. We were more than a day from land at back and none in sight before. It was hard to be sure, from Long-Eye's wooden manner, what variety of rough weather threatened, yet the feel of the air was bad.

Presently the sky darkened to an iron green.

"She is coming," Long-Eye said.

I never in my life had met so briefly ominous a sentence.

This was where my blind quest had brought me, my dream of power that would lead me straight to the goal, unhindered.

Long-Eye's face, more than wooden, was serene. He was safe, being with a god.

"Long-Eye," I remarked, "are you supposing I am about to work a wondrous spell to subdue the elements?"

He shrugged, and this supernatural, indifferent confidence shattered the last vestige of my lethargy.

Then the storm came, the hurricane.

The voice of the wind swept toward us over the sucking roll of the waves. It was like the howling of an enormous flesh-and-blood voice box—and made less pleasing by this resemblance to something human or animal—growing impossibly larger and more imminent with each second. Such a noise had no place in the real world, but it was unmistakably here. It was the kind of clamor to run from, save there was no place to hide. Then a tree of lightning flooded up the shadow sky, branches and claws slitting the overcast from horizon to horizon. From the lightning's roots sprang the storm itself, a sheet of solid yet preposterously volatile lead, that smote the skiff one hammer blow straight on her back. She leaped, as the flying fish had leaped, as if to get free.

The sea hit me. My mouth was full of water. I tried to take a breath and that was water, too.

The wave passed on with another riding behind it. The boat bravely attempted to chase up the length of it. The vast swell—black shot with green like a bolt of rotting Eshkirian silk—slammed under the keel. The skiff swung, poised on her tail, and capsized.

So the invincible god was to be drowned after all. The invincible god could not swim.

The black water gushed up over my head; I was bottled in it. My panic was indescribable; there was no sequence as I thrashed and choked in that stranglehold of heaving ink.

Long-Eye, taught to swim strongly in a poisonous blue river one swallow of which meant death, hauled me up. He dragged my hands together around the floating mast.

A moment of precious air was followed by fifty seconds drowned in the vitals of a roller. The wind screamed in my eyes and ears.

Even through the dark, I had a glimpse of Long-Eye's face, as blank and noncommittal as I had ever seen it. When the next big breaker smashed over us, he clapped his palm across my mouth and nostrils and stopped me taking on a fresh lungful of water. With the cordage of the sail, he had lashed his left hand to the mast. Somehow, now, between the surges regular as heartbeats that thrust the sea at the sky, he contrived to lash my left hand also to this life raft.

"Fool," I said, "you chose the wrong master, fool of a slave."

By way of a change, the black sky fell down on the black sea.

The hurricane lasted in fact, in the first portion, for about three hours.

How we survived it, I had no notion. I quaffed deep of the sea, that much I knew, and brought it back again. The buffets of water and wind numbed me, though I felt my ribs crack in the old place. There was no feeling in my feet and legs up to the crotch, but there I had grown painfully erect as if the sea indeed would couch me. The flesh of my face was flayed like the hide of a whipped man. My hands turned blue as they grappled the mast, and the left wrist was braceleted where it was tied with my own raw, bloody meat. Long-Eye was in a similar case, or worse, his cheeks peeled open and half-blind. We learned soon enough that both his legs had been broken by the force of the waves.

But for his trick with the lashing, we should have been fathoms down some while before. Even with it, our bruised and battered carcasses were fair set for death. I had fed on fish, now fish should feed on me. Barely conscious, I clung to existence—the mast; survival reduced to pure stubbornness, abstract motives literally washed away.

After those three hours of hell (I reckoned the duration only later from the positions I had vaguely noted, when I could see them, of the sun), I appeared to myself to be drifting up into another sea, the water grown so level I thought it had congealed, so level it actually nauseated me after the turmoil that had preceded it, and to which I had grown accustomed. Then, lacking the frenzied beating of the sea, my numbness began to wear thin, revealing a hundred bursts of pain of variable intensity.

The hurricane seemed spent, the ocean abruptly flat, the sky pastel and very bright with low sun. The unnatural lull was, however, the vortex, the storm's eye that travels at its center—merely an interlude, the cat toying with the mouse.

This fact Long-Eye presently told me. Even in my half-wit state, his fortitude appalled me.

I glanced about, illogically glad of the lull despite its transience. The sun was lying over in the west, on my right hand now.

"If you are in the mood to curse me," I said, "do it."

My speech sounded like a drunkard's, blurred and thick.

"You will act when you are ready, lord," Long-Eye said imperturbably.

"When I am ready? Don't you see yet, fool's slave? I am incapable. Behold, I manumit you. Curse me."

He said, "Mast not enough to save us. Without the lord's power of will, we should not still be living."

Apparently he continued to believe I had illimitable abilities, yet did not reproach me for not using them. What he imagined me playing at, I cannot guess.

I rested my face on my arm over the mast. My mind was blank.

Suddenly, between one breath and the next, it reached me. It was like a voice calling, far back in my brain—*Here. Look for me here.*

All your life you must be ready to change course, open for it. Then, when the signal comes, you are prepared. When I was a boy in the krarl, learning to hunt or to ride and mainly my own teacher, for the environment was hostile to me, I must continually go over the actions of what I did: *Now, I set my hand so, and now my foot.* One day, a great surprise—I found I had done everything by instinct without thinking it through first: I had learned. Something like this occurred in the storm's eye, as I have later concluded. At the hour, it was as if a black window broke in me and radiance streamed through it, a revelation, such as men say they have of their gods or their destinies. It is only their own wisdom, maybe, catching up to them at last.

The light was bronze now, and the sides of the waves like jewelsmith's work, heavy seas of amber and beaten gold.

Something ran molten together in my chest. It was the break healing in my ribs. Dead flesh flaked from my face and hands, which had knit whole beneath. I broke the lashing on my left wrist. Then I did what magicians dream of. I got to my feet, easy as a man rises on a boat's deck. I stood upright on a floor of choppy brazen gold, and I walked on the ocean.

I analyzed this, after. When it occurred, a sort of aberration came with it, precluding reason. Analysis told me, however, only one fact. Belief is the root of this power. Not to tell yourself you may, but to know you *can.* I have journeyed far enough since, in the seasons of my life, to understand by now that the skill is not as exclusive as I then supposed it. The sorcerer-gods are only those born knowing the key to the brain's inner rooms. That is their luck, but beware—the meanest may search out the key, or stumble on it, and become gods also.

Having achieved one miracle, the rest seemed little more than a process of mathematics.

I kept my balance lightly, as a charioteer does, levitating

my body without effort, my feet braced on the smooth toiling of rollers. The sky was veiling again; the wind threatened from a different quarter.

I stared at sky, at sea, one with it, master of it.

Power gives wings, and fire. Power is the wine after which all other wine is mud. To control the raging elements becomes explicit and simple. Rope the wind, disperse in fragments the hurricane that bounds the vortex wall. Pressure to pressure, thigh against thigh, the mind wrestling briefly with the insensate motive of the storm. The blows are diverted and the vast forces quenched.

The hurricane died over the sea like a huge, ghostly bird.

Ultimately, the act had been swift, positive.

Behind the storm was a green cloud, out of which a quick rain fell. I could see Long-Eye, horizontal on his back, capturing sufficient of this rain in a leather water bottle of his own—the clay pots had been smashed and lost. I watched him with a certain prosaic interest. As I walked on the water.

Gulls flew over, refugees of the storm. The air was charged with ozone and a scent of iodine from floating stirs of ocean weed. Nothing seemed strange in the sunset; the apotheosis was in the man, not the world about him.

Long-Eye lay unprotesting and observed me till I should remember his plight. Gods were selfish, their right and their failing.

In the end, I collected myself and went to him.

I healed his broken limbs, the bruises and wounds at a touch, as before, feeling no virtue go from me. I asked him if he noted anything when I did this, any pain or curious sensation. I was hungry for facts, could not get enough of my talents. He said it was like a tremor of electricity disturbed in an animal's coat in summer, nothing more. I placed my fingers on his face to renovate the skin; he said it was like spiders running. His legs were stiff and needed massage before he could work them. Once he was able, I unstrapped him from the mast, and told him to get up and follow me.

His face, almost invisible now, for the night was black and the moon unrisen, scarcely altered.

"I am the lord's slave."

"If I tell you to do as I do, you shall manage it."

Left in the water any longer, he would die of it. His devastating trust, his human wits by which he had saved me, were things I prized with a sudden and emotional fervor new to me. I grasped his shoulders.

"You know I can equip you to do this."

"Yours is the cloak that covers me," he said. It was a ritual phrase out of some primeval and obscure ancestral past.

He let go the mast, the wood was mostly sponge by now, and set his hands out as if to balance himself. By his shoulders, I drew him up to stand, as I did, on that faintly swelling, calm night sea.

Thus we remained, between heaven and ocean, the clouds pouring slowly over above, the waves tilting gently beneath.

Long-Eye began to weep, without shame or restraint. Then he bared his teeth and threw back his head, staring up at the sky, grinning and crying. After a minute, he rubbed his palms over his face, and looked at me. He was again as passive as I had ever seen him, as if he had rubbed expression away with the tears.

I turned, and began to walk due east, the direction the storm had driven us to as if some fate were still in it. He followed me, as I had instructed. His faith never wavered. He fixed his eyes on my back and trod unerringly across the sea.

Now that I had a power beyond any man's hopes, beyond even my own, I felt neither confusion or excitement.

It was as if a million hands had clasped with mine, a million deep vaults given up their treasure and their secrets. A sense of omnipotent loneliness more absolute than the desert of space, a sense of omnipotent continuance more definite than if an army of my forebears had stretched away from me, each linked to each and culminating in this final existence which was mine.

Yet I was not thinking of my father. Neither did I think of her, the lynx woman, save as a lamp somewhere before me, which, armed with the thunder, I should one day extinguish as she had extinguished his dark light.

I was thinking of what was in me, truly, of my *self*.

Old beyond age, younger than the chick, I strode across a mosaic floor now black and silver, now splintering into yellow as the sun rose like a wheel from the east. The night had passed like a folded wing.

And I saw the ship on the farthest edge of distance, etched there, immobile, as if awaiting me, almost as I had seen it on the shore of the island, behind my eyes.

2

To the people of the southern ocean, the sea is the woman; what rides her and must be stronger than she, that is the man. So the ship was masculine that rode at anchor in the bright morning, storm-blown a great distance from the trading routes of the south.

He was a tall galley, this male ship, towering up from the water on his double oar-banks, twenty-five oars to a bank, fifty to a side, a hundred oars all told. The two high masts, stripped spar-naked after the hurricane, striped the dawn-burned sky.

When he sailed, he had been a brave sight, twenty-four man-lengths fore to aft, a vessel painted blue as a summer dusk over his ironwood planking, the prow gilded, and the vast curving whale's tail of the stern. The sails were indigo figured in ocher, with a triangular wind-catcher or shark's-fin sail at the stern. His name was written on his side in southern picture writing:

Hyacinth Vineyard.

He had gone west of north, the ship, swallowing up red amber and black pearls, jade, cloth, pelts, purple dye, and antique bronzes from the archipelagoes of Seema and Tinsen, before he turned for home.

One morning, out of sight of land, the wind dropped. The oar-slaves, every back scaled like the backs of reptiles from the beatings that fell on them like rain, day in and out, grunted and sweated up their hate and agony on the iron-bladed poles. It is the only death sentence that crucifies a man sitting, and may take ten years or more, if he is sufficiently tough and maddened, before it kills him.

The beautiful ship, courtesan-colored, pretty as a fancy boy and named for one, and for the earth rather than the sea, powered by a heaving of pain and fury in his oar-gripped bowel. He met the hurricane at midnight, the one stranger not to be bargained with.

A night and a piece of a day the galley fought the tempest.

The sails were taken in but presently broke lashings, rent,

and were stripped. The oars, unusable, were belayed. The rowers' station, though decked over, was nevertheless awash from the hatches, and dead men lay about in the untidy and unhelpful manner of the dead, for the overseer had tried to outrun the weather and paid for it by breaking the ribs and guts of others.

The ship staggered and wallowed at the mercy of the boiling cold sea and the black gale. He was well built for such work, or he would not have lasted.

About noon they passed into the cool eye of the storm. The sailors, of whom many were additionally slaves and recent landsmen, ignorant as I had been and thinking the fury done, lay facedown on the deck praising their amulets, as they had similarly lain wailing and puking at the storm's violence. Others, knowing this lull to be the vortex and worse to come, were for throwing the precious cargo overboard as offerings to the sea. The officers, their greed larger than alarm or superstition, decreed otherwise. The naval instruments were broken or mislaid; no coast was visible. The master took stock, unsparing of his amber-necked whip.

Even at the tumult's height this man, the master, Charpon by name, had been grim rather than disturbed. Charpon was a "Son of the New Blood," thus, however lowly, a bastard fragment of the elite, the ninety-year conquerors of the great city that was home to the ship. His emotions were limited to avarice, obscure but definite pride, a certain brutal, unimaginative intelligence, and a liking for the flesh of boys.

While the *Hyacinth Vineyard* hung gently rocking under him, oddly becalmed between the two walls of the hurricane, Charpon, his face like a fist, stood in the bow, whip in hand, on lookout for the returning storm. He was not thinking of death but rather of the abacus in his brain that was clicking away his profits in lost slaves, lost goods, a foundered vessel. He owned the ship; it represented the twelve years of his life he had labored to buy it.

Then, the hurricane failed them.

After two or three hours, the sky clearing into deep gold and the sea smoothing into a silk finer than the dyed stuff in the galley's holds, the crew descended to their knees once more to give thanks to the ocean.

Smoke was burned before an image in the raised forecastle. It was an effigy of copper, depicting a male warrior-god grasping lightnings and mounted astride a lion-fish with enameled wings of blue and green. This was the demon of waves, Hessu, the spirit revered by the Hessek sailors of the "Old" Blood. Charpon did not bother with it.

The ship put down anchor to lick his wounds. Parties were herded up to patch and hoist the sails, stop leaks with heated bitumen, and sling overboard the useless dead. The master and his seconds prepared for the task of plotting their course afresh.

The day went out in night. A watch was set about the vessel; ten exhausted men, still half afraid the hurricane might attack again like a tiger in the night, superstitiously telling the little red beads of Hessek prayer-necklaces, promising sweets to all the spirits ashore.

[illegible] sun, having circled under the sea, rose from it in the [illegible]ddenly one of the watch yelled out in terror, "S'wah [illegible] that roughly means, "May my gods guard me," and [illegible]ter repeated the plea with vehemence. A whistle was [illegible] and sailors came running. By now the watch had col-[illegible]sed on the deck, whining. Soon Charpon arrived, whip curled in hand.

"What does the piss-brain say?"

The sailors, having caught the plague of fright, yet aware of their master's irreligious and mundane preference, hesitated to tell. A kiss from the whip, however, loosened their tongues.

"Lauw-yess." (It was a Hessek word, expressive of respect and obedience.) "Ki says he saw a man, in the sea."

At this Ki, appearing demented, began to mutter and groan and shake his head.

Charpon struck him.

"Speak for yourself, worm."

"Not a man, Lauw-yess. A god. A god, the fire-god of the Kings—Masri, Masrimas, dressed in fiery flakes of the sun. I saw him, Lauw-yess, and he walked. He walked on the sea."

The sailors gave off a shuddering murmur.

Charpon gifted Ki a second blow.

"My crew has gone mad. Maggots in the head. There is nothing in the sea. Take this worm and shackle him below till the fit soaks out of him. He shall not feed or drink till he's sane again."

But, as they were taking the unfortunate Ki away, another of the watch shouted. Charpon's head jerked up. The sailors clustered at the rail, gabbling. This time, no sorcery. Two men, no doubt wrecked survivors of the storm, floating in the troughs, one splashing feebly to attract attention.

Charpon nodded. He did not see survivors but replacement oarsmen, if they lived. Some recompense, after all, to be measured on the clicking abacus in his head.

Knowing I might cross the water afoot, reach the vessel, observe some two hundred men stricken on their faces with alarm, or else riotous and searching out weapons with which to attack me, I had preferred discovery in the image of a helpless destitute. I had heard the man scream his terror from the side, and that had been warning enough. I lay down in the sea, and Long-Eye with me. Levitation had surmounted the need to swim. I buoyed us up and let the swells drift us toward the blue ship.

At length ropes were thrown us. We threshed a[illegible] dered and were dragged up the iron-wood planking[illegible] picture-writing of the galley's name, onto the deck.

Charpon's black shadow fell on us.

He was a tall man, the "New" conqueror blood showin[illegible] his height, huge bones, and russet skin. His hair was clipped and oiled until it resembled a cap of black lacquer. His teeth were white but unevenly set, like shards stuck haphazardly into cement. In his left ear hung a long, swinging earring in the shape of a golden picture symbol—the sign of Masrimas, the fire-god.

Charpon prodded me with the handle of his whip.

"Strong dogs," he said, "to have lasted the storm. We shall see." He fingered his earring and said to me, "Speak Masrian?"

"Some," I answered slowly, not wishing to seem too proficient, though Masrian came as easily to me as the other languages I had met. It was the conqueror tongue named, like the conqueror race, for their god. Charpon nodded at Long-Eye. "No," I said. "He is just my servant."

Charpon smiled dismissively. My days of possessing servants were obviously numbered.

"Where do you come from?"

I said, "Northward, and something westward."

"Beyond the wall of rock?"

I remembered the great cliffs across the sea. Probably the traders had heard of northlands, but had not gone so far for centuries.

"Yes, The shore of ancient cities."

"Ah." He seemed to recognize it, contemptuously. No

doubt he knew little of it, poor trading land, a jumble of barbaric tribes and ruins.

I could smell his rough cunning, his shrewd greed, foresaw, with no recourse to magic, that he would use me where and how he reckoned most profitable. And I wondered briefly if I could read his mind—I did not know my limits, my power might stretch to anything. Yet I shrank from that ultimate intrusion, that floundering among the swamps and sewers of another's brain, and did not attempt the feat. Reluctant as I was, I hardly think I could have managed it in any case.

Charpon did not seem inclined to question my grasp of the [illegible]asrian language. Probably he believed the whole world [illegible] speak it, to the greater glory of his illegitimate sires. [illegible]ed with the whip handle, and a sailor brought me a [illegible]ater with some bitter alcohol mixed in it. No offering [illegible]en Long-Eye; when I shared the ration with him, [illegible]n seemed tickled.

[illegible]e can't conduct you home," he said to me. "We make for the Sun's Road, the way to the capital of the south. You'd best come with us. It will broaden your experience, sir." He was attempting polite, sarcastic humor. His four seconds, well-dressed bullies, one missing an eye, grunted.

"I agree to that, but I can't pay you," I said. "Perhaps I can work my passage?"

"Oh, indeed you shall. But first, come to the ship-house, sir, and share my dinner."

His smiling and unlikely courtesy would have warned the slowest fool of tricks in the offing. Yet, in the capacity of intimidated flotsam, everything lost, adrift on his clemency, I thanked him and followed him, companioned by his bully boys, Long-Eye a pace behind me.

The ship-house lay aft, constructed of iron-wood and painted indigo, but the door was pure wrought iron with brass fitments. I could hardly resist the idea such a door had mutiny in mind. Inside was a great beamed room with plush couches built in along the walls, and piled with spotted and striped pelts, and cushions and drapes better suited to a brothel. A luxurious twist to Charpon's granite. I could picture the master lolling at his leisure, the incense burners smoking and his whip to hand, ready for action of one kind or another.

The obligatory statuette of Masrimas, gilded bronze, fine work, stood in an alcove looking on with eyes of nacre shell, a flame fluttering before it.

We sat at Charpon's table, I and the four seconds; Long-

Eye he let crouch near my chair on the rugs. Three youths brought the food. Conscripted in childhood for this hell of a life, they were bound to it for ten years by Masrian law unless they were sharp and desperate enough to run away in some port. Two were handsome under their dirt, and one knew his luck. He flirted a little, surreptitiously, with the Lauw-yess, brushing the master's arm with his body as he set down the platters in their scoops. Charpon pushed him aside, as if irritated by the proximity, but he was taking note. The boy was clever, if he could make it last. Though small and slight, of the old Hessek blood to judge by his sour-pale complexion, he had already got a Masrian name: Melkir. [illegible] looked at me with cultivated scorn, the precariously s[illegible] [illegible]ting himself from the damned.

[illegible]ds had fallen part-dead on the ship's deck [illegible] entered the storm's eye. The sailors had wr[illegible] and now served them up stewed. The worshipe[illegible] did not sully fire by putting carcasses in it to c[illegible] [illegible]eat boiled in water in a pot, or baked in a container, [illegible]wed, thus keeping it the required distance from the god.

Charpon urged me to gorge, for, as ever, I ate sparingly; he told me I must get back my strength. Yet, he remarked, I was certainly no weakling to have survived; my servant, too. How long had I been in the water? I told him some lie of the boat's capsizing later than it had. Still he marveled. Most men, this much in the sea, would be spoiled for anything. Masrimas had blessed me and preserved me for the ship.

I asked him, casually, what work I might do about the galley to recompense him. He supposed me scared, no doubt, trying to learn my destiny by degrees. He said I should not do common crew work. Then I knew for sure he meant me for the rowers' deck.

I turned and said to Long-Eye in the tongue of the Dark People, "He intends us to embrace the oar. Watch him."

Charpon said decidedly, "You will speak Masrian."

"My servant speaks only his own language."

"No matter. It's better you do as I say."

His bullies laughed. One said to me, "You must have been a fine prince among the barbarians. Did you save any jewels from your skiff?"

I told the man I had nothing. Another put a hand into my hair.

"There's always this. If the young barbarian lord were to

shear his fleece, there's many an old whore in Bar-Ibithni would pay a gold chain for a wig of it."

I moved slightly to look at this man—his name was Kochus—as he fondled me. His eyes widened. He snatched his hand off as if he had been burned and his face went gray. The rest were drinking and never noticed it.

Since the miracle in the sea, my abilities seemed loosened in the sheath, more ready. I was confronted by choices. I could mesmerize the roomful of villains, kill or stun them with a white energy of my brain, or perform some other magician's trick of terror to set them gaping with fear.

Feeling myself omnipotent, with leisure to spare, was my [illegible]ness. A sudden scuffle from behind alerted me, but too [illegible]mething struck me on the skull, hard enough to jar [illegible]s.

[illegible] sufficiently aware, however, to realize I was going to [illegible]ow-decks after all, a substitute for some storm-death. [illegible] was dragged. A hatch was pulled up, some words were exchanged regarding new flesh for dead flesh. I was lowered and left to lie in a stinking dark, the anus of despair. The oarsmen stretched in corpse-sleep, groaning and mewing as they rowed in their dreams. Long-Eye tumbled close to me. The hatch slammed shut.

After a while, lamplight shone through my lids. The Overseer of Oars was bending above me, together with the Drummer—the man whose task it was to beat out time for the oar-strokes. A pace behind them stood one of the two "Comforters," those essentials of any slave galley, their work being to patrol the ramp between the rowing benches, and "comfort," with their flails, any who fell behind in the labor. Compared to those flails, Charpon's whip was a velvet ribbon. Every instrument had three strings to it of corded leather toothed with iron spikes. My eyes were shut and my head clamored; I formed a cerebral rather than a physical picture of these men through their mutterings and movements, and later from my own experience. It was partly disappointing to me to find them so exactly predictable. Like a child's drawing of a monster, each was inevitably what one would expect, barely human, a perfect prototype of depraved viciousness and myopic ignorance.

"This one is very strong," the Overseer remarked, kneading me like a hard dough.

The Drummer said indifferently, "They don't always last, Overseer, even the strong ones."

Somewhere, one of the rowers called out indistinctly for water, in a dream. There was the crack of a flail. The nearest Comforter laughed.

Long-Eye was examined next, and the same words were brought out. Presented with a line of fifty unconscious potential rowers, no doubt they would have mouthed the inanities over and over: This one strong. Even strong ones don't last.

Two Comforters picked me up. They handled me indifferently, without interest since I was not yet properly aware, alive, receptive, the love affair not yet begun between us. Th[illegible] t[illegible]gh, stubborn slaves they liked the best, the men wh[illegible] [illegible]d snarling at the flails, struggling in their shackl[illegible] [illegible]t free and kill the tormentor, to no avail.

[illegible]gh, they found an empty place for me. [illegible]lying under the bench in his chains, hi[illegible] [illegible]and creaking as he slept. His dead mate [illegible] [illegible] and got rid of some hours ago.

The [illegible]eek from the benches was thick as mud in the nostrils.

The Comforter bent near, fixing the irons to my legs, and securing these in turn to the bench. Both limbs were constrained. Later, an iron girdle about my belly would link me with the oar itself.

Before he went away up the ramp, one of the Comforters struck me across the back that I might wake to the full taste of my new life. I was returning fast to myself now, and reaching upward from my thought, healed the stripe immediately, which he did not witness in the gloom.

The shackles were of tempered blue iron, alcum as they call it in the northlands. I felt them over gently, wondering, as ever, if I could or could not. Then the rivets opened like warm putty. I laughed at my mage-craft softly as I lay under the bench, and the sound of the laugh, unfamiliar to the man beside me, my oar-mate, roused him.

To judge from his cries, his brain had been full of a dream of death, drowning in cold seas, weighted to the inescapable intestine of the sinking ship. He was a Seemase, sallow-pale and with curdled black hair of the Old Blood, like wool. He had a year of life left in him, and barely that. He looked at me, coming to himself, with a malicious pity, sorry another should share his rotten fate, and glad of it, too.

"Luck wasn't with you," he said to me, speaking the argot

of the seaways, part Masrian, part Hessek, part ten or so ancient tongues.

"Perhaps it's with you, then. How do I call you?"

"Call me," he repeated. He coughed and spit to clear his lungs. "I was called Lyo once. Where did they catch you?" he added listlessly. He was not curious, this being merely a ritual, the new victim who must be questioned on a reflex.

I said, "They didn't catch me, Lyo. See." I showed him the broken chains about my ankles. The alcum-iron looked melted.

He peered, then had to cough and gargle up more phlegm before he said, "Did you bribe them not to fetter you? They [illegible]ill still do it."

[illegible]ed a piece of the chain in my fingers; it fell apart in [illegible] his eyes. He blinked, trying to puzzle around the [illegible]

[illegible]ould you like to be free, Lyo?"

[illegible]Free," he said. He looked at me, then at the piece of [illegible]ain. He coughed.

"You're sick," I said. "Two months, and you will bleed in the lungs." Something went over his face, the thought of the oar in a high sea, his ribs broken, a tearing in his chest like cloth. His dull gaze flickered up into fright, then faded out.

"Death's no stranger. Let him come. Are you Death?"

I reached over and put my hand on his belly. The sickness swirled up like a serpent trapped under a stick. He choked and caught his breath, and jerked away from me in terror. He gasped and put his palms over his face.

"Say what you feel," I said to him.

Presently he said quietly, "You are God."

"And what god is that?"

"Whichever you say."

"You will call me Vazkor," I said.

"What have you done to me?"

"I have cured your lungs."

"Free me," he said, "free me, and you can have my life."

"My thanks. You offer what is already mine to take."

He kept his palms over his face. It was a ritual gesture—humility before the Infinite.

"Pretend nothing has happened between us," I said. "Later, you shall go free."

He lay back, weakened by the shock of healed strength flowing through him. It was strange to work a magic this vital, without even a sense of pity or sympathy having moved me.

I was cautious now, and did nothing further. Shortly a Comforter found me still in my place, unchained. He called one of his fellows. Next, the Overseer came, and shouted like a bad and unconvincing actor that they should know better than to shackle a man with corroded bonds. I vacantly gazed at them as they brought fresh fetters and did the work anew. Lyo laughed and a flail slashed him across the neck.

Not long after, the order came to resume oars.

The *Hyacinth Vineyard* was turning home.

South, no longer east. As I had seen in that flash of pre-nition on the island, the ship was the fate that me toward my goal. I would find her in the sout ven in this city they named Bar-Ibithni, wh the god of fire. What did she do there? Or s ther to find Uastis Reincarnate, my mother n this reflection, I made no effort to escape oars was sufficient to know I could get loose when wished. Besides, I was young and proud, and full again of my vow of hate, and somehow that mood was fitted to those huge, grinding pulls and thrusts upon a blade of iron and wood.

You row from the calf to the groin, from the groin to the pit of the skull. Only the feet rest easy, and then not always. A boy put to the labor when he is still growing will emerge, if emerge he ever does, with the body of a toad, a vast chest and arms and a goblin's squat, tapering lower limbs. Here and there about Bar-Ibithni you might see such a man, survivor by incredible luck of a shipwreck or sea battle between pirates, who had subsequently bought himself off by bribery of a priest in some Temple of Sanctuary.

Yet the toil was nothing to me. I could have carried the enormous oar alone and made a jest of it, and later did.

Presently a Comforter came by to check my fetters, currently intact. He gave a grunt, stepped back, and, for mere sport, raised his flail. I turned and looked in his pupils.

"You should know better, dog, than to pick up snakes."

A lightning of fear flickered in muddy irises. He felt the flail writhe in his hand, and let it fall with a cry.

"Poor dog," I said, "you are sick. Go vomit, dog, till you are dry."

He lurched about, clutching his belly, and staggered off in the growing gloom and began to puke. Lyo giggled excitedly.

Judging a disturbance, another of the Comforters materialized at my elbow.

"Give me water," I called to him, "water, for your god's sake."

He grinned and stared me in the eye, and made to beat me, and lashed himself across the face instead. He screamed with pain and stumbled to his knees.

"Now you will give me water," I said. I put my palm on his shoulder, keeping the oar going easily single-armed. He took his hand from his injured face. "Water in a cup," I said.

He crawled away, and returned with an iron bowl, his own, filled with mixed water and grain-liquor. I drank, and [illegible] him the cup back with a bow. Bloody, he shambled to [illegible]on, apparently unaware of his hurt.

[illegible] Drummer sat drumming the time of the strokes, a [illegible]ot seeing. The Overseer was above.

[illegible]ion had tightened over the rowing lines. The oar does [illegible]eal kindly with the mental process; only a few had taken [illegible]what had occurred. Even so, a febrile alertness had spread like a new smell through the deck, and a rampant, gnawing memory of the first aspirations of the slave—mutiny, rebellion: freedom. The inexorable pendulum had faltered. Not one of them but did not sense that much, and fasten on it with a cloudy prayer for change to whatever gods they still forgave and reverenced.

And none of us missed a stroke.

3

It would be a journey of seventeen days, so they reckoned, to regain the ship-roads and reach the city, for they had been in the outermost regions of their travels when the hurricane caught them. Seventeen days, too, was an estimation that took into account continuous use of full sail and oar-power together. For this, each rower worked a third of a day alone at the big pole and one third in harness with his mate. An hour following the sunset, when the quarter-lighted black of the underdeck thickened to an unbelievable second depth of darkness, a portion of sleep was allowed, and the slaves tumbled down into that abysmal, muttering unconsciousness by which any man, having once heard it, could tell such a spot blindfold ever after. At the midnight bell, the flails would rouse the lines again to toil in shifts till sunup.

For one day I perversely continued my slavery, after which I had had enough of it.

At sundown, before the last shift was done, I broke and kicked off my chains, and stood up leaving the oar to Lyo. The two Comforters I had had dealings with before retreated from me, shouting. Immediately the shouting spread, the rowers snarled around from their poles like hungry, angry beasts, yet still with not a stroke missed. Plainly the Comforters in my path did not wish to touch me. I met their eyes, and they crouched gradually down on the ramp, like men bowed b [illegible] normous weight upon their backs. The Drummer, n [illegible] rvant on this occasion, had left off his beating and [illegible] to get his hammer ready for a blow. I called to him [illegible] Put away the drumstick, or you shall break yo [illegible] with it."

[illegible] en the paralysis of authority had not affected the o [illegible] grisly clockwork toy, the motion kept on, though their faces were craned to me.

The Overseer lay in the below-decks cabin, nursing a pipe of Tinsen opium.

"Get back to your bench," he said thickly. "Who sent you here?"

"Don't be troubled," I said. "You are having a vision from the poppy seeds."

"You are no vision, stinking slave," he whispered, smiling at me through the thin mist in his head. "Who unchained you?"

"I am Vazkor, and you are my servant. There is no doubt. Accept it."

"If I do not obey, what then?"

"Be disobedient, and learn."

He lapsed back.

"You are a slave," he said.

I looked into his drug-blind eyes and made him know that I was not, and went out, leaving him in an abject, speechless idiocy, the idiot's smile still sewed on his face.

I did not imagine I should need to sleep, but sleep I found I must. I chose a spot for it, confident in the fear I had inspired, and in fact no one came near me at that hour, or tried to take me.

The slumber itself was crowded by dreams, nightmares that

angered me, the first for days. My cleverness had outgrown such wretchedness, or surely should have done. Lying on the roughly padded bunk in the Comforters' warren below, I met even Ettook again and every one of the old frustrations, and one new damnation, which was a girl hanged in her own yellow hair. I was not a mage, asleep.

Near midnight I woke.

I thought, *It is no longer thus. I have changed, I have dislodged the past.*

A shadow had bent near me that lurched sideways at my stirring.

"I meant no harm, Lauw-yess."

The Comforter with the lashed face—he would carry the [illegible]e rest of his days, however short or long they might [illegible]ut to be—accorded me Charpon's title.

[illegible]t no menace from him, but I held up my palm and the [illegible]y shone through it, and sent him to kneel pleading in [illegible]lack that I should do him no harm. I had become clever [illegible] the energy, able to portion it out in various strengths and forms.

It would be no problem to discipline my servants. Also, no problem to kill my enemies now perhaps, not as it had been in the wildlands beyond Eshkorek, the pale glare and the sick agony after it.

I dropped into another sleep.

There was another dream. I dreamed of my father.

He rode through a white city, lighted up in fits and starts by the bonfires of a sack, and I rode beside him. I could not see his face against the red fires, but I saw a white cat seated on his shoulder, and continually it darted with its paw and slashed at his breast, over where the heart was, and the black shirt was bloody. He did not cry out at these stabbings, which raked ever nearer his life, but he said to me quietly, "Remember it, remember the vow you offered me. Do not batten on my will, which made you, and forget."

From this I woke calmly, as one does not generally wake from such a thing. But all the grim jokes I had derived from my Power aboard the ship, and all the endless mistakes I had made, had soured like wine kept too long in a cask.

I was not a child but a man, the son of a man. His death hung like a leaden rope about my neck at that moment. My father would not have clowned with his destiny as I had done with mine. His ruthless ambition, his iron mind, his ability had been better employed. Was I then to ape Ettook, the futile boasting of the red pig in his sty?

The midnight bell sounded above. Ignoring my absence, as the crowd ignores the passage of a leper—shrinking aside, yet speaking of the day and the state of trade—the lines were being roused to their work by the brotherhood of the flails.

I rose, and went out and climbed up the ladder from the rower's deck, and those awake watched me with their glinting, awestruck eyes.

I passed two of the watch on the upper deck, and had them before they could challenge me. Once I would have [illegible]d a weapon or a blow; to make a man stone quiet wit[illegible] [illegible]yes is a curious deed.

[illegible]rpon's ship-house was dimly lighted, with on[illegible] [illegible] red lamp. By another of the laws of Masri[illegible] no kindled flame might be left uncovered, sa[illegible] [illegible]od. The room smelled of incense, and of a stable. [illegible]ster, russet as a bull in the lamplight, spraw[illegible] across the handsome boy I had seen make up to him earlier. The boy's face, curd-white between the ruddy cushion and the master's ruddy flesh, stared straight up at me with a pared and vicious horror, like the white mask of a rat cornered by dogs.

"Lauw-yess," he cried, seizing Charpon's arm, frantic between fear of angering the master and a worse fear of me.

Charpon growled. The boy shook him, hissing a stream of faulty Masrian. With a curse, Charpon heaved around and made me out. His fingers slipped along the couch to his knife-belt. I let his grip close on the handle before I educated him. This time I saw the bolt shoot from my hand. It caught him about the wrist, soundless, but Charpon roared and jolted sideways, letting go the blade half-drawn. The boy squealed and jumped off the couch, flinging himself into a corner. I felt sorry for him, his fortunate night wrecked by the unexpected.

"Melkir, run for seconds—" Charpon shouted.

I said, "It will do you no good. Before the boy gets to the door, I will kill him, and you shall be next, I promise you."

I let him have another bolt between the ribs, as I would have cast a spear but one year before. He doubled up, retching, among the exotic pelts.

The boy Melkir began to snivel.

"You will spoil your looks," I said. "Shut your mouth and keep still, and you will live to ply your wares ashore."

He turned off the tears instantly, and made his eyes soft, in case I might be susceptible. Having been the pupil of a hard school, he was apt for quick lessons. Even the sorcery was less compelling than violence, of which it was obviously merely another branch, something to be avoided, placated, put, if possible, to use.

I crossed over to Charpon and rolled him onto his back. He wiped his mouth and showed his irregular teeth.

"What are *you*?" he asked.

"What do you suppose?"

[illegible] suppose mischief. I send you to the oar, and you are a [illegible] of tricks—a priest perhaps? I have heard of such [illegible] being the property of priests."

[illegible] was a swift rodent scuttle through the draperies—the [illegible]caping out of the door. Charpon swore, knowing quite [illegible] would get no help from that quarter.

[illegible]Well," he said, "what do you want?"

I met his little black eyes, which froze with no struggle. Finding me more than his match, Charpon wasted no effort on resistance.

"Your ship," I said, "your service. Whatever I instruct shall be done. We will call your officers in and tell them the happy news."

Outside, the night tasted already of the faint spice balm of the south, and the stars described different patterns between the sails.

I had mislaid my memory of Long-Eye, but presently recalled and had them release him. He came limping from the chains and stood beside me.

I remembered how I had valued him and was at a loss to find him once again only a piece of what was all around me, a mortal wasteground peopled with beings no more akin to me than is the tinder to the flame that strikes from it.

I clothed myself with light in order to impress them, which it duly did. It was easy to do so, as had been the other things, unnervingly easy. It was not surprising that in after days I found myself reluctant to experiment with the Power that had abruptly burgeoned in me, afraid of its enormity, so suddenly unleashed. However, I became lord of Charpon's ship, and ninety-seven men offered me fealty that night, kneeling bewildered and afraid on the upper deck.

I felt neither hubris nor exaltation. I felt, for those moments, as afraid as they. I found myself on a pinnacle, neither king nor magician, nor even god, simply one man isolated from the race of men. Alone, as never in my life before.

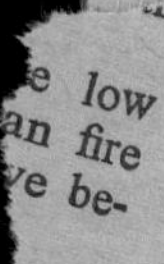

Part II

The Sorcerer

1

first city I came to was a dead one, Eshkorek Arnor, lden Skull. My second city lived, a shining anthill, im- ous it seemed to disaster, degradation, the scouring pas- of the winds of time, and to every one of those things t had eaten Eshkorek alive. I remember that, despite the events that led me there, I was still humanly young enough to gape that seventeenth morning, when the *Hyacinth Vineyard* drifted on her oars and dipped sails like a blue moth into the Bay of Hragon.

The summer came early to Bar-Ibithni; against the backdrop of an indigo sky, five hundred palaces let down their reflections in a sea of sapphire glass. West, where the great docks began, gold and green alligators of ships covered the water. At the innermost point of the bay stood a statue of gilded alcum, flashing like a fire some sixty feet high: the Masrimas of Bar-Ibithni: Hragon Masrianes, the first conqueror-king, who raised the city to its might, also raised up the statue. It had cost a thousand Hessek slave lives to do it, but slave life, as ever, came cheap. The god statue wore the pleated kilt, generous draped breeches, and knee boots of the conquerors, and also the massive collar and shoulder-pieces and the spiked helmet of a warrior. This gear—imposing on the tall Masrians, serving indeed to make them seem giants among flies—was but another symbol to the people under their sway that to dwarf a man is usually to best him.

A hundred years before, in the "Old Blood" days of the Hessek kings, only the embryo of a city had stood here, Bit-Hessee, or Sea's-Mouth. Inland lay three Hessek provinces, and over the water to the west, Hessek Seema and Tinsen. The Hessek kingdoms had contrived to persist some centuries, a culture ancient and sufficiently rotten that the thunder of war soon shattered it.

War came from the east in the form of a young people thrusting west and south. The old world crumbled where they passed. The little empires were consumed one by one, broken, annexed, and remade in the name of Masrimas, Flame-Lord.

The fire-worshipers were a formidable race, large in frame and huge in military numbers. Their legions, or *jerds,* were matchless. Disciplined to iron, clad in burnished bronze, and equipped with horses, the like of which animal had never before been seen in the south, they poured across the map in their hunger for ground. Starved in their arid home of snowless crags and raw desert, the Masrians [illegible]overed [illegible] south with its rivers and alluvial plains, and t[illegible] ing withstood this change, as ever, stubbor[illegible] were thrown down and savaged with all the re[illegible]

Seduced, however, by the bride they had [illegible] riors rebuilt the old world, dubbed it the "New," [illegible] trinkets of architecture on the ruins. Bit-Hessee, a mere oc[illegible] port of the Hesseks, was razed and re-created, a model city for the Warrior-Emperor Hragon. Bar-Ibithni, as she became, instantly rivaled, then soon outshone, the Masrian cities of the east. Palaces were built by the sea, temples, monuments, theaters, which swiftly reduced the former capital to the artistic level of a cow-byre. The invaders had become occupants of a land of plenty, and were learning its ways. Where the jerds marched now was in the drillyard and the court; they stacked their arms in taverns and by the couches of women, till half Hessek was impregnated with Masrian seed. Presently the Masrians mellowed into that intellectual and sane enjoyment of life that heralds the decay of human strength.

The *Hyacinth Vineyard* paid her toll, and entered under the bar into the docks. Such quantities of shipping passed into and out of the harbor that the port and dock together ran for a mile or more. Behind lay the vast storehouses and Fish Market, landmarked by its two golden fish high on their pillar of granite. Here Amber Road began, which led in turn to the Market of the World, where was sold them anything that could be got in the empire, from transparent silk to green Tinsen tobacco to candied bees. Off from this colossal pool of commerce the lesser markets flooded away, the dealers in horses, cattle, and slaves, and here, too, the hostelries and wineshops and whore-palaces commenced.

I left Charpon with three of his seconds to sort the ship's

business as he would among the merchants' offices about the quay. With a guard of ten Hesseks, Kochus, the remaining second, conducted me through the Fish Market and up Amber Road to the Dolphin's Teeth. This place, named for the sea as city ships were named for the land, was a gaudy hospice, catering to wealthy brigands, and well supplied with such. Even Hessek pirates flocked there if they had silver money chains enough to pay for their board. Yet it was a Masrian house by inclination, aping conqueror ways, though I do not imagine a man of pure Masrian stock had ever entered it.

Kochus led me up the yellow marble steps of the Dolphin's
h with the pride of the landowner returning to his estate.
pillars, painted a blue and red fit to spear the eyes,
up a roof of white stucco. The tiled walls bore pictures
arily of dolphins.

arly drinkers, ships' masters and sea bandits, were swag-
ing into and out of the vestibule with detachments of ruffi-
s. Kochus, exhibiting the true sentimentality of the sadis
grinned black molars and embraced acquaintances. Seeing
stand modestly to one side, a scarred devil with an armful o
gold, and missing the obligatory eye of the pirate, remarked on my out-city bumpkin appearance. Kochus flashed me a look of fear.

"This is a lord from foreign parts. The whole ship is in his debt."

"What, Charpon in a man's debt? Hey, you, girl-eyes, what did you do for him? I'd have said you were too tall for the master's taste."

I said offhandedly to Long-Eye, who stood behind me, "You see the noisy one there? Go over and strike him for me."

Kochus cowered aside; the pirate stood nonplussed, not believing his ears, till Long-Eye, obeying me without expression and without a second's delay, hit him hard in the mouth. Gold-Arm did not like this greeting and raised his meaty fist to flatten Long-Eye before coming on at me, while everywhere around the traffic through the hostelry halted and watched with interest. Thus I made my first impression on Bar-Ibithni. I loosed a white energy from my palm, clear as a lightning bolt. It connected with Gold-Arm in the region of his neck and felled him like an ox. He crashed on the floor of Masrian tiles and rolled a couple of yards, woundedly roaring, while over the crowd passed that simultaneous involuntary gasping sound with which the magician comes to be familiar before he has got very far in his career.

To augment the proceedings, all our ten Hessek sailors dropped to their knees and groveled before me, and Kochus crept near, imploring I do nothing else.

Gold-Arm stopped rolling on the floor, and peered up in flinching amazement.

"I had hoped to spare you that," I said to him. "You may remember in the future that it is better to let my servant strike you than I myself."

A constrained hubbub broke out around the edges of th hall. Seeing I was not about to fling lightnings in indiscri nate directions, curiosity had outweighed panic. Such civilizing effect of city life upon men. It kills the instin replaces them with extended noses.

Just then a figure came floating along the vestibule. Hessek by race, scented, creamed, and powdered wit cheeks, and earlobes tinted to the shade of fine pink c eyes shaped with blue kohl, hair curled and sprinkled with ver dusts. A trailing of gauze and green silk, and a pair of high-heeled slippers with tinkling disks to accompany a gliding gait like a smoothly oiled wheel running downhill. In two narrow white hands was the silver cup of welcome this pretty, mannered house offered to arrivals.

It was so unexpected, it took my brain a moment to come up with my perception. A beautiful girl. Without breasts. And she was close enough now, offering me the cup and looking under the butterfly lids, that I could see the cat's jaw would need shaving before the paint was put on it, for they do not castrate their boy whores in Bar-Ibithni.

"Drink, my lord," said the voice, carefully schooled into a softness that gave away nothing, except that no woman was speaking. "And you, Lord Kochus, welcome to the Dolphin once again. Is lord Charpon to come later?"

"How could he keep away?" flirted Kochus, putting his hand, with no preliminary, inside the loose draperies on the smooth, meticulously depilated flesh. "This is Thei," he added to me, "highly recommended comfort of the inn. And this lord, Thei, is a foreigner, a sorcerer, as he has just demonstrated. Be careful the management doesn't overcharge him, or he'll tumble the house around your ears." He still looked liverish with fright, despite his antics, striving to align himself with the earth-shaker, and fool the world and himself into believing his trembling was an integral part of the quake.

Gold-Arm had scalded off among his friends like a bull into a thicket.

The hall hummed, and the curious Thei led us away.

A room at the Dolphin's Teeth. Three walls washed dark red and one lavender. Lamps in cages of leaded lavender glass hung up among bronze cages of tweeting pink and white birds, the whole ceiling a riot of light-flicker and bird-flicker. A Masrian fireplace, the length of the second red wall—an odd affair, since worship of Masrimas means a naked flame must not be seen to burn. The faggots were invisibly lighted behind an intricate lattice of iron, which [illegible]ently altered to the color of the fire, and glowed with a [illegible]ing, venomous heat through the cool city nights of early [illegible]r. In the lavender wall was a single large window with parchment blind to let down, thereby turning the room [illegible]. Outside, the view of a small court, orange trees, and a [illegible]e basin containing striped fish.

In this location I sat, and gave myself over to the modish appearance of the city. Aristocrat, merchant, bandit, all looked much the same, providing they could afford it. For it was an expensive thing to be in the mode.

They chop off the hair at the shoulder and the beard close to the jaw, and curl what remains with reedlike tongs. For the bath, they show you forty essences and recommend forty others they do not have on them. Three tailors come with garments readymade and cloths uncut, and spit and bicker between themselves, and the jeweler slinks up and produces a silver collar, two hands broad and with lion epaulets, which you have reason to suspect has been recently around the neck of some pirate-prince just now sent to be measured for a piece of rope instead.

At length the noon meal is brought in, and you discover platters full of gilded stewed seafood with raisin stones among quinces, and miniature joints that turn out to be baked shrews and their gods-know-what besides, and tall thimbles of black koois, the rum of the south. Everything, in short, that such luxury-loving sharks as Charpon might desire.

These novelties so far came as a flamboyant credit, extended to each of Charpon's officers. Where I was to pay in cash, I borrowed from Kochus, who accepted every fresh excursion into his coffers as insurance against my wrath.

In the early afternoon Charpon presented himself, having turned meantime into as much of a dandy as I had, and with his cropped pate covered by a wig of blue-black curls.

"I hear you're sending my men on your business, sir," he said. He looked me over, taking in the New World elegance, "And spending freely on my credit."

"Lord Vazkor has been using my money, Charpon," cried Kochus, anxious to show loyalty to both his dangerous superiors.

"Charpon," I said, "if you wish to dissociate yourself from me, get out."

"You are aware, sir, that I am as much your slave as any of my Hessek rabble. I am only surprised, after your treatment at my hands, that you let me live."

"I have no wish to kill a man without cause," I [illegible] Through his eyes I saw pass, under the layer of cauti[illegible] unstruggling surrender, the contempt for my suppose[illegible] and my lack of years, which even my sorcery had not [illegible] him of.

I had had sixteen days as the *Vineyard* sailed and [illegible] gratis in Charpon's ship-house—sixteen days to formulat[illegible] plans. Which were simple enough. If my bitch-dam was he[illegible] in the south, as my sense of precognition led me to believe, I would need funds and cunning to seek her. For sure she had hidden herself. Talk with the sailors had not revealed any notion of her; clearly she had not elevated herself to a position of influence, as in Ezlann when she was my father's wife. Supposing her here, she might even have lost herself in some backwater of Bar-Ibithni itself. It seemed to me one way to flush her out was to make a stir, in my father's name. I meant to become the sorcerer and healer Vazkor, and I meant to amass some wealth, too, putting my alarming gifts to work for me. With sufficient reputation and coin, my investigations could be facile. If she fled, or if I failed to come on her, I must simply cast the net more widely.

2

Charpon dismissed, I went out into the dove-wing heat of the city, which in late summer would swelter into a furnace. The Amber Road continues from the Market of the World along the western side of Hragon's Wall, that bastion which divides the aristocratic portion of the metropolis from the vulgar.

Bar-Ibithni was four cities. Its hub was the vast commercial area of port, docks, and markets, which clambered into suburbs across the uplands in the south. Beyond Hragon's inner wall lay the fortified citadel on a natural hill called the Pillar, a military edifice situated within two square miles of bronze-faced outer battlements, and capable of accommodating seventeen jerds, somewhere in the region of seventeen thousand men. Away from the Pillar, to the east, stretched [illegible] Palm Quarter, its terraces of gargantuan temples and [illegible] mansions culminating in the Heavenly City, inaccessible [illegible]—the Emperor's stronghold.

[illegible]ime, beyond a tract of marsh far to the west, where [illegible]rmed like a scum around the ancient and abandoned [illegible] was all that remained of Old Hessek Bit-Hessee (pop[illegible] known as the Rat-Hole), a warren of slums worse than [illegible]at clotted the outskirts of the New Capital. Half un[illegible]ground, frequently fever-ridden, dark as dusk at noon[illegible] pitch-black by night, no man, warrior, or imbecile vis[illegible] there unless it would cost his life to stay away.

Amber Road ended near Winged Horse Gate, the main entrance through Hragon's Wall to the Palm Quarter. Here, on the west side of the wall, the fashionable part of the commercial area began, squares with fountains and stucco houses with painted columns, and the Grove of the Hundred Magnolias. To the Grove those with the time to idle come at this hour of the day, to parade up and down the smooth lawns, and breathe in the perfume of dusty, full-blown magnolia blossom, while conjurers performed tricks and caged beasts roared in arbors.

As Kochus and I, with the usual precautionary band of accompanying roughnecks, strolled up the street to the Grove, Lyo sprang out on us from a shadow.

"Lord Vazkor," he said urgently to me, speaking in his own Seemase tongue, which only I could entirely follow, "there shall be three."

While I had lounged in the hostelry, Charpon's Hesseks had been about the town, on my orders, to spread word of the sorcerer. (My dealings with Gold-Arm the pirate had probably found their own voice) Lyo, however, I had sent with a man who knew the undercurrents of Bar-Ibithni, to inquire after those sick in need of an extravagant cure.

"Three," I said. "Good."

He grinned; he had been running around on my errands, pleased with the sound chest he now had.

"It's to be this way, Lauw-yess. An old woman will approach you on the second lawn, selling sweets from a tray. She will stumble and fall in your path, crying out loudly so everyone can hear. She is well known and has a crippled spine, though she panders to it in order to win sympathy."

"Will she, then, not object to being healed?"

"Ah *no*, Lauw-yess. She says if you are magician enough to do it, she will be able to exhibit herself as your handiwork and get more coins than ever. She asks"—he grin[illegible] again—"if you could not make her young again, too."

"And how much did she cost us?"

He pursed his mouth.

"My apologies, Kochus," I said. "Tell me the rest, [illegible]

"Once you have worked the miracle for her, ano[illegible] come, a young man known to be blind in both eyes[illegible] the youngest son of the merchant Kecham, but his fathe[illegible] him off when he would go live with a strumpet, and no[illegible] strumpet is the only one who cares for him. She will bring him on the cue, but she is worse than the old sweet-seller, wanted three pieces of silver for it, for she lacks faith. She will see. When that is done and the boy's eyes healed, Lauw-yess, the crowd should be primed. But to be sure, I have passed the word among the gate porters of Phoonlin's house—he is rich, half-Marsian, and superstitious, and his wife gossips with the maids and is more superstitious even than he. He has a rock near his bladder that is nearly killing him with the pain. He has called on priest-healers before, of the Masrian temples, and of the Old Faith, too, so I hear. If he knows there is a magician in the Magnolia Grove, he will go to discover. Then, after a wonder or two, he will throw himself down before you and beg."

"You did well," I said. My other errand boy had by now come up, and Kochus paid them both without demur. We crossed Winged Horse Square and went through the old wall of the Grove, which had been a Hessek garden a hundred-odd years earlier.

The lawns rose in four levels, flecked with pink magnolia shade and dotted with pools. A fine spice of dust smoked from the winding paths where the merchants and their like went up and down.

There were few women on display. It was basic to Hessek morality that the female is a jewel best kept in a box. Ladies might venture out with their husbands only under cover of darkness, and then veiled from the nose to the ankle. Even the poorer women, of necessity abroad, covered half their faces and all their forms in this manner; only the Masrian girls went bare-faced, but they were mostly over in the Palm Quarter. Commercial Bar-Ibithni was a hotbed of mixed blood, Old and New, and though the men put on the draped breeches and the airs of Masrians, they preferred their women in the old style, safely tethered. But there was a predominance of masculine courtesans of Thei's ilk. More than once, before I grew accustomed to it, my eye was caught by something too much a girl to be one.

On the second lawn a red tiger was pacing about its post in an open enclosure above the path, staring with practiced hatred at the crowd of fools who patronized it. A single weak link in its alcum shackle would have meant a different game.

Kochus said, "She's coming, the old woman. Over there. I've seen her before, Lellih the crook-back."

I turned and looked for her. She would recognize me, from some description Lyo would have given her. Her hair was uncovered, gray and sparse, and her eyes sewed up in snarls of skin, but she also had hidden her lower face with a bit of a veil. She was tiny, shrunk little even for a Hessek, and her back rested over her like a small broken mountain. The wicker tray that she wheeled before her on a solitary wooden wheel was loaded with delicate confectionery that seemed to mock her unsightliness.

She got within a couple of yards of me, calling in a thin wail for custom. Then I realized why she had demanded money, for part of her act was to be that all her trade of sweets be spilled, for dramatic effect, at my feet. As the sugar gems rolled, Lellih swung herself awkwardly down, flopped over in the grass, and began to shrill with a ghastly, damaged anguish.

The idling crowd drew aside, alarmed by the proximity of this distress. Kochus, unable to restrain his mirth at the play, had begun to chuckle, till I warned him to be silent.

A figure ran over, somebody's drab, thin female servant, who presumably knew the old woman. She crouched down by her, trying to take her arm.

I walked to where Lellih was folded on the lawn, screaming, and the servant girl stared up from dull eyes, and cried, "Don't harm her, sir. She can't help herself. She'll be better in a moment, see if she isn't." She spoke in faulty Masrian for my special benefit, I supposed. I was of Masrian height and tanned very dark, and in my fashionable gear I probably seemed to be of pure conqueror-blood.

"I don't intend to harm her, girl. If this is Lellih the sweet-seller, I mean to heal her."

The servant gaped; the crowd around us hovered. Only one man laughed, catching my words. Lellih of the crooked back, meanwhile, turned her bird's head and squinted at me with an eldritch wickedness.

"How can you heal me?" she asked, having got it pat from Lyo, and managing besides to make her squeaking heard a fair distance. "All my years I have carried the gods' curse on my shoulders."

I bent and lifted her up. She was like a wisp of brittle-dry straw, ready to flare alight in the heat of the day. Her head came no higher than my belt.

"Don't mock me, my fine lovely lad," she shrilled out. "How can you heal a cripple who has been bent in a hoop since she was birthed?" Under her breath she maliciously added for me alone, "And just let's see you do it, for all your boasting, you devil out of Hessu's sea."

"Hush, granny," I said softly. I put my right hand flat on her spine and my left under her chin, and I straightened her, as I might straighten a stick of green wood.

I had felt little or nothing the other times. This time I felt a surge come out of my palms, and she screamed aloud once, in earnest, and her twisted spine crackled like cinders underfoot. Then she was upright, her burden gone and her rags hanging hollow on her back, and now her head reached to my rib cage.

The crowd made its sound.

The servant girl hid her already three-quarters-hidden face.

It was Lellih who turned up her predatory eyes and said, "Is it as it seems? Is it? The pain went through me like red-hot whips, but now I am straight as a maid. Say, handsome priest-fellow, will you make me young, too?" She glinted at me, sly as a gray fox. "I was a fair sight when I was young, saving my hump, truly fair I was. Will you do it?"

My flesh crept, as it had for a moment when Lyo first told me her words. If I could do that, pare off age, remake youth, that was a vision indeed to catch fame. But I was not sure. It seemed a thing no man, magician or priest, should aim at—half unholy. It got me superstitious, where I was not, to think of it. I said, nevertheless, and very quietly, "You've had your medicine for today; besides, I work no miracles without ultimate profit, granny-girl. If I did what you ask, you'd be my tame monkey thereafter, part of my sorcerer's credentials, a peepshow; I waste nothing of my work."

"Make me a girl, and you can have me for whatever purpose you like," and she plucked my sleeve and cackled and said, "Make me a virgin, too; seal me up again. And then break the seal yourself. Will you, will you, eh, handsome?"

Kochus took her sticklike wrist and began to move her on. I said, "Gently." She looked sufficiently fragile to break in his paws. She flashed her eyes at me for that, turned suddenly and started off over the lawn, trampling her sweets, leaving the wheeled tray and the servant who had run to help her, and the whole crowd gazing, crying out like a child as she went by, "See me, how straight I am, and how tall!"

I had considered that the blind boy and his prostitute might prove reticent, having taken the money and disbelieved the promise, but they had come to taste the water, and finding it sweet, were ready to drink. Two or three seconds after Lellih was gone, Kecham's son was pulled forward by his doxy—not female, despite Lyo's use of "she," but another Thei, and not so winning. Kecham's son had a conjunctival disease a good doctor could have cured, if he had been set to it in time, but I guess the girl-boy did not have the riches that buy physicians. It was an easy matter for me, nevertheless, and with no particular sense of passage. Yet when the boy found himself blind no longer, he started to weep, and his lover fell on his neck and wept too, which made a pleasant show.

However, if I expected next some sight of the wealthy Phoonlin, with his kidney stone, I was to be disappointed. In fact, I had no need of him. The idlers in the Grove of a Hundred Magnolias, whispering and screeching, had bethought themselves of their own personal ailments, and were rushing on me from every side, kissing my boots and kneeling in Lellih's ruined confectionery.

I stood my ground and worked my magic. I must have saved three score lives at least in those hours, and stemmed a host of minor troubles, and still the crowd swelled and implored me. Word had spread thoroughly at last. Men came running, the well-to-do with the poverty-stricken, up Amber Road, through Winged Horse Square, and into the Grove.

Kochus stood in a static green-faced panic at my side, protesting that we should be mashed beneath a berserk mob.

My strength, greater it seemed than at any moment in my life before, buoyed me with a kind of cold exhilaration that had little to connect it with the marvels I was performing. I had no unease at the size of my clamoring audience, nor any compassion. If anything, it was a variety of scorn that kept me there to lay my hands on them. Their miseries were like black worms wriggling at the bottom of some enormous depth, clearly perceived, far removed, valueless. Till I grew bored with the phenomena, I should remain.

How I proposed to make my escape, I have no idea. Perhaps I would have metamorphosed suddenly from savior to destroyer, and struck a path for myself with killing energies. Instead, another authority resolved the puzzle.

There came a yelling and thrusting from the edge of the mob nearest to the square and the Winged Horse Gate. Shortly, over this hubbub rang the commotion of iron hooves and a bellowing of horns.

Near me, one of the Hessek crew who had remained at his post began to shout, "Jerdat! Jerdat!"

Kochus gibbered, "Someone's told the citadel. They've smelled riot and turned out the garrison."

The crowd, no doubt aware of what was good for it, was parting down its center, and through this parting came galloping some two hundred mounted soldiers, the fifth portion of a jerd.

The horses were all salt-white, one or two with a freckle of chestnut or black, and trapped in white. The jerdiers were dressed in the way of the Masrimas statue in the bay: boots, wide trousers, and pleated kilt of white leather, the latter reinforced by strips of white metal. Above the belt, their color changed. Red leather chest harness with pectoral plate of bronze, collar and shoulder-pieces of bronze, bronze sleeves to the elbow, and gauntlets of red kidskin. The spired bronze helmets were grafted onto a wig of brass mesh like the hair of some curious clockwork man-doll, and striking, mated to black beards. It was well known from the annals of the Masrians that their first military advantages were won in horseless lands because of this mode of kitting the cavalry. Each white to the waist and showy red and gold above and mounted on a white horse, they blended into the animal and looked, from a very slight way off, to be a race of four-legged equine monsters. Such days of glory, however, were gone.

The jerdat commander reined in his gelding and the fifth

of a jerd pulled up immaculately behind him, spectacle perfected at a million practices in the drill yard.

In the way of such things, the press was sidling off from me, leaving me space to greet official wrath alone.

Shining in his bronze, the jerdat took in the scene. He was near my age, my man's age at least, and constructed in a manner to please his women. Finally he thought he might speak to me.

"You, sir—are you the cause of this disturbance?"

"You, sir, are the cause of it, not I."

Plainly, he did not care for my answer.

"Express yourself afresh, sir."

"Gladly. You have ridden your troop headlong into a peaceful gathering, thereby creating something of a riot. I hope I make myself clear."

The jerdat nodded, as if an assessment he had privately formed of me was showing itself as accurate.

"Be good enough to tell me your rank and your blood."

"I am a foreigner to Bar-Ibithni."

"Yet you talk like a Masrian. Well. And your rank?"

"I am a king's son," I said.

At that he smiled.

"Are you indeed, by the Flame. Well, then, and what is this foreign princeling at, stirring up a mob of Hesseks?"

"I am a healer," I said, "among my other powers."

"You dress mighty fine for an amputator of warts. I'm wondering if you're a thief's son rather than a king's. Maybe I should offer you a night of entertainment in the Pillar jail."

Supremacy, once established, must remain constant, and I could not afford to let these soldiers best me in public. I was weary, too, and he riled me. I watched his face smiling, and I watched it alter as I let the slender bolt of light from my arm, which had been itching with it, into his plated breast.

He almost toppled down, but, rare horseman that he was, he kept his seat while the animal itself neighed and danced with fear, rolling its eyes between the silver blinkers.

The crowd stood, huge-eyed.

The soldiers broke ranks and started a rush at me, but the jerdat checked them with a shout.

White-lipped, he accused me with the truth, "A *magician*!"

I said, "Order the people home; they will go. I am done with my work for today."

At that there were wild entreaties on every side. I held up

my hand and got silence, as normally only a fifth of a jerd would get it.

"I said, for today I am done. There will be other days. Captain," I added, not taking my eyes off him, "I cede the matter to you."

The crowd fragmented at the urging of the jerdiers, and bubbled away over the lawns of the Grove. There was no violence, and few lingered between the trees to molest me, afraid the soldiers would chastise them.

The jerdat and three of his subalterns sat their horses at the perimeter of the grass while this went on, below the enclosure with the tiger in it. Their mounts, schooled to beasts as they were schooled to an assortment of terrors, were stony-still as the red cat prowled and growled above. Presently the captain rode back over to me. Obviously, the blow still pained him and he was half stunned, but he meant to have it out with me.

"You have dishonored me," he said. "Not content with that, you did it before a mix rabble off the Amber Road, and before my own men."

"And what had you in mind for me?"

He said, "If you're a stranger to the city, I must ask if you know the code of the Challenge?"

I said, "A challenge to what?"

"To combat, you and I."

"Ah, warrior matters," I said. "Do you think you can match me?"

"If you will abide by the code. You claim to be a king's son and appear at least to be a gentleman. I will take so much on trust, for redress I will have, magician." Shaken as he was, he lost his control, and rasped out at me with his eyes burning, "By Masrimas, you shamed me, and must give me *something*!"

"If I refuse?"

He smiled, reckoning he had my weakness, and not far off at that.

"Then I will personally see to it that the whole city understands, sir, that you are afraid to meet me, doubting your powers. Which will do your trade no good, I promise you."

"Assume I accept. That thing I did I can do again. What weapon can enable you to best a sorcerer?"

"If you have any honor, you will observe the code of combat and use only the weapon that the code permits—a sword.

If you prefer jackal's tricks, you may find me more ready. I, too, have had priestly training."

A feature I had noticed casually a moment before now disconcerted me. Despite his Masrian coloring, his eyes were blue, and I recalled hearing that this was a mark of the Hragon kings.

"You had better tell me who you are," I said.

He said steadily, "You guess already, by your face. It makes no odds. I am the prince Sorem, son of the Emperor. And the challenge still stands."

"You must think me mad," I said, "to invite me to kill the heir."

"I am not the heir," he answered coldly. "My mother is his former wife, and he has cast her off. You need expect no trouble from that quarter—I am not in favor. I will see you have safe conduct besides, if you harm me. *If*. Don't worry too greatly on that score. You will hear from me inside the month."

He turned the horse smartly and rode off, the column of men falling in behind at a parade trot.

Glancing about, I saw Kochus's face and nearly laughed.

"Courage, man. I am to fight, not you."

He gabbled something, saying it would likely make my fortune if I slew this superfluous prince who was out of favor. All the princes constantly warred with each other in the citadel and out of it. The heir himself, nervous of his future, as most heirs have cause to be, would find means to reward me for Sorem's death—one less threat to his throne. As for the Emperor, he had fathered too many to keep count, had grown obese with age, and cared only for the tricky adolescent boys he took to his bed, and then, the tale went, could do little with.

This chat of the imperial court, which seemed much removed from my own destiny, bored me. I was only astonished at the twist to the afternoon's work. Besides, there was a disturbing element in Sorem, something that recalled to me my own self as I had been, still was, perhaps—hotheaded and young and out of temper with my life. (I wondered idly if the cast-off second wife was ugly, that she had been cast off. It seemed to me the woman who mothered him had had her share of beauty, for you saw it there in him. But no doubt the years had dealt unkindly with her. It put me in mind of Ettook's krarl, of Tathra, of all that wretchedness I had thought left far behind me.) Regarding his commission in the citadel, the jerdat captaincy, it was probably a bone thrown to Sorem in better days. It was apparently not uncommon for the royal house to place its princes in the army, the ancestry of the Hragons being a military one. Yet he handled himself well and was an excellent horseman. He had mentioned a priest's training, too. Maybe all these things were fruits he had plucked for himself. His men were loyal to him, you could not miss that. He had used what came to hand, and used it well enough, but his birthright must have been gall rather than honey to him, such crowds before him, and such crowds looking on to see if he would fall, to mock him when he did. No wonder his pride was raw. Hearing of a Hessek mob in the Grove, he had come out like a young lion for action. Finding me, he felt his gods had set him another test. He would kill me if he could. I had no option but to deflect his purpose. And it irked me.

3

When I left the Grove, the sun was low, sinking brick-red behind the piled roofs, into the distant western marsh.

Bar-Ibithni took on a new color in the sunset, a feverish, sullen glow of burning lacquers and dyed plaster walls. In the high prayer-towers of the Palm Quarter, the Flame priests sang out their hymn to Masrimas's fiery sun.

A man loitered by the wall of the Grove. When he saw me he bowed and touched his fingers to his breast, the Masrian greeting to a religious leader.

"Illustrious sir, my master has sent me to entreat you to visit him. His house is your house, he will give you anything you desire, if you can cure his agony."

"Which agony is that?"

"It is a rock, holy one, above his bladder."

Phoonlin, the rich merchant Lyo had promised, was gambling on me after all.

I said I would go with the man, Phoonlin's steward, no less, and told him to conduct me.

If any were watching for us, a fine reassurance it must have been for them to observe, sauntering up the street, one tall young dandy surrounded by a crew of three villainous and overdressed ship's officers and six filthy and crazed-looking Hesseks. Small wonder if they had barred the gates against us; yet they did not.

The house, situated in the fashionable area, was as close as Hragon's Wall and the Palm Quarter as it could get. A mansion of stucco and tiled gables, it lifted itself on heavily gilded columns carved to resemble palms, out of a garden court of black sculpted trees. Here the hot afterglow was fading in a narrow strip of pool. A lion fountain of white stone stared down into the water; it had a woman's breasts and the wings of an eagle, and through its bearded lips, pursed as if to whistle, jetted a glittering string that created the only movement and the only sound in the quiet.

No lights had been lighted in windows of the mansion.

A veiled figure opened the door and pattered away ahead of us on little naked pale feet.

The stewards asked if my servants would remain below, and took me upstairs to the second story. Here, as we waited for the girl to return, he said, "Forgive the lack of light, sir. It is my master's whim."

"Why?"

He seemed embarrassed.

"It has something to do with the Old Faith," he said. "I beg your pardon. We thought you to be a devotee of the Hessek order."

"Do I seem a priest? I'm not. But this is a Masrian house."

"Partly, sir. But when a man is desperate, he will turn anywhere. And if you are not of the Masrian canon yourself—"

"I am a foreigner," I said. "Tell me about the Old Faith."

Before he answered, something went through my brain, some intimation, a memory of talk on the ship. The Old Faith. Darkness as opposed to the clear light of the Flame, the sun and the torch symbols of Masrimas, something arcane and occult, a mildewed dust from the tomb of ancient Hessek.

"Myself," he said sturdily, a fellow who felt his sense and his reason affronted by the persisting doubt in his bones, "myself, I don't credit such superstition. I, too, have Masrian blood, and if I incline to any god, it would be the Flame-Lord. That's clean. For the other, it's rife in the old city over the marsh. Bit-Hessee. . . . Did you know, not even a jerdier will go there after sundown?"

"Give me a name for this god of the Hesseks. I thought they worshiped the ocean or some such."

"Yes, sir," he said, "but it's not a god. It's a—an *un*-god. I'd rather keep quiet. I've said too much. You understand, my master Phoonlin turned to the idea in desperation, and he doesn't grasp the fundamentals of it. I've heard them say you must be pure Hessek to do that. . . . Here's the girl coming, sir."

He broke off, and the veiled servant ran up on her white mouse feet, and whispered that the master bade me enter.

It was now very dark. I went in at another door and stood in shadows. I made out breathing, harsh from pain and excitement—or was it fear? I read his fright, glimpsing him with the inner eye rather than my sight, a fat man wasted to his skin, a blade of pain in his side, death on his mind.

"Be calm," I said. "I am the sorcerer Vazkor, and I have come to heal you."

There was a lamp on a stand. I crossed to it, opened the glass panel, and put my hand in, letting the energy rise gently from me, as I had learned to do, enough to heat the wick and set it burning. Phoonlin caught his breath. The flame shot up, scattering lights about the walls as I closed the glass on it.

Now I could see him. He lay in a chair, blinking at me. The curled wig was threaded with silver, and there was a silver fringe on his robe and great rings on his fingers, but his face was naked. He would sell me everything, I could see, for an hour without pain. Here was my wage.

"I have tried several," he muttered. "All failed. I wasted good cash on them. You, too, perhaps, in spite of your trick with the lamp." He glared at me with dismal rage. "You're just a boy."

"It is your discomfort that makes you forget yourself," I said. "So I will relieve you of it, and then we shall do business."

The minute I put my hand on him, I felt the stone, "saw" it through my palm, like a black knot in a white branch. I thought, *This I will leave you for today. Only the hurt I will take, till I have what I want.*

Rich Phoonlin became rigid. He gripped the sides of his chair, and paused, to be certain.

"It has—gone—" he said. His face was full of entreaty.

"You are not yet cured," I said. "That's for tomorrow, if you'll pay my fee."

He sighed and shut his eyes.

"Even for this," he said, "I would reward you. By the

Flame, how sweet it is. If you can make me well, you may name your price."

I had questioned Kochus briefly concerning the merchant, and was well primed.

"I name my fee now. Ten balances of gold, to be weighed at the market rate; fifteen of silver. Also a brief interest in your business dealings, corn and vineyards, I think, and pearls. I ask only enough to provide me an adequate income while I am in the city, say twenty percent of each current measure, vat and gem—at the market rate, of course."

"You dog," he said. "Do you judge me that wealthy? You will batten off my blood, like a parasite, will you? What right have you to ask this of me?"

"As much right as you suppose you have to live. Choose."

"You'll ruin me."

"Death would do it more thoroughly than I," I said. "I will return tomorrow; you may tell me then if my terms are to be met."

I felt no pity for him, trying to keep hold of his life and his hoard at once. It was not my time for pity, at least, not for men such as Phoonlin.

Torches burned along the front of the Dolphin's Teeth, in funnels of blue and yellow glass. Inside the vestibule and corridors, I passed no one who did not stare.

The story had got around, as was to be expected. They had heard everything, the episode with Gold-Arm, the hours as healer in the Grove, the jerdat-prince turning tail with his two hundred men. What would the sorcerer do next?

The sorcerer went to his apartment. Here I was presently disturbed by Kochus, coming back from his supper with a frightened face.

"Charpon, Lord Vazkor," he blurted, his eyes darting nervously. He was about to betray his master to me, and the thought scared him almost as much as I did.

"What of Charpon?"

"It's the ship, the *Vineyard*. The Hesseks say he means to get aboard tonight, very late, and sail with the dawn tide. That he means to tell you nothing. The other seconds are to be with him, and all the crew he can gather up so fast. The oar-slaves are still aboard. I hear he's sent them starting rations—the meat and wine they're given before a voyage."

I let Kochus rattle on, explaining this and that to me, Charpon's foolishness, his own willingness to serve me, how dangerous it had been for him to go against the master and bring me the news. I did not want to lose the ship and did not mean to. Charpon, who seemed almost deliberately to have set himself to be a thorn in my side, had reached his terminus. The only way to stop him and surely end his trouble to me was to kill him.

Having decided that, then I must face the other thing, that I did not want to kill him, or any man for that matter, not in that one infallible way I had, by use of my will. This was no ethic or moral stigma. It was pure fear. I feared the Power in me. At such times as I feared it, I felt some demon had possessed my brain, the sort of dichotomy that would drive me from my wits. So now I shirked it.

I sent Kochus out, thanking him, and he slunk away to the bed of Thei, furtive with his anxiety not to appear furtive.

Long-Eye, who crouched at my door immobile as a wooden sentinel, I called in. I told him of Charpon's plans.

Before I need say anything else, Long-Eye said to me, "I follow Charpon and kill him."

"He won't be alone," I said.

"No matter. All Hessek men reverence Lord Vazkor, before Charpon."

"You know I could do this myself," I said, goaded by the bizarre guilt of it. "Don't you question that I ask you to manage it for me?"

He gazed at me blankly. Gods were inscrutable. He looked for nothing else. He slipped away into the night without another word.

He saved me in the sea from my death, that man; I sent him to his own.

I sat before the purple window till dawn rained indigo through the black, and red through the indigo, and the birds sang softly in their cages.

It had not been a night for sleeping. I had thought, *Is it now he kills Charpon, or now? Maybe the Hesseks adhered to their master after all. Maybe judging Long-Eye a robber, they have killed him instead, perverse jest to round off this lunacy. For it is foul, it stinks. If a knife must be used, why not my knife? I have slain a man before, I suppose. This is delegated murder.*

Eventually, a knock. The door opened, and I jumped to my feet as if it were I who awaited the executioner.

It was not Long-Eye, but one of the Hesseks, who promptly groveled, obeising himself hands over face.

"The Lauw-yess—" he began, and broke into a gabble of ship's argot.

That was how I learned that Charpon, walking with five Hessek sailors, had halted in a winding alley, a shortcut leading from the Fish Market into the docks, saying someone tracked them, some footpad, who must be dealt with. The Hesseks accordingly concealed themselves in the narrow mouths of warehouses that stood about, and Charpon stationed himself alone, facing the direction they had come. The footpad, presumably sensing trouble, failed to appear, so Charpon presently went back a way, with a drawn knife.

From the gloom of the street there rose suddenly a strangled animal scream, another, and another.

While it was true that most storehouses in the Commercial City employed guards, it was also true that they recognized their duties as being within rather than without doors. No one therefore emerged to interrupt Charpon as, leisurely and bloodily, he killed Long-Eye, the messenger he had been expecting.

Of the Hesseks, three took to their heels. Two stayed, gummed to the shadows, trembling and muttering. Eventually the cries, and the whining note that had replaced them, ceased. Charpon reappeared, a red-armed butcher, and he said to the Hesseks plastered flat in their fear to the doorways, "And shall I do the same for the slave's master, this reptile Vazkor, someday when he sleeps?"

Then there was a noise, like a bird disturbed on a roof, and Charpon's head darted up and met some swiftly moving thing that flew to him like a bird. The bird flew into Charpon's eye.

When he was dead, which was not quickly, the Hesseks stole over, and saw this bird was a long piece of flint, filed sharper than a knife. They had been careful, prudent from years on the uneasy perimeter of law and safety, not to look for whoever had avenged Long-Eye from the warehouse roof. Yet I got from them, when I questioned them later, that it must be a Hessek, a pure Old Blood Hessek from the ancient city, Bit-Hesee, over the marsh, for such slingshot was what they carried there, to get duck or gulls from the reed-beds. Having been prohibited by Masrian law to carry blades, they had invented all manner of devious toys to compensate for the lack.

The sailor, having recounted his tale almost on his face, now glanced up. The varicolored lights from the dawn window caught his expression, not of nervousness or secrets, as I had anticipated, but a curious sort of frightened pleasure.

"Find Kochus and the rest," I said, "and send them to me."

According to his story, he had not glimpsed the "footpad" Charpon had slaughtered. No doubt he had been particular in not glimpsing him, as with the unknown assassin on the roof. Any master of a galley was to a certain extent hated by his men, and Charpon was no exception. Probably one of the three who had run off had put the occasion to his own use in settling an account. A mystery not worth unraveling.

The master had owned his ship; it would be easy to supplant his rights with mine (a chain of gold cash in a suitable official area), hand the command to Kochus, who would puff up with the delight of an unwholesome and evil boy, and be my creature willingly, as even now he was.

The thorn, by whatever means, had been plucked from me.

It was settled.

But for Long-Eye, what? Son of a short-lived people, he had lived no longer in my employ. He had saved me from the hurricane that I might give him to Charpon's knife. He had believed me a god. Perhaps he died in agony, believing it.

I sat and spoke with Kochus, and listened to the three terrified seconds summoned back from the ship. They had obeyed Charpon in spite of me, and begged me again and again to overlook the lapse. All the while I visualized Long-Eye's hacked body in the alley near the docks. I knew that as I gave out my orders and my clemency, the mundane rats who dwell here and there about any port were coming from their houses to a feast.

4

That day I returned early to Phoonlin's house, and cured him of the kidney stone. He railed against me, as before. He told me, as before, that I was a dog to bicker over his life. Still, he had had the papers drawn up, and got witnesses ready—he had no choice. His pain had come back, as I had meant it to, and I would not lay a hand on him till I was paid. I thought sourly then that he could not call me any worse name than I had already coined for myself the previous night. I told him he would not dare cheat his tailor, why should he expect to cheat me?

A crowd had gathered about the Dolphin's Teeth soon after sunup. It might have been anticipated—the poor, the sick, the inquisitive. When I came in sight, there was uproar. My fame had spread faster even than I had reckoned on. Despite the efforts of Kochus and the Hesseks, I could make no progress for clutching hands. I stopped and looked around, moved by my shame and by disgust, at them, and at myself who traded on their desperation and naïveté.

"I will heal none of you here. Go back to your homes, and at dusk you will find me in the Magnolia Grove. That is my last word."

Then a woman rushed toward me, shrieking in Hessek, and Kochus struck her aside. This turned my stomach, but I dared not help her or they would be bawling again.

Without another glance about, I walked straight on up the steps, and the crowd gathered itself out of my path, save for a rough swarthy fellow who grabbed my arm. But I let him have a shock from my flesh that sent him off howling, and I was not molested further.

By noon, Charpon's death at the hand of robbers was news at the hostelry. Charpon's seconds, who must surely guess my part in the matter, were too awed to voice their suspicions, and helped spread the tale of a mysterious party of thieves from Old-Hessek-over-the-marsh. There had been crimes in the docks before that had found their origin in Bit-Hessee.

I saw to the business of the *Vineyard* as quickly as I could, putting Kochus in charge of the vessel as my captain. The man grinned and mouthed his pleasure, yet with a pane of profound unease over his eyes. He only balked once, at my command that the *Vineyard*'s rowers be unshackled and permitted the freedom of the deck, though under the care of a hired ship-guard, and that these hapless cattle be paid and decently fed. He argued that slaves were violent and prone to flight. Most of those I had seen had looked too broken to attempt it; if they did, I reasoned we could get more. Should the ship be long in dock, I did not want the oar-crew dead from lack of exercise and clean air. Lyo, my former oar-mate, who I had long since freed and used as my servant, aboard ship and on land, I delegated to oversee the act and report back to me. It earned me a fresh name in Bar-Ibithni; this time for foolish charity.

That, my second day, was altogether a busy one. Phoonlin's agents visited me to arrange payment of my wages, and I spent the remainder of the afternoon in renting for myself rooms fashionably east of Hragon's Wall and on the fringe of the Palm Quarter, near to the money belt of the city. Everywhere I went my guard of Hesseks went with me, and Kochus, or one of his fellow pirates. Now and again, some group of supplicants would approach me, but I would not break my rule, and rough treatment sent them off. A public benefactor is everyone's property but his own. I dreaded my evening reappearance in the Grove, the sickness and entreaty, the healing they pressed from me, which brought me no joy, only commerce in reputation and coins. I thought, *This is to be sucked dry by leeches. And are they the leeches or am I the leech? Who feeds upon whom?*

It had all come to me too quickly, this I could finally see. But there was no stopping now. I had to remind myself hourly of my goal, my anchor of purpose—requite my father's name, be worthy of it, slay a white witch.

At dusk the people were thick on the road, their little lamps of tallow under filmy greenish glass dotting the way as far as the gate of the Grove. I did not look about, but straight ahead, for I had learned that to catch a man's eye meant he would begin to plead and fight to reach me. The people opened a way for me to let me through and fell in behind to follow. And they were very quiet. Even when I entered the Grove and walked up the lawns, the crowds there were silent, a massed darkness all of the garden's dark, except for their lights and the fireflies in the bushes. I remember I had some fancy that they knew I had ordered a man's death the night before, indirectly the death of two men. But it was more simple than that. They had heard how I intended to "live Masrian," the other side of Hragon's Wall on the edge of the Palm Quarter. They guessed this was the last I should consent to be with them. There was no riot, no shouting, and no prayer that I abide. They had accepted that they could not influence anything of mine. They moved by me, I touched them, they received healing and melted into the shadows like a ritual. They were like ghosts. I seemed to see through them to the transience of their persons, the brevity of their days.

It was a black moonless night, and became cold as the nights of early summer do in Bar-Ibithni.

I was exhausted. I wondered how they could yet draw strength from me.

Quite suddenly the crowd began to thin, to fade away, the cloudy lights and moanings and pressure of fingers, like a dream. I saw with vacant surprise that the sky was lightening, transparent with dawn.

An old woman stood at my elbow.

"Make me young," she whispered.

"Now, Lellih," Kochus said. He had been slumbering beneath some arbor. He yawned, waiting to see if Lellih would amuse or annoy me to discover how he should react to her. The remaining crowd, since she was recognized as a thing of mine, had drawn back in awe to let her through.

"Young," she said, clawing my arm, "young, and virgin."

"She's a saucy old piece," said Kochus.

I stared at her in the slaty light. Crinkled paper on a face of wire bones, but her crooked back straight as a sword from my hands. I had been expecting her to return.

"Why not?" I said to her. She cracked. "Not yet," I said. "Before witnesses. Do you agree, granny-girl?"

Her face smashed into laughter, like a child's. She smote me a blow with her cobweb hand.

"Done!"

I went to the inn and slept like the dead, save that I dreamed. (Maybe the dead dream, too, and forget their dreams when they are born again, as the Masrian priests declare.)

When I woke I had forgotten Lellih. But she had not forgotten me. She stood in my court, screeching maledictions on me for a fraud who promised her youth and withheld it. Kochus had threatened her with blows and she threatened him with her teeth. She said better men than he had died of her bite.

It was noon of the middle day of the Masrian month of Nislat. As good a day as any to remove my diverse household from the Dolphin to my new rooms.

Kochus had seen to the domestic arrangements, hiring a cook from the inn and a couple of girls to feed us and keep the place clean. He also brought Thei and installed him in his own quarters, whispering to me that if ever I felt the need . . . I kept my guard of ten Hesseks, paying them now, from

Phoonlin's bounty, a daily wage. For these the largest area, the outer yard and stables, was turned into a makeshift guards' barracks. Shortly, a black dog began to be seen here. which—they said, eager as children—they meant to train against robbers, though mostly they seemed to train it to beg scraps from their fingers.

There were nine rooms in all, built about a couple of courts, Masrian style. The better of these courts I kept for my own use, the other was divided unequally between the luxurious Kochus and the downtrodden domestics. Kochus's brother seconds and the residue of the ship's rabble I had released from my service. Even if I wished to crew the ship tomorrow, I would find men in the Market of the World or the dock eager for such work. For the seconds, they were glad to go, still sensitive to Charpon's slaughter. I never saw any of them again.

Beyond my own household, I kept five men in my pay, Lyo being one of them. I allotted them portions of the city. Their instructions were to nose after stories of sorcery, legends of an albino woman who could heal and harm as I did. They were to mention my name, Vazkor, to see if any ripples stirred. Only Lyo dared say to me, "Is it a sister of yours you're seeking, lord? Or a wife? She must have angered you, lord. Don't vent the anger on me."

"No sister," I said. "She's twice my years. A white withered hag with cold eyes. Find me word of her, and I'll see you rich as the Emperor."

Thinking of it, as ever, brought back the old poison into my veins. My dreams had been all of her, that white thing with its silver lynx face, or the black face of the shireen. My instincts, which roared to me of her presence near at hand, could surely not be wrong. I could do so much, I must be able to find one bitch.

By sunset, twenty-three messengers had come to my barely settled apartments. The rich invalids of the Palm Quarter had been awaiting my arrival. Some spoke of gifts to come and others sent me gifts; the outer room grew bright with bits of gold-work, silver dishes, and money chains, over which Kochus gloated lovingly.

The messengers bowed to me, a couple kneeled down. Their masters were dying of a variety of incurable afflictions—boils, gout, headache, palpitations, the illnesses of overindulgence and refined nerves. I told them I would visit them, and stipulated times. I was prepared to travel to and fro, to spy out as much of this opulent landscape as I could. Anything might be of use to me; the maddening thing was not knowing quite what.

I had also sent one messenger myself, having first seen him dressed in the black livery tailored for my servants at one of the better shops in Bar-Ibithni. He had carried my letter to the Hall of Physicians. It required an audience of them, at which, I assured them, I intended before witnesses to turn a crone (Lellih) into a girl.

It seemed too fine a stroke to miss, since her gods had set her in my hand. I no longer wondered if I could do it. Moment by moment I saw myself commit acts that one year before would have had me gawking if another had produced them. Out of boredom, I had raised the wine jar from its courtyard corner where it stood cooling in the shade, raised it without use of hands, by will alone. A voice in my brain had said to me then, *It is the time to beware when you begin to work miracles from ennui.* Had my father, Vazkor of Ezlann, ever done so frivolous a thing as raise a jar up in the air that he might hear the kitchen girls shriek? I imagined not.

Lellih was in the first court, Kochus's area, shielded from the Hessek barracks by a porphyry wall, a grove of young cypress trees, and a gray marble fountain. A friendship had been struck between Thei and Lellih, a means, I suppose, of preserving the artificial sustenance of their lives. Now they crouched like a couple of cats over a Masrian board game of red and blue checkers, drinking koois in little enameled cups and smoking little female pipes of green Tinsen tobacco.

My shadow fell on the board, and Lellih sprang around to berate me. I cut her short.

"Tonight you will go with me to the Hall of Physicians."

Lellih screamed.

"They cut up Hessek women there, and pickle their parts."

"No doubt wise. Beginning with the voice box."

Lellih cackled her cackle. "Is it to make me young, young before witnesses, eh? Is it?"

"Yes. It may kill you."

"May it? Then he would raise me, would he not, my lovely darling?"

Magicians work wonders on the living; demons raise the dead. I did not like her words.

"I agree no bargains of that sort."

But she was already back to the old song.

"Make me young. How young will you make me? Make me fifteen, fifteen and a virgin."

Thei laughed. The laugh was disconcertingly a boy's.

"She has no modesty."

Lellih squeezed his waist, her elderly lust tickled by anything toothsome, its sex random.

"We'll make a pretty pair."

I hired horses and a carriage. By conqueror law, no man but a pure-blood Masrian might ride or draft white mounts. Therefore, with the contrariness of my years, I chose blacks. We made a small procession, going down through the Palm Quarter to the Hall of Physicians, the carriage with its gilt and enamelwork, the six black outriders. I heard the tremor of sound start up all about: "There is the carriage of the sorcerer Vazkor." Truly, I had not done badly in three days to get myself into such a quantity of heads.

The thoroughfares were crowded. The Palm Quarter seemed never to sleep by night, lamps burned till daybreak.

Women with faces in veils of paint instead of cloth leaned from their balconies; torchbearers, each torch in its cage of iron or glass, ran before some lord on his way to a theater, bisecting the road with streamers of gold smoke. On every side, pillars reached up with their round fingers to grasp the cascading panoply of roofs. The prayer-towers murmured at the death of the light, their tall minarets like slender starry war-spears massed on the blue-green dusk, while at the center of the rising terraces, suitable far toward the sky, the Emperor's Heavenly City made a distant black diadem.

The Hall of Physicians was crammed to its doors. They had come to mock, as they were telling each other, to deride this obscure showman who dared try to deceive them with some common trick. The talk had an oiled quality of deprecation and laughter, but when the usher led me across the mosaic of winged horses that served as a floor, a silence fell like the night.

The Master Physician peered at me through a spyglass of topaz while the usher announced me, for all the world as though none of them might guess who I was. There was then a discussion between this fool and that, the purpose of which was to keep me loitering. I broke in.

"I am aware my name and my intention precede me," I said, "or I should not have been granted audience here at all. Thus, gentlemen, shall we get on?"

Kochus and three others escorted Lellih in. Two underlings of the Hall were selected to strip her, for the physicians' observation, to a dry, curd-colored nudity. Lellih leered about her, unabashed, from inside that case of flapping dugs and bald loins, still irrepressible. Brazen as their scrutiny was merciless, she poked their well-fed sides for every touch she got from them.

The Master Physician spoke.

"I doubt you can do more with her than soften her flesh a little with some oil or balm, such as Tincture of the Princesses. For her teeth, perhaps an artificial set of ivory or whale-rib. The breasts might be cut and padded with membrane, but there is a risk of infection and this practice has grown unpopular."

"Sir," I said, "don't presume to teach me cosmetic medicine." The ponderous old wretch was unaccustomed to plain arrogance in others, and could not collect himself sufficiently to reply. I said, "The woman is eighty years. I mean to make her young, a girl. And without recourse to any such rubbish as you mention."

Affronted, he dropped his spyglass. An usher bounded to retrieve and hand it back to him.

Lellih meanwhile screeched, "Tell the frog to sew up his jaws. He shall see, he shall." And she drew the attention of one sleek young man who had attracted her notice to the straightness of her spine, she, who had gone crooked from birth till I healed her.

At last I inquired if they were satisfied, and the physicians drew away, shaking their heads, smiling, gesticulating, saying I was deranged, every man tense as a bowstring. I had a stool brought and set Lellih on it. She would keep up her chatter; I put her in a trance, as much to have peace as because I thought she might feel pain at what I did. I motioned the assembly to stand as close as they wished to me, and to her. The Master Physician had stopped looking through the topaz, and leaned forward in his chair so far that he was almost out of it.

I placed my hands on her little skull. I thought, as one does suddenly when there is no road back, *Maybe I shall find now I cannot do it.* But something in me struck the hesitation aside. *You are a god, Vazkor, son of Vazkor. And you do this thing not only to make a path to a witch's hiding place, but to prove to men what has come among them.*

I had never completely felt the true pride of what was in

me before, not even when I had turned the storm, had walked on ocean. Hubris had mingled with surprise that day. Now, it stood alone with me.

I was flooded with a surge of Power, of life itself. I felt the flood sear from me into Lellih under my hands, bright as a bursting sun.

Not intending it, unguarded, I glimpsed her brain, the squawking crows in their mind attics, the dusty cerebral mansion of an old woman's soul. Then the light had scattered the dust and crows. I drowned that inner room with it. I gave her my Power for that instant, let her feed from it, and felt the dying tree tremble in its bark.

The nearest physician uttered a cry, and actually ran backward.

Lellih's skin was crackling and twisting like paper in a fire. In the prosaic seconds before the sense of glory came on me, I had never anticipated anything this showy, the flesh sloughing from her like plaster from a wall. Her left hand appeared first, like a pale flower pushing up from dead roots. One perfect woman's hand with almond nails and a lotus palm.

"Stop," the nearest physician, no longer so near, shouted. "This is a blasphemy. Stop, you will kill the woman."

I kept my fingers on Lellih's head, and watched him till he dropped his eyes and averted his whole person in fright. I could feel her thin hair lifting by its roots under my fingers. The left breast, rounder than it had been, juddered with a heartbeat quick as a sparrow's. Her flower hand lay on the yellow twig of her knee, which gradually peeled like a split chrysalis to let out the firm new limb of a girl.

Abruptly she rose to her feet, leaving me, going forward, stepping out of herself like some strange woman-serpent rearing from the expended skin.

I had never in my life seen anything that abhuman, that terrible. It thrilled me; *I* had made this happen.

The physicians were shouting and pressing away from Lellih as if she carried plague, yet were unable to take their eyes off her.

Her hair was growing up, spilling from her skull like black water from a fount, thick black Hessek hair, girl's hair. Like gray scales the old body rained into dust on the mosaic. Her back was white and smooth rising from its vase of white ample buttocks. She moved, I saw the outline of one breast, perfect to its candied tip. The profile was polished alabaster, black eye, a mouth to entice bees, white little teeth. She looked over her shoulder at me. It was an unexpected face, alluring, yet cold as unheated metal, the colors too fresh, unlived in.

She was young as the world before the world knew men.

One of the physicians went on his knees. She turned to look at him, as if he offered homage to her, which indeed perhaps he did. And as she turned, her eyes rolled up in their sockets. She fell forward without a sound across the wings of the jade horse in the mosaic.

It was known all over the Palm Quarter by sunrise; all over the city by noon. A crone changed by magic into a maiden in the Hall of Physicians.

She lay in a stupor in a room of the second court, by the porphyry wall. She lay there five days.

I half thought a mob from the Commercial City might come to the gate, but they did not. They were afraid of the devil-sorcerer Vazkor.

I had meant to kill Charpon simply in order to be sure of transport; I had most definitely killed Long-Eye by making an assassin of him. Presently I should have to fight and kill Sorem, one of the Hragon princes, a youth I had barely spoken with, a youth who reminded me of my own self. All those things came about through my Power and my quest, my cowardice and pride, my inability to strike a balance in myself between man and mage. And still, I had used Lellih in yet another of these games of mine, these random games that resulted in self-fear and guilt.

Those five days when she lay insensible, I had other matters to handle, for I must visit the rich about the Palm Quarter, heal their ills and garner their coins. These sophisticates did not fear me. They welcomed me, hungry for something different. It was a gaudy drudgery. The fine houses, the costly furnishings, the whining of fat patricians whose Hessek slaves—all Masrians, it seemed, had Hessek slaves—lay in half-starved heaps about the lower kitchens or scurried to obey, with purple whip-scars on their necks.

Besides this, no word came to me of the woman I sought, the sorceress. I would lie awake in the nightingale nights of eastern Bar-Ibithni, and I would tell myself I had mistaken her, the smell of evil that I believed an indication of her presence. It was the city which was rotten, that and my deeds in it. The glory had paled. Any sunset, no matter how glamorously bright, means the sun is going out. And with myself, also, a period of inner dark had followed the light. I seemed trapped in my own careful plan.

I had been waiting, too, on edge, for Sorem's formal challenge. By the aristocratic code of honor, a certain season of days must elapse from insult to battle, so the participants might burnish their skills and see to their affairs. This time of pause was now over. I had noted that the rumor of Sorem's altercation with me had flickered out in the city. Some dampening force had clearly been at work there, hushing up the business. The Emperor's men, perhaps. It scarcely mattered; I should have to meet Sorem, finish him. At least on this occasion it should be clean and with a blade. I would keep to their ludicrous code because I was surfeited with magic, sick of myself.

Then, the challenge did not come. No band of jerdiers with set faces slinging some parchment scroll on the floor and marching out. I wondered what kept him, if he had been forbidden this duel.

There was a silly woman, the wife of one of my patients. She had been sending to me constantly. She was pretty enough, and she wrote in delicate Masrian script, unlike the picture-writing of Hessek, describing how she would die and see that I had the blame for it if I did not tend to her. Her servant, a foxy fellow with an earring, informed me that I should find her in the white pavilion of her husband's house, and, wanting distraction, like a fool I went. She was dressed in true Masrian style, skirts of flounced brocade and a jacket of beadwork, and where there was not guaze or silk or sleeve or flounce, there were bracelets, necklets, rings, and ribbons. It would be easier to strip a porcupine.

I stayed with her till the red shadows of afternon turned to blue on the white lattices of the pavilion. She told me I was cruel not to care for her when she had betrayed her husband in order to pleasure me. It was the sort of stuff countless stupid girls had meowed in my ears since first I began to lie with women. She told me, too, that I was not a god, as her Hessek slaves had said, but only a man, and would wish for her again. I did not need her lessons.

I went back to my rooms, hoping for some tidings there of any sort.

There were tidings.

Lellih was gone.

Lyo stood in the court. He said, "She slipped out at dusk,

they say. But there's a man gone also, one of your sailor guards."

I asked him who. He told me the man was called Ki. The name nagged me till I remembered Ki was the Hessek Charpon had imprisoned below deck because he swore he had seen me walk on the ocean. I had had the story from Kochus.

"Another thing," Lyo said, "at your door."

He held up before me a black crow, or the corpse of one, its neck severed to the spine. It was some while since I had seen a bloody carcass, and obviously this had not been slain for its meat.

"Why that?"

Lyo winced.

"The Hesseks say it is a token of the Old Faith. An offering."

"To whom?"

"To you, lord," he said, "to you."

I did not instigate a search for Lellih. She had shown my powers to the Physicians Hall. It was enough. I did not need her value as a peepshow, despite what I had said. Something in what I had done unnerved me. I was almost glad the proof was missing. Where she had gone and what she did, I did not speculate on. Only the memory of that half-turned face—that primeval, virgin, wicked face—disturbed me, that and the dead crow left at my door. Sacrifice to a god. Not Masrimas, for whom they slew white horses at the midsummer festival, but some darker effigy, the Ungod of the Old Faith. I questioned Lyo briefly. A Seemase, he could tell me little. The Hesseks, when I spoke to them, gibbered and muttered. The vanished Ki, they admitted, might have known how to tutor me in the ancient religion of Old Hessek.

I sat in a chair and surrendered my mind to a black wasteground of profitless reflection. My past and my chaotic present ran before me, and the unanswered question of my future.

5

A brazen bell rings in the Masrimas Temple of the Palm Quarter at midnight. I heard it struck, and roused myself, and heard another thing. The black dog was barking, for a carriage on the lonely midnight road had halted at my gate.

One of the Hesseks came into the court and rapped for me at the door.

"There is a rich woman in the first courtyard, lord. She gave us gold so we should let her in to you." He showed me the chain of money and grinned nervously.

I imagined it was my doxy of the afternoon, risking her lofty name and her husband's indulgence in pursuit of me. For a moment I meant to pack her off, but, aimless as I had become, thought better of it. If her scented flesh and pigeon's chatter could come between me and my mood tonight, all to the good.

I told the Hessek to bring her, and sat down again to watch her rustle in, full of pleas and threats and endearments, her skirt of flounces scraping the doorway.

The lamp was burning low, yet when she came, there was no mistaking it was another than the one for whom I had looked.

She was tall and she held herself, moreover, very straight, with a pride unusual in a tall woman. Her garments were black, and she came into the red light like a fragment of the dark outside, and for all her flounced Masrian skirt with its fine beaded sweat of gold drops, she was veiled like a Hessek woman, even her eyes. I could see only her hands, long, slender, hard brown hands, like a boy's, so that for a second I wondered, Bar-Ibithni being as it was. Yet I could tell she was a woman, even veiled, her breast hidden in the drapery, and when she spoke, I could not miss it. A somber, smoky voice like the color of the lamp.

"You are Vazkor, the man they call the sorcerer?"

"I am Vazkor, the man they call the sorcerer."

She seemed, from her tone, accustomed to prompt replies and obedience in others. Yet now she hesitated. There was a little bracelet, a snake of gold, on her right forearm, which flickered the light as if she trembled. But then she said, clear and steady, "I hear you deal honestly, if the payment you receive is high enough."

"Are you in need of healing?"

"No."

"What, then, do you require of me?"

"I want to know what price you put on a man's life.

I had risen, intending to adopt Masrian courtesies belatedly; now I set my hand to the lamp to brighten it.

"It would depend on the man," I said. "Some men come very cheap."

I heard her draw in her breath slowly, to steel herself. I already knew what was coming. The flame leaped up yellow under the rosy crystal, and she said, "Sorem, Prince of the Blood, son of our lord the Emperor Hragon-Dat."

The light did not pierce her veil after all.

"Sorem's life is obviously dear to you, madam. Why do you reckon it in jeopardy from me?"

"He has challenged you by the code to fight him. You will use some device or some trick, and kill him, and he is too honorable and too proud to see this. I ask you to avoid the fight. I will pay what you suggest is necessary."

"And what of my honor, madam? Am I to acquire the name of a craven? He promised me I should if I did not meet him."

"You barter and sell your magic, if such it is," she said contemptuously. "You cure a man for a chain of coins, and leave him to die if he has none. What is one name more?"

"You're unjust to me, lady, and ill-informed. As to Sorem, I can do no other than he's bound me to."

She stood there a moment like stone and then, in a theatrical, angular gesture, again oddly like a boy's, she gathered the veil up in handfuls and thrust it off.

And so I saw her.

Her hair was black and curling, shiny as glass, piled on her head Masrian fashion with pins of polished blue turquoise. She had no other jewels save for the little snake on her arm, only the flawless copper of her skin, which came from the black case of the beaded jacket like honey from a jar. She was slim, but slim like an iron blade, her hips and waist narrow as her hands were narrow, except at the rise of her breast where the terrain was altered, half revealed by the Masrian bodice, two full amber slopes powdered with gold dust like pollen, which spangled in the light as she breathed.

But her face was something else again. I vow I looked at it and thought her ugly one whole second, confronted by those aquiline features, her age, which was some years in excess of my own, the black anger that masked over her eyes; nothing soft anywhere. Then everything was changed; I saw the beauty that this face really was, beauty like the point of a knife.

"I do this that you may discover who I am." She had been like a lightning bolt to me, yet no revelation came with it.

"I assume you are the mistress or the wife of Sorem," I said. At that she smiled, not in any womanly way, but sardonic as some prince forced to be courteous to his enemy. Through the kohl and the black lashes of that extraordinary gaze, the lamp found out blueness.

"It appears you also are ill-informed, magician," she said. "I am Malmiranet, the cast-off of the Emperor, but still blood of the Hragons for all that. Sorem is my son."

"I beg your pardon, madam. I didn't realize I had a royal woman in my house. Be seated."

"And you be damned," she said, fast as fire. "I am not here to play empress with a dog from the backlands. Tell me the price of my son's life and you shall have it. Then I will leave."

Her eyes were surely blue, but dark as sapphire, darker than his. The looks that shot from them would wake a man part dead.

"You go the wrong way around this, madam," I said quietly. "You presume me a jackal and a wretch and a fool. You will make me one, then there'll be no reasoning with me."

"Don't tutor me."

"Nor you me, madam. I have spoken with your son. He won't thank you for the shelter of your skirts."

She made a gesture that said, "This is irrelevant, unimportant, providing he *lives*."

"And if I refuse?" I said, as I had said to him.

"There are ways."

"Have me murdered, Lady Malmiranet, and the whole city will say your son did it out of fear. Besides, I wonder what assassin could overcome me when I can kill a man with my mind alone."

She observed me unansweringly, but her hands were trembling again. I could smell her perfume now in the little room, a faint incense, smoky as her voice. Suddenly she dropped her lids and the words came out broken.

"Do you think I estimate my son a coward that I came to you? If he were that, you might have him. It is his bravery I fear, and your *sorcery*. If you can do one fifth of what they say, he will die. Why does a sorcerer want this duel? The notion of honor amuses you. Very well, let him believe you ran from him. What do you care for such a thing? You are a man, and young. Use your powers to make yourself a lord elsewhere, and let Sorem live."

I went up to her, this empress who had fallen from her high station for some reason that was beyond me, seeing her as she was. True, she was not quite a girl, but that face, carved so purely and without compromise, would never have been a girl's face. For the rest, even this close, you would need to be witless or blind to pass by. Her brows were nearly level with my own. I took her hand, the hand with the snake wrapped above it. The palm was hard from riding; the hand of Sorem could not be that much different.

"For you, then," I said, "he lives. I forego the dubious sweet of killing him."

Her eyes flashed up, wide, blue; deep enough they looked to go bathing in.

"Tell me your price."

"Nothing."

It was worth something to me to see her stare.

She withdrew her hand and began to pull at her veil.

"How can I trust you if you'll accept no fee?"

"That's one problem you must solve yourself."

She paused and said, "Are you the son of a king as the rumor has it?"

"Ask them in Eshkorek," I said.

She turned away, impatiently pulling at the veil till she was swathed in it again. She went out into the court quickly, without another word, and a minute after I heard the carriage wheels and the hooves of the horses on the road east.

Sorem's formal challenge came the next morning.

Two blank-faced jerdiers, his lieutenants, brought it: One handed me the bronze scroll-case and stared in the air above my head while I read the script.

Sorem Hragon-Dat to Vazkor, generally named the sorcerer.
An invitation to swords.
Tonight, the Field of the Lion, by the northern altar.
The hour after sunset.

"It is acceptable?" the jerdier asked of the air.

I told him it was.

They swung around like clockwork, and strode out.

The courts were full of whispers that day—Lellih, and the fight to come, and the veiled woman. In the middle of the afternoon a ragged man carried his child to the gate, and begged me to help her. I did not have the heart to refuse it, since there were only the two of them. The child was whimpering with agony in his arms, but went away laughing and skipping about the man's feet, he in tears. It moved me, and I caught myself thinking, *She should have seen that, the court lady with her talk of money chains and barter.*

I had not wanted to strike down Sorem, by whatever means. Having abandoned the scheme, now it did not seem such a very difficult feat to turn aside his challenge and end the nonsense. Nor did I mean to leave Bar-Ibithni to do it.

The way she had secretly come to me—from the Heavenly City, which was a legend for its guards and bolts—must have been dangerous for her. She had not known what to expect of me, either. I might have exacted any price, the sum of her wealth, her jewels, use of her body; I might have killed her even. Since all she had heard of me was rumor, the rumors would have postulated that, too—in some tales I was a savior, and in others a monster. She was brave and she was strong, as only something fine and tempered can be strong. I wondered if her amazement had lasted her, to find me a man and not offal in a gutter.

About a mile from the Pillar Citadel lay a stretch of open land, given over to vineyards and orchards but falling off northward into rough wooded country that ended only at the seawall. An altar place stood up near the wall on a low hill, a briar-grown pile of stones, sacred to some pastoral goddess common to Hessek slaves and poor Masrians alike, who crept here at dawn to strew bread and flowers for her. Beneath this hill lay the Field of the Lion.

I went by backways, and on foot, muffled in a cloak. For company I had Lyo with me and no other. I would have been glad of Long-Eye, his obdurate silence and discretion, his lack of curiosity at my strange deeds.

A ruined palisade, remains of some Hessek Fortress, ran along the outskirts of the fashionable streets, dividing the Palm Quarter from the vineyards at its edge. The sun was just down, the light hollowing with the flushed blueness of first dusk, when I passed through the palisade and took the path toward the northern wall.

Swarms of bats went dazzling through the cool sky, and in the black-green stands of cypresses the ubiquitous nightingales of Bar-Ibithni tuned their silver rattles.

Stars came out. The path wound up, then down into the woods, and I began to hear the sighing of the ocean as the soft wind blew it inland, serene as the breathing of a girl asleep. I thought, *What a night to go murdering on, what a night to slay a man.* And from that I came suddenly to notice that my perceptions had been altered by half an hour's argument with a woman.

Lyo was alert for robbers, and flinched at every sound. A fox barked three or four miles off, and his hand quivered full of knife. I laughed at him, so mellow had I grown. Next instant a man stepped from the shadow of trees. But he was one of Sorem's jerdiers, who nodded to me and beckoned me to follow.

The Field of the Lion was a rectangle of turf between juniper trees that filled the air with their scent. Northward the ground folded up from the wood into the altar-hill, the shrine at its peak, like an uneven jet doormouth cut in the wide twilight. I wondered how many aristocratic duels she had presided over, that obscure deity of the hill, with the dead poppies around her hem some slave had thrown there.

They had brought four brands in iron shieldings, as yet unlighted, and stuck them in the ground. Sorem stood by one, with a couple of his officers, dressed in the casual wear of the jerds.

It was getting dark in the field, but I glimpsed his face well enough. I saw the look of her there in it, as I had seen his face in hers.

He nodded to me, curtly, polite as my guide had been, and told the nearer man to light the torches.

"Welcome, Vazkor. I hope you agree the arena."

"Most picturesque," I said. "But there's another thing."

"Well, speak. Let's settle it."

The torches started to flare up behind their metal guards, changing the soft colors of the clearing by contrast to thick violets, greens, and leaded black.

"I did you wrong," I said. "I acknowledge it, and will recompense you as you wish."

"I wish to find recompense here," he said, "with this." And

he tapped the sword the lieutenant held for him, still in its scabbard of white leather.

"I won't fight you, Sorem Hragon-Dat."

He let out an oath, partway between scorn and amazement. "Are you afraid? The sorcerer afraid? The mage who turns crones into girls?"

"Let us say, I don't want your life."

The last torch caught with a gust of sparks and his anger sprang up with it.

"By Masrimas, you'll fight me, and I'll feed you steel before you tell me that again."

I showed him my hands, which were empty. He turned and shouted to his men for another sword. They brought it. He drew it and offered it to me. It was sharp and good. Next, he drew the other, his own, from the white scabbard. This was blue alcum chased with gold about the hilt, but no better edge on it.

"Since you have forgotten your blade," he said levelly, "choose either of these."

"You're too generous," I said, "but you must accept that I have no use for a weapon."

He looked like the tiger just before its springs.

He slung his own sword, point down, in the ground at my feet.

"Take it, and be ready."

"I decline."

He raised the soldier's sword, saluted the hilt, and came at me.

I had been tensed for it, yet he moved very fast. He knew his business evidently. *Here is a warrior*, I thought, with a kind of tribal stupidity. Then I lifted my hand and let the bolt from it. The light blazed out in a thin pale ray and the jerdiers yelled. It caught the darting blade and smashed it from his grasp.

He halted, stock still, about a yard from me.

"Magician's tricks after all," he said, very gently.

His eyes widened and went blind. I had barely time to think, *What now?* Something filled the air, a cold burning. I felt it strike me, and then the ground heaved up and tossed me over on my side.

I lay there for a heartbeat or two, dazedly aware of Lyo crouched near me with his wavering knife inexplicit for my defense, while I dragged the inner strength from myself to purge my brain and straighten my legs.

I had dismissed the delay, the extra days that had elapsed before Sorem's formal challenge was given me. Now I realized how the time had been spent. He had threatened me once with his priestly training, and he had been renewing his acquaintance with it. Sorem, this prince of the Hragons, could also wield Power.

I staggered to my feet. He had made no further move to attack me.

"I see how it is," I said.

"Good," he answered. "Now we fight. In whatever fashion you prefer, sword, or—that."

But it had cost him dearly to act the magician. His face was drawn and pale. It had sucked him dry as a gourd already, that one white blow, weaker than any of mine.

"Sorem," I said.

"No more talk," he said. He ducked lightly aside and took up the sword again. I thought, *I am shaming him further every second I refuse him. Surely I can fight him without killing him. Tire him out, then let him wound me perhaps; what's one wound more that heals at a wish?*

So I, too, reached down, and drew the sword from the ground, the alcum sword that was his own.

I had had swordplay in Eshkorek; you picked up such things there as you might have lessons in an instrument of music. Nor had I been sedentary long enough to have lost the skill. However, for my plan of coddling him, that shortly went from my mind. He fought me as the snake fights—swift, unlooked for, and lethal.

The blades ran together, and the force of his strokes rattled my bones to the arm socket. The red-hot iron of the torch-shields lighted up his face and showed me his determination, which I did not need to see. He did not hate me; it was more deliberate than that. Hatred would have been handier to deal with.

Presently he struck me in the side.

Not a killing stroke, but raw. We had been beating up and down, each giving ground to each and then retrieving it. The lick of steel in my flesh made me mad. No man likes to be whipped this way when he is thinking himself cunning.

I shut the wound like a door. If Sorem noted that, I do not know, for I gave him small leisure.

I thrust him back, the blade going like two or three meteors, and he grinned as he retreated.

"Better," he said, "better, my Vazkor," and he jumped sideways so only the tip of the alcum kissed his shoulder.

"You shall have better yet," I said, and cut under his guard, hitting him in the forearm. I had not intended this five minutes ago, but my warrior past was catching up to me.

I did not want to kill him, and maybe I should not have done, though by now the fat was near enough the fire to burn of itself.

As he was closing with me, I heard a man cough beyond the torches. Not a sound to alert anyone, unless he had heard that unique noise before, unlike any other—the choke a man must give when a knife blocks his windpipe.

Sorem apparently recognized it, too. Instantly we fell apart, staring through the glare of red iron, our pedantic fight suspended in the face of quick reality.

They did not keep us waiting, the fourteen men in their garments of black.

Sorem had brought four companions with him, I just one. If we had reckoned on treachery, it should have been from each other. But here stood fourteen men who had crept in on us, garbed for night work, and around their feet lay four dead jerdiers, Sorem's officers, dispatched with professional competence. Only Lyo stood upright and unharmed, gaping at me, as well he might.

One of the black cloaks stepped forward.

"Lord prince, your pardon for this interruption." Then he turned to me a battered, shuttered blob of features, myopic to life, a look I had seen often on the faces of professional homicides. "Sorcerer. Your pardon also. But I've been watching the duel and it seemed somewhat dilatory. Perhaps you'd like my help in ridding yourself of the prince. How would it be if two of my men held him while you ran him through? Much less exhausting, I'm positive you'll agree." He snapped his fingers, and someone tossed him a velvet bag that clinked. "Then there's this," he said. "We heard your price was high. My master—nameless, I fear, as all good masters are—offers you one hundred gold chains, here in the bag. Feel free to count them. You understand, of course, that having slain one of the Blood Royal, it would be wise for you to leave the city? Though, I may add, the Emperor will not weep long for this unfavorite son. Three or four months, say, and you'll receive a pardon."

Obviously, they, too, had had their doubts as to whether I should kill Sorem. It appeared that someone wanted him killed very badly. They intended to aid me and let me take the blame. Possibly silence me, too, later on, to consolidate their lord's innocence. I had a high price, did I? Higher, maybe, than they anticipated.

I glanced at Sorem. He thought himself finished, but he stood there, contemplating us, his eyes like blue hell, ready to take as many as he might into the dark with him.

"Well, sir," I said to the black cloak, "I appreciate your kindness. But I prefer to settle my own accounts." I swung the sword and stabbed it in his guts and twisted it, for all those men I guessed he owed the pleasure of his pain. As he fell, squirming and crying, I unleashed the force that had started up in me. It went from my palms and from my eyes, searing and half stunning me, that white light of Power.

Then, my gaze clearing, I saw ten corpses taking their ease on the turf, and three survivors gathered about Sorem in a squall of knives. My brain for the moment seemed spent of its energy; besides, he was in the thick of them, and I could not aim and miss him. The black cloaks were screaming as they fought, terrified, yet sworn to his murder.

A sword is no weapon to meet knives, too large and slow. I ran and pulled a man back and sliced open his neck for him. One struggled on Sorem's blade, trying to extricate himself, to ignore the mortal wound and go on living. Sorem held him aside, and kicked the legs of the second man from under him. As he went down, the other also crashed over, taking the sword with him out of Sorem's grasp. Sorem turned and saw the kicked man on the ground, who was surging up again with his knife poised for throwing. A pale shaft erupted from Sorem's eyes, the lightning flash that had hit me earlier. To observe it in another was uncanny. The black cloak rolled sideways from the blow, and got his own blade in the chest as he fell. Then Sorem dropped to his knees and hung his head like an exhausted hound.

6

The dead lay everywhere. Only Lyo had remained alive, and he was gone. I did not altogether blame him for that.

I made sure of the black cloaks swiftly. I even found the

bag of "gold," checked it and discovered it to be full of pebbles and the gilt imitation coins with which children play.

The night had grown abruptly soundless; even the sea held its breath. Then the nightingales began again, eastward and west, four or five of them, indifferent, as they had a right to be, to the battles of men.

Sorem had recovered himself a little and pulled himself to sit, his back against a juniper tree. I did not know the extent to which they were trained in the temple precincts of the south, if he could heal his own skin. But the wound I had given him in the forearm still bled; his sleeve was scarlet from it. Stunning the last of the black cloaks with Power had left him half dead himself. With some surprise, I became aware that I felt no debility, as I had before when I had used Power not to disarm but to take life. It seemed I had outstripped my own humanity yet once more.

I crossed to Sorem, and he said, "Some god must be laughing somewhere."

"Some god is always laughing. That is, if you believe in them, which is surely enough to make them laugh."

"What now?" he said.

"If you're able, close that wound. If not, I will."

"Will you?" he said, and smiled slightly. I saw he could not help himself and I set my hand on his arm, and watched the skin draw and refashion itself till only a faint bluish mark was left there under the rusty sleeve. He gazed at it a while, then he said, "I perceive I am the novice and Vazkor the master magus. But you puzzle me. For so much gold, why not let them kill me? No doubt they were not to be trusted, but with such talents you have no need to fear black assassins. My thanks for your aid, but why?"

"Why not?" I said. "I don't hanker for your death. Neither am I to be priced so readily, like the bull in the market, and certainly not with trash coins."

"There may be others searching for me. My life's a debt I owe Basnurmon. You had best get going and leave me, unless you want to tangle in court matters."

"Consider me tangled. On your own, you could hardly hold off the ravens. Do the priests teach you no healing?"

"Some," he said, and shut his eyes, which were swimming from weakness, "but the other is simpler to learn and refurbish. It's always more simple to harm than to cure."

I placed my palms on his shoulders, and let the healing pass into him. I felt it go this time, yet no lessening in myself.

The matter between us was changed. He saw, as I did, that the enmity, the sparring of two hawks who meet in the sky and suppose it their business to fight, was a thing of smoke that had blown over.

I showed him the bag of mock gold.

"Now tell me," I said. "Who is this shyster Basnurmon that seeks your life and wants me as his unpaid dupe?"

"Yes," he said slowly, "I owe you that at least." Feeling his strength return and partly astonished at the recovery, he was at sea, and took a moment to collect himself. The torches were guttering and the light came and went across the empty dueling place and the bodies sprinkled there. He looked at those, and then he said, "You understand that my father is the Emperor, Hragon-Dat. His seed began me and I carry his title; beyond that, nothing. He got me on my mother when she was barely a woman. She was his first wife then. They were cousins, both of the Hragon blood, but she was as proud as he, and he did not like her pride. Nor does he now. After me, there was no other child. I think she took care there should not be. Presently he put her aside, and chose another wife to be Empress of the Lilies, not royal, but out of one of the priestly families. This bitch gave him three males. Now he's finished with her, too, but she keeps him sweet by acting as his procuress, selecting for him boys and girl children scarce old enough to walk, let alone bed. Of the two empresses my mother is named second, his cast-off. Me, he has disowned in favor of the first son he had by his priestess-wife—this son, the heir, in Basnurmon. And here is the stumbling block. The whole city knows I am pure Hragon stock come down from Masrimas the Conqueror on both sides, sire and dam. Basnurmon is Hragon only through the sire, his priestess mother has none of it. This makes him anxious. All my life there have been plots. I am safer in the Citadel among the jerds than in the Emperor's Crimson Palace. I can imagine that hearing of my challenge to you, Basnurmon must have wanted a say in things. He thought he could be rid of me tonight, once and for all. The Field of the Lion is common dueling ground, no trouble to his dogs to find me here, and I was too much a fool to dream of it."

"And when he learns he's not rid of you, what?"

"That intrigues me, Vazkor. He's never been so open. He's risked much on this throw and won't like to have lost. For the Emperor, he'll turn his usual blind eye."

There came a sudden dull clatter of harness and mail from

the wood at our backs, and riders with closed Masrian lanterns showed between the trees. Sorem smiled.

"Yashlom and some of my jerd, from the sound of it, a minute or so too late, if it had not been for you. Still, we'll have a safe conduct to the Citadel."

The party of soldiers reined up, and the leader called out to Sorem. Even spies had been spied on, apparently, and these fifty jerdiers had been dispatched to intercept Basnurmon's men, rather too late, as Sorem had observed. Now they inspected the dead, and gathered up their own. Presently the captain, Yashlom, brought up Sorem's white horse, and he, courteous and graceful as the lord's son at a feast, offered the animal to me.

I thanked him, and told him I did not mean to break Masrian law by riding white, and added that I could make my own way back into the city, being well able, as he might have noted, to protect myself. I had in fact no wish to cause a military stir on my return home; I was too far in the plots and snares of the Heavenly City already for my entire liking.

Sorem nodded, probably aware of my reasons. He took me aside and said, "I have my life because of you. We met as enemies, but that's done. I won't forget this night's work." He offered his hand, which I gripped Masrian fashion. Then he mounted up and rode off with his men toward the Citadel and his precarious safety. Tomorrow she would hear, that blue-eyed lady, that he lived through me.

I had no fears of the dark disgorging further enemies, and went up the hill to the shrine of the unknown goddess, and sat down there in order to think. Yet my thoughts were aimless enough. This city of the south seemed intent to trap me and keep me from my purpose. Its women, its scheming. With some uncharitable bitterness, I reflected on the loyalty of Sorem's men, the four who died for him in the Lion's Field, the others who had burst on us with strained, angry faces, anxious for his defense. I was remembering the warriors of the tribes, even those I fought with in the Eshkir ruin, who forgot my leadership so swiftly. I had very often been aware I had no man I could trust my back to, and had none yet. Charpon the shark, and Long-Eye, dead. Even Lyo, my slave, had run away.

Then, looking down the northward slope to where the faint line of the ocean was penciled in above the seawall, I put reflection aside. A green light had opened there, and against its color shapes were moving. I was to have company.

My psychic armament was recharged in me, though I had retained one of the black cloak's short blades besides, which I now drew and kept in readiness. Soon I could make out the foremost of the several men who climbed toward me—Lyo.

He raised his arm and shouted to me in Seemase, "Lord! Wait, Lord Vazkor." He ran the last yards and flung himself down before me. "Your Power," he said. "I feared your Power, and ran away."

"I thought it was fourteen men and their knives you feared."

"No, lord." He lifted his head and stared at me. "I saw you kill them."

"Who have you brought with you?"

"Hesseks," he said. "Lord Vazkor, they were in the groves, watching what you did. They kept back till the jerdiers were gone."

"Yet more spies," I said.

"No, lord," Lyo said. It seemed to me he looked frightened, not of me or the watchers who had returned here with him, but of something less tangible, less avoidable than men.

The others were coming up now. There appeared to be five of them, but their own lamp was shining behind them, which I did not care for.

There were withered flowers lying on the altar stone, black opium poppies filched from some merchant's field. I loosed the energy from my fingers to set this offering burning and give me light to see by.

The Hesseks halted at once. A brief whispering went over them, like dry leaves blown down an alley. They were not speaking Masrian or Seemase, or the Bar-Ibithni argot so many got by on, but Old Hessek. I hardly needed the light after all to show these were not slaves or free scavengers from the docks, but the semi-outcast denizens of Bit-Hessee-over-the-marsh.

Ragged dirty garments, which had initially been greenish tunics not of Masrian style, were open at the arms and sides and laced with rope lacings, rusty belts of green copper links without knives in them—the law—yet strange morbid toys dangled there, catapults and little knotted strings and pipes and pouches of flints. Otherwise they wore no ornament, not even the Hessek prayer necklaces of red beads common to the dockland. Their hair was long, matted, and wild enough to break a wooden comb, if they had ever tried one on it, which I doubted. Their skins were the swarthy white of all true Hessek flesh; even their marsh-hunting had not tanned it.

I had never come on their like before in the city, at least, not dressed for their part openly. One of them I had certainly met previously, camouflaged in sailor's gear, later in my own livery. I recognized him now straight off: Ki, the man who saw me walk the sea, who vanished with Lellih out of my courts, who had left a dead and bloody crow at my door.

He moved near to me, kneeled, and touched the earth with his forehead. From that position he said, "You remember Ki, my master? I was your first witness and I was not believed." It was ridiculous, this speech delivered by a man on his face with his rump in the air. I told him to get up, and asked him what he wanted.

"To serve you," he said. "Let us serve you. There may be danger from the Masrian lords. If you wish a safe hiding place, we know of one."

He did not need to tell me where.

They smelled of danger, of lawlessness, those men, and of suspense and religion, too. It was not hard to find the pattern. Ki had spread legends of me, and taken Lellih to his people as a proof of my magic. His was a race like Long-Eye's, accustomed to gods, perhaps awaiting them.

I did the thing then that had been on my mind to try to do some while, the thing from which I shrank. I looked deliberately into his thoughts to be sure of him.

I had glimpsed the brain of Lellih briefly, but then I had been armored with hubris, the contact accidental and vague. Now I only brushed the surface of Ki's inner world, yet the alien country turned me cold to my groin. To enter another's head was no trip to be undertaken lightly or often. Still, having done it, I learned something.

For an instant I was Ki, saw through the eyes of Ki. What he was seeing in me was a god, a god darker than shadows.

Events, my own meditation, had unsettled me. There stole up on me a feeling of dread that must be explored.

I nodded to the Hesseks.

"Bit-Hessee then," I said, "Let's visit this outlaw city of yours."

7

Their green lantern burned on the seawall, where crumbling steps led down into the water. The remains of a watchtower stood there, its beacon long unlighted, and at the half-rotten pier were moored two ghostly boats, sailless Hessek craft constructed of the bound tough stems of the great marsh reeds. Poles rested on the thole pins, of some notched black wood, their blades muffled with swathes of cloth.

Three of the five Hesseks got into the nearer boat, Ki and another man took the oars of the second vessel and offered the passenger's place to me. As this went on, Lyo broke away and fled up the slope. I told them to let him go, which they did. He had been at best an unnecessary companion, whose nervousness put me out of patience.

The papyrus boat was rowed from shore a few moments later onto the black breadth of the ocean.

The Hesseks steered their course about three quarters of a mile out to clear the shipping and the docks of Bar-Ibithni. There was no moon, the liquid dark almost absolute except on the left hand, where the coast glimmered with the silver fog of lamps that marked the city and the port. Nothing lay in our path save two tall galleys anchored outside the bar, which presumably had been unable to make dock before sunset closed the toll-gate. They had the deathly stillness of all benighted ships, only the red signal lights popping on their rails and spangling in the sea. The Hessek boats drifted between them, unchallenged, on the muffled oars. Unwelcome in its own country, Old Hessek had learned caution to the last letter.

Farther west, the coastline was pleated into the obscurity of night, and the lights scattered there grew few and indeterminate. At length nothing showed but the glimmering, barely audible sea, companioned on one side and gradually swallowed away into a featureless shore.

Presently the salt-fish odor of ocean faded into something saltier and less pleasing, the reek of the marsh.

The boats began to turn inland at once. The water became

turgid and scythed off from the oars in a soup of vegetable flotsam. Soon reed-beds opened out before us, glowing unnaturally, not from the lamps of men but the phosphorous illumination of the landscape itself. The current swerved, guiding the sea and the Hessek craft together through a sinuous delta that slowly narrowed into the blackest of black channels. On either side reared up the marsh of Bit-Hessee, which was in essence the child of some older thing, a remnant left aground from the morning of the world.

Swamp rather than marsh, a swamp uniquely deficient in the noises of night birds or small water-life, yet perpetually susurrating. This insidious papery rustling reminded me, against my logic of the movement of vast reptilian wings aloft and similar reptilian scratchings below—doubtless no more than the stirring of the giant reeds and spiny leaf blades. There were insects, however, making an endless chatter. And occasionally a mouthing of bubbles uttered glutinously from the mud-banks where the trees rose.

I thought them palms at first, these trees, but they seemed rather the pylons of primeval ferns. In the faint dungeon glare of the phosphorus, their fibrous stalks, diagonally scaled, soared into a massive invisible umbrella of foliage.

"Ki," I said.

He looked up over the oars at me.

"Lord?"

"No birds, Ki. Yet I heard Bit-Hessee hunted these marshes for the pot."

"Birds farther east, lord. Nearer the New City. Hessek hunts there when it must."

Something flopped in the water ahead of us, and then passed alongside with a treacly wavering of the channel. Just beneath the surface, itself dully luminous, shone a saurian beast, part alligator and part bad dream.

"This swamp is old," I said.

Ki smiled, an ingratiating smile, but due to the circumstances, tacitly menacing.

"Old as Hessek," he said.

"And how old is that?"

"Old as darkness," he said.

The other man, alerted to our speaking, watched me with bright hollow eyes.

"Ki," I said.

"Yes, lord."

"Give me my true name."

He started slightly, then said, "We are cautious with names."

"Still," I said, "you imagine I am he, your black Ungod of the Ancient Faith." I did not want to delve in Ki's skull, nor any man's but my mind was still sensitive from the previous contact, and the images cast up on the skim of his brain were abnormally distinct. "You call him the Shepherd of Swarms. Don't you?" Ki lowered his eyes, the other man stared; both continued to row as if their arms moved independently. "He's the god of flies, of crawling things and winged creeping things, of tomb-darkness and worms. That's what you worship here in your swamp-sink."

"There has always been the dark," Ki mumbled, some ritual phrase.

"Shaythun," I said experimentally, and the faces froze above the rigidly grinding arms. "Shaythun, Shepherd of Swarms."

No one spoke. The enormous trees went gliding by and the insects sparked and ticked. The reeds, each thick or thicker than a man's wrist, came down into the channel and the boats pushed through them, causing the tassels of green-bronze, which passed for rush-flowers, to rattle like corrupt metal.

"If I am Shaythun," I said, "surely I am permitted to say my own name. But why should I be Shaythun? If I am a god, then why not Masri?" I said to Ki, remembering those cries he reportedly gave when first he saw me in the sea, that I was clothed in flakes of light, that I was Masri—Masrimas—the conqueror's god.

"You make fire and leave it to burn free."

I thought, *That's true*. No Masrian would light an unshielded lamp or even a camp fire without some covering and an invocation, let alone burn an offering on the altar of a cheap floral deity. And, perhaps ineptly, one supposes their Masrimas would not either.

"Why not Hessu, then," I said to Ki, "your sea god?"

"Hessu is no more. The Masrians drove him out."

"You have an answer for everything," I said. "I am Shaythun, then?"

"It is to be proved."

The reeds parted suddenly. The channel lay open ahead, broadening immediately into an irregular lagoon bounded by swamp growth in three directions, while to the west, about a quarter of a mile away, a fungoid whitish promontory stood clear of the salty pool—remains of the wharf and dock of the old city.

As we neared the dock, the skeleton of a ship appeared around the winding bank: a vessel of Old Hessek, unlike the galleys of the Conquerors, narrow and serpentine, green now, and sinking in the ooze. Beyond the dead ship, an avenue of wreckage, the ribs and timbers and rotting prows of countless other hulks, with weeping trees clinging among them. There had been good trade here, it seemed, before the harbor silted up. From this marine graveyard, broad steps clotted with slimy algoid gardens showed the way aboard the land.

The green lantern, extinguished all this while, was rekindled. The boats sidled to the steps and were dragged around among concealing undergrowth. Ki led me up the stair, carrying the lamp.

Black walls shot forward on the lamplight, rubble, slender blind windows. Bats flickered in crenellated gutters, under pointed broken eaves.

In the midst of the ruins, the path snaked downward, and abruptly the charcoal smell of smoke was mingled with the stench of the marsh. The winding street, whose upper stories embraced each other, presently became a tunnel, and into this pitch-black foulness we went.

Unexpectedly the lamp caught a white rat transfixed in its glare, and I called to mind the nickname Bar-Ibithni gave this area: the Rat-Hole.

It was a warren, such as rabbits make for themselves, but noisome in parts as the mansions of foxes. Here and there the tunnels were open to the sky, against which the deserted upper city ruinously crowded or the encroaching stems of the giant trees; mostly the road plunged beneath brick overhang or through the guts of the earth itself, where the hard mudbanks were hollowed out and shored up with stones. Stagnant salt canals roped away in the gloom of it, and the roots of growing things intruded. In this incredible vileness, men lived.

Shadows, crowding against mud walls that gaped with little entrance holes; the mouths of caves, subterranean house cellars, and rooms excavated from the swamp. Not rabbits, not foxes. Termites, rather. Termites who could make fire, and let it burn naked (Masrian blasphemy) in earthen pots by the "doors" of their macabre hovels.

I had never seen quite such degradation or such sinister eccentricity. Hessek had truly gone to earth as the hunted animal will.

Pale fire caught pale faces. There was not a man there I saw to whom I would have turned my back of choice, and for the women, I would rather lie beside a she-wolf.

I noticed a child on a ledge, who had a plainly gangrenous foot, but who did not cry or fret, only stared down at me with a hatred he must have learned early. Maybe captive Masrians had been brought here before—the children at least would think me captive probably, and in some degree no doubt I was. I reached for the child, an impulse to heal him taking hold of me in my disgust at this hell-pit. For a second I thought he inappropriately smiled before a set of yellow teeth were clamped in my forearm.

Ki shouted, and the four other Hesseks yelled also.

The child gnawed on me like a ferret, and I had a fancy he drank my blood. I struck him thrice on the head before he let go and fell down with a red mouth and rolling eyes. Then I put my hand on his leg above the festering wound. And no healing came from me.

Evidently my nauseous revulsion drove out the benign aspect of my sorcery—not in regard to myself, for I healed instantly of the filthy wound the child's fangs had given me, but in regard to others. I could have killed the poor little brute with Power, but nothing else.

The Hesseks relapsed into soundlessness. I motioned to Ki to go on, but asked him where he was conducting me.

"Not far," he said. "A place holy to us. Shall the child die, lord?"

"He's almost dead now. Be more specific about your holy place."

"A tomb," he said, as naturally as another would say, "My neighbor's house."

I no longer glimpsed his brain; its turmoil had faded into obscurity, and though I had felt no trepidation before, invincible as I seemed to have become, the dark and stink and misery began with no warning to eat away at me to the point of allergy.

About three minutes later, we reached our destination.

The warren came up against a Hessek cemetery, once exclusive to the city above. A gate of ornate and rusty metal introduced a stone corridor, intermittently lighted by uncovered torches burning in low sallow spurts.

The end of the corridor was blocked by double doors of copper, gone to a bluish talcum with age. which gave onto a rectangular burial chamber hung with draperies of ancient cobwebby silk. Against the farther wall of this cozy nest were three couches of scrolled stonework, decorated with green human bones, as casual as you please.

It is not generally delightful to arrive so in the odorous house of death.

"Ki," I said, "this isn't the safe place I should want lodging in."

"I beg your patience, my lord," Ki said. He lifted aside the fragile drapes. A second room lay behind them, similarly torchlit but empty.

I went through into this room and the drapes subsided, leaving me alone. Ki was gone, and the rest of the Hessek party.

Simultaneously a trick door appeared at the far end of the chamber. Eshkorian stratagem. But through that entrance something approached that stopped me thinking of Eshkorek.

A figure in black came first, a man's figure, yet crawling on all fours, his head down like a beast, and a leash about his neck. Behind him, holding the leash, was another, also black-garbed but upright, his bare face patterned over with designs of what looked to be brilliant emerald beads. Last, came a woman.

Her smoky hair was woven with a colony of vipers. Jewelwork they were of polished bronze, yet they looked real enough, and for a moment too real, catching the shifty light and seeming to twist and shiver. She wore a robe of flax-linen, very thin; the torches soaked through it like water to her silver limbs beneath. At her waist was a girdle that bled with green and scarlet gems.

She halted, covered her face with her hands, and bowed before me. She wore no veil and no paint. When she raised her eyes. I knew her. I had reason to.

Lellih.

8

The man-creature on the floor growled. He lifted his face. It was smeared with black markings like those of a tiger, and his teeth were filed to points. His eyes wandered, savage and unhuman. He was in the grip of some possession, induced or haphazard, that made him suppose himself a beast. The beast's keeper, the man with the mask of green beads, spoke to me.

"Welcome, lord. We rejoice you are here, that you came willingly."

"And did she come willingly, too?" I said.

Lellih smiled, and cold fingers walked on my shoulders. She was indeed beautiful, this girl I had re-created out of senile flesh. Too beautiful, remembering what had gone before, that pristine primal alabaster countenance, unmarked as a new born child's.

"She is to be our priestess," the man said, "our symbol."

"Symbol of what?" I said.

"She was old; you have made her young, strong, and blessed. Hessek is also old."

"And I'm to make Hessek young and strong, am I? Because I am this devil-god you worship."

I perceived now that the emerald dots on the man's cheeks and forehead were not beads after all, but small, shiny mummified beetles, glinting in the torchlight. He seemed to be a priest of sorts, the gem-insects and the man on the twitching leash sigils of his authority. My priest, then, presumably. And Lellih my priestess.

"Even you, lord," he said, "may not grasp your destiny, the will of the One that is in you. If you permit, we will take you to the Inner Chamber, and discover."

"And if I don't permit? You know I can kill you where you stand, and any others who might come for me."

"Yes, lord," he said. It was difficult to be sure of his expression through those insects stuck there. I had heard Masrians say with contempt that every Hessek was alike, and in the filtered gloom of the burial place, this seemed to be so. This man was a composite of his race rather than an individual. Stare at him as I might, I felt that, stripped of his devices, I would not know him after.

But it was Lellih who had an answer for me.

"The omnipotent are curious concerning men," she said. "Go with us and satisfy your curiosity."

I had not heard her maiden's voice before. There was nothing of the old Lellih left in her. Her words were elegant. Even the brain that formed the words was changed. I wondered if she actually recalled who she had been, her dismal life as hunchbacked whore and crippled seller of sweets. As to what she said, I could not deny a clammy, reluctant desire to see what was brewing, the very sensation that had brought me here.

For all my cleverness, I half believed then that they had bewitched me.

"Well," I said slowly, "we had better be going."

The man bowed to me, my priest, then to Lellih, and when he spoke to her I became aware he added the Hessek honorific "years."

"You are wise, Lellih-yess."

She smiled, a smile I did not take to.

The priest went out, she after him. I followed her along another corridor, hot and fetid as only a grave shaft could be; and under the growling of the leashed tiger-man, I said softly to her slender back, "Continue to be wise, granny-girl. Don't try tricks."

"You wrong me," she said. "Besides, what should you fear, who are brave and terrible? They tell me you saved the life of a Hragon prince tonight. Is Sorem your lover that you hold him so dear? I thought Vazkor was a man for women."

Her gauze gown was showing me all it might, but here was one girl I did not want and never would. A sort of loathing came over me at the notion of lying with her. This she did not realize, as I noticed from her mode of walking.

"You made me virgin, too, just as I asked. And the seal's intact. Not a man for women, Vazkor?"

"Whatever else," I said, "not a man for you, lady."

There is no swifter way to make an enemy of a woman. You may tell her she is a clod or a bitch; as long as you lust for her, it will be forgiven. But say she is the wonder of the world and show her cold loins, and she will hate you till the sun goes out. This I understood well enough, but reckoned Lellih not much, if her people were a little more. It was, in any case, plain honesty, and put to the test would not altar.

She said nothing further, and I, too, kept quiet.

There had been a prophecy for ninety-odd years in Bit-Hessee; the priest spoke of it later. Like many a conquered people made slaves, beggars, and outcasts in their own land, they were dreaming of a savior who would redeem them from the oppressor, and reinstate the ancient Empire of Hessek over a million graveyards of dead Masrians. Their former gods, who had failed them, they cast down, even Hessu the sea demon, mythological founder of Bit-Hessee itself. Though Hessek sailors and slaves still offered lip service and perfunctory offerings to deities of ocean, field, and weather, no scrap of this natural religion lingered over the marsh in the old city. As the metropolis went to ground in darkness, so did its mysteries.

Hessek was aged, used up, decaying. It began to be said that when the barren tree put on green the savior of Hessek would come—a cynical enough maxim under the circumstances, which grew more naïve and auspicious as the years of thralldom marched by. Yet Lellih, the barren tree, had put on again her green girlhood. Inadvertently, I had fulfilled their dream with that game of mine, which had used her as its pawn. I had thought, when she came whispering to me of her youth in the Grove, that her gods had put her in my hand. Maybe they had.

The Inner Chamber seemed to lie at the core of the cemetery, accessible via a labyrinth of passages that passed among various boneyards and tomb closets, where piled skulls leered in the half-light and the air was putrid.

I expected some menacing of freakish greeting at the end of the journey, and was not disappointed. An arch revealed to me a large space packed about the walls with black priests and ragged Bit-Hessians, and deserted at its center, where burned a tall bronze tripod lamp of the open Hessek sort. Lellih passed in before me, and the priest with his unpleasant pet. As I entered, a screaming shout emanated from the throng and split the hollow roof in echoes. It had in it the pent-up hysteria I had heard women break into in a death chant among the tribes. I did not like the noise of it much, and missed the words of the cry till they came again. What they were yelling over and over was: *Eiullo y'ei S'ulloo-Kem!* ("The invisible god is made visible in his son!)

I had named myself a god more than once; I had had my reasons. But to confront this fanatic horde and hear that shouting chilled me through. It was like standing in one of the powder cellars of Eshkorek's cannon and striking flints.

I thought, *I am on trial here. If I fail them, they will go mad, and if I am what they want, this same madness explodes in my face.* I did not know what test they meant to set me. It might be anything, judging by their demented fervor.

The priest brought silence by raising his arms, and the jewels in Lellih's girdle splashed green and red fires up onto her breast and neck as she bent above the tripod lamp.

The floor at the center of the chamber was figured in a white circle of running beasts and muddied over with brown stains; blood, no doubt. In the strange agitation of the light Lellih was conjuring the beasts seemed to run, each snapping at the animal in front. It put me in mind of a herd running headlong to escape the stinging of a swarm of gadflies. . . . Something in the circle drew me. I felt the pull of it, and I said to myself, *I can match any power of theirs.* And of my own will (I imagined), I chose to enter the circle of running beasts, and wait there for what might come to me.

Tell yourself, as you will, that you are god and demon. Come in the presence of either, and you see your error. To this day, I do not know if he was really there with me, their devil-deity, master of the dark. Perhaps the conjuration was so ancient, so much a part of Hessek, that it had become convincing, or maybe the insistence of their frantic belief had truly caused the thing to be, as pearl forms about grit in the oyster's shell.

The white beasts ran, real now, three-dimensional and upright. I could smell their odor, feel their warmth, and see the spit fleck from their jaws.

Then the floor dropped from under me, not suddenly, more as if it melted. And I was alone in a place without light or sound, and he was there with me.

I did not see him, or hear him, this being they called Shaythun, Shepherd of Swarms, but I was aware of him, instantaneously, like a breathing next to my ear. I remember I gathered my Powers against him, like a hedge of thorn dragged around the krarl to keep the wolves out. But this was a wolf I could not keep away. There is no man so holy that you cannot find one black thought or one black deed in him, however small. And that deed or that thought is the gate through which devils, like the devil of Hessek, come and go.

I began to see, without light, and hear, without sound.

Out of smoke, another smoke poured. It was composed of a million tiny atoms that I saw to be his creatures. Winged beetles, flies, black moths, locusts, and below these, the grounded messengers of his kingdom, the maggots and the worms, the spider-folk hanged on their wires of steel. They fell and crawled across the inside of my shuttered eyes like rain across a paper window-blind. I seemed to have no choice but to admit the illusion; my Power was chained or numbed by the pressure of Hessek's worship, and because I had no positive fear with which to fight.

After a moment the insect vision passed and the featureless half-dark with it.

I was in the Inner Chamber, which was now empty save for the ring of white beasts. No longer mobile, they had turned their great heads to look at me. Running, they had resembled lions somewhat in the body, but those heads were more like the heads of horses, though far heavier and scrolled with flesh about the neck, and the short legs, muscular pillars beneath the low-slung bellies, ended in five-toed pads. Their smell was of the swamp's beginning, some hot initiating ooze now centuries cold.

They stared, lolling their thick brown tongues like dogs after the hunt.

Then a darkness came between me and the beasts—a shadow growing up on the air. I knew it was not the Hessek's ungod, for he was not to be visualized, despite their shrieking. Real or phantom, he had no actual masculine shape, which this presence did. I realized suddenly that my own mental energy, held in check by the religious passion of Bit-Hessee, had turned in upon itself, and produced some archetype of my own brain, as if to counter theirs.

I believed him, for an instant, to be the mirror image of myself.

A tall man, large boned, hard and lean, tanned very dark, his blue-black hair long as mine had been when I was a brave among the krarls, if more kempt than mine. He wore black, and black rings on his hands. His face was mine, yet not mine, some difference in the eyes and mouth; most would never note it. My blood clamored in my head and my sinews loosened.

I forgot Hessek. There was a salt tingle in my mouth, terror that was not terror churning in my guts, and I faltered out the words as a child would falter them.

"Vazkor. My father."

He did not answer me. But, ghost or hallucination, he gazed at me as if he saw me. Nothing in the past, no dream or reverie, had prepared me for this, not even the promise and the fiery shadow on the island. He seemed live enough to touch. But I went no nearer to him.

"My king, I have not forgotten. I swore a vow. I will keep it." My legs trembled and the sweat rushed down me. "What do you want of me, other than I am sworn to?"

From being solid before me, he began to disintegrate, which was now unnerving and horrible.

"I cried out, "Wait—tell me what it is you wish. Javhovor—king—*Father*—"

But he was gone, and through the place where he had stood, so finely noble and so evident, a great barred cat leaped toward my throat.

I rolled across the ground, wrestling a tiger, in my hand the knife they had not taken from me. I slashed the neck of the tiger, and its scalding blood ran on my breast, all this in a daze with my mind crying out in me still.

The cry burst upward but was not mine.

I was on my feet, within the circle of painted white animals at the center of the Hessek cemetery. The flame of the tripod lamp blazed up, showing me a crowd on their knees all about, immemorial groveling of men before their gods. Lellih also was outstretched, and the beetle-decorated priest, and one more figure lying near me. I had not killed a tiger after all, but the lunatic on the leash who thought himself one. This was their true form of sacrifice, to lower a human into a beast and then cut his neck veins, and I had officiated for them—the bloody knife was back in my belt.

It was the priest who crept to me on his knees. He grasped my foot and mouthed it, and I kicked him away and broke a tooth for him. He looked up at me, not appearing to register his hurt.

"It is proved," he said. "The Power of the circle revealed it, as it must. Your guiding principle, the burning shadow." He whispered, "You are Shaythun made manifest, Shaythun made flesh. Command us."

"Be thankful I don't kill you," I said, low as he.

"Kill me. I am ready. I offer myself to the death you will give me, Shaythun-Kem."

Lellih had raised her white face also. She tore open the gauzy linen and scored her breasts with her nails, her lips parted and the vipers glinting in her hair. She offered me other things, choosing to forget what I had said to her.

"Command me," the priest repeated.

"Then take me to this lodging your men brought me over the marsh to find." I got this out in as prosaic a voice as I could muster. The blood, the magic, the corpse-smell, and the shifting light were sending me faint as any silly girl. I had had enough, and meant to have no more.

The priest rose and bowed and obeyed me.

I came into the room and found it unoccupied, clean and wholesome-smelling after the other. A couch with rugs stood by the wall. I fell on it, and into the gray country of sleep.

A dream woke me, the dream of a white cat, drinking my blood.

I started up into a confusing twilight, and saw, crouched at my feet, the selfsame monster from the dream. There in a terror unlike any other; it eats the mind. But it was the dawn in the room, broadening, and in a second I saw the thing for what it was, and kept my sanity. In a white robe, a white veil over her hair if not her face, Lellih the priestess ceased to be my private haunting come to devour me.

This room was near the top of the Bit-Hessee warren, presumably, and sunup was finding a high thin window under the beams and filling it with a sugar-pink confectionery of rays. Lellih stretched in the fountain of the pink morning, letting the veil fall, and the loose robe after it.

"See how pretty you made me. But, oh, Vazkor, I should not like to have such dreams."

I comprehended immediately that she knew the dream, in all its detail. No doubt I had cried out aloud in my sleep, but the conviction came on me that she had read my thoughts, unperturbed, as yesterday I had read Ki's with such uneasiness. In that upper room I experienced again the draining energy of something ancient and perverse. For all my avowals of strength, my healing had failed me here, and I had entered that circle of theirs as the cattle go to the butcher's shed, and more willingly. If I let go my caution their Power would creep in on me to sap my own, to make me part of them and their belief.

Lellih laughed, showing me her nakedness.

"They gave me the treasures of Ancient Hessek to wear—the Serpent Crown and the Girdle of Fires, but I have more fabulous treasures, do I not? Don't hesitate," she said. "He is to visit you with his green face, but I have instructed him to be slow. You have time to lie with me before he arrives." She came crawling up the length of me as I lay there, like the embodiment of that other thing I felt steal in on my mind.

Presently she hissed in my ear, "Sorem the Masrian *is* your lover, then, Vazkor Shaythun-Kem. You should have made me a boy, like Thei."

"Take your weight off me, priestess, or I'll send you back to your god, who you say is my father, with this knife."

"Oh, a knife, is it?" she whispered. "That is all you are able to stick in me? And such a tribal barbarian still, equipped to slay with light, yet preferring a thief's blade."

I thrust her aside and held her and hit her, so her head

rolled on her neck, for it did not suit me to be afraid of a woman. It seemed she had read my past with the rest, to know my origin.

"Your people revere me. You had better get the habit."

She looked back at me. Her eyes were all surface, like polished iron, without dept. One cheek was red from the blow, and she put her hand to it, gently, as I have seen girls tend a sick baby or a kitten. Indeed there was nothing of the old Lellih left in her. Though she was the figurehead of a faith, I saw in that instant that she alone of her heritage set no store by me as a messiah. I had every one of the clues then, and missed them.

She slid from the couch, drew up her robe, and laced it with the odd side lacings the Hesseks affected. The veil she let down over her face and hid her look in its white smoke, and went out.

The beetle-priest entered a moment later. He had been waiting on her as she bade him.

He kneeled at once on the floor, and I instructed him to rise. I took a high-handed attitude, for my nerve was gone, and I would gladly have been in most spots but there. I asked him straight out what he wanted. He bowed and recounted the legend of Hessek. He spoke of the savior I must be, who would lead the outcasts from the swamp through the wide white streets of Bar-Ibithni, striking down walls and gates and men who stood in the path, installing Bit-Hessee at the hub of the Heavenly City and in the Crimson Palace of the Emperor, made crimson indeed by a liberal spillage of Masrian blood.

As he intoned all this, the beetles, following his facial movements, scurried on his cheeks and brow. It was a strange thing, for I could see he genuinely reckoned me what he called me—the Shaythun-Kem, god-made-visible—while imagining he might yet instruct me as the instrument of Old Hessek. Thus a real messiah would be, I suppose, the hammer of his people's hope rather than a man.

I say this now, calmly. At the hour, a sea of panic was sweeping in on me. I felt the burden of their demand and their hunger, their malice, their ungovernable hate. To be five years old and surrounded by foes out of a nightmare, that is what set on me in that high room of the swamp city.

There went across my inner eye that scene in the docks as it must have been: Charpon murdered simply because he opposed me—the flint in his brain their gift to me, like the bloody crow, the tiger man.

My only weapon remained constant: mundane, flat logic.

"Are you finished?" I said to the priest. He lowered his head. "Good. Listen, then. I'm not your prophet, neither your savior. I am the sorcerer Vazkor. No religion and no religious power will alter it. You may fear me. I'll allow you that, since I can kill the pack of you, when and how I please. But for a leader, search elsewhere."

He did not glance at me. "Why have you come among us? Why have you done as you have if you are not the one we wait for?"

"Ask Shaythun," I said. "Now. Step away from the door."

He stood rooted and murmured, "I cannot, my master. You must stay with us. You are ours."

I moved toward him, and he straightened and grappled me about the waist.

He was a muscular man. His breath smelled from some drug or incense, and through his open lips I saw the tooth I had chipped. I did not want to use the Power on him. The sorcery of this hell seemed to feed from mine. I had played at being Shaythun, and I had augmented Shaythun's influence in doing it. I had gazed inside the skull of Ki; Lellih had scoured my own. A demon's shadow had remodeled itself as my father's. Loose the energy of death here now, and, I wildly surmised, it would assume another form to destroy me.

So I wrestled the priest and struck him from me. He gripped my legs to pull me down, and I leaned and stabbed him. ("Tribal barbarian . . . equipped to slay with light . . . preferring a thief's blade.") He groaned like a man turning in slumber, and let me go.

Outside, the corridor lifted itself upward to the left, as I had dimly remembered from the previous night. Dayglow suggested itself on the slope of the wall. I ran toward it, and no one prevented me.

9

Despite my hubris and my ability, I went to the Rat-Hole of the south under Hessek witching, and I abandoned it part crazy. No man is weaker than one who believes himself invincible, and even the sting of little wasps can kill, when they gather in great numbers.

I found myself, after an interval, wandering among the ruined upper tiers of Bit-Hessee. How I got above I had forgotten, and how I should escape across the uncertain swamps and lagoons I could not for some while reason out. Eventually I recollected Hessek's boats stowed along the fringe of the silted dock, and the ships' graveyard where, if other plans failed, some beggarly raft could be constructed from oddments. To walk on water I never contemplated. I wished just then very much to be merely human. An eye seemed to be watching me, the eye of Old Hessek. Be Shaythun and I should call Shaythun. I shuddered from fatigue and horror, and could not pull my wits and impulses together.

So I proceeded, staggering along roughly northward, and overheard the wrecked black stacks of Hessu's port staggered in rhythm with my stride.

The heat of the day came, a slaty pressuring of low sky. Once something shrilled in the marsh among the towering fern-trees. And once, between the buildings, I sank to my knees in a gaping mouth of mud, and dragged myself free with difficulty.

I saw no men and no beast. Neither did I reach the dock or the shore.

At first I lay down in the shade of a wall, full length in the muck and reeds, with no watch for enemies. (He was everywhere. Why trouble to look out for him?) Their Power contained mine. They kept me in. I had fled the warren and was now caged on the surface. I muttered with a sort of fever, dozed, and tossed about, a pitiful object if there had been any to take pity.

When I recovered myself, the light was fading in slashes of madder and bronze behind the crossed swords of upper foliage and the broken roofs. Something shifted against me, and

I found six or seven leeches oozed from a pool in the street and supping on my calves. I tore them off me, rending them and myself. In the smoking dusk my blood welled, and the wounds did not heal.

In Masrian theater, the storm always comes at such a moment. The melodrama of thunderclap and red lightning hyphenate the bellows, prayers, and poetry of the doomed hero. And so it was. The sky blacked over, building to a mountainous pressure, which was suddenly carved by three white blades and a crash of battling clouds. The rain fell hot as my blood on the antique cobbles.

I blundered into a doormouth and leaned there inside the shadows. The rain hung like a curtain outside; I could see nothing through it. Thunder rang across the sky, and my head cleared abruptly. Vitality and intelligence seemed to wash back into me. I looked at the leech-marks and they were sealing. Now was the time to break for the dock. The natural storm had sluiced off their sticky magic, and I might find the lagoon and a boat, and reach open water.

Behind, something whispered my name. Not my chosen name that was, but the name my krarl had given me.

Tuvek.

I turned around slowly, not wanting to see, though I left the uncleaned knife in its sheath, accepting its uselessness.

A hall went back from the doorway, uncertainly lighted by crevices in its walls, featureless, save at the farthest end of it there was a white shining. I could not distinguish what it was, but even as I stared and held my breath, soft fibers came drifting out and fastened about the pitchy walls, the roof, interweaving, methodical, ultimately floating around me also. An enormous web. And at its center, in the pale luminance, a spider?

I began to walk that way, toward the white core of the web. It was not so much a compulsion as a deadly, angry knowledge that I could never get away in the other direction.

The threads of the web fluttered as I broke through them, and re-formed, fastening me securely within. The touch of them was like an icy kissing. I could observe something seated in the light now, the center of its whiteness. I think I had begun to believe it from the hour I woke to Lellih at the couch's foot, telling me my dream.

I had anticipated finding Uastis, had cast my net for her. But she had grown more astute with the years, the sun of my whole lifetime, in which she might have prepared her weapons. What better and more hidden place for my mother to choose for herself than Bit-Hessee-over-the-marsh? What better kingdom, rotten, masked, vengeful?

She had twice my years, perhaps a little more, but she looked, as I had suspected she would, far older. Her face was, as ever, covered, on this occasion in the Hessek mode, with a figured veil of heavy white silk. Yet her arms and throat were bare, the stringy harsh albino flesh gathered on the bone, and under the robe, the shape of the two withered dugs that never suckled me. Her white hair was plaited and held with silver links, and the long talons of her hands were enameled the color of dying fire.

I could say no word. I had sworn to slay her when I discovered her, but I was helpless. I gawked like an idiot, and she spoke, this hag, and her voice was young and fresh and beautiful, and harder than blue alcum.

"I was rid of your father by means of my hate. You also I may kill. Unless you consent to serve me."

"If you wanted my service, you should have kept me by you."

"You were his curse on me," she said.

"And I am still."

"Hessek is mine," she said. "Obey me. Lead my people to victory, and I will spare you and reward you."

Suddenly my brain revived. I perceived that none of this made sense.

"Shlevakin," I said, "they are *shlevakin*. Rabble. Hessek is nothing to Uastis the cat-goddess of Ezlann. This is some further trick of Shaythun's priests." Before I properly guessed it, my hand had shot out and snatched the veil from her face.

I jumped backward with my eyes starting from their sockets almost. It was not a woman's face at all, but the head of a white lynx—its fur had brushed my palm as I wrenched off its covering, and I had scented the rank perfume of its mouth. Pale green irises like diluted jade, brown teeth striped with old blood.

I knew it for an illusion, but it seemed, in every particular, quite real. At that, in panic, I drew the knife from my belt and thrust it at the nearer gleaming right eye. Reality met the unreal, as the knife pierced tissue and she screamed. And vanished.

The web trembled, became what it was: cobwebs. Of the spider-hag-cat-queen nothing remained. The knife lay on the floor, but it was stained new red.

I went out into the rain, and walking down the flooded street, got easily to the shore and the dock. I found a boat with equal ease; there were about ten of them pulled up among the reeds. I unshipped the oars and rowed into the lagoon. The thick water spread in slinking rings under the splintering rain. The thunder had sunk northward, scud following it in procession over the darkening dusk sky. I did not consider that I should lose myself any more, even in the many channels of the delta. I was guided to the ocean by an instinct such as that which sends the fish to warmer waters at the year's end. Besides, by a foolish, unpremeditated act—the ham-fisted blow of a terrified tribesman—I had torn the web of Old Hessek. Before it knit again, I should be gone.

Not that the affair was done between us.

The rain ceased, and the papyrus boat slipped through the slender giant trees toward the sea, as a ruddy hunter's-bow of moon was painted in on the emptied night.

Although the hag they had shown me had been only the illusion of Uastis, I was now grimly convinced that she was somewhere near. I saw her strategy in the wickedness of Old Hessek, the poison of her enchantments like a powerhouse that they might tap. True, she was indifferent to the aspirations of Bit-Hessee, but she might use them to destroy the threat which was myself. She had known I would seek her, and she had left pitfalls in my road. Well, she had taught me a lesson. In the future, I would be more ready.

As for the Rat-Hole, a notion had come to me. If she were watching out to see me tumble, she had better beware, the bitch.

About an hour later, the reeds opened on the vista of the ocean, pure salt air, fish leaping, and, far to the east, the jewel haze of Bar-Ibithni.

10

I gave the city and the docks as wide a berth as had my Hessek guides on the previous journey, since any craft spotted on route from Bit-Hessee might arouse the suspicion of the Masrian watch. Sheer marble walls, palace parks, and the ornate grounds of Masrian fanes stretched down into the sea all along the coast east of the bay of Hragon, and I had no choice but to come ashore in the garden of a temple. Here, amid the incense of the night-blooming scarlet lilies of the south, I stove in the papyrus boat and sank it in the black water under the temple wharf.

I met a red-robed priest in the garden, who took no more note of me than if I had been a prowling cat. Perhaps worshipers commonly came here after sunset, or, more likely, lovers, to keep trysts in the bushes.

It was close on midnight when I reached my apartment house and found all the courts in darkness. This was unnatural anywhere and at any hour of night in the Palm Quarter, and I trod with caution. No need; violence had come and gone before me.

The outer doors were broken off their chains, the inner doors similarly forced. Trampled drapes lay about, and smashed crocks, and the black dog my sailor guard had been keeping had had its neck snapped and been thrown in the gutter outside for the street sweepers.

Of Kochus and my men no trace remained, and I could guess the fate of the women.

I had such a variety of enemies by now, I was unsure of who these visitors had been. As I was staring about, I heard a noise and whipped around, to find a figure at my elbow, one of the kitchen girls.

"My lord," she squeaked, "oh, my lord."

Her face was smeared with tears and fright, of me as much as anything. I sat her on the broad rim of the fountain, and gave her a drink of koois from a silver flask that had been overlooked; most of the other valuables, the alcohol and the wine, had disappeared.

Amazement at being served by the master of the house pulled the girl together, and she poured out her tale without preamble.

Trouble had arrived sometime in the hour before dawn, when she was already up to light the oven-fire behind its shield, and fetch the water for the bath-tanks from the public well.

The Hessek guard had been whispering together and acting oddly all night. (Most probably, I thought, they had got word I had been persuaded over the marsh. Just then, all Hesseks appeared to be in league against me.) However, despite their agitation, or because of it, their watch was not thorough. The outer gates were suddenly shattered, and the yard and courts aswarm with men. They shouted for me, and getting no answer, routed the appalled household from their beds or from the places in which they had hidden. The girl did not see much of this. Accustomed to calamity from an immature age, she had taken refuge in the great tank that fed the faucets of the bath. She had long been acquainted with this tank, having had to fill it every day with nine pitchers of water from the well. Now it was only part full, and she crouched down in the dark and water, and heard indicative sounds as the strangers beat and took Kochus and the Hesseks prisoner, and presently ransacked the rooms, thereafter extending their quest to neighboring courts. Finding no trace of me, they at last turned their attention to my property, drank my liquor, and lay with the kitchen women, who, the girl prudishly declared, being loose hussies, were apparently audible in consent and approbation.

At length, silence encouraged my girl from the tank. She found the havoc much as I had found it, and no one on hand save the alarmed neighbors, most of whom fled for fear of further activity. She alone had remained to warn me.

Seeing she was braver and more quick than the rest of them put together, I gave her the silver flask to keep and some silver cash I had on me—makeshift reward for all her gallantry. But she blushed and gave me back the coins, saying she loved me and had done it for that. Poor little thing, I had scarcely noticed her, a skinny, small brown waif of poor-Masrian stock, and not much above thirteen. Still, she did not try to give me back the flask. I imagine life had taught her already to put some prudence before sentiment.

I asked her if she could tell who the invaders might be, and she said at once, "They wore yellow and black—the guard of Basnurmon Hragon-Dat, the Heir of the Emperor. Everyone knows his wasp device."

I sent the girl off to her home, after she had surprised me by insisting that she had one. Then I collected up any money-raising portable items that might have been accidently ignored by Basnurmon's morons, and went straight out to the nearby hiring stables, dressed as I was in Bit-Hessee mud.

The man who opened up for me seemed innocent enough, but had heard the news of soldiers sacking my courts, and was nervous with questions to which I did not reply. A chain of cash got a mount from him, and an hour after the midnight bell I had crossed the bright streets of the Palm Quarter and was hammering on the bronze Fox Gate of Pillar Hill, the entrance to the Citadel.

There were three or four decent rooms, the central chamber large and well furnished, more than a soldier's cell, commander or otherwise. The lamps were the plain pleasant shade of the yellow wine that stood by in the crystal flagon. On the lime-washed walls were swords of damascened alcum, and a collection of shields, and bows and spears for hunting or war; and in one place hung a leopard's pelt, something Sorem had taken himself and been proud of. I should not have been ashamed to have got it myself. There was an un-Masrian quality in the lack of clutter, but neither was it unaesthetic. The woven Tinsen rug had all the jeweled colors the lamps did not, and the wine cups of polished malachite would not have looked amiss on any fancy table of Erran's in Eshkorek.

A sleet-gray bitch hound lay before the open windows where the cool breeze of earliest morning crossed the stone veranda. Dim sounds rose up there from the garrison, mingled with the stir and shrill scent of lemon trees in the court below.

They bedded late in the Citadel, as elsewhere in eastern Bar-Ibithni. I had no difficulty in gaining entrance at the Fox Gate; it appeared Sorem had also heard news of the marauders. Some of his men had been sent out to try to intercept me, and the watch on the gate been primed to let me in. Altogether there had been extravagant events in the Citadel, as I was to learn, since we parted with our formal courtesies at the Field of the Lion.

Sorem came in, wide awake and fully dressed in the casual military gear of the jerdat. His face was tense, alert, and he grinned at me with a boy's excitement, which told me more than anything that some fresh game was up. A girl poured us our wine and went away, and we stood to drink in silence, Masrian tradition with the first cup, to show the grape you honor his gift.

This done, Sorem said, "I owe you my life and I pledge you your safety. Beyond that, you had better know this is unlawful ground you're standing on."

"Unlawful, how?"

"Word of Basnurmon's tactics reached the Citadel, and the jerds have declared for me," he said simply. "At least, my four brother commanders here in the garrison and my own under-captains have done so, while I think the soldiery itself has no complaint against me and prefers me to Basnurmon. That puts all those five jerds, which currently occupy the Citadel, under my command. The astounding matter has remained secret from the city itself due to the loyalty of these men. They seem prepared to risk livelihood and life for me. But technically, Vazkor, Pillar Hill is now as much outlaw territory as Old-Hessek-over-the-marsh."

I drank off the remainder of my wine at a gulp. This fitted so perfectly with the wild plan that had been jelling in me that I could almost swear someone's god had a hand in it.

"And what do you know of Old-Hessek-over-the-marsh?" I said.

He was surprised, as well he might be.

"The name they give it here speaks for itself—the Rat-Hole. A sink of wretchedness and corruption. They cling to the old faith of Hessek there, some foul magic, involving, reputedly, human sacrifice. Since the time of my grandfather, Masrianes, who conquered the south and built this city, Masrian rule has tried to stamp out such activities, bring these people from their swamp, and eradicate the villainies they practice.

"And instead of the swamp, you offer them what? Slavery under Masrian masters? Or the lives of beggars in your fine streets."

"That's not my doing, Vazkor. It's the Emperor's code that suppresses Hessek labor, and his tax of Bit-Hessee that insures Hessek slaves. Every year he creams off three hundred children from Old Hessek for slaves, mostly for use in the mines of the east. The priests of the Rat-Hole make no complaint, in fact I have heard it said their marsh could not support more children than they keep, that the tax prevents a famine. Still, it's vile, not something I should want to put my seal on, if I were master in the Crimson Palace."

I smiled at that. I had never seen his ambition before; no doubt he had learned to conceal it. Now, things being as they were, the malice of the heir Basnurmon naked in its intent at last, and the Citadel declared for Sorem, the voices that had been whispering in him twenty years made themselves heard.

This close, and in the steady light of the lamps, I could see him very clearly for maybe the first time.

He was a little shorter than I, perhaps by the width of my thumb joint, not much in it; in build we might have been brothers. Neither of us had lived soft. The palms of his hands were welted in smooth callouses from handling sword, bow, and harness, and there was a jagged white scar I had noted on his forearm, the love token of a boar's tusk, or I had forgotten my hunting. Reminding me of myself, he had taken on a look of familiarity. Even the blue eyes—which reincarnated, at odd instants, Ettook's damnable krarl—Dagkta eyes set in the face of a Masrian prince. Which spelled other things from my past: Both of us saddled by a father, unloving and unloved; the mother thrust aside because she did not bear his rutting; the birthright—of a krarl or an empire—withheld, and in his case given to another.

These weird parallels between our histories had been leading me somewhere, and, coming from Bit-Hessee, I perceived where: To meddle in the dynasty of the Hragons, to redeem my past with Sorem's present, to grasp power and use it. And for what better reason than that, in so doing, I would destroy the thing which had hunted me in the swamp city—the witch and her tangling web.

We sat down, and I told Sorem swiftly what had happened to me since the night of the Lion's Field. He listened intently and made no idiot comment. I did not specify Bit-Hessian enchantments, nor speak of Uastis or my father's image cast up from that circle on the tomb's floor, but still I made him aware of the horror and the darkness, and of their belief that I was their messiah, the Shaythun-Kem.

"The Citadel has declared for Sorem," I said, "five thousand men. And at a word from me, despite anything I may have done there, despite my escape even, Bit-Hessee will declare for Vazkor. How many fighting men do you suppose exist in the Rat-Hole?"

"By the Flame, not men alone, Vazkor. You've seen them. The women would fight too, for this, and their children. It was Hragon-Dat—my father—who forbade them to carry knives, for there have always been rumors of uprisings and prophetic leaders from the marsh. Still, they will have found some way to circumvent the law. To estimate, I would say seven thousand, or eight, if their old ones and their very young fight, too. And apart from those, the slaves would rise in Bar-Ibithni, for a messiah." He looked me in the eye and added coolly, "Do you mean to turn them against me, Vazkor? They won't march to aid a Masrian."

"They'll aid you," I said, "without meaning to. Hear me out, then argue."

I put my plan to him, to the inappropriate accompaniment of some love song a jerdier was singing three courts away.

It was a long night, much going over of the material and plotting of strategies, and drinking wine to fill in the gaps of thought. Presently Yashlom was brought in, Sorem's second, a captain with whom he had been campaigning a couple of years before. They had saved each other's lives once or twice, and liked each other the better for it. Yashlom was a young man, a lesser prince of the Masrian aristocracy, serious and clever, with the stillest, steadiest hands I ever saw. Two other jerdats were also admitted, friends of Sorem beyond where their duty took them: Bailgar of the Shield Jerd (named for some military honor they had won in the past), and Dushum, who had been the first to declare himself Sorem's man after word of Basnurmon's treachery reached the Citadel. They did not trust me immediately, for which they were not to be blamed, but came around to it on the strength of the incident at the Lion's Field. In respect of the other commanders of the garrison, Sorem meant to call a council in the morning, and with this in mind we sought our couches a while before sunrise.

For myself, I slept little, too much in my head for sleep, and hearing the dawn hymn start in the prayer-towers of the city, I got up again and paced about the chamber I had been allotted, going over everything soberly.

Beyond the five jerds in the Citadel, which amounted to five thousand men, there were the three Imperial Jerds of the Heavenly City, exclusive to the Emperor's protection. In addition, nine jerds patrolled the borders of the Empire, Tinsen, and the eastern provinces, and might be called home on a forced march, to reach Bar-Ibithni in two months or less. This seemed poor odds, all told, but with Bit-Hessee slung in the pot the stew should become more appetizing.

For my scheme was this: Pledge myself, after all, to the Rat-Hole; incite them to cast off Masrian oppression; then learn their method, their exact strength, and the hour they would elect to strike the blow. Eight thousand or so religion-mad Hesseks running amok in Bar-Ibithni would insure two things. First, that the Emperor, caught unawares, would have his hands full to deal with the trouble, keeping his jerds entirely occupied, and leaving the military regime of the Heavenly City and Crimson Palace in chaos. Second, Bar-Ibithni, in its terror, would lay the blame for the uprising squarely at the door of Hragon-Dat and his heir Basnurmon, both of whom were known to have propagated laws and taxes under which Old Hessek was outcast and chafed. The Emperor's three jerds would be insufficient to quell the rising, for they were reckoned slovenly. If the riot was permitted to get far enough so that the rich merchants and the Palm Quarter began to suffer from it, Hragon-Dat and his chosen successor could expect no mercy from their subjects. At this point, Sorem, riding out at the head of the jerds of the Citadel, would rescue the metropolis from Hessek menace. (Five jerds—mounted and equipped with Masrian crossbows and longswords, fully armored, trained, and alert for the event—should be a match for a half-starved rabble with blowpipes and slings from the marsh.) Sympathy and approbation should swing to Sorem like the pendulum, and the uprising squashed, the path could be laid for the overthrow of Emperor Hragon-Dat and the elevation of Sorem to his place. As Sorem had said himself, the whole city knew him to be pure king's blood on both sides, sire and dam.

This much I was prepared to help Sorem to, out of liking, for I liked him well enough, but also because I foresaw for myself the temporal power that could be gained through him. Become his brother in this campaign and I could choose my station afterward, without magic or trick, on merit alone. A slice of the Masrian Empire was no mean prize. Even the little I had seen of it had shown me that. Slipshod and sleepy as it had grown, two men with their youth and their wits about them could order it differently. I had some dim dreams of conquest, my father's dreams perhaps, the empire he had tried to make but barely held and finally lost through the betrayals of those about him. I had some right to carve from this joint, who had narrowly missed a birthright of kingship myself.

Yet, more than anything, my obsession was to rinse the mud and stink of Old Hessek from the map. To show the witch who had instructed them that I could best her. She had meant them to eat me alive with their beliefs; she had meant me to resist them and perish, or else to succumb to the tug of their rotten fantasies and perish of their filth. I had no doubts she knew the web had almost caught me, had waited eagerly, wherever it was she hid herself, for graveyard news of me. But I had disappointed her, got free. This time she would reckon on anything but my consent.

She should die with them if she were in Bit-Hessee, a fraction later if she were elsewhere. I remembered well, irony of ironies, how I had sent *Hesseks* to search for her. She had kept them ignorant, or they had lied. I must be careful now of the Power in me, for it was her beacon, and she fed from it and used it against me. Therefore, I had turned to armies, weapons of steel, human subterfuge. I should end her, one way or another. In doing it, I would become a prince of the Masrians. Everything she had denied me, I would have—a revenge in itself.

For the rats of the Rat-Hole I cared nothing, nor for the soft and luxurious populace of Bar-Ibithni who should shortly feel the nip of rats' teeth. One could not play at wars and tremble at dead men. The human lot was death; soon or late it fell. To have what I must have, it would fall now. This was what my life had taught me. As the Masrians say: Only those who live in the sugar-jar think the world is made of sweetmeat.

We had the council, which was brief and lucid. They were intelligent men, the oldest, Bailgar, not much above thirty, not yet stuck in his ways. I suppose, too, they had seen the rot set in on Bar-Ibithni, the army stagnating in its forts and barracks, the occasional minor flare-up on the borders all that kept it in trim. It was to their credit that the legions of the Citadel were finely drilled and in excellent battle-order, not a thick gut or a smeared buckle in sight. I gathered from general talk that the jerds of the Heavenly City could not boast as much.

Concerning my plan, they marveled, looked me over, and at length came to approve of it. They knew my reputation already, and asked me questions. I gave them straightforward answers where I could, and answers that seemed straightforward where I could not. Their patent loyalty to Sorem no longer irked me, now that I could put it to use. He had the knack of getting himself liked and well thought of, and was man enough to back it up with deeds, so none need be shamed to call him commander or friend. For me, I saw that morning that he could shoot straight as a hawk's flight, for we took some exercise in the great Ax Court of the Citadel. I imagine the jerdats were testing me, and I was sufficiently clever with their kicking iron-shod bows and the other games that they could find no fault. Bailgar even grew lavish in his praise, clapping me on the shoulder, saying his eye was going for shot and it grieved him to see such a keen one as mine.

While this was going on, my brain was worrying at different matters.

There was that ship I had bought at the cost of Charpon's good health, the *Hyacinth Vineyard*, lying at dock in the harbor. I had a notion that some of Kochus' ruffians might still be aboard, if Basnurmon's raiders had not gone there, too, and though the ship did not seem as important to me as before now that my course was changed, I had a mind to seek out a man there from among the Hessek crew. Having no wish to return to Bit-Hesse in person, I stood in need of a messenger.

I talked it through with Sorem, presently. My face was too readily known in the city; had I not seen to it that it should be? It appeared I must effect a disguise, not quite for the first time in my life.

Bailgar was brought in on this jaunt and four of his Shield jerdiers. Beyond the commanders, it was officially unrecognized in the Citadel that the jerds were no longer the Emperor's property but Sorem's, to command wherever he chose. However, it seemed to me that several guessed what was afoot. There was a general feel of conspiracy, the promise of action. Unrest must have been on the bubble here for months or years, Sorem's popularity and the Emperor's stupidity unfailing tinder, requiring only the final spark. Everywhere I looked, men overpolished their gear, meticulously shod their horses, acted out crack drills, or else laughed and indulged in the sort of horseplay that springs from waiting and nerves.

Even the six priests, who appeared like a spell in their midst and passed out through the Fox Gate an hour before the noon bell, excited no particular comment, only quick grins or the solemn blank masks of sentries very much in the know.

The six priests were of the order of Fire-Eaters, an obscure sect that had a small temple or two in Bar-Ibithni. An offshot of the worship of Masrimas, they claimed to receive the blessing of the god by swallowing live flame. This was considered blasphemous by the bulk of fire-venerating Masrians, who consequently, as a rule, avoided the orange robes of the order.

The priests rode on mules, for, like many another of their calling, they were a slothful lot. Trotting down the wide avenues of the Palm Quarter and through Winged Horse Gate on to Amber Road, they received no attention, but in the more commercial area an occasional blessing or curse was flung at them, while a small girl selling figs in the Market of the World stole up politely and offered her wares as a gift. This, a priest (Bailgar) refused graciously, pressing some copper cash in her hand. Despite her Masrian piety, she was part Hessek. I had been thankful to see only Masrian servants in the Citadel, but since I was actually seeking Hesseks now, I must recover my judgment. I was plagued by a recurring image, though not Lellih or the cat-headed demon, not even the tiger-man I had sacrificed for them . . . it was the child who sank his teeth in me when I meant to heal him, and drank my blood, and would not let go of me. He had become for me the symbol of that place of tombs.

The smell of the Fish Market recalled for me my arrival in Bar-Ibithni, the simplicity of my planning then, the clear-cut issues, the lonely sense of godhead and invincibility. The two fish glinted on their pillar against a lapis lazuli sky as they had glinted on that morning. No change, yet change everywhere, unseen.

The *Vineyard* lay calmly in the dock. Her sails were stripped, and her blue and weathered gold refurbished at the erstwhile order of the glamour-conscious Kochus. The hired guards were gone, however, not caring to be about now that I was Basnurmon's target, and the deck was alive with filthy, ragged children, fighting and swarming the ropes like black monkeys. There had been other visitors in the dark, for I could see at a glance where various fitments were missing. Even the enamel wings of the watch-god's mount in the forecastle were gone, and the whale-tooth tiller had been wrenched apart and carried off by night.

Bailgar pulled a wry face in his hood.

"You'd better work some magic, Vazkor," he said, bluffly enough. "Whisk your property back out of the thieves' paws. That'd make them jolly." I said nothing, for he meant no harm, and next told two of his men to seek the harbor-master, and tell him to reinstall a guard on the sorcerer's ship. "If he argues," added Bailgar, "say Prince Basnurmon has an interest in it and doesn't want it spoiled. That should bring the bastard to his wits again."

The two remaining Shields, Bailgar, and I went up the ladder—left in position by some idiot—and got aboard. The children, mixes and dock brats, fled in all directions, some even jumping in the green water and swimming for distant wharfs. In about ten seconds the deck, save for ourselves and accumulated garbage, was bare.

"A shortage of Hesseks," I said to Bailgar. "I must scour the port after all."

We searched around, nevertheless, even below in the rowers' station, now vacant. The oar-slaves had taken their chance and run, at which I could scarcely be outraged. Charpon's deck-house had been despoiled of its cushions, silks, and pelts, and also of the gilded bronze Masrimas statue. Male lovers had used the couch and left tokens, and decomposing fruit had enticed out rats, cockroaches, and similar guests. And this was but one or two nights' work. A miserable sight.

Outside, one of the Shields called. I went to see and found him with another miserable sight squirming on the deck, which squirmed harder and tried to bury its head in the planking when I came near. It was none other than my faithful and devoted Lyo.

"I found him in the hold, sir," the Shield told me. "Thought I was Basnurmon's scum and kicked up a rumpus. Frightened of the dark, too, for all he was down in it. And scared out of his pants of you, sir."

I told Lyo to get up, which eventually he did. He choked up some tale of fleeing my apartments when the wasp guard broke in the doors, and seeking refuge on the *Vineyard* as being the only other place he knew in the city. He was half out of his mind with fear of this, that, and the other, and mainly of me, recalling how he had made off twice on the night I went to Bit-Hessee.

I observed him without pity. I saw only something I could use, if it would leave off whimpering. He owed me his life, did he not? Let him earn it.

I took him to the rail, and set him there and looked at him.

To use my Power, after what had gone before, unnerved me, but this seemed a small piece of it. I mesmerized Lyo swiftly. His whimperings stopped and I felt his brain flicker out under the force of mine. I spoke low to him.

I was aware of Bailgar and the Shields standing about, staring, not sure what I was at, concluding that it was some sorcerer's method, and keeping very silent.

Finally, Lyo walked off the ship and away through the port, going west. I was convinced there would be watchers, in the dock and at the opening of the marsh. They would guide him over, finding he came from me. I did not even think they would kill him, for he was a Seemase, not a Masrian, part kindred of Hessek. Besides, he would inform them that their messiah, having struggled with himself, had bowed to the will of his destiny, and would lead them. Shaythun-Kem, *God-Made-Visible.*

Bailgar's tough red-tan face had altered toward me, no longer so bluff. Until then he had only heard reports of what I managed.

"It's done, then? Well, you know what you're at. How will they get word to you when they're ready?"

"Lyo will tell them I lodge at the Citadel. He is to say I trade on my friendship with Sorem for my own protection, also to lull the Masrians and to discover the strength and weakness of your armies. The Hesseks know I saved Sorem's life, and the rest follows naturally. If I'm easy of access to Hessek, even in the Citadel, I shall have word."

Bailgar glanced at his soldiers and back at me.

"I'm glad, Vazkor, that you've no desire to be the messiah of Bit-Hessee. I suppose you haven't? Just so I can sleep at night."

"Of all the things I have ever wanted," I said to him, "this I do not want."

I surmise my expression and my tone carried some conviction, for he believed me.

Part III

The Crimson Palace

1

Having climbed out of the morass into which I seemed to have fallen, the atmosphere of the Citadel appeared to me as wholesome and sound. Two square miles of bronze-faced outer battlements, manned by sentries in the red and white of the jerds, were like a shining shield against Hessek. For, though I never quite admitted to myself my utter fear of Hessek, my fear of what it had brought me to—a powerless, blundering animal—it was a rare night hour that did not bring some dream of it. Finding a spider's web in a crevice of the Ax Court wall, I crushed the undeserving beast and its sticky lace with a cringing malice, as a child would do it.

Another two days went by, my tenth and eleventh in this land. (Only eleven days, and so much in them.) We had our provisional plan as fine as we could get it now. Old maps were sprawled on the cedar-wood table, showing the thousand roads and avenues of Bar-Ibithni, from the marsh gate in the west to the old northern seawall beyond the eastern vineyards, and south into the folding suburbs. The campaign was plotted like a war, even before we knew for certain the routes the Hessek rabble would take. Bailgar, eating raisins, suggested to me that to draw the rats up one way would be to insure their decimation; Denades and Dushum demanded another ambush somewhere else; and Ustorth of the fifth jerd gave harsh voice to my own opinion that to sacrifice a little of the city to the rats would make certain of its gratitude after. Rescue, effected too soon, might as well not be a rescue. Against this, Sorem argued. I had mistaken the extent of his ambition, for his honorable nature and his basic compassion overruled opportunity. He did not want to see butchery and rapine in the streets, he said. And all the while he had half a hedonist's ear and eye for the musician girl, with her hyacinth locks trailing on the Tinsen lute she played poignantly in a corner. There were several girls about the Citadel, but they were free women and well treated, though seldom alone at night, I imagine. I saw no girl-boys, but like most armies, this one would have had its own traditions in the matter of that.

Stupidly, my nerves like knife-points, I was looking for a signal from the marsh almost immediately after I sent Lyo to them, but, as yet, there was no stir. We heard only that Basnurmon had given over his search of me, and assumed he had puzzled out where I must be. At the close of my third daylight on Pillar Hill, we had the proof.

Sorem and I were on the mile-long racing track of the Citadel. Here I was riding "white" despite my earlier protest, and both of us putting a couple of young horses through their paces to pass the time and relieve tension. I had never ridden anything so fine, save once or twice in Eshkorek. It was a pure-breed white, one of the Arrows of Masrimas, as they called them, sleek and lean as a great racing dog, the color of snow in sunshine, and with a fountain tail like frayed silk rope. It bore me proudly, broken to its destiny, but unready for a fool. I could feel the steed waiting to see if I mistook myself, or it, but finding I would master it and yet be courteous, it accepted me as a woman will who is of that temperament. Presently I won our race and swung down. Yashlom slipped the red cloth on the stallion and gave it a piece of pomegranate. Sorem came up and laughed at the horse eating.

"If you care for it, it is yours," he said.

For all my scheming, this caught me off balance. He gave as a boy does, charming, generous, and very casual. A rich boy, perhaps I should say, and to one who had grown up with little he did not wrest from others by dint of fighting, it had a ring that set the teeth on edge. No fault of Sorem's, nor of mine, and I had learned enough to get the knot from my throat, thank him, and accept.

He said, nevertheless, as they led the horses off, "To give is easy, is it, Vazkor, but not to take."

"Waiting on Bit-Hessee has soured my temper and made a clot of me. I beg your pardon."

"No matter," he said. "A horse is not much to offer a man who gives you your life. I was ashamed of my gift not matching your own, but since you thought it large enough to be angry over, I feel better."

Just then we saw the sentry running up. He came from the Fox Gate, where a small party of Basnurmon's men had apparently craved admittance in the most polite manner. It was no trick, the sentry avowed, merely a steward in the wasp livery of black and yellow, mounted but unarmed, accompanied by two servants with a box of carved wood, which all three claimed was a present from the heir Basnurmon to his royal brother Sorem.

Sorem looked at me, and grinned.

"And now, Vazkor, I'll show you how to receive a gift. Let them up to the Ax Court," he added, "and give them a royal escort—twenty men with drawn swords should be sufficient."

We walked back to the court ourselves, and into the red-pillared colonnade that ran behind the target-fence. Sorem's bitch hound trotted up and flopped down among the tubs of lemon trees. Yashlom and Bailgar followed her out, but the court was otherwise devoid of men. It was coming up to sunset when no Masrian draws a bow unless he must, for the old superstition has it that the shaft might hit the eye of the sinking sun. This, though considered a joke, is adhered to, as men touch stones or wood in other lands to appease spirits in which they no longer quite believe.

Into the empty Ax Court there was shortly marched a nobleman, escorted by twenty jerdiers and their swords.

This being recovered himself as best he could, and bowed to Sorem.

"I approach you from the Crimson Palace, my lord, bearing the gift of your illustrious brother," he rasped, "and am I offered rough treatment?"

"Not at all," said Sorem, smiling. "The swords, I assure you, are for your protection. We've heard of treachery, sir, assassins abroad in the city by night, and we wish only to safeguard you."

Bailgar laughed, and Basnurmon's ambassador screwed up his face uneasily. With a snap of his fingers, he summoned the two servants, who hurried forward and deposited a box on the ground. It was carved oak, with handles of silver and inlay of mother-of-pearl, and I wondered if it contained some exploding matter—primed powder or the like, though the Masrians did not appear to use it—or maybe a nest of scorpions.

Sorem surprised me by asking the wasp steward, with faultless civility, to open the box himself. But then, I thought, he had lived twenty years in the midst of this, and would not have lived five if he had not been schooled.

The steward, through confidence or ignorance, flung off the enameled lid with a flourish. What was revealed brought him up short and changed his color for him, after all. Not death, but insult. It was a porcelain statuette in the box, about eight inches high, painted and executed with intricate detail. I was interested as to how it had been done in the time, for it was almost an exact replica of myself, of myself and Sorem. The position in which it showed us was the one they name "Hare and Dog" in the male brothels of Bar-Ibithni.

I was angry enough. I would have been angry to see such a toy constructed of myself with a woman, and this I liked even less. I reasoned later, when I had got cool again, that it was a ready-made carving, with the heads smashed off and the new ones, Sorem's and mine, fashioned overnight, molded and stuck on in place. I believe, too, that it was so excellent a likeness, if I had studied it, though at that moment I was pleased to study anything but.

Sorem's face went dark with blood, then pale, and I could hear Bailgar cursing. The steward, too, seemed far from joyous.

Having a premonition of this tableau going on forever, I said, as blandly as I could, "Basnurmon confuses our tastes with his own. For the workmanship, I've seen better in the Market of the World."

"My lord—" the ambassador began to me; then, presumably recollecting tales of white rays and other magics, he fell on his knees to Sorem. "My *lord*—"

Sorem said in a voice I had never heard him employ before, "Take this filth and conduct it back to the filth that sent it."

The ambassador did as he was bid, and I seldom saw a man move so fast. In less than a minute he was gone, box, servants, and escort of jerdiers, right to the Fox Gate, and very glad to get there.

Bailgar and Yashlom, in some unspoken agreement, had walked off along the colonnade, and the bitch hound, aware of trouble, had come to Sorem and leaned on his boot anxiously.

He looked sick with anger, and his hand shook when he reached down to quiet the dog. My own temper was cooling already; I could see something of the joke of it.

"He'll pay dearly for that jest of his," I said. "Let's not get as riled as he would wish us to."

"Let's not," Sorem said. He did not look at me but played with the ears of the dog. "One thing I deduce from this token of his is that Basnurmon knows the Citadel is spoiling for a fight. The sooner Hessek finds its yeast, the better. We're losing ground." He glanced around and called Yashlom back. "Meanwhile, my mother would do better here than in the Emperor's city. Till this evening I thought her safer there, not implicated in these intrigues of mine, but now—" Yashlom had approached, and Sorem said to him, "The lady Malmiranet. Take two of your men, and go and get her. She's aware that a quick departure from the Palace may be imminent and will make no delay. Use the Cedar Stair, and give her this ring. It's an agreed signal between us."

To say I had not mused on Malmiranet since that solitary meeting of ours would not be quite true. I would have remembered her more often, if other items had not come in the way.

Yashlom was about to depart.

"I elect myself for your two men, Yashlom," I said to him, and to Sorem, "If the wasp prince means business, a sorcerer might be of more use than a pair of heroes."

Sorem stared at me a second. He spread his hand.

"I perceive you've sworn an oath to put me in your debt."

"Say that when your empress-mother is safe."

I reckoned he might be glad of my help, and, in any case, I was curious as to the byways of the Heavenly City. The memory of Malmiranet had flared up in me, too, reaction against webs and tombs, the plot and the waiting.

Perhaps I would discover her differently tonight, eating sweetmeats like the baker's wife, starting up distrait with alarm, that strange voice of hers (indeed I recalled her very well) rising to a shattered shriek. Well, let me go and see.

Yashlom had paused for me to catch him up. We went across the barrack hall toward the stables, with no chat.

More disguises. There seemed a wealth of them in this place. This time the gear of clerks, plain dark breeches and jacket and short cloak, and a pair of dusty little horses to mount on, absurd after my white Arrow, and fractious to boot.

Yashlom was familiar with the path he would take, and told me, before we rode out in silence, what I needed to be aware of. We left not by the Fox Gate but a back door of the garrison in case of watchers.

The sky was growing red behind us, and silver flecked with birds rising from the prayer-towers at the sunset hymn.

There was a pleasant tightness in my guts; I did not visualize that she would start up shrieking, after all.

2

Two miles of terraces rose toward the high walls of the Heavenly City, crowded below with the Palm Quarter and all its lights, clothed toward the top with groves of cypress, mountain oak, and the bluish larches of the south. They said often in Bar-Ibithni: As easy as to get in the Heavenly City, when they meant a woman was not to be had. But in fact, as with most impregnable fortresses, there will always be some way.

There were patrols of Imperial soldiers in the groves, but busy with gossip and counter games and wine; we got by them easily, having left the horses about half a mile below, tethered outside a small temple.

The walls were sixty feet high, in some spots more, black as ink, with purple guard-towers and gold mosaic horses set in along the top. Superb and unbreachable they seemed, without unevenness or crack, the only entrance being the huge gates on the northwest side facing overcity to the harbor, which from here looked as little as a pool, afloat with lanterned dragonflies for shipping. All Bar-Ibithni was visible from the high terrace beneath the wall, a jewel box of colored lamps well worth staring at, if I had had the leisure.

Yashlom had picked us a track around to the east. A stream splashed out here from the rock that underlay the terrace, with a massive cedar, centuries old, leaning above it from the roots of the wall. In the shadow of the tree was a dry well down which we climbed. It had footholds in plenty if one had a guide to indicate them, though it was dark as the pit. Presently, the luminous evening sky a sapphire thumbnail pinned above onto the black, and our feet in sponges, slimes, and disturbed frogs, we had some play with a trick door and got into a passage. Yashlom struck a flint to show me its length and the steep stairway at its end, then blew out the name (with the proper Masrian apology to his god for using naked fire) and we crept on and scrambled up the stairway blind as two moles. I did not relish this, imagining sentries at every cursing step. But it was proved clever to travel lightless, for the stairway surfaced in the Emperor's grounds, next to the inner wall and with no camouflage but wild thickets of red mimosa.

So I entered the Heavenly City for the first time, and understood nothing of it, catching only a jumbled impression of dagger-leafed trees, pale pillared walks and mounting lawns, far-off lights and twang of music, and everywhere the smell of night-blooming flowers and the vacuum enclosure of a vast private garden.

A path ran between poplars and through an avenue walled in by hedges higher than a man. Somewhere near a lion gave a throaty growl and had me almost out of my skin.

Yashlom said quietly, "The Emperor's beast-park is close by. That one is safely caged." The lion gave another sulky grumble as if to bemoan the truth of the statement.

The avenue opened onto a wide court, which fell away at its northern end in steps. There were five men here, lounging by a tank of ornamental fish, trying to catch them for sport. These imbeciles wore the deep red and gold of the Crimson Palace, Hragon-Dat's Imperial Guard. As Yashlom and I crossed the wide space, our hooded clerks' heads modestly bowed, they yapped out ribaldries concerning our supposed calling and our destination. Yashlom had informed me earlier that Malmiranet, trained by her father as a prince would have been to intellectual learning, frequently employed clerks, historians, and similar scholars. These men were seen coming and going about her apartments at all hours, for she was forever at something, reading and dictating notes upon this tome or that, or having herself taught some obscure tongue of the southern backlands. She spoke Hessek, Yashlom had told me, and all the seventeen dialects of the east. Hence, two gray clerks hurrying to her rooms would not excite undue speculation. It had seemed to me a dry occupation for a woman of her appearance, and I had concluded it doubtless an excuse and cover for other pursuits, less dry. As apparently the Imperial Guard had also concluded, judging by their noise. They did not molest us, however. We got down the steps and came to a cluster of buildings of stucco and white stone on a sloping lawn.

The great wall was out of sight in distant trees, but it was there. I wondered, as I had before, how she had got free of this pretty jail to search me out that night. Surely not through the portal of the slimy well, in those elegant clothes and with a carriage and horses?

Yashlom broke his silence to murmur, "Those in favor with the Emperor live close to him."

Malmiranet, self-evidently, was as far from him as she or he could get her, in this tiny pavilion. But its convenient proximity to the Cedar Stair had struck me. Probably she had chosen her home with that in mind. There were acacia trees in a cloud about the unlocked gate of the first court. A guard sat there on a marble bench, and I could tell at once that he was tame. A jug of liquor, a cup, and a plate of fine food. He had loosened his belt, and, noting us, only gave a greasy smile and waved us on. It occurred to me that she had been oiling him against such an hour as this.

A colonnade led from the court onto a wide terrace. Tall alabaster lamps burned a soft light that turned the darkness more blue by contrast, and in the midst of this glow was a scene such as painters strive to capture for the walls of palaces.

There were two girls with her, both half-lying on the rugs and cushions spread before her chair. The nearer girl played a rectangular eastern harp, the notes visibly running off like water as the lamps flickered on its disturbed silver strings. She was a Masrian, amber skinned, with black curling hair about her jeweled shoulders, and she wore the jacket and the flounced skirt of the Masrian lady, in a shade of bronze satin that seemed to match the hair of the other girl. Though tanned, this one was clearly of different blood, those bronze tresses of hers falling smooth like a wave over her breasts and the black Masrian clothes, that in turn complemented the musician's black ringlets. Like a couple of beautiful paired hounds, they reclined at the feet of the woman seated behind them.

I had remembered her imperfectly. It is hard to carry such an image about with one intact, like trying to memorize a landscape, every flower and stone and blade of grass. There is some feature one would mislay, something forgotten.

She wore copper silk and a necklace of heavy gold, but that I scarcely saw. She was listening to the harp music, her eyes half shut and far away, idly caressing the bronze hair of the foreign girl who leaned against her knee. The face of

Malmiranet would tell you many, many things, but you would not be certain which of them were true, until she chose that you should know.

The last note fluttered from the harp. It had been a strange melody, neither glad nor sorrowing. The Masrian bowed her head, the other girl lifted hers, and Malmiranet, bending sinuously, kissed her intently on the mouth, which set my blood fairly racing.

Yasholm and I had paused in the shadow of the wall, I to gape, he, I will presume, for courtesy.

Now Malmiranet rose, the lampshine snaking down the length of her silks. She came along the terrace lightly, stopped by a pillar maybe four feet from us, and said, looking out at the night, "Can it be my illustrious husband has sent someone to murder me at last?"

There was something essentially dangerous about her, like a coiled serpent, all immaculate immobility; till it strikes.

Yashlom went straight up to her, bowed, and held out the ring Sorem had given him.

She took it without a word, examined it, and gazed before her. Her face had hardly changed, but she said, "As bad as this?"

"As bad, madam," Yashlom said. She was as tall as he. I recalled her eyes had been nearly level with my own.

"No more questions, then," she said, and turned to look at her women. They had stood up, and were waiting for whatever she might command. Both were very beautiful, but, beside her, like a painting of fire beside the furnace.

"You hear Captain Yashlom," she said to them. "Is the wine jar ready, Nasmet?"

The Masrian girl smiled slyly.

"I will see it is, Empress."

"And you, Isep, you had better go, too."

"Yes, my Empress."

The other girl bowed deeply, and both slipped away between the columns, with a clinking of bracelets.

"Madam," Yashlom said, "we should leave here at once."

"I beg your pardon, Captain," Malmiranet said, "but that is the only thing we must not do."

"Your son—" Yashlom began.

She broke in with a gentle insistence. "My son would tell you that in this you must be guided by me. Did you notice five fools kicking their heels in the Fish Court above? My husband, Captain, has increased his guard over me for the first time in years, influenced, no doubt, by Prince Basnurmon's caution. To leave dead Crimson Palace men about the grounds after we quit them would be a pity, since the midnight patrol would find their bodies and an outcry follow. Nasmet and Isep are intelligent girls. They have become acquainted with the guards against just such a possibility as this ring you gave me. We will have to wait perhaps the third portion of an hour. Please be seated."

"Madam—" Yashlom began again.

"Yashlom," she said, "two lovely young women and a jar of drugged wine will deal with five guards surely and discreetly. Far more so than the knives you and your comrade would attempt to insert, however subtly, in their backs."

"Are your women to be trusted?" Yashlom asked.

"Completely."

Her conviction carried him and he said nothing else, and sat down when she again requested him to. At any rate, her girls had titled her "Empress," which would be neither common nor unbrave, things standing as they did.

She had taken no note of me, very likely thinking me some subaltern of Yashlom's.

"Now I said, "What of the guard in the courtyard, is he to be drugged also?"

She turned around again and came over to where I stood, not seeing me yet for the darkness beyond the lamps.

"You needn't fear for Porsus. We're old friends, he and I. I have left this place occasionally in the past, with his connivance."

Yashlom was seated at the end of the terrace, minding his own business, so I moved out where she could see me.

"I was wondering how you managed it, that night you sought me in the Palm Quarter."

She caught her breath and took a step back, as if finding me like this frightened her.

"What's this?" she said. "Not gone, as I suggested, from Bar-Ibithni?"

"You should ask Basnurmon," I said, "as to my whereabouts."

She said angrily, "No word-games, sorcerer. It isn't the time for them. I knew your lodging, in fact. Am I currently to believe you my son's errand boy?"

"If you wish. I am here with Yashlom to get you safe from the Heavenly City to Pillar Hill."

"By the Flame," she said. She stared away from me, frowning. "I don't like you in this enterprise."

"You trusted me before. Trust me again. Sorem lives; I gather you know why. But when you are alone with him, lady, since you misunderstand the news you get here, you should ask him what happened on the dueling field."

"If Yashlom vouches for you, which he does by his presence, I will accept that."

"You are too gracious," I said.

"When I am gracious, young man," she said, "you should beware."

And she went away across the terrace, speaking briefly to Yashlom as she passed him, then going up a little stair to some apartments above.

It was a fine night and the view was pleasing, but to sit and wait there on the whims of capricious females suited neither of us particularly.

Yashlom maintained his calmness, but his eyes had begun to fidget if his hands did not. For me, I soon got up and paced about.

It was not a long sojourn, though, for suddenly the Masrian girl came running down the colonnade, red cheeked and merry, with a story of Crimson Palace guards sprawled among the bushes, apparently drunk. Isep, the bronze girl, came behind more slowly with a face like stone, and I pondered if they had had to give something more than wine, these two, that the Masrian liked to give and the bronze girl did not. Both went up to the rooms above, but did not linger. Presently three boys came out, who you realized were women when the light caught them in a certain way. Malmiranet and her girls in male clothing, and carrying nothing.

"Madam, these ladies," said Yashlom.

"Do you expect I would leave Nasmet and Isep here when I have left, to endure whatever punishment that hog and his heir might vent on them? You observe that we have no fripperies to burden you. We're ready, and will make no fuss."

"We must use the Stair and the well," Yashlom said.

"Of course. Why do you think we are in breeches? Come, come. Why this delay?"

"You carry nothing. Is there no jewel you want to take?" I said.

"Against my poverty? I am supposing that Sorem will get my riches back for me." And she turned, and led our way for us through the colonnade into the outer court.

Her tame guard, fat Porsus, came shambling over, and kneeled down at her feet, and gazed at her with such canine devotion you would take him for her dog.

"The carriage has already gone through the gate, madam, as you instructed, empty, but otherwise just as on the other night. The gate guard pocketed the bribe, but I judge the information has already been relayed to the Palace. The heir's men will be out to follow you, as they think, in the carriage."

"Clever and dependable man," she said to him. "I would have died without you," at which the clown blushed and mumbled. "Will you take care when I have gone?"

"I'll be safe," he promised her. I thought him a wretched idiot and her a wicked one, either to dream he could escape suspicion after all this connivance with decoy carriages, drugged guards, and the like. But I did not mar their touching farewell.

About an hour later than we had planned it with Sorem, Yashlom and I escorted three women up the slope, by the snoring Crimson guards, and finally edged down the pitch-black stair under the mimosas.

To be just, our charges were serene as ice and nimble as three mountain goats. And somewhere in the dark, as we waited for Yashlom to work the stone door into the well, a pair of smooth arms came around my neck, and a wine-sweet mouth with sharp teeth gnawed gently on my lower lip. I thought it was she, for one mad second, but it was the Masrian girl, who whispered in my ear some promise for the future. I heard Malmiranet laugh at her antics, and I thought to myself, *Do you care so little for me, lady, that you must laugh aloud to prove it?*

Everything was well, no hint of vigilant patrols, pursuit, or altercation till we reached the temple half a mile down the terraces outside the great walls. Here the two horses had been tethered, enough for two men and one slim woman, but not enough for a couple of extra girls.

"No matter," said Malmiranet. "We may get horses here. The priest has a small stable and is amenable. If one man will stay to protect me, the other can see my girls safe to the Citadel."

"Madam," began Yashlom.

I asked myself when he would leave off these polite beginnings and tell her to do as he bid her.

"Isep is a matchless horsewoman," averred Malmiranet.

"Nasmet shall ride behind the man on the second horse, which should be a joy to both of them."

"Lady," I said, "our purpose is to conduct you to your son, not half your retinue. How do you know the priest will give you horses?"

"He has done it before," she said. "Are you afraid to stay with me here? I heard the sorcerer could overcome multitudes."

She was adamant as any woman used to obtaining her own way. I looked at Yashlom.

"Do as she says. Take the girls and get them to the Pillar. I'll follow as swift as I can with this one."

"Sir—" he began. Now he was starting his tricks with me.

"Remember the ten men on the Lion's Field, Yashlom, the ten I killed? Do you? Good. I am better protection for this lady than any army, and if she has sense in nothing else, she has the sense to recognize that."

She had got me to blustering and boasting like the cockerel in the farmyard. But Yashlom, taking the words at their basic value, nodded and mounted up with the Masrian, while the bronze swung into the saddle like a young warrior and trotted off down the jagged scarp toward the gem-lamps of the Palm Quarter.

Shortly I stood alone with an empress outside the temple portico.

She draped her cloak around her, and said, "I look enough like a boy in this dark; I've fooled the priest before. Tell him we're lovers and that my father will whip me if I'm late home, and he finds I've been out again playing Hare and Dog with you in the terrace groves."

"Will that work?"

"It will. He has a soft spot for boys and their men, particularly when a silver cash or two comes with it," and she tossed me a purse, which I tossed her back before I went in at the leaning entrance.

The instant I was in the door, I felt the trap and spun about.

Too late. A hand came on my arm, and a voice said, "Placidly, Vazkor. A man already has your companion in his charge. You would not like her to die, I think, after such measures to protect her."

Then the dark was erased by a flourish of torches, each lighted with its muttered invocation; religion before all, even murder.

I kept quiet and glanced about. I was not amazed to discover some fifteen men packed in the dilapidated fane, the iron-wrapped brands glaring on their weapons and on the black and yellow livery of Basnurmon.

The voice behind me spoke again.

"If you're looking for me, sorcerer, I'm here. I came in person this time."

Thus I faced around on the Emperor's heir, with whom I had had such a quantity of invisible dealings.

He was oddly familiar, which disconcerted me, until I grew conscious of the likeness of all Masrians with their curled hair and beards. Even I, who had taken up the fashion, would slightly resemble Basnurmon. I had been expecting I do not know what, for we tend to model the faces of our enemies before we regard them in certain ugly, infantile ways. To confront this ordinary object, handsome, clothed in fine dandified garments of cream and gold, unremarkable, grinning like a fisherman who has caught two fish on the hook when he anticipated only one, was curious. And the more curious when I acknowledged that he would kill both her and me, or worse, because he, too, registered enemies when he beheld us.

"You called me sorcerer," I said. "Do you believe it?"

He let his grin sour as if he ate lemons.

"Oh, I believe it. The wild priest from the north who slays men with light. But if you will turn your head, you will see the mother of your beloved. Malmiranet's life, for Sorem's sweet sake, is incomparably dear to you. You won't risk her."

Two of his devils had her by a pillar, one with a long-knife against her neck. She looked amused, tolerant, and she said direct to me, ignoring the rest of them, "There is a foul smell in this shrine. I wonder what it can be."

The guard without the knife raised his hand to strike her, and Basnurmon barked at him to be still. He wanted unspoiled goods to present to the Emperor, or for some private revelry he had in mind. Yet I could see that whatever move I made in here would cost her life or mine. A struggle had begun inside me, too. Despite my boasting of my armory of Power, Bit-Hessee had left me fearful to use it.

I tried for Basnurmon's eyes but he was shifty in that, maybe cognizant of tales other than rays of light. He walked over to Malmiranet instead and put his hand on her breast.

"I shall have to inform the Emperor, my royal father, how I caught you with your lover. That's very treasonable. It may merit the Mutilation of Cuts; first these," and he squeezed what he held, "and later that fine nose which, for too many years, has been thrust into matters that did not concern it."

"Little boy," Malmiranet said, "I comprehend you could not help coming out this dirty, from the dirty silly bitch who whelped you."

"Shut your mouth!" he shouted, cowering like a whipped puppy, like the thing she had named him. When he came away from her his face had fallen in strange, petulant lines. She had been his earliest gall, no doubt, but I did not reckon she would have stooped to attacking him as a child, if he had not begun it at his mother's urging.

I thought, *This woman is as brave as any man, and as sharp. She guesses he will take her to her death, or does she hope I can save her? She has had weaklings around her since her father's passing, that much is obvious, and even Sorem is more gold than steel.* My fear left me at that, the sepulcher fear of Old Hessek. I felt a pride come up in me like Masrimas' dawn, for she was worth a battle, and I due for one.

They herded us out into the night. Probably they had removed the priest, or he was in hiding; I got no glimpse of him. Horses stood behind the fane, and the wasp men mounted up. They had found a spare horse for me, but not, it seemed, for Malmiranet. Basnurmon told one of his cutthroats to tie her hands and take her up behind him, and I recognized what I must do.

The city gleamed through the trees; there was even a nightingale, as ever, speckling the dark with chimes.

The man with Malmiranet had drawn the rope that tied her wrists through his belt. I called out to her, "It may be a bumpy ride. You had better hold on tight, Empress."

I saw from the flash of her eyes that she took my meaning, and then I let the energy from me in a molten burst that sent my guards squealing and tottering down on either side. Basnurmon yelled with a scared puppet face, and the bastard who had her roped to him swung around with his dagger raised. I caught him in the breast with the white ray that had brought two thirds of my fame in Bar-Ibithni, and kicked my horse in the side. It ran into his, and, even as he fell, I slashed the rope free of her hands with the energy in my fingers that I had used to light lamps. I leaped from my mount onto his, before her, as his place became vacant, and gave the beast, too, a touch of fire to start it off.

She kept her head, as I had trusted she would, and clasped her arms about me.

To ride the terraces below the walls of the Heavenly City is frequently done, but sedately and with care, for as each ledge gives way to another, step-fashion, there will come here and there a drop into space, with the Palm Quarter some hundred feet below. Directly at the lip of the temple terrace, where one of these same drops occurred, I now drove the horse. It plunged and tried to veer, but I cut it around the neck, and with a scream of terror and a pottery clatter of sparks and stones kicked off beneath its hooves, it sprang out from the hill into the enormous void of air.

For a woman who could sound like a man, she now gave a little squeak, like a mouse.

"Hold me, and keep faith," I cried back to her. Her arms never loosened.

The horse pranced screaming beneath us, striking the sky with its feet while the stars wheeled. I seized with my will on its brain, open on the nude chaos of its fear, and welded it to obedience and silence, while I held us, all three, aloft, effortless, as I had held the wine-jar in the court to make the kitchen girls stare. Shivering to the roots of its extended limbs, as I gripped its flanks with my thighs and its brain with mine, the horse rested motionless, on nothing.

There had been some roaring on the terrace behind us, but now a huge gag had stopped their mouths.

The jewel windows lay below, tiny as beads. The horse's mane stirred in the breeze of night, still tractable to every law of the weather and the world but one.

I was young, and I was a god. The Power in me was like a golden shaft.

"Do you yet live?" I said to her.

I felt the movement of her head against my shoulder blade as she nodded, unable to say a word.

I tapped the horse lightly, sorry I had had to beat it. With a vast flying bound it stretched itself, and again and rode over the indigo air as if it were a summer pasture.

That ride, brief as it was, shot straight from a myth. There were stories after, in the city, of the sighting of a falling star, a comet. In the folklore of Bar-Ibithni I think there may have grown the legend of a prince and a princess, borne over heaven on a winged horse. I cannot tell if any truly watched that flight beyond the crowd below the Emperor's walls, who had their motives to forget.

Quickly and coolly I began to reason. I shunned the idea of such an arrival in the Citadel, I am not sure why. Too much furor perhaps, on top of the other; or possibly I considered how she might feel, dropped from the clouds into the lap of her son. She clung to me tight, with some cause. She did not cry out again, or entreat me. She felt what I could do, and had surrendered herself to me, this much I knew. Her surrender was very sweet in the moment of my triumph, the renewal of my godship.

I brought the horse down, drifting soft as a lady's scarf, in the open country just outside the Palm Quarter, near where the vineyards start.

There was an aroma of magic everywhere, or so it seemed. The night, the velvet groves, the outline of the old palisade and the glimmering of lights beyond. I let the horse stand for a minute in the long, dark-scented grass, and it put down its head and cropped there, as if we had come from market.

I said to her, mundane as the horse, "Someone betrayed you to them, Malmiranet. Someone who had observed I was with you, and who knew your mind well enough to guess your action at the temple."

She said, in a husky fierce voice, blaming me, "Sky-flights, and he speaks of betrayal. I shall lose my wits. Oh, you are right, I shall die of it."

She let go of me, and slipped down from the horse and walked away a step. I supposed her crying for a second, before I heard it was laughter. I dismounted and dropped the reins over the horse's head; it was in no mood for running off. I went to Malmiranet and drew her to me and kissed her.

I had been crazy indeed to mistake another for her on the stair, however momentarily. She did not taste of wine or scent, but of the smoky pulsing of the night itself. There was no mouth like hers, and no perfume, and her body shaped itself to mine.

She waited only a heartbeat before she put her arms about me, and held me strongly as she had held me in the sky. Then at length she pushed me gently back, and looked at me, and smiled.

"They told you the koois gets better with aging, did they?"

"Sorem is to be king in the Crimson Palace," I said to her. "I will make him Emperor. How will you reward me?"

"So little," she said, "for so much. I am too old for you,

my magician." But she went on smiling, not melting but dangerous as high-banked flame. Now she kissed me, holding me by the hair, and the fastening of her boy's shirt came undone so willingly that I think she had been there before me to help me on my road.

It was the horse which roused us, snorting and pawing at the ground.

I turned, and saw how the western sky was red at its bottom as if the sunset had begun again. I smelled burning, and a low far thunder came abruptly on the wind.

"Fire!" she exclaimed. "It looks to be the docks. What can have caused it?"

A cold snake, running on my skull, made me answer, "Bit-Hessee."

3

The horse galloped, not through air, but on the hard flagged paving of the Palm Quarter. Crowds scattered before our headlong progress. The bright streets were more full than usual, rippling with an insidious alarm, and the balconied towers bristled with leaning figures, peering northwest toward the scarlet bonfire of the burning docks.

They did not know what had broken loose; they thought it only conflagration, accident. Those with money in ships grew pale and wrung their hands, and ordered their slaves to run that way and get news. There was, too, an uneasy, superstitious, ridiculous thing, the Masrian embarrassment at these blasphemous uncovered flames.

The horse hurtled down the thoroughfares. Bells were mourning on the west wind now, and a taste of ashes. In my mouth also. I was afraid, as if Old Hessek sucked my soul from me. This, coming when I had not been ready, after all my readiness when I waited and they did nothing.

We clattered up the track of Pillar Hill, and the Fox Gate was drawn back for us without a challenge. The vast inner yard of the Citadel was massed with jerdiers and horses, and the red-hot iron flare of caged torches. The men made little sound, but the clamor of bells was louder here, and a distant roar, of fire or voices.

One of Bailgar's Shield captains came running over and led us through and up into the Ax Court.

Sorem was in the pillared walk, flanked by his fellow jerdats, Dushum, Denades, and the rock-faced Ustorth, and an ever-moving crowd of rank and file was coming and going about them.

Yashlom appeared, and politely aided Malmiranet to dismount, while I heard her demanding if her girls were safe. He said they were. Then Sorem came up and took her by the arms and thanked his god that she was unharmed.

"We met Basnurmon on the way," she said.

"By Masrimas, I thought it was more than horses delayed you."

"The sorcerer took care of it," she said. "Shall I tell you the wonder now, or save it? You seem busy, my handsome beloved. What goes on here?"

"Sit in on the council and learn, Mother. Vazkor"—he gripped my hand—"you have all my gratitude, but it must wait. You saw the fire?"

"The whole city sees it," I answered. I felt leaden, devoid of energy, which the activity about made worse. With an effort, I drew myself together and added, "I conclude that Bit-Hessee counts me an enemy, despite my playacting. They moved without sending word."

"Oh, they sent you word," he said grimly, "had you been here to receive it."

"A Hessek messenger, and your men let him *go* before I returned?"

"Not quite."

He called a young jerdier over, who had been loitering by the target-fence. The boy looked nervous and gnawed his mouth; when Sorem told him to speak to me he blurted out, "I was on lookout, sir, on the left tower of the Gate. It was just getting dusk, but I saw them come up. They looked like lardy beggars, sir, but after the orders about Hesseks—I calls down, in a friendly way, do they want anything? But they runs off. Still, they've left a basket under the wall. I sends one of my mates for it; he brings it in and we open it. Oh, God, sir, I've seen some things in my time, but that—"

The sentry was a Shield, and Bailgar had come up behind him and taken him by the arm.

"Don't make a drama of it. It was a head, Vazkor. A child's head, and the teeth had been torn out."

"Torn *out*," the sentry repeated, as if appealing to me against the injustice of his having had to discover such an item.

My gorge came up in my throat. I swallowed and said, "Yes, I think I can imagine which child it would be."

"Once the rest is settled," Bailgar said quietly, "someone should avail himself of the opportunity and burn that stinkhole out."

I took a short walk along the colonnade, beyond the torches. My head was ringing as it had in the fetid tomb that night in Bit-Hessee. The child who chewed me with his yellow teeth. His toothless head, their gift. Yet if they had accepted me as theirs again, why not wait till I acknowledged their sacrifice? Unless—unless I *had* acknowledged it.

The Power, again. The Power. I had used it, great power, enough to ignite my darkness, and theirs. For the white witch had trained them in her ways; now they could read me, feed from me, as she had. That psychic firework of the flying horse had been my beacon to them; sensing it, they took it for my intentional command, and they had risen, making me their Shaythun-Kem, eating my strength, their hunger tapping my brain and my life.

It must stop. Now, before they destroyed me, for I was not theirs to devour alive. Neither hers, Uastis', however much she might wish it. I, who walked on water, who stilled the hurricane, who rode the sky, surely I was master of myself, and of these *shlevakin*.

I must have cried out, for, when I turned, they were staring at me—disconcerted, anxious, and bemused. The man I believed a friend, his eyes blanked over by his shocked unknowing of me, and this woman I had come to want beyond all other women, averting her head with angry pride, not to let me see she was afraid of me.

But I was done with bellowing like an ox above the slaughter-pit, and done with leaning on a pillar.

I went back to them.

"What is it?" Sorem asked.

"It's done," I said.

A man burst into the court, shouting for Sorem.

"Jerdat, the port's alight, and the grainhouses along the commercial side. Twenty ships are burned, and a mob is on the Amber Road; Hesseks, my lord, for sure, upwards of three thousand, and others farther west, so the watch says."

They erupted from the marsh like a festering wound, a pack of wild dogs rather than rats. The port guards who saw them coming took to their heels. It was like a tide of mud running into Bar-Ibithni, the overbrimming of the swamp, and the surface alive with poison. A band of twenty men—police from the dock who tried to hold Fish Street, an alley that led east toward the Bay—were slain in moments by a black spray of darts and stone slivers. The tide had its unlawful knives, too, homemade, primitive instruments of sharpened flint, not even bound. At each thrust they cut their own hands to the bone, but did not hesitate. Anything that came in their way they slew, man or woman, child or beast, and what they slew they trampled over. They were of one mind, one heart. They made no sound as yet; it was their victims and those who fled them who filled the air with their hubbub.

Inside a quarter of an hour sheer terror was communicating itself along the arteries of the New City. Amid the tolling of warning bells, lighted by the red horizon, the rich merchant section rushed from its fastnesses. Winged Horse Gate became a point of exodus, through the inner wall of Hragon to the supposed greater safety of the Palm Quarter. The scanty guard there, some thirty or forty jerdiers, thrown into confusion and without orders, tried to bottle up the stream of shrieking citizens in the Commercial City, holding the gate against them as if they, rather than Bit-Hessee, were in revolt. Though not till a great bolt of flaring thunder shot up the sky—the storehouse of whale-oil in the Fish Market set ablaze and its vats exploding—did the jerdiers jam home the alcum doors of the gate and shoot the valves. This act of idiot and compassionless bureaucracy led, inevitably, to a worse panic.

The merchants and their households, whores in their tinsel, mixes and Masrians alike, fell on each other in an effort to get free, not only now of the Market of the World and Amber Road, in which the closing of the gates had shut them, but of the crushing press that had accumulated against Hragon's Wall. Men attempted to scale the wall itself, toppling back on those below.

All this while, sparks spread the conflagration behind the crowd to the gaudy brothels and inns that scattered the fringes of the Market, and all this while, too, the Hesseks poured nearer.

There were almost four thousand on the Amber Road,

three thousand more had split away to enter Bar-Ibithni to the south. Some went in their papyrus boats to beach among the gardens at the foot of the Palm Quarter, as yet undetected. Despite these apparent maneuvers, they had no actual plan of advance; the distribution of their forces was so far random, and the more appalling for its randomness. They struck where and how the urge moved them, men and women, young and old alike, flooding the Masrian streets, firing them as they fancied.

Tidings reached the Crimson Palace late. Invulnerable behind those high black and purple walls, brooding on smaller plots, its jerds indifferent to action, sluggish, unprepared. The Emperor, too, was slow to rouse. I would never have dared to hope he would show himself to his people in so poor a shape. He did not accept the tale of a Bit-Hessian uprising. When they showed him the glowing sky, drew his attention to the pealing of bells, the Heavenly City on its eminence seemed removed from these matters. He stirred himself at last, and sent out one of his jerds, a mere thousand men. He also sent for his scribe and penned a brief letter to Sorem. It read, succinctly, as follows: *Jerdat, we have been woken by a riot in our city, and is the Citadel yet asleep?*

Sorem was already like a madman in his rage to muster the garrison jerds, and ride down to the aid of the commercial area. We had held our last brief council, one extra there, Malmiranet, who listened to it all and judged it as a man would have done. Currently, she—along with Ustorth, Bailgar, and the rest—exhorted him to wait. Seeing the Emperor's letter, she tore the parchment across and said, "Now he remembers he has a son here who is a commander of men. It has taken this for him to remember." When Sorem cried that while he held his hand, the shipping in the port was burning, after our cold counseling, it took her passion to say, "Let it burn. They've let you burn these twenty years."

We had posted scouts along the various thoroughfares; these rode in at intervals to bring information. Not till we knew for sure the strength of Hessek, nor where it ultimately proposed to throw that strength, could we confidently move. To dash out like heroes and lose everything was not in my plan. Bit-Hessee would die tonight, with no errors made. If Sorem wanted kingship from it, he must rein his soul and wait.

Observing him, anguished and white-lipped there, I

thought, honor and friendship aside, though I might near enough call him my brother, yet he was a fool. She had the right of it, she had the ambition for him that he had not, and was more the prince than he. Malmiranet had kept on her man's gear, her black mane loose on her shoulders, and stood on the north wall of the garrison, red-lit by the angry sky, one arm about the bronze girl Isep, who seemed moved as she was, leaning forward with bright cruel eyes and lips parted into the smoky wind. Nasmet, the pleasure-lover, scared and exhilarated at once, drank from a wine cup, pouring libations to obscure sprites, and weeping.

We got word shortly that the fire, at least, had been constrained in the dock. The Hesseks held to nothing they took, but came on and left the way open behind them. Fugitives had formed a water-gang along the bay, bucket-passing from the ocean to quench the flames, and had done some good. During this time, I had waited moment by moment for a cry that the Hessek slaves of the Palm Quarter had risen. That cry was late in coming, but very loud.

The Emperor's stingy battle offering, the one jerd he had dispatched, was clattering down toward Hragon's Wall and the Commercial City, and making slow progress, for the crowds in the Palm Quarter, thoroughly alarmed by now, impeded it. This jerd of the Crimson was arrogant, reckoning itself sufficient to quell the riot, and not fully aware of the numbers with which it must deal. Its way led across the Fountain Garden, one of the large parks that greened the Masrian sector of the city. The jerd was about a third the distance across the tree-lined avenue that bisected the garden when the lanterned groves on either side burst alive with figures.

A huge party of Hessek slaves, got free of their masters in the confusion or else sent out voluntarily for news, had congregated here to intercept the passage of the Imperial Guard. Probably they had expected more soldiers. No one had numbered the slaves. They were in rags or the futile pretty clothes their owners hung on them, but they had snatched up kitchen knives, stones, or concealed barbaric weapons they themselves had constructed, knowing this night was imminent.

A thousand men in full armor, equipped with swords and bows and mounted on pure-bred Masrian horses, caught lazy, dreaming, and stupid by wild animals who fought with teeth and claws when other tools were gone and seemed possessed by devils. Those soldiers who escaped told stories of the bellies of screaming horses ripped open by bare hands, of girls of twelve years or less with blood-red hair pulling down shrieking jerdiers, and covering them as bees cover spilled syrup. Those who witnessed the evidence later, what remained there in Fountain Garden, coined a fresh name for the avenue: the Beasts' Run.

Till this incident there had been no noise from the Hesseks.

Now, the Commercial City awash with them as they cascaded like black ink into the Market of the World, and appeared abrupt as death itself on the wide streets of the Palm Quarter, they began to call a single thing, over and over.

"Shaythun-Kem! Shaythun-Kem!" And after it, that other howling, *"Ei ulloo y'ei S'ullo-Kem!"*

I heard it, borne to the Citadel, even above the din of the bells, and my skin crept on my bones. I needed every iota of my former resolve to keep me sane.

Then, in the midst of their wailing, a more mundane racket made itself noticed, a hammering on the Fox Gate, and the hoarse blustering of rich men in fright.

Sorem stood in the room that led from the colonnade of the Ax Court, rubbing the head of the gray bitch hound, his face the face of a man who, fettered, hears his woman tortured in an adjoining chamber.

Bailgar and Dushum stood by him, relating how seventy-odd dignitaries had arrived to plead the garrison gate for the help of Sorem, which was, of all signals, the surest.

Sorem straightened from his dog and gazed about at us.

"So you permit me to go out now, you five kings of Bar-Ibithni? Now that the city is on its knees, I may put my lesson books away. School is over."

"My lord Sorem," Bailgar protested. "This was agreed between us, for your own sake—"

"I never agreed *this*," he shouted. "*Never*, do you hear me?"

"Then, Sorem, you should have countermanded their orders, and done what you thought fit," I said from the door. "We are pledged your vassals. We offer our advice; if you take it or not is your choice."

He spun around to me, and I thought he would come to me and strike me in the face, as a girl would have done, but he collected himself in time.

"Your advice," he said, "your advice is excellent, but it takes no account of human life. The dead, they tell me, are piled in the streets."

"Then now is the moment to finish it."

"Why now? It could have been seen to two hours back."

"I will remind you of the itinerary. The purpose of the wait was to gauge the proportion of the Hessek rabble and the direction of their attack, to show the indifference and weakness of the Emperor, while at the same moment lessening what power he has. Last, to bring the city to your door, Sorem, to beg your help in spite of Hragon-Dat. These things achieved end the waiting."

He looked at me. He said, very quietly, "You began it, Vazkor. You end it."

I thought, *Where did this start? Was it Basnurmon's gift, the statuette from the brothel, fit only to laugh at? Or does he guess I lust for his mother, and has the eternal boy's dislike of me for that? Or is it that he has never truly seen blood and fire all around him, those toy campaigns of the Empire too tender meat to wean him to this night?*

I had put on the full gear of a jerdier since my return to Pillar Hill; now I took up the helmet with its brass ringlets and set it on my head, and went up and back to the wall.

The rich lords of the Palm Quarter were massing beneath, the track glittering with them and their lamps, their wealth piled about them, everything they could drag here, in bundles, in carriages, in the arms of menials. There were even a few Hessek slaves, looking as frightened as their masters. Perhaps they were mixes, or irreligious, but I would not risk them.

"The Citadel will give shelter to Masrians," I shouted down. "I speak for Prince Sorem Hragon-Dat when I say no Hessek will be admitted."

"And what of the city?" bawled the spokesman of the throng, a portly man with much gold on him, and some eloquent rubies besides.

"The Emperor has charge of it. The jerds of the Crimson Palace are even now, so we hear, laboring in your defense."

"*One* jerd!" yelled the rich man. Others parroted the yell. "And *that*, sir Captain," he screeched, "that one destroyed by slaves!"

"Incredible," I said.

The multitude assured me it was not.

The scene brought on an urge to humor. Though clearly they did not know me in my unfamiliar soldier's garb, I had recognized, here and there, former patients of mine, men I had rescued from sure death of toothache and indigestion, and even, beneath the fringed parasol-roof of a lady's traveling chariot, my overdressed lover of the white pavilion.

A man of Denades' jerd approached, and told me quickly that fire had been spotted southward among the suburbs, which pointed the whereabouts of a third portion of Hesseks like a sign post.

The Fox Gate was being opened, and the jeweled escapees grumbling and thrusting their way inside.

The man with the rubies got himself up the wall-stair and planted himself before me.

"Where is Prince Sorem? Is the city to be burned to cinders? Surely the Emperor has instructed him to lead the jerds of the Citadel to our defense?"

"My lord," I said, slowly, so he should not miss any, "Prince Sorem does not enjoy his Imperial father's confidence. You may have heard talk of a plot against the life of the prince, engineered by the heir Basnurmon, and winked at by the Emperor." I certainly trusted he had heard it. We had taken some pains to spread this truth around the city the past two days, using the paid gossips of the metropolis, who will put any rumor to seed, honest or otherwise. "However, moved by the plight of Bar-Ibithni, and not at one with his royal father's sloth, the prince is gathering his forces to quash the Hessek rabble."

Rubies swallowed my speech whole, and made fish-eyes at me. I bowed and went down the stair. The jerds were forming up through the gate yard and the adjacent courts, glad to be employed at last. I made out Bailgar, Dushum, and the rest riding up with their captains around them. I thought, *If Sorem does not come now, he will lose everything.* Then he came.

He rode into the yard, fully dressed for battle, and on the white stallion with its trappings of white, that old Masrian illusion, a man-horse in the dark red torch glare. He looked a king if he was not yet an emperor. One would not entertain the notion that some minutes back he had raved like an angry baby, and as well one would not.

It had been agreed from the beginning that I go with them, my own part an essential one, something I had determined to do, yet which made my mouth go dry, realizing I had reached it. A jerdier led over my horse, the white Arrow that Sorem had given me this very afternoon, which seemed years in my past. I swung up and found Sorem had set his mount in front of mine.

"Vazkor," he said, "will you forgive my foolishness? I spoke in haste to a man whose advice I value and whose judgment I have no quarrel with. You will understand, my grandfather built this city. I did not like to see it destroyed all about me while I hid in a bolt-hole."

It seemed to me he forever begged my pardon, or I his.

"You said nothing to me that I will recall with rancor, Sorem Hragon-Dat."

The rich citizens were crowding up on the wall to watch us go forth, the saviors of their city, and their gold. The gates stood wide, and from the parapets above brass horns were sounding. A jerd is a fine sight, five jerds, by deductive reasoning, one supposes must be five times finer. I rode with Sorem at the head of his jerd and my pulse was slow as sleep.

I felt I stared at it, this brazen passing of legions, this pealing of light on white swords and the red-blood splash of leather, as the mage-priest stares, in the old mural on the temple wall, at the world in a sphere of crystal. Even though my mouth was dry because I went toward Old Hessek, I seemed to have no part in my own fear.

A woman stood on the parapet, a woman in man's clothing, with a little gold snake wound about her wrist. Malmiranet also watched us from the Citadel, regarding the show as a lioness regards from a rock the dawn of fine hunting weather. But she, too, I beheld in the crystal. In a hundred years, or much less, she would be dust in a tomb, and I a dead god.

Hessek slaves, left outside, whimpered and implored and slunk away.

Then the city was before us, raw with its fires, and I was back in my body, a man again, and an enemy ahead of me I meant to kill.

4

Dushum's thousand galloped east through the Palm Quarter; Denades' jerd and Bailgar's Shields took the highway south to stem the haphazard advance three thousand Hesseks had made upon the suburbs. Ustorth's jerd went south, then west, crossing into the Commercial City where the line of Hragon's inner wall came to an end, turning finally north to liberate the port and close in the Hessek four thousand from the rear, cutting them in the flank where possible and driving them forward to meet Sorem's jerd along Hragon's Wall itself and at Winged-Horse Gate.

The desperate crowd on Amber Road, getting no mercy from that closed gate, had already cascaded south before the Bit-Hessian thrust, leaving corpses thick on the ground, all slaughtered accidentally or in panic by their fellow citizens. The Market of the World and its neighboring alleys, markets, shops, and warehouses, were alive with the rats of Bit-Hessee, or blazing where they had flung their fires and run on.

But something was slowing them now. Not the greed or curiosity of the invading army, pausing to loot and rape, or simply to gawk at the alien treasures on which it comes. Old Hessek appeared to have no interest in these ordinary diversions. It was the lack of a leader which turned them lethargic and aimless. They had risen at the will of Shaythun-Ḳem, they had sung their chant to him in the thoroughfares, but God-Made-Visible was nowhere to be seen.

I never thought that I had betrayed them. I saw only filth to be wiped away, a nest of vipers to be crushed.

The forty jerdiers who had held Winged Horse Gate against a frightened, innocuous crowd lay dead from Hessek missiles. Beyond the bastions of the wall the light jumped, now scarlet, now flaring black, and a second wall of smoke obscured the near distance, out of which rose the intermittent crashing of timbers, cries for help or of pure agony and terror. The Hessek mass milled before the Gate, at least a thousand of them packed up to it, with a makeshift ram—the doorposts of some nearby inn wrenched off for the purpose—thudding on the alcum barrier. Over this nightmarish scene, so like a disturbed colony of ants at work upon a carcass, had descended this strange pall of slackening blank-eyed silence. Their shouting was done and their inspiration quiescent.

They noted the advent of armed men on the slope the other side of the wall, and left off battering, but the pale "Old Blood" faces were all the same it seemed to me, wells without a floor, imbecilic almost, with a dreadful unyielding imbecility.

The jerd reined in and waited, glittering clean as new bronze in the coming and going of the light.

As I had arranged it, I rode forward alone, up the ramp to the wall's head, and onto the crown of Winged Horse Gate. I removed my helm as I went, and glad enough to do it for it was stifling me. My palms were clammy and my guts cold, but the iron was still there in me, my sanity, my pride. They had turned my Power against me, but I would master them. They must finish here. After them, one other must be finished.

I dismounted, and stood alone on that high place, gazing down. Presently the voice of some hag shrieked out my name and the name they had allotted me.

"Vazkor! Ei Shaythun-Kem!"

Only she; no other perpetuated that calling, but their faces altered, raised themselves to me. I had seen women who thought they loved me look at me that way, and wolves which were hungry.

The pressure built itself inside my skull.

I lifted myself upward, levitating from the wall into the spark-ridden murk. There was no effort, as with the horse, the storm, the ocean-walk; it had the ease of the perfect thing, what is meant to be.

They watched, their faces tilting like pale plates, after the rising of their star. I struck them, even as they worshiped me.

The fire that sprang from me was no longer white, but red, blinding, a hurt, a sheet of scarlet hate that wrapped around them and me.

I slew three hundred or more with that first blow, six hundred at the next. Death shot from me in vast waves of sightless brillance, and they fell like dolls of melting wax, not attempting to evade me, motionless till they toppled, then motionless once again.

I remember everything that followed with great clarity.

The jerd was moving, had opened the Gate and raced

through it, over the mounds of blasted human flesh. I, regaining the wall, caught the bridle of my horse, which shied from me, squealing, till I touched its brain with mine. I mounted and caught up to Sorem's men, and went through them and beyond, unaccompanied, into the fire-fog that swirled before us.

They had their own strong sorcery that night, the rats of Old Hessek, for somehow they became instantaneously aware, scattered as they were across the length and breadth of Bar-Ibithni, that in that second their messiah had rejected them, and that the bolts of his lightning were turned on them. I broke the spine of their rising with the first blow I dealt them at Winged Horse Gate, but did not guess it, and besides, had not done with the beating.

To fight an enemy in a trap, in the dark, to feel his stranglehold on my windpipe, and then abruptly to discover a knife under my hand, that was how it was. I struck him again and again, my foe who could no longer cloud himself with shadow, shield himself with my own body. Long after the stranglehold was broken, I stuck that red knife in his side.

In every direction, crackling fires, the voices and the shrieks, and before me a carpet of dead Hesseks. I left the jerd small need for swords or bows. But they had a city to rescue, fire to tame, honor to win. That was their portion, Sorem's garland, not mine.

There was eventually a different luminance in the sky. Dawn in the east, the color of decaying leaves from the smoke. A huge quiet descended with the darkness into the marsh.

The streets were coming out of the night clad in soot, charcoal wrecks leaning on the air, and up and down them the damned were journeying, some with their garments burned from them, others with the skin similarly gone. I healed no one and no one came to me for healing. Probably, my face smeared with grime and my eyes red, like the faces and eyes of all those about me, they did not know Vazkor. I must have appeared, too, a man capable of murder, but not of compassion. For, to this hour, that act of death has left its sign on me. That act and the deeds that pursued it.

Presently, some order emerged with the city from the darkness.

The fires were dying, for it had begun to rain—a boon from Masrimas perhaps, his seal on the victory of the light.

Though quite a few believed the sorcerer ordered the rain down from heaven.

It was the first dawn I had seen in Bar-Ibithni and no morning hymn had risen from the prayer-towers in the Palm Quarter. Everywhere the priests were busy doctoring the injured (I even noticed the orange fire-eaters genuinely abroad, with baskets of salves and amulets), or else they had gathered their temple riches and hidden themselves.

The rain splashed through the sullen dawn. Soldiers were collecting the unclaimed dead, Hessek and Masrian, and throwing the bodies into road-sweepers' carts harnessed to mules. There was a great traffic of these carts. Despite the rain, such a quantity of unburied business could not be left long in the midsummer heat of the south.

Some Hesseks still lived, those who had had no part in the rising, mostly of mixed blood, scared of the whole world now, of Masrian and Bit-Hessee alike. Generally, the only Hessek to be found that day was one the sorcerer had slain, or the jerds, if one traveled farther south or east.

Denades and Bailgar had routed out the three thousand in the suburbs. The menace had gone suddenly from them, the soldiers would tell you; as if under a spell, they dropped their weapons and offered themselves to the shafts of crossbows and the blades of longswords. Like rats that had been poisoned. Denades returned with dawn to Pillar Hill to report his success, for the damage was not vast southward, only an inn or two burned, which he dismissed as nothing. In the Palm Quarter the tale was much the same. The slaves' uprising had been contained in the Fountain Garden, due to the grisly exercises carried out there by the Hesseks on the bodies of the Emperor's jerd. Aimless, and without any leadership, the slaves had abandoned themselves to the wild orgiastic dream of the slave, and gloried in the mutilation of this symbol of their slavery, nine hundred and sixty Imperial Guards. Dushum's men had witnessed a feast of blood, of vampires and ghouls, and not one slave in the park was spared.

Of other Hesseks wandering on the terraces, most were brought down on sight. A handful fled to their boats, surprising the jerdiers by their speed and will to survive, for the majority made no protest at retribution.

Northward, Ustorth had mastered the docks and port swiftly, reorganized its police, and commenced cutting the escape path of the Hesseks and forcing them back upon the swords of Sorem's men. He, too, found Bit-Hessee, however, apt to perish. By dawn he had started on the second task, to set chaos in order. Having argued for the sacrifice of certain portions of Bar-Ibithni to add weight to Sorem's deeds, he had been well prepared. Ustorth had forseen the wreck, and made plans for alleviating it before it even occurred.

Only Bailgar's Shields sent no word, till a savage streamer in the west spoke for them. Now it was the Rat-Hole's season of fire, for Bailgar cauterized the wound of Bit-Hessee as he had proposed.

The snarling glare thinned and swelled alternately till the rain and the swamp licked it from the sky.

Nor had Bailgar's Shields been idle elsewhere. There was something he and I had settled on the day before, that clearly had been effected. A gold cash or two had insured that as we rode back through the Market of the World, with half a jerd behind us, voices began to extol Sorem, yelling his name and authorizing for him the favor of their god. Shortly the whole wretched mob of homeless, shocked, and sick gathered there began to echo these paid praises with weak hysteria. In the Palm Quarter itself, where small harm of any sort had come save to the hapless Imperial jerd, the praise was louder and more definite.

Denades rode out to meet us below Pillar Hill.

"Listen," he said, grinning through his soot. "I wonder if the Emperor hears it."

"I wonder if Hragon-Dat hears anything," I said. "What do we hear of him?"

"A pretty story," said Denades. "Two or three survivors of the Imperial jerd got back to the Crimson Palace, cowards, no doubt, who spurred their horses at the first rustle of the bushes in Fountain Garden. Learning of the situation, the Emperor instructed his two remaining battalions to the defense of the Heavenly City. Every Hessek slave within the walls, whether inclined to revolt or not, was killed. Following that courageous act, his army has manned the watchtowers and there they have taken their ease for the past two or three hours, letting the city stew in its own blood and fire."

"I trust, jerdat," I said, "you've found men to spread this saga of the Emperor's lionheartedness?"

Denades nodded. "By Masrimas, I have. Oh, but there's also a saga concerning you, sir."

"What?"

"Sorcery," he said, shrugging. He was still not sure, this

Denades, what to make of me. "A thousand or more Hessek rats slain with lightning, a magician-priest gone mad; something of this sort."

"And the Emperor's jerds," I said, "have they got wind of that?"

"You may count on it."

Sorem had sat his horse beside me all this while, silent, looking away along the sloping terrace streets and between the towers toward that far outline, almost lost in the smoky morning air, of the Heavenly City. He was as filthy and disheveled as any of us, but no less for that. From the distance at which the vociferous crowds had seen him and even now saw him, he looked only stern and set of purpose. To me, and perhaps to me alone, he looked afraid. Not of any battle or any man, but of circumstances, of this crucial moment which must be grasped before it crumbled. My thoughts had returned to Lion's Field, where he had wielded Power, a power albeit not a quarter for the force of mine, learned in some priests' mystery. I had scarcely considered it after; it had not seemed to fit with Sorem. It had become, in fact, strangely difficult to recall him as anything more than an adjunct to this drama, of which, surely, he was the hero.

Then he was turning to me, saying, "Half my jerd left to bring order to the Commercial City, but half here and Denades' men. We can count on Dushum's thousand, too, if they are done chasing rats. That should be enough." He spoke as a man speaks to get the shape of things clear in his mind, but to me it was as if he cried out, "Now tell me what I must do."

5

We took the Heavenly City, calmly, as I had anticipated, and without a fight of any kind.

The people were in uproar by now, piled up as high as the groves beneath the Imperial Walls, singing out the name of Sorem like a war-cry. For the aristocracy, they had their own code. Their messages came more subtly, not written but in the mouths of servants: "My master, such and such, applauds you, prince, as the savior of the city," and "My master, so and so, pledges his personal house guard, one hundred men, should you have any pressing need of them."

Also, I had been mistaken to suppose the Emperor's two surviving jerds had felt no embarrassment at their confinement. To guard one king and his household, ignoring the blazing confusion below, had got them to a state of shivering, dismal fury. They were a pack of boneless fools, who had lived soft for years on the hog's back. The loss of their brother jerd and the acid, dangerous hate of the Masrian people reduced them to mere jellies. Alarmed at the abuse and threats outside, and sighting some two thousand and five hundred jerdiers with Sorem riding at their head, a group of guards had opened the huge gate, and presently all were on their knees to him. They denied their part, or lack of it. They spit upon the Emperor's name. Several wept. They were but too glad to hand over to Sorem, a prince of the pure bloodline of the Hragons, the single thing they had been detailed to protect.

I had come in like a thief under the wall, previously. Now I rode through those confections I had only glimpsed in the dark. It was a "city" of gardens, of flowering trees and pavilions. After the smoking wreckage below, it struck on me oddly to see the motionless cochineal flamingos in the shallows of the rain-pitted silver lake, the bending cascades of willows, the toy buildings with their domes of enamelwork polished by water. Only the wild beasts were growling ominously somewhere, scenting dead human meat, and the birds, hung from the boughs in tiny cages, had no melody to offer an uncertain world.

The Crimson Palace stands at the center of the Heavenly City. It resembles a temple to the god, with its piled flights of pink Seemase marble, its great wine-red columns, stouter at their heads than at their bases, its cornices of gold lace, and its windows of bright fire. An avenue of winged horses with the faces and hair of beautiful women, each ten-foot creature a huge lamp of segmented alabaster that glowed at night from the burning torches within, led to the door. Before this mosaic door, which was wide enough to admit twenty riders abreast, was a patch of red blood, nearly as wide, a memory of Old Hessek after all, memento of dead slaves, whose bodies had already lined some pit.

Basnurmon had fled; no surprise in that. He had seen the

wind change and he was wise in his villainy. The mother, that priest-princess Hragon-Dat had wed in place of Malmiranet, had also gone, with a carriage full of gems and gewgaws.

The Emperor, however, had remained.

He sat in a lower room with two of his ten-year-old fancy boys crouched by him, both plainly near witless with terror.

I had expected not very much of Hragon-Dat. Till that instant he had been a title and a goal, Sorem's goal at that, rather than mine. I expected not much, and truly, there was very little. He stared at us from the pillows of his dark yellow flesh and from a pair of washed-out eyes no longer blue. The strong and curling hair was a wig, which presently fell off upon the floor as he bowed his head to sob.

"Sorem," he whimpered, "Sorem, my son. You will not slay me, Sorem? I fathered you, gave you your life. Ah, for your honor, you will not kill your father."

Sorem's face was knotted and gray under its weathering and the smut of the fires. This was the thing he had dreaded, which had kept him silent under Pillar Hill. He had foreseen it all.

"You will give me this city, and this Empire," he said. His voice had strength and certainty; it never faltered, nor the strong young hand with its warrior's scars that brought the paper for Hragon-Dat to sign and offered him the Imperial seal, and the wax a frightened clerk was heating. It was quickly done. I thought, *Sorem, Masrian that he is, will never kill his sire, but the man is old and unhealthy. Death will be simple to effect, and Sorem need have no part in it.*

The room was full of exhausted soldiers, and the smells of drying rain and fear and the fatty smell of the hot waxes, and the noise of the Emperor's cries of abdication.

I thought, *Now I have planned another murder, and for another man's sake. I am meshed in this.*

They took Hragon-Dat away like an old, heavy child who has stayed too long at a children's feast, till the children and the adults are weary of him. He cried as he walked, and he had put on his wig askew, which made him, more than ever, a lamentable, pathetic sight. I remember this now with pity, but I am altered now. Then I could only glance aside, out of regard for Sorem's gray pallor.

The two little whore-boys, abandoned shaking on the floor, also were shortly led away, and we were left, commanders of that glamorous treasure-house.

I went somewhere to sleep, some sumptuous chamber. I lay down in my own sweat and grime, stripped of my borrowed armor, on the delicate silk of a bed that had a golden prow before it, like a ship.

What of the *Hyacinth Vineyard*, my galley that had cost Charpon's life, my galley, meant for the hunting? Burned with other vessels in the dock, maybe. What of the hunting, then, the hunting of the white witch, my mother, who surely had not died in Bit-Hessee? I should have ridden there, not here, and applied the torch myself and not left it to Bailgar. He would make no search for white spiders, white cats. . . .

I saw her there in her icy robes, her silver-linked hair, her fiery claws, her cat's head grinning, her left eye green, but the right, which I had skewered with my knife, a bloody crater. She whispered to me gently as a lover, "You will not slay me, Vazkor, my son? I birthed you, gave you your life. Ah, for your honor, you will not kill your mother."

I struggled to wake, for I knew she was a dream. Sparrow, that little minstrel girl of Eshkorek, held me and murmured that all was well. Her grip was stronger than I remembered, and I opened my eyes, not on her fawn and cream, but on dark amber, and an amber mouth that said against mine, "When you are old as I am, you will outgrow such dreams, my magician."

Malmiranet lay along my side, naked as I, but fresh from the bath, scented with water and that incense of hers; even her curling hair, like the hair of a black lion, smelled of rain and musk.

"I am not fit to receive an empress," I said, conscious of the filthy state in which I had lain down.

"You are a man," she said. "Am I to like you less for that?"

Her skin was marvelous to touch, and the slender muscles under it were firm, nothing gone to waste, for all those words of age with which she tested me. Besides, she understood her worth, proud of what she was. She poured her gold on me from choice, not loneliness. There had been plenty before me, men she had selected to pleasure her, and put aside when she grew weary of them. I never before had one like her. She used sex like an instrument, not by means of games such as they teach in Eshkorek, but out of a beautiful, uncluttered lust. She had measured her own ground, explored it through. This thing was no surprise to her, as to some women it eternally remains, but rather an ancient way, old as earth and as bountiful. She required of it no speeches, epitaphs, excuses; she required only me and her own self.

It was later she spoke of what she knew of my days in Bar-Ibithni, and of my dealings with Sorem. Her information was full and accurate; she had her own spies in the Citadel, so it would appear. She had heard from the beginning that I was a king's son, but I believe she cared not a jot. If she had liked me and I had been the groom it would have been well enough. She did not need the lineage of others to bolster up her own.

The day broadened and began to wane behind the silken window shades. If it was bright or overcast I never discovered. I was done with intrigue and armies, at least till suppertime. At length there began to be lamplight under the door, and a girl's voice, Nasmet's, I thought, called softly in to her that the commanders meant to feast in the Hall of Tigers.

Malmiranet answered, saying she would come out presently, but never moved from me. After a minute, she said, "I would not have Sorem know of this."

"Are we to carry on with it in secret, then," I said to her, "like brats stealing apples behind his back?"

"It will not last long, this apple-stealing."

"It will last," I said.

"So you think. Be at peace, my love. I must let my girls sample you before I chain you to me. You might prefer Nasmet, who is exceeding anxious that you should like her. Even my Isep has a kind phrase or two for you, and generally she does not care for men."

The voice came again from outside, with mischief in it now.

"They have brought your clothes chests, madam. Am I to lay out the red silk or the white?"

"White, and begone, you hussy," she cried.

"Do you trust them to keep this hidden, then, those girls, if you would not have Sorem hear of it?" I said.

"I trust them. With my life, as you saw."

"Someone betrayed you last night, Malmiranet."

"It was Porsus," she said, frowning at me through the brown twilight. "He bartered his health for mine to Basnurmon."

I recalled how he had simpered at her feet, and I said, "I will insure his suffering."

"I have done so already," she said, and kissed me.

I would have kept her longer if I had not heard Nasmet's stifled laughter beyond the door.

6

The *Hyacinth Vineyard* had not burned. Knowing it for my ship, as the Hesseks had seemed to know most things, everything, in fact, save that their messiah would fail them, they had thrust it out of dock, tied it by ropes to their papyrus craft, and rowed it free of the blazing harbor. There had been two hundred and eighty ships in port that night, vessels from the Empire's margins, east, west, and south, and sixty-five of these had gone up in flames and their unloaded cargoes with them. The Hesseks' careless advance, which allowed for the water-gangs with their buckets, had saved the rest, coupled with the sluggish wind and the dawn rain.

For days men of the Commercial City patrolled the borders of the marsh and the delta outlet to the sea. They watched the smoldering ruin of Old Hessek as the rat-catcher keeps watch on the hole. When a rat emerged, which was rarely, they clubbed him down and to death. Some even went through Bit-Hessee itself, venturing over the broken pylons and through the black tunnels, blacker and more broken now from Bailgar's torches. They found nothing much alive, and what they found did not live long.

There were horror stories. Ghosts howling in the marsh, dim wraiths with bloody claws, and women's severed heads, all snapping yellow teeth, bouncing like balls through Bit-Hessee. The rat-catchers, unnerved by their own fantasies, retreated back to Bar-Ibithni. Once again, the proverbial warrior would not cross the swamp by night, out of fear of evil spirits—where before he had feared only the drab evil of men.

Bailgar's act, the Masrian blasphemy of unleashing naked fire, was spoken of with censored approval. Masrimas had cleaned the dark with his light, the Shield jerd being his instrument. Bailgar, tossing off koois by the jarful, harking back to his landowner's stock, would put forward plans for silting up the whole marsh, reclaiming it, and growing melons there and salt-rice and the green water-tobacco which flourished in the muddy valleys of Tinsen.

Bar-Ibithni itself responded to the disaster, once it was safely over, in a mood of complaining gaiety. Sorem had thrown open the Imperial coffers to aid the destitute, and enable all who had lost property to make some claim on the state for restitution. Soon, every gorgeous brothel that had had a tower burned in the fire attempted to procure funds to build on two, and every merchant whose cargo lay in clinker on the harbor floor was filing petitions at the exchequer gate concerning three times what had gone down. This led to perpetual investigation, perpetual argument, and a crop of fraud cases in the courts of law. This wearisome business, both the dispensing of money and its retraction, fell on the shoulders of Imperial ministers well used to their burden, for the Emperor had given time to nothing save his pleasures. Now that Sorem stood for him, more active in affairs of law and state, youthful and alert, these recalcitrant ministerial rabbits would clutch their dignity and their scrolls, squeaking that everything might be left to them as it always had been. Most were thieves and had skimmed off profit from the Emperor's purse for a decade or more. Sorem went through their ranks like an ax-blade. But despite his concern for it, such business bored him, and having cleared the undergrowth somewhat and elected people he could reasonably trust, he gave it into their hands.

He was not yet Emperor. He was what they pleased to call the Royal Elect, that is, Hragon-Dat's functionary. The papers which had been drawn up in the Citadel, and which Hragon-Dat had signed and sealed that rainy morning in the Crimson Palace, had been shown at the court, copies sent among the aristocracy, and finally posted up throughout the city. They declared Hragon-Dat's voluntary abdication due to humiliation at his own weakness in leaving Bar-Ibithni naked to the Hessek threat. His beloved son Sorem—child of his earlier union with the lady Malmiranet, former Empress of the Lilies—he now recognized as prince and savior of the city, and fit to conduct its affairs in the abdicator's stead. Of Basnurmon, the Heir, only one brief sentence, scrawled on the parchment in the Emperor's own hand: *This beast abandoned both the city and his Imperial father to die.* A pretty touch.

Thus, Sorem was lord of the Empire in all but title. Masrian titles being weighty things, they must be conferred by priests, the brow smeared with oil, the robes sprinkled with water from some holy vessel, while a white horse is given to the god. Then, and only then, does the Royal Elect become Emperor.

Meanwhile the messengers rode out, and presently rode back, bringing the letters and the gifts of Empire lands, which swore loyalty to this new master, with cages of white peacocks sent to prove it. The nine out-city jerds, from their border fastnesses, sent their standards rather than peacocks, which, at the ceremony of anointing, their representatives would receive back (a typical Masrian show). There was to be no hint of menace from this far-flung soldiery. They, too, declared wholeheartedly for Sorem. To know the hub of the golden wheel they guarded was rotten wood has often been familiar and foul news to the periphery legions of several kingdoms. Sorem's rule promised better.

Seeing yet again how he was admired, his leadership accepted by veterans and novices alike, my mind went back to his outburst in the Citadel, his boy's heroics and anger, his look of bewilderment and despair as he gazed up at the Heavenly City, imagining his father's sniveling, letting the precious seconds slip. It was the Masrian way to revere what was beautiful and honorable, every knife in a sheath of fine brocade, that is if you must carry a knife.

If I had not been with him, what? I thought. With five jerds in the Citadel he could have rescued the city, but would he have ousted Hragon-Dat? More likely he would have been a god for a day and assassinated on the next, and countless thousands of women, and as many men, would have wept as his gilded sarcophagus was borne through the streets. The Royal Necropolis lay on a high southeastern hill, perhaps a fifth city of Bar-Ibithni, sugar-white domes and gildings. They had made a poem of death. Masrians say: The gods slay those they love that the world shall not have them. But Masrians were not always romantics; it took the honey of the south to soften them. And nothing breaks more swiftly than corroded steel.

A month went by. It was the lush flowering of the summer, the trees of the Garden City still founts in the blue air, and the Palace bathed in its red shadows, and the lions making their lazy thunder from the park. All this has combined into a changeless, never-ending afternoon in my memory. Afternoon when, with the connivance of her women, Malmiranet and I would lie close as garments in some fiery chest while her son was trapped in Palace business with his council. Though there were also nights. At the feasts, each supper being a feast in the Heavenly City, Sorem would occupy the king's chair, the Royal Elect, I on his right hand and his commanders about, and the notables who would expect their places. Malmiranet, Empress of the Lilies, in silk of snow or gold or wine, would sit at the table's farther end. Exactly where she had sat twenty years back, fifteen years old, Jointress of the Empire, Hragon-Dat's unwanted consort. They had seen her grow big with child, some of these same old goats and their wives who littered the banqueting hall under the frescoes of tigers, that child who was to become Sorem.

She had here a queen's apartments, hung with gauzes and beaded curtains, yet on her wall, too, were an ivory hunting bow and crossed spears burnished by old use. She said she never used them now. There was a tall palm beyond her window. She told me she had climbed it once, when she was six or seven, having seen a slave do it. She told me indeed all about her life, between the milestones of our lust that marked out our nights like shining blades. Her life was as I had supposed it, though not for an instant did she seek pity. She was proud and cruel, having been well taught, but to those she loved, generous and fiercely giving. Between her love for me and her love for Sorem, she was hard put to it to find a remedy. I thought it foolish, this clandestine way of going on, but would not waste our time in persuasion. I thought, *I will speak it through with him, some evening when he is free of court nonsense, and then she shall see.* Still, I put it off.

In fact, I put off much. It seemed a usual contrivance here. Even Hragon-Dat was left alone in some secluded underroom; why not everything else?

I had grown lethargic in all things but love. It will happen when you have been fighting long, and it had occurred to me I had been fighting most of my days. Now, here was the sunny island in the wild ocean, and I lay upon it, forgetting that the sea encircled me still.

It is difficult to remember the sea, however, when you can no longer hear it. The threat and the fear had gone, died, as I had intended, on that night of fire.

Bit-Hessee in ashes, only a few ghost stories to emphasize its passing. It appeared to me, in these amber days, that my nightmares had been purged and would return no more, every nightmare, even those of the white witch.

True, I had sworn a vow to a shade, or to my own conscience—to my father if I would have it so. But maybe she was gone with Bit-Hessee, Uastis the cat. Yet if she hid and lived, there would be better methods of ending her, with all the resources of the Masrian Empire to help me to it. Vengeance was a dry gourd after all; surely my father would wish greatness for me, even if it delayed her death? There was space for everything.

Caught in the slow pacing of Masrian court preparations for the Ceremony of Anointing, I came to move slowly also, as if through warm water, the beach always in sight. I, too, had swallowed southern honey.

So, with a little hunting and riding through the enormous inner parks, and many a bee-buzzing formal council, and the feasting, and the hours of love, this crimson afternoon poured on into a lengthening shadow of night I never dreamed would end it.

The day of coronation, devised by astrologer-priests for its auspiciousness, was fixed. Into Bar-Ibithni, bright with its fresh paint and brickwork, flooded a concourse of people, anxious to see the show and batten on it where they could. From the outlying townships and minor cities, from the coastal plains and the archipelagoes, from the arid rock castles of the east. Lords and little kings coming perforce to offer homage, peasants to stare, traders to sell, and itinerant robbers to slit purses and drunkards' throats.

I knew little enough of the surrounding geography, having spent my days so far in Bar-Ibithni alone. This diversity in peoples and beasts to be observed in the streets took my fancy, more sweets to please my languid hours. Particularly I liked the notion of the eastern tribal clans, whose women veiled their faces in transparent gauze that hid nothing, and went bare-breasted into the bargain; or the black men, traders in ivory and sapphires, who rode in from southern jungle forests on gray angry monsters of pleated skin, which had a horn in the snout, bloodshot eyes, and ugly manners, a sort of misshapen unicorn, prone to defecate without warning. (For this, the poor loved them, dung being useful in a variety of ways. I rarely saw these grunting unicorns without a train of hopefuls, complete with shovel and bucket.) From Seema, too, came magicians with faces muffled in red veils and swords like butchers' cleavers in their belts, who would dance with ropes that came alive, or seemed to, in the Market of the World, or else fold their bodies into minute packages of knotted bone and hide. I had gone to look at them with some of the Citadel men, and seeing me, the Seemases bowed almost to the earth, an action that amused me, having lost its significance in a drowse of calm. Noting that even foreigners honored me as the sorcerer, the crowd laughed and clapped. They did not offer me the love they offered Sorem, but knowing my part in the crushing of Hessek, there was often a clamor when I went by—though never anymore for healing.

As I was turning away, one of the magic-men came up to me and twitched my sleeve. I could see only his eyes above the red muffling, but sometimes that is enough.

"Your power is beyond the power of men," he said to me, using some outlandish language that would be nonsense to all about us, including the educated aristocratic officers who were my companions. If I had needed a reminder of my powers, this surely was one, to know at once, as ever, what he said and be able to answer as if in my mother tongue.

"My Power is beyond the power of most men I have met," I said.

"Truly. But there is one other. Not man, but woman."

If he had drawn his handsaw weapon to slice off my head, I hardly think I would have started more than I did.

"Which woman?"

"The one you sought, lord of sorcerers. White as the white lynx. Uast."

Denades, who was next to me, seeing my face, said, "What does the fellow want, Vazkor?"

"A personal matter," I said, "an ancient feud of my forebears." Denades nodded and stood aside. Secret debts of honor, family feuds, these were understandable Masrian commodities. To the Seemase I said, "How do you know this, and what is your purpose in coming to me with it?"

"In my own way, lord, I, too, am a magician," he said somewhat ironically. "They relate strange tales here of the burning of the Old City over the marsh, of the ghosts there. Not all are ghosts. I seek no profit, nor to entrap you, lord. If you will come to my sri, I will show you."

Denades caught the word "sri"—the Seemase traveling wagon—and said, "If he's suggesting that you go anywhere with him, I'd advise not."

"I have no choice," I said to Denades. "He has information I want. Don't trouble yourself. I'll be safe enough, and so will the red-veil, if he's civil."

The Seemase understood; I saw from the creasing of his

eyes that he smiled. While he was still smiling, I reached out and into his mind, a contact brief as ever, for I would never learn to like such plumbing, but sufficient to reveal his honesty, and a deal of genuine mystic lore besides.

"We will wait here for you, then," Denades said, "or shall I, or any of us, go with you?"

"My thanks, but I'll go alone."

"Sorem will put me to the sword if any harm befalls you," he said.

His eyes were playful. He meant me to have all the meaning of that. Denades would follow Sorem into any battle and guard his back like his dog, yet he, too, made jokes, and I was tired of them.

"Lead me," I said to the Seemase. He bowed, and we went off across the marketplace, stared at by every pair of eyes that could see, and also by a couple of "blind" beggars.

The Seemase magicians had made their encampment in a rented field adjoining the horse market. Six black wagons, strung with scarlet tassels and amulets of copper and bone stood in a half-circle on the horse-cropped grass. A small fire burned, covered by an iron grille out of courteous deference to Masrian custom, and two women were cooking the midday meal on it. They were richly dressed, with necklaces of golden coins, their faces bare and only their hair hidden in red turbans. Strange tradition to reveal the woman and mask the man, but I supposed it was to do with their magic.

Five large white oxen were lying in and out of the shade of a tree, gazed at askance by the horses on the other side of the fence. There had been no horse in Seema till Hragon Masrianes claimed the territory, and the light sri wagons still travel in a chain, two or three at a time, linked together by couplings of brass, and hauled at the front by a yoke of oxen or bullocks. The land route from Seema to Bar-Ibithni is long and hazardous, and would have absorbed more days even than are found in a Masrian month, leaving no margin to arrive before the ceremony of coronation, so I concluded that this party had come here by ship—men, women, wagons, animals, and all.

The women by the fire gazed and giggled softly. One kissed the air at me. My guide seemed unperturbed.

"You allow your women great freedom," I said.

"No," he answered. "God allows them that, and the men of the Sri do not presume to take it from them. We are not actually of the Seemase race, Lord Vazkor, but an older strain, and our ways are rather different. We have a saying among the Sri: Keep what you can, and what you cannot keep, let go, for it is already gone."

We went up into one of the wagons. It was dark, but pleasant smelling from bunches of herbs hung in clusters from the hoops above. He lighted a lamp, then took down a copper disk from a peg and set it on the rugs. We sat, and he drew my attention to the disk, which was highly polished as a girl's mirror; in fact, I had taken it for that.

"The lord has seen my mind," he said, "but the ways of the mind are muddy, even to those who must live in them. Therefore I offer you this means, the copper. This is the way of the Sri, between adepts. Thoughts projected onto the disk by one mage are revealed to the other. There can be no chance of deception, neither any intimate contact of the brain displeasing to both."

I sat and looked at him, despite the rest, unsure. Unsure, I believe, because I completely trusted him. For all I could have mastered him with my powers, he made me feel a boy before a man. From his eyes and his hands, I judged him in his fiftieth year, strong and agile, his wisdom a natural weathering and sharpening such as wind and rain produce upon the rocks of the desert. Sitting before him, I had that same sense of impermanence as I had known on riding from the Citadel on the night of the rising, the sense that far too soon a man is in his grave, and how small are the hurricanes and mountains of his life—vengeance, love, might, and conquest—compared to that tiny heap of bone dust at its end.

At last I recollected what I had come to find, and bowed my head over the psychic copper, and concentrated my will upon it. In a moment my blood ran like ice and my metaphysics left me for sure.

They had come by sea, as I had reckoned, and their tall galley had passed by the unlighted shore of the night marsh with dipped sails. From the rail, scenting sorcery as the hound scents lions, the man of the Sri beheld this on the shore: A white shape, dwarfed in the distance to the size of his small finger.

I beheld in the disk, as he beheld it, that whiteness, and I experienced, as he had done, the smoke of force that rose from it. It was the force of hate. He had shuddered to feel it. He had heard of the burning of Bit-Hessee and of the things that haunted there, but this thing he knew to be no phantom. A white woman, with white hair and white hatred growing from her soul like a huge tree. And her Power was as great as mine.

Scattered near her on that muddy open shore were dark shapes with gray Hessek torches in their hands. The breakers and the creaking of the oars and the sails of the ship hid any sound they made.

The old miasma came slinking over me.

The copper was suddenly empty and my host was holding out to me an agate cup with liquor in it.

I drank and he said, "I knew her name. She had written it on the night for any who could read it. I knew also she had marked you for her evil. The mark is on you like a brand. Yet, lord, this whole city has been marked. Not only the men who razed Bit-Hessee, not only the men who dreamed of razing it. Truly there is a black cloud above the golden towers of Bar-Ibithni, the Beloved of Masrimas. A black cloud which shall hide his sun."

I stood up and my limbs were trembling. I suppose I must have looked like death.

"How can I match her?" I cried out stupidly, not actually to him. "What Power I use she feeds on. *She.* I tried, I was rid of her, yet she persists. Whatever I do is turned against me." My mind was racing. I thought to go straight to that shore, the avenue of dead ships, the blackened ruin, and kill her there. It was what I had vowed to do. Or perhaps I should become the quarry. She had marked me, then let her follow me. Leave Bar-Ibithni whole, Sorem its Emperor, and Malmiranet, my woman, on the Lilly Chair of the Crimson Palace, thinking I had fled like a coward. . . .

He took my arm.

"I am a messenger," he said, "no more. I can offer you no counsel. But my name is Gyest, if you should require my services."

I wished he might have helped me, but despite his own acumen of strengths, I understood too well he could not. Paradox. My ability towered over his, and I was a shivering baby.

I thanked him. His eyes were fatalistic. The city was under her curse and he remained in it. *What you cannot keep, let go, for it is already gone.* Life also, presumably.

Outside, the sky was as blue as the sapphires the black men

brought from the south on their ugly unicorns. No cloud in sight.

Denades and a couple of his captains had remained to wait for me. He raised his brows and said, "Bad news, then. I hoped not."

None of them knew anything of my life beyond a few necessary minor items, and were always anxious for the chance to learn more.

"Someone lives whom I had calculated dead," I said.

"Oh? What now, Vazkor? Can it be you'll adhere to our customs, the code of the challenge?"

"The challenge is already offered, and accepted."

Denades stared at me, between approval and distrust.

"Hardly a fit moment, however, my Vazkor, two days before the anointing of Sorem for Emperor."

I spurred my mount up through the market, so bright with noise and color and show under that unclouded sapphire sky. Denades kept pace with me.

"Does Sorem know?"

"He will, inside the hour."

He frowned and kept quiet.

I had put a bold face on it, perforce. Nausea pervaded my body. There was a dream I had as a child, later in another form, some wild animal I had come upon on the hunting trail and slain, only to have it start up again, bleeding from its gaping mortal wounds, and leap for my throat. Presently Denades spurred his horse off to the Citadel, no doubt to spread the news.

I would have to fight. There was no other choice. Fight and fight again, however many times the dead beast came at me. It was not this city I gave myself to rescue, no, nor the life or the esteem of any man or woman in it. It was my own terror. I would rather meet the sickening thing head on than turn my back to it. I had thought her dead, or of no consequence, space to seek her, maybe space to forget her even. How Uastis must mock me in her ruin.

7

I entered the Crimson Palace, as it always seemed I did then, in that eternal afternoon. The sun, swimming into the apex of the tall western windows, crucified the rose-red walls and pink marble floors with long nails of pollinated light.

Sorem was with the council and the priests, learning off his actor's lines for the coronation. On the day preceding it, he must enter and abide within the Masrimas Temple, tradition prior to the ceremony. I had seen little of him in any case, since we took the Heavenly City. We had gone hunting once after the wild boar that were tamely bred and let out of cages into the game park for the sole purpose that the nobility might chase them—a dissolute, idiot sport it seemed to me after, though I had not chafed then. Sorem, disliking it as I did, had promised me better hunting in the southern hills, puma and lion and various water beasts in the vales there, when we should have days to spare for it. He had been always promising me things through this month of afternoon, and sending me gifts when he was away with the council, so I could not ungraciously refuse them. I had barely noticed, being with his mother more often than in my apartments to receive them, but now I had begun to ponder if he mistrusted me after all, and tried to keep me loyal by bribes.

Nasmet ran up to me on her gilded feet as I lingered, looking drearily at the sun. She put a flower in my hand, which was Malmiranet's signal to me. Nasmet appeared to have no envy, playing out this liaison which was supposed to be ours, but which led me to her mistress. Usually I was eager enough, and glad to see the girl.

She took in my difference, and said, "She would not have you with her if you have business elsewhere."

"Business with you, maybe," I said, my fear giving everything a perverse flavor. "You'd like that." I put my hands on her waist. I did not want her, yet I would have had her if she had been willing.

But she said, "I would like it a little. But not to displease Malmiranet. I love her more than I will ever love any oaf of a man, however handsome he is, or clever in a bed. Besides," and her eyes altered, "she would kill us both." Her loyalty and her amused spite—mixed as it was with an almost unnatural pride, as if, with Malmiranet's knife in her heart, she would have said, "See, here an *Empress's* anger"—brought me to my senses. I think I should have been embarrassed if other things had not weighed on me like lead. I asked myself, as I followed Nasmet, if she would recount my cloddish courtship to Malmiranet. I imagine some part of me wished to tear desire and liking out of me, flesh and brain and heart. It would be easier to die without it.

Then the doors were opened, and I saw her, and everything was altered, as I might have reasoned it would be.

I think I had never come to her and found her quite the same. Always there was a subtle variance in her mood, the setting of the chamber, her garments. It was her cleverness, mannered or instinctive, to be changeable yet unchanged, like seasons in a garden.

I remember how her thin white robe of Tinsen gauze, catching the red reflection of the sun on the painted wall, seemed to smolder on her skin, pleated smoke caught in by a girdle of ruby silk. Her hair was knotted up loosely. She would tie it this way sometimes that I might unfasten it. She had been playing with a leopard cub, a little tawny mewling devil that rolled on the mosaic, gnawing at the ends of her silk girdle. Turning to me, the light behind her, all the dark slenderness of her body rimmed with fire, I thought suddenly of Demizdor, a contrary thought, for they were not alike in any fashion.

"Well," she said, "I have heard a curious fancy. You are to fight another duel."

I had lost my puzzlement at the quick roads of Masrian gossip. Besides, I had meant to tell her.

"Yes. Something I can't avoid."

She loosened her sash and let the cub have it; then she came to me and set her hands on my shoulders.

"I acknowledge that you have brought my son to the Emperor's Chair, that without you and your wicked genius he would be corpse-cold, and I sport for some wretchedness or other. I recognize everything and I obeise myself. So don't do this thing, now of all times, two days or less before Sorem is anointed. He trusts you, values you. If you die, some part of him dies also. I am silent in the matter of my own distress."

Even she knew nothing of my past, beyond what was common talk. We had come to love too simply, and with too few lies; she had demanded no detail of my life the way most women will, as if every incident recounted is a link that binds, as if you should have had no life indeed, but what you live of it with them. Malmiranet had nagged no history from me, yet she knew me, as I was.

Seeing my face, she said quietly, "Yet you will do it, will you not? No pleading of mine can dissuade you."

"No. It is beyond your words, or mine. Beyond all of us."

"Will you say what it is that drives you to this?"

"If it would help us, I'd say. It would not."

She drew me to her, and held me, and said, "Well, then. I'll ask nothing else."

If I had ever wept in all my years since I had been a man, I would have wept then. I foresaw my death, and hers, as clear as I saw the sunlight on the red wall.

It was not a moment for harsh sounds, yet the door flew open, and the bronze girl Isep ran through it.

"Empress," she rasped, "my lord, your son—"

She had no need to say the rest. Sorem appeared behind her.

He was wearing black, some modest custom before the coronation, and it made the rage in his face twice as evident. He grabbed the bronze girl by her hair. She winced but made no noise.

"Yes," he said to us. He looked at Malmiranet, at the thin robe and her nakedness beneath and his color rose. At me he did not look.

Malmiranet stood away from me.

"Isep," she said, "please take my leopard cub and have him fed, that is if he requires anything after eating my girdle." She spoke lightly, as if nothing were happening out of the ordinary. Almost involuntarily Sorem let go of the girl, who darted forward, scooped up the cub and the girdle together, and ran out. Sorem, with great deliberation, shut the doors.

With his back to us he said, "I find everyone in the palace informed, except for me, that this has been between you. I'd heard you were lusty, my Vazkor, the darling of the beds of the Palm Quarter. But I am surprised you donated some of this lust upon the body of my mother."

"Let us get it right," I said. "Is it your notion of honor to creep up on her bedchamber to make certain she remains celibate?"

He sprang around, snarling out some oath.

Malmiranet said to him gently, "My beloved, I haven't taken the vows of a priestess, as well you recall."

"Yes, you have chosen men," he said. "It was your affair. But this one, this northern dog who has sprinkled his lecheries like spilled wine—"

I had been at a low ebb and passed from that to dull anger. Now I could have smiled sourly. Here was the irrational brat broke loose again. What possessed him?

"You had better names for me a month ago," I said.

"I trusted you then, though I should have been undeceived. Five hundred men and women dead on your instructions, Vazkor, when the city burned and you persuaded me that it must."

"We are remembering that once more," I said.

"I have never forgotten it."

"There is only one thing you forget," I said to him. "Yourself."

"By Masrimas," he barked, and took a step toward me. His eyes were blazing, half mad. "You would have made yourself king in my stead if you could," he shouted. "Treachery is your ablest weapon, that, and the tool between your legs which you used on *her* to such effect. *That's* the way you mean to climb, is it? Onto my throne by way of a woman's passion?"

"Who had been talking to you?" I said.

He controlled himself with an effort, and replied, "One of Denades' captains reported to me that you had been seen conversing with Seemase magicians in the market. I am aware of your ties with Seema—that man Lyo who was your slave. I don't know what plot you hatched, but be warned, Vazkor, I have guarded against it."

"A pity you were not more guarded against foolish chat, sir," I said. I wondered if the captain had also told him of my dealings with Malmiranet. Several must be conscious of the facts, and it had been doubly unwise to keep it from Sorem, since this was the result. Still, I could not fathom the roots of his fury. He railed at me like a child, or like a drunken girl.

He had grown pale as ash after the fire has died. He said again hoarsely, "I trusted you. I would have made you my brother, my friend." He strode across the room and struck me in the face. I had never yet let any man do that unanswered if my wits and my hands were free, and be sure I answered him.

He sprawled on the mosaic, just where the leopard cub had sprawled in its game, with the fringe of the red sash spilling from its jaws. The red that spilled from the corner of Sorem's mouth was blood.

He got up slowly, leaned on the wall and looked at me, and his eyes were full of water. Then he called, and Yashlom and six jerdiers walked into the chamber.

Malmiranet had moved away from us, twisting the gold serpent bracelet on her wrist, staring from the window at the giant palm tree as if not to add her witness to his shame. Now she murmured, "No, Sorem, for my sake." Her voice was uneven as on that night when she asked his safety from me. I could hear that she was not asking for her sake, as she said, neither for mine, but for his.

"Madam," he said, "I put down your own deeds as due to weakness. Don't make me involve you in his treason."

At that she turned to face him. I had had that look directed at me once, and I recollected it well. Sorem flinched and averted his face. Not glancing at any of us, he instructed the six jerdiers to conduct me to my allotted apartment. It was the most elegant phrase I ever heard employed in sending a man to a jail.

I had not gone armed to her room and had neither knife nor sword about me. I was slow, too. That spell from the marsh had made me sluggish for a whole month of idleness, and I could not thrust it off quickly enough to snatch up some handy weapon—the stool, one of the hunting spears from the wall. It seemed, in the settling of my inner despair, hardly worth it. As for Power, I dared not. Of a selection of devices the readiest and most effective, it was denied me. For a moment I thought, *Perhaps this, too, Sorem's idiocy and anger, are of the witch's making, to fetter me. If I use the Power in me, she will feed on it and utilize it to destroy me. If it remains unused, she will come more leisurely to my death. But still, she will come.*

It was an elegant dungeon, a set of chambers in one of the western towers, decorated in enamels and marble, with a whole wall of books, a cabinet of wines and liquors; the bed was borne on the backs of four crouching lion-women. Nothing is straightforward in Bar-Ibithni; no lion statue without a woman's head and breasts, no horse without wings, and no man without dual natures in his soul.

I did not keep my head. I was young and a dolt. I sat on

the pretty couch and got drunk on koois and red wine. I had never been able to get drunk, for more than a little either of food or drink made me ill, which this presently did. After that was over, I closed my mind to the world and slept.

I woke in the morning. The birds were singing in their cages under the tree boughs. I was in a daze, so far gone in not knowing what to do I no longer bothered with it, and lay abed, watching the sky beyond the windows. Each window was latticed with iron, a memento of Eshkorek and my stately prison there. And, as once in Eshkorek, I faced my death with morbid languor, almost laziness.

All remedies were valueless. Even that duel of sorcery I had planned could end only one way. I would not go to the marsh to get my demise when I could wait more comfortably for it here.

I dozed.

A man, one of the Crimson Guard, brought me food at noon. He was afraid of me, and at some pains to show me there were five of his fellows outside the door. I swung off the couch, and he lumbered backward and unsheathed his sword.

"Be at peace, my friend," I said. "The teeth of the sorcerer are drawn."

But he rushed out, and they thrust home bars to lock me up again. If I had felt free to set my Power on those bars, they would have been in a delicate mess.

The food was excellent, and I ate some of it and drank some water, the memory of wine making my belly gripe.

I did not believe that Sorem would have meted out to Malmiranet any of the bitter judgment he had vented on me. All the while I had been reckoning that it was his anger, suspicion of me poured in his ears by others, his jealousy of her, fear of my strength and how I had been before him on that night of fire.

This was the day he was to fast and pray in the Masrimas Temple. No doubt his honorable heart was full of much besides tomorrow's anointing. All at once it made me sorrowful, the drunkard's sadness, to recall that brief comradeship of ours. Sorem the one man at last to whom I could trust my back.

I had found a three-stringed eastern viol, along with the other commodities of the room, and had set about the work of returning it, having nothing better that I might put my hand to in that prince's tower.

Just before midnight, the bars scraped up from their sockets and Sorem came into the chamber.

He was dressed in the yellow robe of an acolyte, the hood of which he now pushed back. He motioned them to shut the door, and when it was done, stood in the lamplight alone with me, staring at my occupation with the viol. I thought, *By my soul, has he come to beg my pardon yet again?*

"I am not actually here, Vazkor. I am in the Temple, before the Altar of the Kings. You understand?"

I looked up at him and said, "I understand I'm past joking with you."

He spread his hand, that gesture of his, magnanimous, at a loss.

"I don't know what I should do with you, and that's a fact. I don't mean to kill you," he added. I must have smiled at the absurdity of his rescinded threat under that sword hanging in the sky. He caught his breath, and said, "Don't laugh at me, Vazkor. You deceived me and you've made me nothing in my own eyes. You've done enough."

"Prince," I said, "I am weary."

"Listen, then. Tomorrow at dusk, provision will be made for you to leave the city. Your wealth and your portable property shall go with you. I'll retract no measure of your just earnings."

"At dusk, then. And so farewell."

His lip curled. Probably he had seen some actor do it.

"Since you entreat me for news of her, my mother is unharmed, and keeps her apartments with every recompense I can give her."

"Why should I entreat for news, Prince, when you say I took her only as a means to the Emperor's Chair? As for recompense, Prince, I should guess she'll scarcely notice it."

He crashed his fist down upon the table, so the wine cup spilled its draft of water.

"Tomorrow," he grated out, "you ride with my cortege to the Temple. The people expect to see you there. You will be guarded, and there will also be priests in case you should try sorcery. After the ceremony, you'll wait till sunfall, when you will be escorted from Bar-Ibithni."

"Very well," I said. "What's one day more or less?"

"You speak as if the world will end tomorrow," he said

acidly. "I assure you it won't, despite any machinations of yours."

The lamp was burning low, the room nearly in darkness. He suddenly shivered, then came over to me and set his hand on my shoulder.

"Vazkor," he said very softly, "this enmity is ridiculous. If you will swear to me, by your own gods, that you have never plotted against me—"

I met his eye, and I said, "I am finished with your kingdom, Sorem. And I have no gods. Do as you wish."

His eyes blurred and his hand gripped my shoulder as if he could not stand without it, and then he walked away. But I had seen what I had been too blind to see before—I think perhaps because I had not wanted to.

"I will grieve for this for many years," he said, "that you would not swear and cleanse yourself of suspicion."

Then he rapped on the door and they let him out.

I tightened the last peg of the viol. Somewhere nightingales sang, but it is possible to tire even of nightingales.

Part IV

The Cloud

1

The flies came with the morning. I woke, and the air of my chamber buzzed with them. They flickered across the panes of the windows inside the lattice and crawled along the table—ten flies, or twelve, or more; it was hard to be certain, for they were forever in motion. Their noise and agitation disturbed me, so I turned slayer of flies till the rooms were quiet again.

A girl brought me a Masrian breakfast, fruit stewed in honey, sugarbread, and similar stuff. She did not seem afraid of me as my male guard had been; perhaps she did not know who I was. Then, as she set down the silver platters, she saw the corpses of the flies and cried out.

"What is it?" I said. I felt sorry for her; I seemed to see only decaying bones where she stood, emblem of approaching death. The whole city had such a look for me that day.

"The flies—" she said, "everywhere. In the Horse Market the herds are mad with flies. One woke me at sunrise, crawling in my ear."

"The summer heat, no doubt," I said, but she put her hand to her lips and said, "The blind priest who begs by Winged Horse Gate—he said it is the god of the Hessek slaves, the dark one they call Shepherd of Swarms. His vengeance—a plague of flies."

"Well, there could be worse things," I said. "See, I've killed them."

I could eat nothing when she had gone.

The bells were ringing in the Palm Quarter. The sun shone bright as a dagger on this day of coronation.

An hour later they brought my ceremonial robes, cream-colored linen embroidered with gold and silver, the kilt diagonally fringed with indigo, the boots of white bull hide studded with red bronze. There was a heavy collar of gold and alcum set with blue gems, and the border of the looped cloak of scarlet silk depicted a whole boar hunt, done in silver, green, and blue thread. Nothing had been omitted, even the theatrical sword with its soft golden blade and hilt warted with pearls. I was to be shown favor before the people, Sorem's brother, the sorcerer. He did not lack cunning in his own way. What tale did he mean to give them to account for my abrupt departure tonight? Not that he would need to give it. Not now.

The invisible sword above the city would fall today.

I felt as sickly numb and as deadly indifferent as only a man can who is going to his execution.

Bales of crimson silk had been set down all along the tracks and the roads that led to the great southern Masrimas Temple. They bloomed like a river of poppies before us; after we had passed they were in rags from the booted feet, the wheels, and the trampling of horses, but still the people ran to them, and ripped the rags into smaller rags, and bore them away as trophies of this imperial moment. Even before we got outside the gate, I could hear the cheering and cries of the crowd. They had filled the groves, hanging in the trees to watch. Men had even climbed the ancient cedar that leaned above the secretive well. As the tracks bore around and descended into the terrace streets, the throng stood in a crush so thick they could barely move their arms. They gaped and shouted as if we were their sustenance, a vicarious show that made them all kings for a day.

As tradition dictated, Sorem had remained in the holy precinct. He would come out to us, dressed in plain black, meeting us in the open square before the Temple. Here, the spokesman of the council would greet him, a man of eighty-odd years, strong, tough, stubborn old fool who reveled in such customs and the part they gave him. Sorem would ask why we had come to him, and be told we had come to make him our Emperor. Sorem would immediately refuse, pleading his unsuitability. The council would then severally state his virtues and fitness for the job, and we should troop in the Temple to effect the matter. This theatrical imbecility, a ceremony that had evolved two hundred years ago, or more, was Hessek custom rather than Masrian, incorporated by

Hragon-Dat into his own coronation, apparently to please the mixes of the city, but more likely to titillate himself.

In the rays of the young sun, the Temple was a pile of shining light, everything of it faced with gold or bronze. Massive pillars of yellow marble, broadening slightly as they rose their thirty feet, supported a portico roof of brazen god-figures. Six slender pointing towers fenced in the vast central dome, which was a wonder of gold leaf and jeweled enamel. All about the Temple square reared winged horses of cast bronze, on this day garlanded with late blue-black hyacinths, roses, and similar flowers. Flowers had been thrown on the red silk roadway and on the stairs.

I looked at the scene as intently as if I must learn it by heart, as if remembrance of it would comfort me in my grave. Actually, I saw only an empty concourse, the crowd all gone to brown bones, and ravens perching on the upper parapets of the Temple, with scraps of flesh in their beaks.

I had been paralyzed, my brain empty, already dead. I have observed insects in this condition, stored in the spider's web.

Malmiranet had ridden somewhere ahead of me in the procession. At occasional turns of the road I had glimpsed the lily tapestry of an empress, which traveled before her on its silver poles. Her skirts were of emerald and purple, fringed with gold, and her gemmed bodice flashed like a fire. She wore a tall diadem, a veil of purple brocade pleated from a sunburst of gold. She was borne in one of the low open chariots, drawn not by animals but by men, each naked save for the skin of a spotted panther around his loins and the silver horse-head that encased his own. A girl in white held a fringed parasol above Malmiranet's head, the color of yellow asphodel. All this I could see with no difficulty, but not clearly the face of Malmiranet, which seemed expressionless.

I thought dully, *Does she feel this, too, the mechanism of our lives running down?* Then again I would think, *Why bother to act this out?* But I was past original action of any sort, or so it appeared to me.

There had been some trouble with flies. They had irritated the crowds, and the horses. But the light seemed to lick them up, dry them off the earth, as the day grew hotter and the sun higher.

The procession came to its halt in the square, among the

bronzes and the thronged people. Ten priests emerged from the Temple porch, with Sorem walking in their midst.

There had been enough jokes to tell me. Even she had known, my lover who had birthed him. There had never been a father or a brother for Sorem to respect, and among the men about him whom he valued, not one who would stand in the way of his decisions, not one who was sufficiently discourteous to make his own rules, to be stronger and more able than a Hragon prince. Maybe it was simply that, that he had liked me, but the woman in him had wanted to be mastered. God help him, any other man in Bar-Ibithni, I think, would have been more accommodating than I. It was their fashion; they were part bred to it. Even those who would marry and get sons might have their fancy boys on the side. I think, too, he did not realize it of himself till Basnurmon opened his eyes with that statuette of porcelain. His change to me had been suspicion of himself rather than of me. He had condemned me out of frightened desire, not because he believed the stories of a plot.

I looked at him as he stood there, speaking intelligently and calmly the absurd phrases of the ritual, making it more than it was by the strength of his own worth. It was true, he had everything to tempt me—his looks, his valor, the basic soundness of his nature which, molded carefully, could have been made much of—everything, in fact, if I had not been myself.

Anyway, he would not suffer it long, that shame of his and that denial.

The old ass of the council was puffed up and ranting his lines like a third-rate orator of the lowest Masrian school. Under that noise was a stillness such as comes on a mountain when the wind drops, the silence of desert and wilderness. Not a murmur from the city, the crowd peculiarly quiet, not a bird singing, not a dog to bark. It was apt. Bar-Ibithni in the spider's web was waiting, paralyzed, motionless, and without a whimper.

A shadow passed between us and the sun.

It had been so bright, that sky-torch of Masrimas; it had seemed impossible that a cloud should blot it out. But suddenly the golden light turned dun, then brown; the gilded bronze facings of the Temple ceased to burn and faded to a leaden yellow, and the air was sodden with darkness.

The council orator broke off in full spate. He felt the chill to his marrow, and tilted back his old man's head to stare.

The mass of people rippled and surged, muttering, thousands of heads tilted back similarly. Then a burst of cries and imprecations. Then again, silence.

I, too, had lifted my head, and gazed as they did.

A streamer of cloud, like a bolt of cloth spun off a huge loom in the western horizon, was unfurling over the deep blue of the sky. A black, curiously flickering, curiously dazzling cloud had spread across the sun's orb, masking it, smothering it, while all about the blue sky shaded into umber.

Some pointed in the crowd, without necessity, for all looked upward. Some started to pray, afraid of this phenomenon; indeed, it would be hard to regard such a sight without fear. The black-sequined dazzling of that cloud seemed not to pass, but to gather there, directly above, swelling larger with each moment.

The horses began to toss their heads and stamp nervously. The priests on the steps behind Sorem swung their censers of gold and chanted aloud to Masrimas to push aside the veil from his face. But the cloud did not lessen, rather broadened and deepened. The square became dark as evening, and women screamed, and stifled their screaming.

There was a new sound now, the sound the cloud made as it descended toward us, a high-pitched singing buzz.

Then the black cloud fragmented into many million pieces, and fell on us.

Flies.

Like a rain of mud, quivering droplets of mud that spangled and adhered to whatever they touched; the air swirling like a pool in which the sediment had been stirred up. Into the open eyes the black sentience dashed, into the ears and nostrils. Open one's mouth to cry out and this cavity was also packed with seething blackness. Limbs thick with them, hair crawling as if water ran through it. Choking, blind, and in mad terror, horses and men thrashed in the maelstrom.

My own horse reared up, its eyes clotted as if with black gum, and I glimpsed its fore hooves smash in the skull of my nearest guard as he struggled from his saddle. Then I was on the ground amid a forest of such hooves.

I got a kick in my side, not a bad one, but it set me rolling. I was brought up against one of the bronze horses, itself black and glittering with the flies, which, finding it unliving, abandoned it, only to be replaced by hundreds more. Here I tore the silk cloak off my back and wrapped it about my head, mashing what swarmed beneath it into a treacle of death on my face, gagging and spitting out what had invaded my mouth. I was capable of action after all. I cannot say *thought*; what I did was purely reflexive.

It was Tinsen silk, the cloak, just fine enough that I could see through it a little. What I saw was horrible enough. Not a yard from me a man had gone crazy, and had been flailing about at the flies with his knife, mutilating or killing those men and women who blundered into him, till he himself toppled and was trodden under. Presently I stumbled into a child choked to death by the insects that had poured down his screaming throat. I saw several in this condition, several more thrashing in wild spasms on the paving. Here and there, one had done as I had, wrapping up his face, but, without the benefit of thin silk, could not see, and blundered hither and thither, or else, lifting the muffler in panic, was again overwhelmed by the flies. Some beat on the doors of adjacent houses, but the houses were also infested through their many unshuttered summer windows.

Where the procession had halted was a mass of shrilling horses and floundering soldiery. I could not be sure of a great deal through the blur of the red cloak. I was trying to force my way through to where Malmiranet's chariot had been; Sorem I could not discover anywhere.

The buzzing, whirring noise of wings was like some ceaseless engine.

Again I stumbled, this time over a Temple priest. He lay full length, and near his hand, where the golden censer smoked, was a little island of free air. The flies avoided the perfumed vapor. I wrenched off the lid and exposed the burning coal and crumbled incense sticks under their grille, next swinging the censer by its chain in an arc about me.

I made out the Empress Banner of the Lilies first, one pole caught in the chariot wheel, which kept it partially upright, the other on the ground. Malmiranet herself stood inside the chariot, a landmark to any who had tried to find her. She, too, had muffled her face and the face also of the girl beside her—Nasmet—who had held the parasol in the purple brocade of the diadem veil. These two were pressed together in their wrapping, neither making a sound, quite still, and the flies jeweled their arms and shoulders like beads of jet. Even so early, I had noticed the preference of the flies for living tissue. Briefly they would crawl on metal or cloth, discarding it instantly for flesh.

By the chariot was a final proof of mindless fear. The men

who had drawn the vehicle, their heads protectively cased in the silver horse casques, had torn these off in their alarm and bared their facial orifices to invasion.

I got into the chariot, which rocked unsteadily, and put my hand—itself gloved in insects—on her waist.

"Malmiranet—" I said.

She jerked as if she had come alive.

"You—are you here?" She put out her fingers to me, then flinched them back, shuddering at their burden. "Where is Sorem?"

"Close," I said, to reassure her. "We must get into the Temple; there will be some windowless place there we can take shelter."

"Is that a smell of incense?" she asked hoarsely.

"Yes. Take the censer and keep it near your face. These black ones dislike the smoke."

She did as I told her, but when her palm crushed flies between itself and the chain, she gave a low thin groan. Nasmet started to sob.

I guided them from the chariot and toward the great stairway, where a dead woman lay among the sprinkled flowers with flies massed on her in a shining mantle.

When we were halfway up the stair, a horse bolted past us, shrieking in that terrible voice that frightened horses have. Its eyes closed with insects, and insane with terror, it ran head on into one of the massive columns. The smack its skull made turned my guts over inside me even after all I had witnessed. The horse wheeled up and crashed over on its back, and the disturbed flies poured in on it again like a tide.

Nasmet's sobbing had turned to breathless gasps. Malmiranet muttered to her, soft, coaxing love words special to women, and kept her moving up the steps. Beyond that one cry, Malmiranet herself had not faltered.

We reached the portico and went in. The lamplight gloom of the Temple made it almost impossible to visualize through the cloak, yet there was a noticeable alteration, for gradually, as we felt our way slowly on, the whining buzz of wings grew less. A strangeness on my arms and chest told me the things were dropping from me in clusters. The incense smell was strong here, and dim ruddy flares indicated countless burning lights. Pausing, I began to hear the whimpering of children, the whisper of human movement in the visionless red dusk.

It seemed the scented smoke had driven back the flies.

Someone shouted, ahead of us. Next instant, a white brilliance pierced through the cloak. A man's voice called.

"Is it the Empress? It's safe, madam; you can unwrap the veil. They don't come here. Masrimas keeps them from us with his holy light."

2

We sloughed our protection and the scene came clear.

Directly in front of us rose the image of the god, pure gold, dressed in the warrior garb of the east, one naked flame before him. High up, lamps of heavy amber glass; the smoke of their incense was drifting everywhere in long blue eddies. There were no flies, save some dead ones that had fallen from our garments or our skin.

A sparse straggle of humanity crouched among the pillars and about the subsidiary altars. Some of the children wept, otherwise there was no disturbance. An anguish too huge for expression had stolen speech, even lamentation, from them.

A priest in the white and gold of the Temple had approached Malmiranet, bowing and smiling through pale lips. He reiterated that the god would protect her and asked her how she was. Her face was black as mine, plastered with insect mortality, as were the faces of all those around us. She stared at the clean priest, who had escaped by means of his location.

"What of the people?" she said, like stone.

"Those who have sought sanctuary here are unharmed, as you see, my lady."

"No one but I had come to aid her; no one aided the frantic crowd outside. The vast Temple blocked out the strangled screaming, the sudden bursts of ominous clamor, the whining of wings.

She looked at me and said, "They don't care how many die, providing they are whole." Then of the priest she demanded, "Where is my son? Have you guarded your Emperor at least?"

"Ah, madam," the priest said, stepping back a way. "Lord Sorem tried to reach you, and was struck a glancing blow among the horses. Nothing of any consequence. Two of his captains brought him here. The shrine physicians attend him."

Malmiranet clenched her blackened hands upon her skirt. If he had not been a priest, she would have struck him, so much was obvious. To the priest also, who hastily offered to conduct her to her son. She seemed to have forgotten me as, gathering the trembling Nasmet in one arm, she stalked after him. But about six paces off, she turned almost involuntarily toward me and, leaving Nasmet huddled there, came back.

Malmiranet grasped my hands, ignoring now the crushed things that broke between our skins. She needed to say nothing, her eyes saying all of it. Then she left me and followed the priest into the warm darkness, bearing her girl with her.

A faint cacophony from the far end of the Temple—a man had plunged in at the door, rushed forward two or three steps, and collapsed. I went that way, toward the vaulted entrance, the slender bluish arch that showed its opening into the nightmare world beyond. The refugees among the pillars scarcely glanced at me.

I had let Bar-Ibithni burn; there had been a reason for that. There was no reason now to hold my hand. I had reacted to the horror outside, not as a magician, not as a god, but as a man. Even if I had dared use my Powers, most probably I should not have thought to use them, caught up in that whirlpool of malignity. Vazkor had become only one more pitiful human creature. I confronted that doorway, the corpse sprawled across the threshold. And, from moving sluggishly, I began to run, winding the protective cloak about my head.

What I intended, I am not sure. To pick up the struggling and fallen and carry them bodily into the fastness of the fane, to herd the rest, like berserk cattle, up the stair and through the arch. My body was stretched like the athlete's as he poises himself upon the starting point. Thrusting out from the vaulted door, I beheld that the race was already done.

Under the lightening sky, the square and the streets that led from it had the uncanny, semi-mobile quality that attends a battlefield when the armies have withdrawn. From the black blanketed piles and heaps of the dead would wave a hand or an arm, exploring for its freedom. Some, actually free, crept forward on their knees. Many who could not see, their eyes sealed or damaged by the flies that had attached there, groped about calling barely audible pleas, curses, the names of friends that went unanswered. Everywhere the flies, in glistening mounds, like an enormous spillage of black sugar, were growing quiescent.

Occasionally a small spiral would rise, spin listlessly for a second as if stirred only by the wind, and fall back upon the rest beneath. Rivulets of flies had trickled along the Temple stair. I trod on their motionless husks as I descended. Those not dead were dying by the instant. One drifted from the air onto my open palm. I looked at it, a thing half an inch long, its legs stiff as wires, its black wings lusterless, harmless in its solitude.

A blinded horse lay against the bottom stair, feebly kicking. I took the knife of a jerdier laying nearby and finished it quickly.

A man, crusted black as were each of the figures in that appalling place, limped up to me and caught my arm. He babbled that another horse had fallen across his wife's body, but that she was alive. I went to help him and managed to lift the horse sufficiently that he could drag her from under it. Then he sat down by her, and held her head in his lap, cheerful that she felt no pain. But it was bad, for her back was broken, and I could perceive she knew it as well as I, though she smiled and patted her husband's hand.

I turned away to help another, glad they had not recognized the sorcerer and begged for healing. I could have done nothing. The Power in me was no longer fettered—it was gone. Such a thing I could feel, as the woman felt the incurable wound in her body. As I bent to my fresh task, I was aware that what I did was, in any case, superfluous.

This man we brought out living, but part choked. I laid him on his belly and worked upon him till he spewed a black vomit of flies and commenced breathing.

Standing, I looked up. The sky was empty, the sun blazing through a steely haze.

Observing what I had done for the choked man, a trick learned on most ships to clear a man's lungs of seawater, I was in demand from every side. So I turned healer in this rough-and-ready fashion. If any knew me, they said no word.

I worked right through the morning and the noon, not pausing to meditate. I understood very well that this was not the end, but had no notion what the end might be. A strained normalcy was struggling to repossess the city. The rain of flies had fallen everywhere, from here south and east, and to the western dock, not a street or a house had been missed, but only here, about the Temple, was there such a harvest of death.

A few had noted the potency of incense, and by early afternoon there was hardly a byway that did not have a brazier set out, smoking up heady blueness from its grille. The faces in the windows were wooden with fear, and on some was a rigor of grief held in.

It was Shaythun who had sent the flies, this they all believed, even those who could not give the name of the ungod of Old Hessek Bit-Hessee. Shaythun, Lord of Flies, Shepherd of Swarms.

Long before sunset the sky was darkening, the sun a smear of bloody heat through the incense smoke. Men climbed about their sloping roofs, sealing cracks and chimney outlets. Often they gazed westward for another swarm.

Bailgar had taken charge of the Citadel, mounting a watch on the high places, the towers and parapets of the city.

I had got down as far as Winged Horse Gate. There were fewer casualties that side of the wall, though a deal of panic and ghastliness. I went through and washed myself at the public basins in the Market of the World. One of the unicorn beasts of the black men, attacked by the flies, had run bellowing, smashing the booths and pavilions, till some artery burst and it slumped against the wall of the basins. Two black men stood beside its body, periodically ululating and trying to force the beast, which was quite dead, to rise.

A sense of purposelessness had come on me again, my services dispersed to their limit among the people, and forgotten. Priests were moving about, as I had seen them do in the aftermath of the fire that day after Hessek's rising. Lamps were already burning, for it had become so dark from the smoke and the abnormal overcast. The sky had become a thick lens interposed between Bar-Ibithni and the light. With an awareness of irony, I turned my steps toward the Grove of the Hundred Magnolias.

On the street, three jerdiers in the livery of the Citadel rode up to me.

"Vazkor—is it the Lord Vazkor?"

It appeared they were not familiar with Sorem's accusation of treason against me and my subsequent confinement, from which I had so incidental and peculiar an escape; they wanted only to escort me to the Palace. I related some yarn of having a woman whose safety I must make sure of on this side of Hragon's Wall, and asked them how Sorem did. The young captain slapped his thigh—that suspect gesture of Orek's, which I recalled as if in a dream where past and present mingled like sands.

"Sorem Hragon-Dat is well. The horse merely stunned him, but the priests carried him to the Temple. The Empress-Mother is also secure. We shall have to make the coronation another day." He smiled at me, charming as a girl, and said, "I remember how you slew the Hesseks, that wild night, like the god himself."

I thanked him. Soon, getting no more from me, they cantered away into the misty, blood-orange dusk.

I had no wish to return to Temple or Palace, to watch Sorem struggle with new gratitude, his raw emotion, yet another pardon. Nor to my woman, though in truth, a portion of me would have been glad enough to seek her arms, what comfort her love and her body could give us both, before the final stroke of the sword.

But there was no logic to it. It would be fruitlessly dreadful to see these grapplings after hope, after life itself, and I partaking of them, when life and hope were done.

I lay down beneath a flowerless tree in the Grove. No stars shone between its branches in that occult sky.

A little after the midnight bell—I had been surprised to hear it ring, this formality and order between the double brinks of chaos—a voice started up not far from me, and went on and did not cease.

I went to look. It was like my omen, and I must seek it.

A man lay in the bushes. He was a thief, out slitting purses even on such a night, and had been counting his gains there. Now he lay on his side, hugging himself in his soiled coat and staring up at me. He shook all over, and he whined, "I'm cold, Fenshen. Fenshen, run to the widow and get some coals. See, I'm cold and I'm sick, Fenshen. I've a pain in my belly like a worm ate me."

As if a bright lamp shone on a word in a book, I grasped the fact.

He shivered, and doubled up his body, and called me Fenshen once more.

"The flies didn't hurt me, Fenshen," he said. "I hid in the cellar of the widow's house, and I brushed them off when they fastened on my arms. But she screamed, the silly bitch, and they went in her throat." Then he laughed and cried and clutched his abdomen, smiling horribly with the pain.

He was the first victim I saw of the plague that the flies had brought to Bar-Ibithni.

3

The plague came to be called Yellow Mantle. Men must name everything, as if, by giving a name, they will decrease the nameless horror they experience. Though it was an accurate title enough. Those who contracted the plague passed swiftly through a stage of lassitude and weakness into delirious fever, accompanied by a purging of blood from the bowels. This was the turning point, for here the purging would either unaccountably stop, the fever cool and the patient gradually recover, or else the hemorrhage would worsen, the entire structure of the inner organs apparently poisoned and breaking down, until death ensued. By this time the body was so drained of blood that the skin of the corpse—in most cases a brown-fleshed Masrian—had altered to a pallid, overtly disgusting yellow. There was no doubt on seeing those corpses piled up on the sweepers' carts that they had perished of some vile pestilence for which no cure was known.

Yellow Mantle came in the night, sudden as only a supernatural curse could be. There was hardly any period while the plague hatched in the bodies of the most susceptible victims. Those who fell sick after, their constitutions being more vital, had simply held illness at bay a fraction longer.

I speak from an intimate knowledge of the disease. I saw all its stages and almost all its variations. I watched the thief die in the Magnolia Grove. He went quickly, before sunrise. I could do nothing to ease him, and indeed had not tried. I knew this for the last stroke of the sword. I think it gave me a strange fortitude to understand that.

By morning, three hundred lay sick of the plague. By noon, three thousand, and there were hundreds already cold.

At first, not properly realizing what had come among them, relatives were attempting to bury their dead in stone grave-chambers, furnished with priestly rites. Soon, vast pits were being dug in the commercial parks, and presently in the open lands eastward of the Palm Quarter. Being a Masrian city, it was two days before an edict was condoned to burn the corpses on open bonfires. By then, the pestilence had spread across every quarter and district of Bar-Ibithni. It was indiscriminate in its choice, sparing sometimes the old, the crippled, killing the young men, brides newly wed, women big with child. While of the children themselves, scarcely one in five hundred escaped.

For myself, I knew I should end with the rest. Each process of suffering I observed in another, I accepted would shortly come to me. I, too, was young and strong, I had survived the venom of a snake, my wounds had healed without a scar, but this I should not survive. The white woman, she I had sought, she I had vowed to slay, had sent to slay me instead. Of all this doomed metropolis I, more than any other, could expect no redemption.

After the thief had died, going down into the smoky, predawn twilight, which had about it already the miasmic half-dark of a plague pit, I encountered a small procession from the poorer area: a group of families who had ventured out, carrying their sick ones on makeshift biers. Their faces were all equally haunted by rabid fright, but they jabbered to each other softly, trying to deny their own prescience. As I was coming up with them, a girl of about twenty, who was walking at the back with a boy child holding to her skirt, abruptly fell down on the ground. The nearer members of the procession sprang about, the women making religious gestures. None went to the girl, and the little boy, tugging at her, erupted into tears.

I went and kneeled down by her, putting my hand on the child's head in an attempt to reassure him. Obviously the girl was in the primary grip of the plague.

One of the women said, "It's a fever, sir. Several have got it. We are going to the Water Temple on Amber Road. The priests are clever healers." The girl muttered and stirred and opened her eyes. There was a glaze over them and she was bathed in sweat, but she seemed to glimpse the child, her brother or her son, and stretched out her hand unsteadily.

"Don't cry," she said. Then she saw me, the blurred face of a stranger bending near, and she said, "I'm well enough, sir. I will get up now." Plainly she could not, so I raised her in my arms and began to carry her after the others. The child had forgotten to weep; he was only about three or four years of age. The older woman took his hand uneasily, and hurried back into the shelter of the group.

Before we had got very far, the girl had begun the bone-rattling shivering that the fever brought, but she was still lucid, and entreated me to put her down. Because of her distress, I laid her on the paving. There in the street she lay for two hours in a pool of matter and blood. She grasped my hand in her agony, and coming to herself again, asked me what hour it was, and died before I could tell her. She had gone more quietly even than the thief in the Grove.

It was very hot, the smoke-laden sky the scorched color of blue cinders, without bird or cloud; a smoldering glare of sun. I did not know what possessed me, unless it was some spirit of guilty contrition. I felt no terror or rage at that point; these had been set by for me. I went on the way the procession had taken with its biers, and arrived presently at the Water Temple.

It was a small building of stucco and red-painted plaster, a Masrimas of green bronze inside, and a magic well, reckoned to be healing. Within the courtyard and the precinct the sick were already packed in rows. They were burning fresh incense here to alleviate the stench—in vain—but one grew accustomed to the nauseous odor after a while, and scarcely noticed it.

I offered my service to the priests, who plainly considered me mad but were yet thankful to find one madman at least who would help. At my stained and draggled finery, they glanced in curiosity, but had no leisure for questions. We fell to our grisly, hopeless tasks. There was no shortage of labor.

I had concluded it was expiation I tried to work out there, and maybe something less grandiose, as if by confronting disaster, I could inure myself to what would come. Truly, I was not inured. My numb state was torn bit by bit into compassion and horror. What I beheld made what I did there the antithesis of my spirit and my humanity. Once I had to go off to vomit, and imagined the plague already in me, foreseeing each paroxysm and calamity I would undergo in the vivid details of which I had by this time watched a hundred enactments. But it was not the plague, not then. Then even my revulsion passed, even my cringing apprehension, so I grew numbed again, as at the beginning.

A day melted into a night, a night into a day. Somewhere I slept, somewhere drank water, somewhere refused the platter of food a priest brought me. These were interludes. The rest was death, and the ever-changing face of death, now a child's, now a woman's. A goldsmith, a rich man brought in from the street, who had a fine house in the upper commercial district and mixie servants, took almost the two days to die. In the middle of his seizures, he recognized me, or what I had been, and clawing at my shoulders, babbled to me to save him. Till then none had identified me as the sorcerer. Goaded by his cries, I set my hands on him, aware it was useless. Finding this, too, his eyes lighted up with hate and he spit in my face.

"May you suffer this tomorrow, you jackal! May you lie in your own filth and blood with these rats in your vitals!"

I told him I expected that I should, but he was raving again and paid no heed.

The sky, like an oven roof of blued heat, baked disease into the city. Everywhere the incense rose in columns; I smelled it in my sleep, over the fetor of the plague. Nearly all the brotherhood of the Water Temple were sick now. Three died by the magic well, pleading for its water, which did not heal them, which they could not even keep down. At length only I and one old priest remained. He drew me aside, and ordered me to leave the shrine and the city, and seek the hills. Many had done this, though, as it turned out, to small avail.

I said I would not go. The priest remonstrated; I had stayed healthy this far and might well be spared, if I would listen to reason. I said I had been forewarned that I would die of the plague, and eventually he left me in peace. That is, in what fragments of peace I had.

Toward the end of that second day we saw the red signature of the plague bonfires to the east and south. I was bemused by then, walking about like a part-resuscitated corpse myself. The pyres put me in mind of some ancient burning, not of Bar-Ibithni, not even from my past among the tribes. It was another thing. I leaned on a pillar of the temple and shut my eyes, and had the vision of a mountain pouring out magenta flames onto a black sky, and a white figure running down a slope with the lava-serpents of this fire going after it.

In the middle of that came a crashing on the courtyard gate. I drew myself together and went to open it, picking my way between the sick. Even outside, the paving was thick with them. Three jerdiers on white geldings stood like tall trees among a world of people on their backs.

"By order of the Emperor's council," their captain said, "all dead are to be burned." Anticipating the pious outrage that must generally have been forthcoming, he added, "The fire of Masrimas cleanses the contagion of the fever, for Yellow Mantle has spread from the ruins of Bit-Hessee." Then he checked and stared at me. He was one of Bailgar's officers, a Shield. "By Masrimas, *Vazkor!* What are you at here, sir?"

Plainly it was ridiculous to dissemble, for we had spoken before.

"I am some use here."

"But have you had no news?" he asked me.

"What news? Only news of the plague."

"There have been men looking for you since morning." He beckoned to me. "Will you step nearer? I've no mind to shout."

"I may be infected," I said, "and probably am."

"Probably we all are for that matter." He swung down from his saddle and came up to the gate. "Sorem's dying."

It shocked me. To see one's death in a mirror. This was what I had run from. Like a fool, I asked if it was plague.

"Yes, plague. What else?"

"When did he fall sick?"

"Sunrise. He asks for you."

"I can't heal him."

"It's not for healing, sir." The jerdier's face was set. He looked away from me and said, "It's little enough. It's a hard death he's having; worse with the strong ones, for it takes them longer. All the same, you had better hurry if you intend to go. The priests have spoken the last prayer for him."

I wanted to ask him if Malmiranet lived, but the words blocked my throat like the black flies. My fate had hunted me down. I should have to watch Sorem's death. Maybe hers. I would have given everything to avoid it.

"I've no means to get a mount." Most of the horses had contracted the plague, the cattle, too; hour upon hour I would hear the mallets of the slaughterers over the temple wall, like a dull thunder.

"Take my horse," the jerdier said. His eyes were bleak with the estimation he had made of me. "You remember the road to the Crimson Palace?"

They let me in at the gate with no delay.

There was not a breath of wind in the garden city. Black spears of shadow lengthened beneath the trees. The pink flamingos picked their way among the shallows of the lake indifferently. No bird had the sickness, neither the smaller domestic animals.

Between the pillars of the incense and the plague fires, the city stretched like one great public tomb. Bodies were tumbled in the streets, since there were few still healthy who would risk carrying them away, though occasionally the death carts trundled by. Here and there a priest or beggar hurried between the shuttered, silent houses and the barricaded shops. In an alley a blind man was tapping with his staff and calling for alms, nervously darting his head to catch the stillness. Perhaps no one had told him that Bar-Ibithni was dying, invisibly, about him. On the steps of a porphyry fountain a little starving dog, some woman's pet, had chewed greedily at a thing from which I turned my eyes.

Sorem's bed faced west across the large frescoed chamber, to where the windows stared into the overcast sky. It had a copper skin, that sky, and a yellow sheen revealed where the sun was lowering itself; no air came through the open casements, only the reflection of the sinking day spilled on the floor. The beautiful room stank, but it was a stink so familiar to me now that I hardly noted it. I could see the bruise still on his cheek where the horse had kicked at him, no other color there but one. He lay on the crimson pillows, which seemed to have drained the blood from him into themselves. Yellow Mantle, yes, it was cleverly named.

I went up to him. He was very near to death; I had barely been in time.

As sometimes happened at the end, the fever and the delirium had abated, leaving him clear. Though he spoke with almost no voice, scarcely audible, yet his words were formed and precise.

"I'm sorry to greet you in this disgusting state. It was good of you to come."

His gray bitch hound was stretched near the bed. Hearing him speak, it raised its head eagerly and beat with its tail an instant, then sank down again like a stone. Sorem was so weak, he could not order his expressions to show me pain, sadness, pleasure—anything. I sat where the physician had put his wooden stool before he went away.

"I was in the Commercial City," I said. "One of Bailgar's Shields found me and told me how it was with you."

"Oh, it's nothing now," he said. "It's almost done." He yawned, as a man does who has lost too much blood, and murmured, "Even the healing of Vazkor could not defeat this thing. But you will live, my sorcerer." He seemed to have forgotten his accusations, what he had said to me in the tower, and before *her*. His hand was moving on the covers, dry and yellow. "I regret we never went hunting," he said. "The white puma and the lion. It's strange," he said, "I never thought of death before. Even that night of Basnurmon's assassins, not even then. I held a leopard on my spear, in the hills once. Any mistake, and he would have killed me, yet I was too busy fighting him to think of it. But this leopard is different."

There was no one close. The court functionaries, what portion was left of them, and the priests, had been and gone. Only the physician was at his table across the room, and a sentry at the door. Sorem set his hand over mine. In the gray parchment flesh of his lids, his eyes had grown more blue, younger by contrast.

"You will not always think poorly of me, will you, Vazkor? It is hard to find yourself, as I did, like some stranger in a dark grove. Harder to find yourself alone there."

I took his hand. I could do nothing else. His grip was feeble. He shut his eyes, and said, "Malmiranet lives. They told her you were in the Palace, and she went away so we might talk privately. I believe she knew me before ever I knew myself. Leave me, and seek her. I'll do well enough for a while."

But I could see he had not far to go. I kept where I was, and said, "Presently, Sorem."

He lifted up his lids, and said quite strongly, "My thanks. It won't be for long. Don't call anyone. I would rather my mother didn't see me die. She has seen plenty already."

So I sat there by him, his hand in mine. A minute passed. The heat was fading, the room growing dank and chill, yet the walls were drowned in the last hot copper-yellow rays of the afternoon, which altered even the motionless dog to a beast of brass, as if the air itself had caught our sickness. Sorem looked toward the windows and his eyes widened, as though he could make out his death rising on the metallic sky.

"The sun is almost down. I shall go with Masrimas then."

I said, for I could summon nothing else, "I envy you your god."

But he shut his eyes again, and his mouth twisted and his hand clenched strengthlessly in mine.

"I spoke merely for custom. There is only the dark before me, and it is too easy to reach it. I have often wondered—"

He did not finish, and stupidly I leaned to hear the rest. But he was dead.

I got to my feet slowly. The physician, employed in mixing some balm Sorem would not longer require, did not turn. Malmiranet stood just within the door. I could not properly see her face in the darkening of the light, but she seemed all pity rather than grief. I suppose she had dreamed him dead a thousand times through the years of intrigue they had weathered here. The reality could not appal her. Only its wickedness.

I was shivering, but, having looked too long for it, could no longer distinguish the demon. As Malmiranet moved across the chamber, the darkness appeared to billow and fold about her. Then I saw that the grieving pity in her face also included me. I tried to say her name and could not say it and sank to my knees without properly knowing how I came there.

Her fingers touched my neck and forehead like wands of ice, and then there was no more.

I was nine years of age and a snake had bitten me. It was in Eshkorek Arnor that this had happened, and the doctors had laid me in a bath of ice to cool my fever. Yet I shouted to them that I was cold, the cold was killing me, and they paid no heed. Eventually my father came.

He was lean and dark, his crow's wing of hair framing his shoulders and his face as he bent to me.

"You must lie quiet," he said. "She has ordered it. I can do nothing. She will punish you till she grows bored with the punishment. Then it will stop."

He showed me, pointing with his long jeweled finger, where my mother stood. Her robes were white and her breasts were bare, the breasts of a maiden, firm and high. Her face was hidden in a cat-mask of gold, and golden spiders spun in her long pale hair. It was from the deck of a ship she watched me, a ship with great blue sails, and from the yard depended a hanged man, and the gulls snapped and clapped their hunger in his vitals.

That was the first dream.

There were only two. In the second, Uastis had shut me in a burning tower, and I roasted there, screaming, for several centuries.

I became aware gradually that the ice had melted in the fire and put it out.

A wonderful stillness filled my body and my mind.

Something shone and gleamed. I puzzled what it could be, but a changing position of her head showed me it was lamp-light on the fair hair of a girl. I did not remember for a second. Then everything was with me.

"Isep," I whispered. At that the bronze hair swung about like tufted grasses, and a face appeared between. "Isep, how well or ill am I?"

She looked me over with a boy's disparaging candor, and said, "Very ill, lord. But better. They predict you shall be well."

It was a small chamber, and our talk had roused the physician. He came puttering up, felt my head and peered in my eyes and laid his hand on my heart.

"Yes, it is remarkable," he said, "a night and a day of the ague, but no purging of blood, and now the fever's broken. Your constitution is unusually strong, my lord, and the god has smiled upon you. You will recover, I swear to that, but you must be patient. They call you a magician, do they not? Ah, yes. Now I acknowledge it."

I felt I could spring from the couch and fly. Why not? I was the sorcerer again. I had survived the curse of death. No god had smiled on me but the gods of my ancestry. I could have laughed aloud, then fear sank through me, and I grasped his arm.

"Where is the Empress?"

It was Isep who answered haughtily, "She has kept by you the entire night, and this whole day, till she was dead herself. Be content, man."

"But is she sick?"

"Sick of you, no doubt, and of your maniac shouting. Otherwise she is herself. They say Yellow Mantle is taking his leave."

"Yes, it's true, my lord," the physician said, bringing a sticky ointment and wanting to plaster my body with it like a joint for basting. "The plague is less. Countless thousands lost, of course, and Sorem, our lord, borne away with them. But fewer deaths this day at least, and no fresh outbreaks, not even among the slums of the commercial area."

I pushed him off me, and told him to spare me his medicinal muck, but he brought another thing in a shallow dish and put it in my mouth. This swallowed, I slipped back into a shadowy sleep where I seemed to swim along the bright shoals of Isep's hair.

When I woke again, it was about an hour past midnight, and my purpose lay intact and absolute before me, as if I had planned it in my sleep.

Isep was nodding at her post, and started alert when I called her, angry as some young soldier caught sleeping on watch.

"What is it, lord?"

"This: Find me some water and some clothing, my own or another's."

"Clothing? By my right hand, you shan't stir."

"Leave off your warrior's oaths, girl. In this room the man says what is to be done."

She turned to run for the physician, and for all I knew, for meatier help, and I was not certain yet if I had my Power again or not. I got her wrist and held her and said, "If you had an enemy who worked against you, and slew those near to you, and would have your life, too, if he could, what would you do?"

"Kill him," she said, and truly I believed her.

"Thus," I said. "That is what I go to do. And since I may have some extra trouble if I am naked, I prefer to travel with my breeches on."

"No," she said, but she was wavering. Finally she asked, "Your enemy is from Hessek?"

"Older than that, but Hessek is in it, too."

She frowned. I knew by her frowning she would do what I asked.

One moment I had reckoned that Uastis ruled them from the swamp itself. I had reckoned her, another time, far off. My indecision, I thought, was perhaps some part of the web in which she trapped me. Not till Gyest warned me had I understood for sure. But then I had been tranced, the net too tight around me for my struggles to break it. But now . . . now I had fathomed her abode; my dream had showed me. Now, better than any portent, I had outlived her sending. This would be the last meeting. If my Power had deserted me, or was not yet strong enough, I would use my hands as any copper-cash murderer knew how. That was all it took.

I was feverish still, but no disaster in that. It only buoyed me up.

I had crept about in her shade, in a terror, paralyzed. But I lived; the ordeal was past. She had committed her worst, and it was ashes.

There were different foul things to be seen about the streets by night, glimpsed in blackness or smoky red glare. What lights burned did so surreptitiously behind blinds, everything muffled, masked. Four fifths of the Palm Quarter, where formerly it had been day by night, had fled to the hills taking their lamps with them. But the plague fires blazed on, and the carts went stealthily up and down to them, loaded with their speechless multitudes. A watchman, drunk on a tower roof, drew back in fear at my galloping horse. Its hooves rang on the paving and the echoes struck ten streets away, as if twenty beasts went racing.

There was a new pyre near the dock, just beyond the Fish Market. The storehouses had been leveled here on the night of the rising and had not been repaired: now human flesh fried and the blue smoke rose in the starless sky to guide me.

The sick were yet piled about the gates of the temples. If there were less of them, as the physician said, I did not ascertain.

But I had a rare wine in my blood. Expiation was over, guilt washed out, terror canceled.

That wild ride, between darkness and red shadow, was indeed what the watchman had retreated from, the passing of Lord Death.

4

It was simple to appropriate a fishing boat, to row out on the black water under the formless sky. No lookout patrolled the quay. The spars of ships were a tangled water forest without birds. Somewhere, raucous music and tipsy voices slashed and mauled the silence, men praying to a flask of koois to save them.

The *Hyacinth Vineyard* stood far out from the dock, where the Hesseks had pulled the vessel with their little craft, to keep him from the fire. My southern ship with its soft southern name and its southern male gender. I had foreseen it would lead me to my witch-mother, all those months and days ago on Peyuan's island.

My strength had returned to me in double measure. The oars were light as reeds, and the somber shore, with its burning fire dots, retracted swiftly. I looked over my shoulder and saw the tall outline of the galley. There was a hard pallid light dancing on the upper deck, showing me three or four black figures, who regarded my coming, showing no alarm, unmoving. Even they had let down the ladder for me. They made no remonstration when I tied the boat alongside and began to climb aboard.

It was not exactly like the dream. The masts had no sails, there was no splendor. The harsh uncovered flame tongues leaped and crackled, painting the deck in fitful bleachings. Six Hesseks about the rail, ten squatting aft, escapees of the jerds, for, as I remembered not all Bit-Hessians had been slain that night of the rising. Perhaps others prowled below. No danger to me, for I could kill them when I had to. The witch had failed with me. She dared not use my own Power against me anymore.

I said to them, in their own tongue, "Where is she?"

None of them answered me. It was another voice that called, "Here, oh beloved."

My hair rose. I spun around, and there she sat, on one of Charpon's couches. She seemed to have arrived by magic; I had not seen her, though I had glanced that way before.

Her whiteness was the whiteness of the torches congealed to flesh, so white it made me queasy to look at her, as if at something bloodless, unhuman; which, maybe, she was. She had masked her face, as ever, this time in a veil of yellow silk that hung from a diadem of silver in her white hair. Beneath the veiling, what? A cat's head, or a spider's? Behind her, almost as I had visualized it in the fever, a man's body depended from among the shrouds, hanging by its feet, and torn by the gulls. The mutilated remnant of a face was Lyo's, my messenger.

"Behold your messiah," the woman said to her Hesseks. "Behold the Shaythun-Kem. Y'ei S'ullo, y'ei S'ullo. God-Made-Visible has betrayed you. Shaythun sent the swarm of his vengeance, and Bar-Ibithni the Beautiful bleeds on its deathbed. But this one thinks he has cheated Shaythun; this one thinks he will live."

Isep had got me a knife, along with the sentry's clothes. I set my hand to it involuntarily.

"See," the woman said. "Barbarian still, calling himself the sorcerer, yet preferring to use the metal blade of a Masrian cur."

The taunt was familiar. It checked me.

"I am the sorcerer," I said. "Then name yourself."

"You name me."

A wave of dizziness and heat went over me.

"Uastis," I said, "the bitch-goddess of Ezlann. My mother, but not for much longer."

She got to her feet, and with delicate mincing steps, she came along the deck to me. She was so little, small, and slender, and yet a force came with her like a huge dark shadow thrown upon the air.

I could not seem to stand back from her or advance to meet her. She halted about three paces from me, and then I noticed how she held her head, somewhat aslant, as if she could see me only from the left side. And, as before, I reached out my hand and snatched off the veil.

A woman's face, not raddled now, but a girl's. Beautiful as a statue, flawless, all but the right eye, which was gone, the scars hidden by a green jewel.

It had taken me till that instant to realize. Whoever she was, she was not my mother, not Uastis Reincarnate, for Uastis had the blood of the Old Magician Race; she would have *healed*. Smoke went over my eyes, like a myriad insects running on a crystal pane. Then I saw differently.

I had chased a phantom, fished for a reflection in a pool.

No, not Uastis. The illusion slid from her as sand runs from an hourglass. The robes were dirty, torn, and of a grayish flax, and her hair was the dull black fleece of Hessek hair, and her one eye a black Hessek eye, the other bound in a rag, and her skin the sallow white of Hessek. But I had dug this pit that swallowed me down. I had been so intent upon the hunt that when a quarry offered itself I never mused it might be other than the one I sought.

"Vazkor is yet Vazkor," she whispered. "He has learned his mistake at last. Not the old witch, but the young. For you made me young, my master and my lord, my stallion, my beloved, and I shall be your death." Lellih smiled at me and slid her arms about me and pressed her body to mine. I felt all its youngness through the fabric of her clothes and mine, all the youth with which I had reenameled it. "In life you turned from me, but in death you will obey me. In your burial place I will work my magic, and lie in your dead arms. Oh, I can't heal my flesh, it's true, but there are more wondrous things. It is you who taught me, my sorcerer. Listen how I talk. Do I sound like an old hag of a sweet-seller, my dove? No. The Power you poured into my brain to recreate my girlhood created me also your equal. A sorceress. A goddess."

A fire came and went across my eyes, obscuring the deck, the shadowy motionless figures of the Hesseks, the pendant corpse. Lellih wound me about like a snake and her mouth on my skin was like the fall of burning rain.

I remembered the Hall of Physicians, her tiny bird skull between my hands, the surge of Power that passed from me to her, illuminating her mind like the sun. I remembered my pride.

Small miracle she had been able to tap my Power ever after, to turn on me those abilities I had inadvertently installed in her. I had been her powerhouse from the first.

"Yes," she murmured, reading my thoughts, as previously she had read my whole brain, my history, my vow, my compulsion. "Yes, you have become my joke, beloved, with your quest for Uastis, who was really Lellih. I took her form to mislead you. You took my poor eye, my lovely eye, in exchange for that jest, beloved. Even that I should have forgiven you, if you had valued me. Then Bit-Hessee might have sunk in the mud for all I cared, and Shaythun, Shepherd of Swarms, sunk with it. There is no Uastis here, and no devil-god either, Vazkor. Only a wellspring of belief I used as my instrument. It is *I* who sent the plague. It is *my* betrayal I punish you for, not the betrayal of my people—Lellih's anger, not the anger of a god. Know this, Vazkor. . . . What?" she asked me then, for I had tried to speak to her. I mumbled something through my frozen lips. She said to me, gently, "No, you'll die, Vazkor, I promise you. Do you suppose of all the numbers who have perished that you alone, who I have cursed twice for every curse I laid on Bar-Ibithni, that you alone, my darling boy, will escape? Believe in the vitality of your own magic which you gave me. You are dying in my arms this very minute."

I knew it to be as she said. She had resealed the plague on me. My viscera scalded, but my flesh was like a layer of wool. I could barely see or hear, only the lower mast between my shoulders kept me on my feet, that and her twining. She had crawled up me to my mouth, and fastened there as if she herself would drain me of my life.

Somehow then, I felt the knife. My hand had not strayed

rom it. My muscles were lead and my fingers water, yet this hand and this arm I could move, if I willed it. It seemed to ake me hours. She was too busy with her grave-cold kissing o heed my hand and the knife. Not till the blade went hrough her back into her heart did she heed it.

I had never killed a woman before, not meaning to, but vith her it was more like crushing a viper beneath a stone. It was a clean blow, despite everything, though she was not inclined to go, and fought an instant, and her one eye stayed wide when she fell upon the deck. She had uttered no final ill wish, having emptied the vat of her perverse hate on me, and to the dregs indeed.

She refuted Shaythun, and maybe she was wise, but something led her to her death, as I to mine.

I stepped over her, and began to stagger toward the rail, but suddenly my eyes cleared, and my brain. I thought, *It shall end here, after all, for me and for the rats who killed me.* The Power came with no effort. I saw the rays leave me, hitting the leaping forms of men, the body of Lellih, and the hanging corpse, the masts, the shrouds, the wall of the night itself.

A torch fell. It caught the edge of Lellih's gray-white garment. It was right this should dissolve in fire, as everything was dissolved in it, Bit-Hessee, the plague-dead, the glory of Bar-Ibithni.

Masrimas' light.

A burst of white flame lighted my way as I crawled down the ladder and fell into the boat. The rope came free, and the small craft, swinging in against the ship's side, swung off again from the impetus, catching the current, drifting out into the fire-flecked sea.

Thus I, too, drifted, into a raging hell of agony, and the world came and went around me, and came and went.

Voices shouted.

A mile off, a burning ship mirrored its tumult in black water.

The face of a man was nearer.

"Vazkor, do you know me? No, Bailgar, I don't think he can speak. It's up with him for sure. So much for physician's prophecies, so much for sorcery. By God, look at the blood he's lost."

Someone else said, "Have a care lifting him. That moron

girl of the Empress, to let him go. Sheer luck I recalled the *Vineyard*."

They were lifting me. I tensed for the pain but it did not come. Someone's rolled cloak was under my head, and through the murk of the sky I thought there was one star stabbed through like a silver pin.

I could recognize Bailgar's voice now, but not who he was. He bent over me, and said, "Try to last, Vazkor. She'll want to see you."

Unaware of who he meant, I shut my eyes.

"It's odd," the first man said, "he doesn't stink, like the others with this filthy thing—maybe it's a good sign."

Bailgar grunted softly, and told him to look at my ship, which was going down.

Her face was a golden mask and her hands were also gold.

"I had them speak our rites for you," she said "I didn't know which were your own and you could not tell me. Can you rest with that? I'll do whatever you ask."

I could not speak—besides, could dredge up no words. I did not know her or where I was. I did not even know it when I died.

5

There was a light.

I had been half aware of it some while—not what it was, its meaning, simply that it was present. In color it was gold, this light, a rich red gold, and here and there flowers bloomed in its path, white and rose and blue.

The light, and the flowers that grew in it, fascinated me.

I had no other sense, only the organs of sight that showed me this.

Gradually the gold broadened, dimming slightly at its perimeters.

It was a roof of flowers, a sky of flowers, and I lay under it.

In a sort of dream that asked no questions, demanded no explanation, my eyes moved over knots of blue corundum, rose crystal, pearls. Flowers made from jewels, and there a arved peacock forever spreading its turquoise fan as the ight discovered it, a horse of white enamel with its feet lost n the dark.

I could see it now, where the light came from, an aperture little way down the flowery roof, about a foot above me nd level with my breastbone. Instinctively then, still without easoning or true motive, I set myself to rise and investigate his source of illumination, and found I could not move.

At first you do not believe such a thing. Movement is your ight. You attempt it several times, each time thinking, *Now.* But at last you come to believe it, that there is a heaviness on all your limbs, your torso, your skull, fetters that have soldered you to the earth.

I was more bewildered than afraid. Writhing there, I seemed able to twist a limited distance inside a kind of case, and at each stultified spasm my own flesh seemed to crumble and flake painlessly away. Meanwhile, the glorious light began to fade and as it faded, by contrast, I vaguely ascertained a heap of dull gold beneath, and how the sides of the flowery roof sloped down to it, and they were narrow sides, very narrow. Each of these things was teaching me. I lay quiet, recollecting everything by swift degrees. I recollected who I was and what had hapened to me. I put on my manhood and my life with all their obligations of sensation and horror. I was Vazkor, the sorcerer. I had nearly died of the plague, but somehow my healing body was recovered. I lived, I breathed, I was whole. And I was in no sickroom I had ever imagined.

Slowly now, in the last of the light, my eyes returned over the jeweled ceiling above me, the ceiling so low and close to me that its every detail was apparent. My childlike wonderment altered to a measureless fear.

I had dwelt among Masrians long enough to glean something of their customs. I had seen the Royal Necropolis on its southeastern hill, the sugar domes, the gilded stucco.

Yes, Vazkor had survived the plague, but had not given evidence of his survival quickly enough. Now I had the lesson pat.

They had thought me dead. They had buried me alive.

Then my stillness left me.

In a maddened blind terror, I began to call and cry out, my wordless roaring filling the great hollow cask so it rang like a bell, and I tried to haul up my arms, to smash my fists upon the beautiful roof of my prison. All the while I screamed within myself to those gods I never admitted I owned, as the gold light vanished on the pitiless staring of the flowers, the peacock, and the white horse.

There was not a vast amount of air in the sarcophagus, only what came in with the sun at that hole in the lid, and thence through the open nostrils and other small vents of what they had bound me in. Shortly, I started to choke and faint and fell back in a muddy swimming of the senses. When the swimming stopped, I was in darkness.

If you seek revenge on your worst enemy, if he has done things for which you believe no punishment sufficient, incarcerate him in a golden tomb, alive.

I do not know how long I lay there, except that I remember the light came and went across the gems twice or maybe thrice. There was no time for me within that box of death. I became a slobbering witless beast, that now and again started into human awareness, to roll and cry and whimper. My seasons were partitioned out in clamor and unconsciousness and the mindless waking stupor that intervened between them.

How I kept my reason is beyond me. If I kept it. For I think the return of intelligence did not actually prove I had not grown insane. Not till some time after did rationality reclaim my mind, and by then I was far from that place and all my deeds in it.

However, my brain did eventually revive, and logic came. It came in the form of a single realization. Something like a madness in itself.

I had not been buried alive, I had been buried *dead.* Stone dead. Corpse-cold without heartbeat, unbreathing, sustenance for the worms. Yet no worm had fed on me. I was entire, even within this tomb.

It was the final gate, the absolute ordeal, the last magical capacity. What I had part suspected myself of possessing, but never dared to test. Having once decided, the facts showed me it was no more than plain truth. For this was undeniable; if I had lain sick enough to seem dead, waking from that sickness as I did in panic and shadow, starved of food and drink, weighted down and shuttered up with barely the air to keep my senses, surely I must have died then if not before. Yet I lived. I *lived.*

My thoughts had cleared like water. I was calm and fear fled me. If I could die and return to life, I could do anything. I had no need to be afraid, I had surmounted the ultimate terror. There was no bone-dust heap for me, no ignominious mound. There was eternity, and the world.

They had piled a tomb on me. They might have piled on a hill, and over the hill, a mountain. It was all one, and mattered nothing.

I used my Power to free myself. The restraints were done with. It never came so easily. A pillar of glowing energy that fired the case within as the passing sun had never fired it. The jewels shattered, the eyes of the peacock's tail fell on my breast. Golden hinges melted and iron cracked. The lid of the sarcophagus rose up into sudden vast gulfs of space and crashed down beyond my range of vision.

It was a fortune they had laid on my body, an armoring of bars and plates of enamelwork, onyx and bronze, a silver helm weighted with enormous palm-leaf rays of gold. No living man could have worn it and walked upright. On my skin, inches thick, was a gilt integument. I had been bandaged in metal, buried like a king. I could only give thanks to hasty or rascally workmen that they had not been completely zealous in the labor. Every oversight, every gap in the wrapping, had been a way for air to reach my flesh and my lungs. Without the air, I might have waited here, animate yet unaroused, till my plastering decayed. A hundred years, perhaps, or more.

There was, too, the round opening in the lid of the cask. For Masrian custom dictated that even in death the corpse would wish to receive the beams of Masrimas' sun.

I split my fabulous armoring by Power. The gold anchors rang as they left me; the skin of gold flaked down in yellow shards.

Stepping naked from my coffin on the floor, as though from some bed where I had slept late, I saw the massive lid on its side a small distance away.

Besides its inner prettiness, it had some outer display—about ten feet of gilding, gems and gold. That I had lifted by my will, a thing that would have taken perhaps twenty men to raise in their arms.

This struck me as amusing. Next I looked about, and smiled some more.

Masrian religious faith comprises an odd dichotomy. They tell you that after death the soul journeys to some unworld, ruled by their fire-god. However, since this soul may linger a while before departure, everything is set out in the tomb for its comfort. Whether any Masrian actually and wholeheartedly credits this I had no notion then, or now. Like Sorem, maybe, the dark was all too easy to reach. Yet, for form's sake, or as some spiritual bribe to their own uncertainty, they did these things.

The chamber was not huge, despite my costly box, yet the floor was laid with painted tiles. A Masrian lamp of rosy glass hung from a silver chain, with flint and tinder set by. On little tables of burnished bone the implements of a thorough toilet were laid out, also a silver bath with accessory tall ewers, filled with water, and crystal vases of oils beside. A fresco on the wall showed gardens of flowering trees, where frolicked monkeys, cats, and birds. (So the ghost should not pine for the gardens of earth? I should have thought such imitation stuff would make it weep.) A couch with posts of gold and cushions of silk was fine enough on which to slumber. Nearby stood sealed flagons of wine, baskets of fruit and sweetmeats, and bread that had gone green. I was starved and ate it, nevertheless; it was vile but nourishing, and the wine helped wash down the taste.

All this time, as I had plundered the food baskets, I had been noting the shape of the tomb. The walls were rounded, narrowing above into a chimneylike shape, where another hole made visible the sky. This hole corresponded mathematically to the position of the opening in the sarcophagus, allowing the sun to shine through one into the other as it crossed the zenith. The upper vent seemed wide to the hazy sky, but a fine grille must cover it or the birds would have been in. All this conformed with the structure of the funeral domes I had seen previously from outside, save at one point. Here the chamber was strangely abbreviated, and presently I grasped that another area had been made here, behind this, a chamber within a chamber. I went looking for the doorway and could not find it. So I axed a passage through with a bolt of energy, ham-fistedly malicious as any vandal. The piece of wall crumbled with a melting of rose trees, monkeys, and honey-yellow doves. Beyond, I saw a second sitting room of the dead.

I had no premonition. Not until I glimpsed the mirror of silvered glass, the cosmetics in their vessels of amber, the slender, much-handled spears. Then I knew.

I stepped around the wall and met head on the coldness of mortality.

The cask was bronze, ungilded and without ornament. Over it was draped the Empress tapestry of lilies.

I stopped where I stood, and leaned on the jagged brick. I

recalled her face floating above me in the fever mist, how she had asked me what rites should be performed for me. She had survived the plague, or it had seemed she had. Yet here she lay.

This was the measure of her regard for me. Fearing I went cheated, my proper rites unsaid, she had given me instead the best of Masrian ritual, the greater chamber, the accouterments of a prince or king, and that tomb of jewels, and all this, in spite of herself. It had been her bed in which I reclined. I had loved her supple unrepentant tallness, her eyes nearly level with my own—yes, her couch would just have fitted me. As for the metallic fortune in which they had cased me, what funds and what cunning had she employed to get it unlawfully for me, who was not even a noble of the city? This done, she took the slave's place, the outer room; dying, she was unaware of the havoc circumstance would play with her gift. Indeed, how could she know I would return from my silence, wake and cry out, stifling in these tokens of her love, her generosity, her pride that denied me nothing of hers, even in oblivion? How could she know, who had expected to become, and had become, only dust?

There was no light in this secondary tomb, save what came in now through the broken wall, and no aperture in the bronze box. What she had done tore inside me like a lion's claws. I turned away from the cask, and walked about the small area, picking up her things and setting them back. Her combs lay on their tray, the kohl she had painted about her eyes. A necklace of jets glittered as I had seen them glitter around her throat. Among her scents I found the vial I knew most readily, and took it up to breathe her in with it—to lessen or increase my wretchedness. But it had no smell of her, merely of incense held in crystal.

Abruptly I moved around, and went to the bronze sarcophagus. There was in me a grim spirit of exorcism, and also that murky human part of me which drew me to stare. The unalterable claim of death. I was free of this end, but I alone. Forever now, and for how long I did not know, I must watch a procession go by me to the grave, and I remain beside the road, impervious, and with no companion.

I wrenched off the top of the cask with my bare hands. The Power filled my arms with a strength I barely felt; it was simply rage. The lid flew away and clattered down, and a musty perfume of balm rose up.

I had anticipated everything, corruption, bones, the stench

of rottenness. I had no means of judging how many days had passed, or months. Yet it had not been long, for her at least, and the sealing of the bronze, which denied her Masrian rites, had preserved her for me to look on.

She was dressed in red finery, but they had not painted her body; so I saw her flesh, which appeared as I remembered it. Thus I learned she had not died of Yellow Mantle, for the unmistakable, awful color of the plague was absent. What then, in the name of her god, had brought her here? I gazed some minutes before I discovered the silver flower over her breast. I had thought it an ornament at first, but it was the hilt of a little knife—sharp, but not of any great length—of the sort that Masrian ladies use to trim their hair before the tongs. To make it do its work, one would have to understand exactly how to strike to come at the heart, and drive it home without flinching.

I imagined then that she had killed herself because of me, such was my vanity and my anguish. I bent nearer and drew a piece of her black hair between my fingers; it was glossy, as if fresh from Nasmet's care. Truly, Malmiranet had no look of death. But my hand brushed her forehead and left a mark there like a bruise, and the black curl came away in my grasp.

It was the broken brick against my spine that halted me, halting also the primitive horror that had overcome me, reminding me of myself.

No longer a man, no longer merely a sorcerer. No longer confined by the natural laws of the world. Now and again the whisper had come, and I had put it aside in fear. But I was beyond fear at last, and beyond half-doubt. Vazkor had mastered death.

I had done everything else, why not this?

No need to stand alone beside the road. The multitudes would pass, but those I selected from among them, these I should keep by me.

I went back to her across the small inner chamber of the tomb. The light was deepening, the open chimney vent dyed a violet rose into the tiles beyond the wall. Dusk and shadow everywhere, save within me, where the shadows were burning.

It was not even hard for me to do. If there were gods, and they were just, there would have been some warning then. Yet maybe there was a warning, some sign I did not note.

It was like a thousand healings I had performed, nothing out of the way in it. With Hwenit, my black witch, I had had some trouble; she had been nearly dead, her pulse faint as the flicker of an insect's wing. But with Hwenit I had not known myself as I should become. With Hwenit I had reckoned myself fallible, human.

Malmiranet returned as the sea returns to the shore. I chose the word "returned" with a little thought, for it seemed she did come back from some dark forest in which she had been wandering. Her skin grew firm and flawless, and the marks of the bruising of decay left her, like the shades of those black death-trees under which she had been walking. Her eyes opened suddenly and looked straight at me. I had somehow not expected that look, so immediately direct, so clear. She raised her hand and put it to her breast where I had drawn out the little dagger, and not finding its blade, the last hurt she had known, she sighed.

She lay yet within the bronze box, which I did not like to see. (Even at such a moment, this obsolete superstition unnerved me.) I took the hand she had let fall, and spoke her name. I helped her to sit up, then lifted her from the cask. She stood before me, as she had stood countless times before me, and her eyes were bright as swords, though she did not speak to me or make any movement of her own.

I led her through into the other chamber, to the silken bed, and poured her wine. At first she would not drink, till I set the cup to her lips. To see the soft ripple of her throat as she swallowed brought home the wonder to me afresh. The responses of sex live close by death—it has always been so, nature striving to replenish the store—and rape has followed the battlefield time out of mind. For all the prelude, I was hot to lie on her now, among the shiny silk. Only her wide eyes kept me from it.

"Malmiranet," I said. "What is it? You're safe and I am with you."

As if at a signal, she placed her hand again over her breast. There was no longer any mark of the knife on her, as I could well see when I leaned and rested my mouth there.

It had not been her practice to be so wooden. At length I told myself I asked too much, and, holding her by me, tried to explain to her the things she must already be aware of, but perhaps could not comprehend. Fool that I was, I even required her to inform me why she had slain herself. I had some notion to shock her from her reticence if I could not bring her to me more gently.

I heard my own voice go on and on, as if I lessoned a child. And she in my arms, like a wide-eyed child, unspeaking.

I was weary, and fell asleep somewhere in my monologue, and woke in the near black tomb to find her there beside me yet. A star stood over the vent in the dome and showed me her eyes, still fixed as gems.

I rose and lighted the lamp that had been provided for my ghostly comfort. In an ivory chest close by, a pile of clothes were lying—my own gear from the Palace; even the jeweled collars in a tray, and the boots below.

I glanced about at her, and she watched me silently.

"I will dress myself as befits a civilized man," I said to her, "since you'll have nothing to do with me. Then we leave this place."

I had no plan; all ways were open but inchoate. My world was centered here, despite my words. I had found I could not quite think what I should do with myself and her. Smash down the wall, that was easy, erupt out into the amazement of the city—or, if I pleased, levitate myself and her to the opening above, destroy the grille and, as once before, travel over a starry nighttime sky. But to what?

There had been a star when I was dying in Bailgar's boat, I remembered it now, one star visible through the murk, like the star in the vent of the tomb. A distant breath of unease passed over me, for even inside safe walls, one may hear the wolves howling.

"Who rules Bar-Ibithni?" I said to her. "The council, or has the old man got back in the chair?" This illusion to Hragon-Dat brought me to Sorem. I had forgotten him, an indication of my true state if I judged myself. Sorem, too, was dead, locked in some gold case. I could raise him, if I felt it proper to my scheme of things. Would he then look at me as she did, and with such bright, unblinking eyes?

I had been examining the chest rather than continuing to gaze at her. Her stare had begun to strike chill on me. The rustle of her skirt made me turn about.

A curious phenomenon. I could survive death, yet my instincts to avoid a mortal blow were as insistent as ever.

She had stolen out as quiet as air and up to me almost as quietly. Her face had not altered, nor her look, but she had brought me another gift. One of those slender hunting spears, which she had raised to plunge between my shoulders.

I jumped aside. The spear flashed down and bit upon the wall and the head broke from the haft. I recalled how she had told me once she had not gone hunting in a long while. The wood had softened, still it was the force of her striking that snapped the shaft. She had meant a second death for me, and to spare.

I caught her by the arms, but she made no other move at me. She was expressionless and she did not struggle. I wondered how I had slept by her and come to whole. Was it some madness of grief or terror on her that drove her to this?

"Malmiranet," I said, "in what way have I done you wrong? Tell me. I will set it right."

I had grown to a knowledge of her face, of her body and its gestures; I could have picked her out if she had been masked and draped among forty women. Now, her body familiar, its contours positive through the silk, and the chiseling of that face of hers unlike any other's, and those narrow hands, one wrist with its wound serpent of gold that I had seen her wear when all the rest of her apparel was gone—now, when she was identifiably one woman only, yet she was not that woman. This was some doll, fashioned in the absolute likeness of Malmiranet, but Malmiranet it was not.

I had let her go, and I had walked away from her, keeping my eyes on her, nevertheless. I took garments from the chest and began to clothe myself. It seemed always so with me, that after the greatest and most miraculous feats of my life, I must be made to feel, by emotion or by circumstance, a whipped brat among Ettook's tents. I could not bear the searing blankness of her stare on my nakedness, like the leveling of a blade. We had been skin on skin too often; it was hard to find winter risen from that fire.

What I had put on I scarcely noticed, some workaday suit of the Crimson Palace, too fine for anything but lounging in. With the jeweled accouterments there was a belt of rare white snakeskin, chased with gold and with a buckle of lapis lazuli—something she had given me. I showed it to her, remembering how she had buckled it on me, and what followed.

She took half a step toward me, her hand outstretched and my heart leaped in my throat, wondering what would come this time.

What came was this: all passivity left her, she flung back her head, her mouth opened wide, and she screamed. Not a woman's screaming but the ululation of an animal, piercing, feral, almost continuous.

I ran to her and pulled her to me. I tried to stop her cries, tried to rock her, console her. The terrible wailing went on and on. When I drew her head against me, she sank her teeth in my shoulder till they met, and still she cried in her throat like a beast, even as she gnawed my flesh.

My blood had grown cold, and I shook as if my death had returned for me. I have no recollection of what I said nor of what I did, until my desperation drove me to that thing I hated and abhored, to seek the reason in her mind.

The mysteries of existence and of surcease remain with me, with me more than with most for, in setting me apart from them, my heritage has denied me, for a while at least, the answer all other men learn too swiftly. The grape of truth is often bitter, but not to taste it in its season would be to waste the vine. One answer I had, there in that tomb with its painted flowers, its clothes chests and its gold. Not mine, but all other human flesh decays, and at its death, what lives within it goes elsewhere. Maybe to some other place, some fiery world such as the Masrians talk of, or to the black pit of the tribes, or to something too wonderful to conceive of, or maybe to nothing, to smoke, to air, to silence. Whatever else, no magician, however masterful, can bring that substance, that element—spirit or soul—back into the vase which held it. Or no, I will amend that I will say only that Vazkor could not, after Malmiranet's death and the failing of her flesh, recall her. Everything of her I had healed. She was whole, her organs sound, she breathed and her heart beat. But she, she was in another country. The creature lived and moved and made its noise, but it was empty as the sarcophagus from which I had lifted it.

The brain I had entered was like a twilight fog at sea. Objects pushed up from the mist, mirages or rocks, the fragmented, now meaningless, remembrances of her brain, like a catalog chipped in stone that the dust storm has eroded. The violence that had sprung from them was basically motiveless, a misinterpretation, a bewildered flailing in the dark. For the creature I had raised was in confusion. A state vague and stupefied, a frenzy concocted of instincts and impulses. Though her brain had retained its melted images of me, the eyes of the automation did not recognize their significance. Its response was primeval. I had introduced this disturbance, and it must denounce me, destroy me. From which it would seem there was some reasoning there, but there was not. As a sail changes to the wind, so this thing angled itself this way and that. No more. All this I know, who searched for a woman inside that skull, and met only the tenantless desert.

I seemed to have grown as vacant as the being I held in my arms, my soul to have left me.

Yet I could not help but be gentle as I reached and stilled what I had set in motion, those ticking clocks within the wooden doll. I gave her back her body's death.

Gradually the tremors of physical life fell quiet, the head slid softly aside, its blind eyes closed. When I had wiped my blood from her mouth, I saw again my woman's face, as I had known it.

I laid her down, not where I had taken her up, but in that couch she had given me.

Her flesh had not yet begun again to die, for this moment it was sweet and perfect. She looked like sleep. I did not ask her pardon; it had not been her I wronged. My trembling had stopped. I lifted up the lid, the huge golden lid I had cast from me. I must use my Power for that, and even as I did it, I thought, *This is the last hour I use it. It has brought me sorrow and folly. I am a child with fire. Let me wait till I have been taught by my life and by the world. I will not be a sorcerer again till I have reined myself and what is in me.*

The shadow enlarged itself over Malmiranet, and hid her. Only the small sun-hole was left. The peacock with its broken tail, the horse, and all the flowers would reflect on her, and when her beauty was merely bones, their whiteness would take color, blue and rose and gold, at the passing of the sun.

The star had vanished from the roof of the tomb. The black was warming into mauve.

One ultimate act of Power was needed to open the wall. One initial step was needed to carry me into my life, which was altered. Something glittered on the silken bed, a bead that had fallen there from the flounces of Malmiranet's red skirt.

I sat and turned it in my fingers, that bead, as the world turned toward the dawn.

6

Human alarm takes many forms. Some appear comic if one's mood is desolate and drained enough.

There was a door into the tomb. They had brought me through it, and she had come that way also. It could not be seen from within, among the branches of the painted trees, but the priests of the necropolis could effect entry when and if they chose. I believe they did not often choose such visits. No doubt they would have foregone this one, if they had not been pushed by decrees other than their own.

I had never thought how it might seem.

A tomb contains the dead, who are properly immobile and unspeaking. Though Masrians leave lamps for the ghosts, nobody expects they will be lighted.

First had come my own muffled yells and bellowings, then the enormous crash of my coffin lid on the tiles, followed by a destruction of masonry and the brazen clamor that marked my opening of Malmiranet's sarcophagus. The domes are solidly built but provide excellent echo chambers with the vent in the roof to let the noise out upon the air. Probably a timorous watch was posted at this juncture, who did not pass a barren night. Maybe they heard me speak, my movements. Certainly, the glowing of the lamp through the aperture would have been noticed. Finally, the snapping of the spear that missed my body by inches. And after that her terrible cries—so terrible to me that they have lingered in my sleep along with all my other hauntings, less poignant but how much more awesome to the priests outside.

They waited till sunup. Bar-Ibithni had had a surfeit of the dark.

The door was flung wide suddenly on the twilight morning of the tomb and on the shadow of my brain; a golden eastern sky gilded everything, and somewhere there was a rill of doves purring, for the priests kept silent a long moment, as if to let me hear them.

There were ten priests in all. Their eyes popped as if invisible nooses tightened on their gullets. Here a hand dropped a magic censer—for purpose of exorcism? There one was turning red with fear, the way some fat men do.

So I had my dismal joke, as I sat there resurrected. I even had the humor to recall it was not the first time I had come back from death to men's eyes, and these not the first priests to marvel at me, though they were without Seel's fury, and this place something finer than the krarl.

Abruptly one of them spoke my name and fell to his knees. It was less a gesture of reverence than a loosening of the joints in fright, but the rest aped him. Presently every man kneeled, every man whispered, *"Vazkor, Vazkor."* (I was back in another place of my past, a fortress-rock in the mountains, seeing the masked city men of Eshkorek kneel before a tribal brave, who was Vazkor, the Black Wolf of Ezlann returned from the grave.)

The joke died, as I had not.

I thought, *I have taken sufficient for one morning.*

I said nothing, made no sign. I walked by the kneeling men and out into the sunny avenues of the Royal Necropolis.

I could have made myself a king that day, Lord of the Masrian Empire. Who could have withstood a deathless sorcerer-god? No man whose name I call to mind. I could have been an emperor, and conquered fresh empires, as my father had meant to do before even he got me, indeed, as he had begun to do, before even he was very much older than I on that day.

But I was beyond empires; I had achieved, or lost, that much at least.

I got out of the pillared archway with no trouble. The guard there, making eyes at the gardener's boy, paid me no special attention, and probably took me in my Palace gear for a noble come to offer in the little temple, for friend or kin.

The streets of Bar-Ibithni, sponged with saffron lights, seemed as when I had first gazed at them: busy, opulent, luxurious. The fringed litters went by, the rich men and the merchants, the boy-girl "Theis" in their tinsel clothes, and occasionally a Hessek slave on an errand. It was very strange, dreamlike, as if the separate scourges, the uprising and its fires, the swarm of Shaythun and the yellow plague, had never been save in some nightmare curtailed by the dawn.

My eyes were dazzled. I had been too long from the sun and too long from men. My way turned east of itself, to leave this enchanted, self-healing wonder behind, and reach the open land beyond the old palisade, the vineyards, and the groves, and perhaps the place where I had flown down from heaven on a white horse, and she and I had nearly missed the signal of the burning docks so deep we were in another fire.

On the road, not far from the edge of the Palm Quarter, I met a woman.

She was obviously an aristocrat's slave, most likely his concubine, dressed fashionably and prettily, and she even had her own slave to walk behind her, to hold a parasol above her curly head, and with a club in his belt for overfriendly citizens. She stepped out from the gate of a great house with green enamel cats along its walls—it was my staring at the cats, my eternal symbol for Uastis, that made me see the girl. She appeared to be set on the same direction as myself, and she was crying.

Till she glimpsed me. Then she put her hands to her mouth and halted, as if at a chasm in the pavement. The male slave, primed to her reactions, strode forward and scowled at me, and told her she should have no insolence from me while he stood by. But she choked out, "No, Chem. Everything is well. This gentleman has done me no harm." Then, starting softly to cry again, she came toward me.

I do not properly recollect what I felt. That she recognized me was sure, that she craved something of me also was evident. My heart beat in heavy leaden strokes, knowing already. She was a Masrian slave, tall and slender. She would have had a look of Nasmet, but for her sadness.

"Forgive me if I am foolish," she said. "It can't be, for they told us he was dead, dead for thirty days now, and buried secretly at the order of the Empress." I could say nothing. She said, "But I have often seen him, here in the Palm Quarter. He was a sorcerer, and he could heal all sicknesses. Or can it be that you, sir, are Vazkor?"

Then I found I was answering her, not meaning to.

"And if I were Vazkor?"

The tears streamed from her eyes. She, too, dropped on her knees.

"Oh, my lord. It's my child. They said you would not heal anymore, but I will pay you anything. My master is rich and careful for me—anything, my lord."

The male slave, who had been standing looking warily at us, now moved up and put his hand on her shoulder.

"It's no good, lady. Suppose he were Vazkor, he could do nothing. Your child died last night. You know it. We all know it, and grieve with you, even the master. But that's an end."

But the girl raised her face to me, running with its tears, bright with them and with a burning hope, and she said, "Vazkor could raise my child. He could raise the dead. Oh, my lord, make my child live again."

A warrior does not learn how to weep in the krarls of the red people, nor can he learn it after in hubris and Power. Yet there will come one day a blow so gentle that it will split the rock and find the spring beneath. The fates are kind to women, or to any that can with ease wash the sores of life in such water. Even when it comes hard, it is a balm.

Yet I had enough of my past still with me that I turned away from her, that she should not see me weep.

Easier to hide a wound than crying from a woman. She knew at once, and at once she was changed. She rose and put her arms about me, and held me like a child, like her own maybe who was gone, and whom I could not give back to her. As if she understood it all, she asked no more of me. Nothing she had from me, yet she would comfort me, and truly, I found comfort there in that leafy street beneath the enameled wall, with the stoical slave idling nearby till our display should be done.

At length the well ran dry. Her own tears she had put aside. She said she was going to the goddess on the hill, that this was a mighty deity, dispenser of calm and consolation, and that I must go also, to be calmed and consoled. Because of the curious thing between us, I went.

The turf was extensively disfigured beyond the old palisade by the marks of the plague fires. This different aspect, the daylight and my own brain, kept it from me some while that I had journeyed this way once before, and that my friend was conducting me to the shrine that stood above the Lion's Field, that dueling ground of princes. I had fought Sorem there, and after him certain others, beneath the eye of the shrine's goddess. Later, I had disrespectfully burned the black poppies on her altar to give me light, when I watched the Hesseks climbing from the northern wall and the sea.

There were no poppies there now but a green-gold ear of grain and some honey in a crock. The stones were briar-grown as ever; I wondered, if they reverenced her, that the slaves never cleared these away. But my friend explained to me, seeing my look, that the goddess preferred the living thing to twine about her. In fact, no offering was set there, even a flower, unless it came of stock already plucked for use.

"She left you strict orders, then," I said.

"Ah, no, she asked for nothing. The offerings do *us* good, for the act of giving, however small, is beneficial." She herself had brought a flagon of cinnamon oil. Her tears returned and she poured them, with the perfume, on the stone; the smell of the oil was pleasant in the clean salt-freshened air. Then she kneeled and whispered on the west side of the altar. I turned away to let her pray in peace, as Chem had done. Shortly, she called to me, and her face was different, not happier, but with a kind of quietness.

She deceived herself into this serenity, thinking the diety had blessed her with peace, but what matter, if she could bear her sorrow more easily? But the girl was there before me again, and she said, "It's not the goddess who takes the burden from me; I find the strength within myself, through her memory that lingers here."

This seemed an advanced, unusual teaching.

"Is your lady old or young?" I asked.

"Young," the girl said. "Something less than twenty years ago these stones were raised to her. And she's real, too; my mother spoke with her. You won't credit me, but thus it is. Shall I tell you?"

I said, glad to humor her, that I should like to hear.

"The city was not so great then. My mother dwelt in the southeast country, among the valleys there and the hills, where the southern lakes begin. She was in the fields, near sundown, when she saw a woman walking between the sheaves. Now you must remember this, the light was fading, Masrimas' sun going out, but still the woman shone and gleamed. It was from her skin and her hair, which was as white as alabaster, and her face—my mother said—was too beautiful to bear."

I had caught my breath.

She did not notice; she said, laughing, "You'll disbelieve it, but listen. The track between the sheaves led by the spot where my mother stood. Soon the white woman had drawn close enough to touch, and my mother, who was afraid, sank on her knees. She was carrying then, with me, and maybe more fanciful because of it. The woman turned, and she said to my mother, 'Will you tell me if there is a town across the hill?' My mother managed to say that there was. She was sure the woman was a sprite, for she could speak hill-Masrian quite perfectly, though clearly she was a stranger. But then the woman, who was looking at her without menace or contempt, said, 'You have a child with you.'

"My mother started, expecting her womb to be cursed, but the woman stretched out her hand and laid it on my mother's cheek, and at once, my mother would tell me, all her fear left her. The woman said, 'When your labor begins, think of me and you will have no pain. The birth will be swift and uncomplicated, and the child strong. Though I fear,' and here she smiled, 'you have a girl inside you, not a man, for which perhaps you are sorry.' My mother was dumbfounded, and begged to serve the stranger, to bring her food or drink, but the stranger said she lacked for nothing, and went on into the dark.

"And now, here is the magic part. When her time came, my mother recalled vividly what the stranger had said. She invoked her name—did I say the woman gave her a name to speak?—and suddenly her birth pangs left her, and I was born inside the hour, the girl she had been promised, healthy as an apple. Doubtless you consider this a foolish romance, but the pain of birthing is not pleasurable, and a woman surely knows when it is gone from her by a spell."

I got my voice, and asked, "Did your mother reckon her goddess, then, or witch?"

"Something of both, maybe. But it was in Bar-Ibithni that I heard the name of the stranger again. Generally it is the poor who cleave to her. They say she came this way, traveling to the northwest—to Seema, maybe, along the ancient route of the wagons."

"To Seema," I repeated, and turned my head westward involuntarily.

"Yes, my friend said. "That is why they have carved her image on the west side of the altar here." She led me aside to show me.

I had not seen before. I had not thought of such a thing; that what I sensed of the presence of Uastis here in Bar-Ibithni was only the memory of her traveling, this ancient remembrance, that while I scoured the city and its environs for news of her, her token had been here upon the hill, where I leaned that night and watched the Hesseks come from the groves and the sea. I wondered if those paid searchers I had set to find her had simply missed this obscure sect of a white goddess, or if they merely did not associate such a mild pastoral deity with the picture I had specified—a white hag out of some hell.

The image was tiny, a hand-span high, a rough-made thing, yet somehow pleasing to the eye, constructed out of white stone. A slender woman in a loose robe, long furl of hair, hands crossed on her breast. I imagined the face had weathered away until I realized how smooth it was.

"They don't show her face," I said. "Was it that terrible?"

"Oh, no," the girl said, "that beautiful. Perhaps some city craftsman could have duplicated her countenance, but a farmer made this. They tell how she descended from the sky in a silver boat, but that story you will never have patience with."

I put my head in my hands. My friend came and stroked my hair. She said she must be going, that she wished she might help me in my trouble, and that she was sorry she had mistaken me for Vazkor.

Her eyes were sad again when we parted, but the healing had begun for her, while for me the wound was torn open on its scars. I never asked her name, but I asked what she named her goddess, and if it were Uastis.

No, that was not the name, she said. They titled her Karraket. Though her mother, she added, had used a different ending for the name; she could not call to mind exactly what.

I watched her go away, Chem, the belligerant slave, trudging behind with the parasol and the club.

I had learned my own road, too, but did not take it till the sun was sinking and the sea had turned the color of koois beyond the wall.

I searched for Gyest in the field by the Horse Market, a hood pulled far down over my forehead. The Sri wagons had gone, all but two, and two white oxen were lifting their pink noses to the cool air of dusk. I had no logical reason to suppose I should discover Gyest had waited on me, or even to assume he had not died of the plague, yet I foresaw he would be there, and there he stood, the dark red magician's veil about his face. He had foreseen also that I would seek him, and when. As I walked to him across the field, he raised his arm to greet me, as if this were the arrangement we had settled on that day we had met. It had been a false image he had shown me in the psychic copper, but not through his doing. He, too, had been deceived, but he had warned me of the cloud of death, the doom, the dark. He had offered me his help.

"Will you eat with us?" he asked me now. He looked at my face, inside the shade of the hood. He said, "You are a boy yet, though you have aged ten years behind the skin. I have heard the tales."

"Did you hear I had died?"

"That, too. I have heard stranger things. And less strange."

"In Seema," I said, "do you have a goddess, Karraket?"

A cook-fire burned in the dusk and pots seethed there, and three red-turbaned women chattered to each other on the grass.

"The people of Sri have only one god, who is neither female nor male, not really a god at all, rather a principle. Karraket is a name I am unfamiliar with."

"Too many names," I said. "I don't know even that I hate her still. I am weary of hating her. What I thought led me here was only the memory of her passing. What I fought, thinking it her witchcraft, was the malice of a human woman infected with my sorcery. Gyest," I said, "I may never play the sorcerer again."

BOOK TWO

Part I

In the Wilderness

1

A road led south toward the outskirts of the city. Shrines and small temples littered the lower hills. Flocks of gray pigeons circled in the air and prayers rose through the dawn stillness; but beyond the walls, the mark of the plague fires was visible between the gardens of villas and groves of palm and cypress, and like a hollow blackness at the center of the sloping meadows. How many refugees died in their hill retreats I never estimated, though no doubt some zealous, sneaking little clerk did so, to leave a record of the Yellow Plague for future generations.

About five miles from the core of Bar-Ibithni, the south road rays into a series of subsidiary tracks. By following the western way we came gradually on the old land route to Seema, which skirts behind the back of the ancient swamp of Bit-Hessee, though in the days of Hessek empire it ran straight to the marsh-city gate. The land route is a hazardous thing. For several centuries the caravans had toiled up and down it, till the advent of the mighty Masrian ships developed the seaways in its stead. For those too poor or too penny-pinching to take to the ocean, the land route remained, however, a negotiable track without alternative. To the Sri wagoners, it was Ost (the Unavoidable). Though groups of them had journeyed to the city by sea, in order to be in time to capitalize on the annointing of a new Emperor, not one went back that way, which would take all their profit in return for a rat's portion of steerage, and the probable death of half their livestock during the voyage.

Ost the Unavoidable goes initially through the dense forestland west of the hill lakes. Here there is game in plenty, fruit and edible roots, and the shelter of the tall trees. But after three days, the forest begins to draw back. A plain opens, well watered at its edges, growing bone-dry on the fifth day. Toward the seacoast there are yet salt marshes, and even the black trickles of the streams that run up into the plain country are saline and undrinkable. By the ninth day one comes to the Wilderness, for this is what all men call the area separating the archipelagoes of Seema and Tinsen from the fertile regions of the central south.

The Wilderness. It is a place of rock, whose mesas and stacks take on a misleading configuration in the distance. By day, under the shifty skies of the summer's turning, now smalt blue, now leaden white, now a hot colliding of blocks of thunder, the Wilderness is bleached as ivory. Yet in the sunset or the dawn, the dust that continually drifts and smokes from the ground makes the sky, and reflectively the landscape, into a giant tapestry of blood and saffron, purple and mahogany. The hugeness and the color seem to suck the mind from the body, and send it whirling through space like a nugget. It is the spot for visions and trances.

And for bandits. However, the Sri are past masters of the grim facts of existence, and pay a tax to any who require it of them on the road, reckoning it less than ship's fees. The robbers, of an appearance that would not disgrace a wild beast, are tickled by the polite and affable handing over of goods and the lack of nervousness that the Sri display, and take from them little, and do no harm. Only the wealthy caravans of merchants, too mean to expend money on a sea voyage or a suitable guard on the land journey, are set on and pillaged to the last wheel and rivet, and the dead left for the orange dog-rats that emerge from their burrows at sunfall. Besides, it is surprising how many of such caravans persist in their attempts to cross the waste, providing thereby a living for its human refuse. Additionally, the Sri are to some extent feared for their magic.

Men and fauna alike give evidence of some water in the desert. It is also true to say, as the Sri say, that any water hole one finds, one shares with the rat, the jackal, the serpent, and the murderer, therefore all must sit down in peace. Even the bone-brown tiger—which occasionally passes over the dust dunes, leaving behind it tracks like menacing flowerheads in the twilight—does not kill its prey at drink. It takes thirty or forty days to cross the Wilderness, longer if you turn south before the Seema-Saminnyo (the large causeway that leads to Seema, an isthmus with its farther body of land broken in islands). To go south before this causeway means one seeks the southwestern ocean, which only madmen do, for the lands that lie beyond it are months away, the weather unsure, and the trade bizarre.

I was twenty-one years of age. Inside my skin I felt a deal older, a few decades, perhaps, yet, at the same instant, callow, unprepared. I experienced the bewilderment of my youth, but I was purged of everything else. It would be hard to dread or to hope, to fear or to love. Inside me was a lion on a chain whose name was Power, and I should not let him free again. The god whose weakness it was to discriminate had gone. The sorcerer-prince who hungered for temporal ascendancy had followed him. Even the man no longer yearned for anything very much.

Only one bright shadow remained, the nightmare dream that had first swung me from my course. I should have been a brave in the krarl to this day, if I had not been haunted and finally mastered by those ghosts of my beginning, one white, one black.

I had nothing to offer Gyest and his people, but they took me in. I made myself useful where I could. Oxen are not horses but you learn their ways and how to handle them. Indeed, I was shortly an excellent groom of Seemase oxen; I have yoked them and bedded them and fed them and led them to water, which they store in belly-sacks, hence their endurance in the waste. Vazkor the groom, drover of cattle, Vazkor who had been villain and dreamer, a healer for a chain of cash, a traitorous messiah, a resurrected necromancer. Vazkor, son of Vazkor. Vazkor, born of a white witch.

The four days of the south road, the forest, the plain's sweet-water edges, went by like one day checked with fragments of night. I slept seldom, my brain laboring in purposeless grindings to rid itself of what it would never lose. Once, after a moment's slumber, I woke thinking myself in the sarcophagus. And I felt no terror.

I would lie in the faint glow of the firelight before taking my turn as watch, seeing the man there doze sometimes, I keeping watch already, though on my back. I would examine the lack in me, the surcease of my fears and longings and angers, which seemed to have died where I had not, in the Necropolis. Presently the watchman would come and touch my shoulder to "wake" me; it would generally be Jebbo or Ossif, the half-brothers of Gyest, and masters of the sister wagon. The fourth night it was Gyest himself—I had considered the figure unusually alert, though motionless, at its post.

"I see Vazkor is also sleepless," he said. I reckoned he had seen it often. "Come, then, let us talk."

He stirred the fire up in a foam of red; it was cool under a fringe of trees, damp with the promise of southern rain. His face showed only the eyes, as ever. Jebbo and Ossif went similarly muffled, even among themselves when the women, of whom there were four, were elsewhere. I, too, had taken to Sri garb. Gyest's generosity had settled on me a suit of breeches and calf-length tunic, both, as I should note, the bleached browned-ivory shade of the Wilderness itself. This camouflage, dispelled by the red head-veil, made me adequately Sri against the hour when we should meet bandits. Nevertheless, I had not aspired to shielding my face and head, the masks of Eshkorek having been enough for me.

I asked Gyest if he would not rather sleep. I even went so far as to suggest his woman Omrah might be missing him. She was a young girl, this one, and a couple of times, mislaying my reverie, I had seen her eyes on me. This I did not care for, for his sake, not liking to think him lessened by a strumpet. He was a deal older than she; no doubt the cause of her glances. Now he surprised me by saying; "My wife is with my brother Ossif tonight, and shan't miss me, I assure you, in the manner you imply."

I suspect I was glad to be surprised, even to be angered in a vague, unextensive fashion, some reactions left after all.

"I remember you told me once that your women are free," I said.

"Not merely our women," he said, "all, man or woman. Those liaisons we form spring from liking, but in matters of sex, our laws do not fetter us."

"When your son is born, does he have the eyes of the next wagon?"

"Oh," he said, "children are not mine or thine among us. They are Sri. Whichever woman has the milk and is the nearest feeds the child, whichever man goes to chop wood takes the child to learn wood-chopping."

"To whom are the wagons left, and the riches of the man when he dies?"

"To whoever is needy. To the Sri. But why concern yourself with death, Vazkor? Of all your troubles, he is surely the least."

"So, Gyest believes Masrian stories."

"I look in your face and see the story there, as I saw before the brand of the witch's curse on you."

"Not the witch I sought," I said.

"We must come to that."

"It's come and gone for me," I said. "Vengeance, ghosts, all ground to dust. No more hate. I don't remember what hate feels like, my friend. I've no motive to seek her now."

"Karraket," he said. "You asked me if I had met a goddess by that name. I've reflected on it, Vazkor, and used the magician's training made mine by the men of my father's generation."

"I am embarrassed by your care of me, Gyest. But I'm done with seeking. Let it go."

His eyes took me in, then hooded as he looked down into the fire.

I had never asked for news of Bar-Ibithni, yet now he told me news, answers to questions I had never thought to ask. As I had felt the dull surprise brush by, now I felt dull interest, dull rage, dull bitterness, but no more. Not even when he spoke names I knew, or of Malmiranet even; there was just a dim, poignant stirring like light behind a muddied lamp. I was aware he tested me, as the physician tests the feet of a man with a broken back, to discover if there is any sensation there, and much the same unrewarding response he got from me as the physician gets in such a case, for the spine of my senses had well and truly come in twain.

It was, too, much as anyone could have reasoned, an inevitable history acted out.

I had been the last known victim of the plague. There was some apt mythological stuff in that they were quick to make much of. Fifteen days after my secret burial, the city was pronounced free of Yellow Mantle. Six days after that, Basnurmon marched in at the South Gate with an army of hill bandits, hastily conscripted peasants of his own estates in the east, and four and a half renegade and opportunistic jerds from the eastern borders. While Sorem and his council had played at coronations, Basnurmon had set vigorously to work. He would have come in any event, but learning of the plague, had let it decimate the city for him, and once his yellow ally was safely away, he rode in on its heels.

Bar-Ibithni, rudderless and at sea, without even the pretense of a figurehead, welcomed Basnurmon, her one-time Heir, and five days later he had been made Emperor from the gathered scraps of Sorem's unused annointing. Patchwork kingship proved better than none. Presently there were reports of the demise of Hragon-Dat, due to ill treatment at Sorem's hands. One could not help but bow to Basnurmon's unsubtle genius.

The day he took the throne, Malmiranet ended her life. She was wise, and acted wisely at the last; no doubt she was more a king than any of us, but Masrians do not acknowledge women in the Royal Chair, for all the other privileges they permit them. Basnurmon had already confined her to her apartments on his entry into the city. Guards stood outside the door, and no one unofficial was let in. Even her girls, who had refused to leave her, were taken. Additionally, her rooms were scoured of anything she might put to use, either against her captors or herself. Plainly the foppish heir had a head on his shoulders, and was aware of her mind, or some of it. What he meant ultimately to do with her is conjecture. There was one tale, that he fancied her, and might have kept her for his bed a while, but probably all her roads would have ended at the graveyard gate, and she had no desire to wait on him or his tortures.

The day of the coronation, discipline was lax, and the guards drinking. Malmiranet managed to bribe these swine. Apparently she wished to procure a hairdresser; with Nasmet and Isep gone she had no personal attendant. The guards concluded she meant to titivate herself for Basnurmon's interest, and were prepared to help her, up to a point, in exchange for a handful of jewels she had somehow hidden during Basnurmon's earlier visits, and thus retained. What they sent her for the price was an old crone, some beldam off the streets of the lower commercial area, more accustomed to curling the tresses of harlots. The guard reckoned this a fine jest, and hoped to have Basnurmon laughing at it before the day's end. At length the cavalcade was heard returning from the Temple, and the guard went in the room and found the hag-hairdresser blind drunk at one end of it, Malmiranet dead at the other. She had used the silver-plated trimming knife, not even silver, as I had supposed, though the pride of the whore-server's collection. Empresslike, she had also left instructions for her burial to be given over to the priests of the Necropolis, where her tomb had been in readiness several years, and she offered Basnurmon her curse if he refused her.

Few men, however cynical by day, yearn to incur such post-mortem bane. Besides, she was royal, more royal than he, being of the direct Hragon line. He did not dare insult her corpse before the city. So he gave her body to the priests, those men who at her previous orders had sealed me up in her own golden box, and who now placed her in the outer chamber. It occurred to me months after, one sleepless night in fact by the steel-blue breakers of a far shore, that that second entrance of priests may have roused me, that extra vital burst of air when the outer door was opened, leaking in through the paint-porous wall that divided her resting place from mine. I had been twenty—six or twenty-seven days in a stupor. Who knows? The whole of this world, by its perversity, nourishes one thing upon the downfall of another, but I do not like to believe her death brought life to me.

Basnurmon, in his way, set Bar-Ibithni on its feet. Indeed, I had seen few scars, as I well recalled. Quick-healing wonder of a city, as if the sorcerer had touched it with his hands. For the rest, Sorem's rebel comrades were courteously offered suicide, Masrian honor and the sword in private, or public disgrace. Only tough Bailgar and five of his Shield captains refused this gloss, daring Basnurmon to show his true colors, and were subsequently tortured for a list of nonexistent crimes, and finally hanged before Winged Horse Gate on the west side of the wall. Denades escaped to Tinsen, so it was said. He had some lover, a rich citizen, who saw to matters. The jerds themselves turned, as any wheel must in the prevailing wind, and swore allegiance to Basnurmon.

Nasmet was imprisoned one day, seduced her jailer, and fled south, where tattle would have it she became a bandit's doxy in a fort above a lake there, and drove the devil to drown himself in its waters from despair at her loving demands. Isep, meanwhile, hearing of Malmiranet's death, pried open the lattice of her tower window and threw herself out upon the paving sixty feet below. She did not die at once, and there were tales of this, too, of certain activities among the guards, who disliked her sexual preference. If any of these tales were true, no doubt her curse at least clings firm to the jerds of the Crimson Palace.

Thus they ended, those people, among whom I had moved: the loved, the loving, and the scarcely known. Masrian gossip had always been a marvel, and I had long ago ceased to wonder at its breadth and swiftness. As for its cruelty, its accuracy, they did not wound me then.

Concerning Gyest's people, none had died of the flies or of Yellow Mantle. It was as if their god preserved them, or else their sheer trust in immunity made them immune. At length, some of the wagons departed. Gyest and his half-brothers (*half* since only the mother was clearly known, in accordance with their custom) had remained. Waiting for me, he said, for he had understood I should come, as mundanely as a man with aching joints understands the rain is near. He believed his fate had elected him my helper. I did not even experience shame, but thanked him, and forgot.

That night, in some moment of sleep, I dreamed of Sorem in his own place of death, some princely dome. I regarded his face through the sun-hole, graven as an image, not unlike my own.

Even in the dream, I thought, *There is my life, and no more to come.*

But the sun rose. It was another day.

2

It was our third day in the Wilderness before I glimpsed our first bandit.

He came bumping along from the south, out of a low line of rock hills there, on the back of a mangy shaggy black pony, and with five of his court bumping after. I saw, with a memory of old nerves, now anesthetized, that they were of obscure Hessek ancestry, though not Bit-Hessian stock, pale skinned and with a clotted wool of hair hanging around them to their backsides, hair which also, in un-Hessek style, sprouted in a scrubby pasture on their entire bodies, as their haphazard garments revealed. I had the impression, that their forebears had sometime mated with some indigenous hairy animal of the wild and here was the result. Still, they were in cheery mood, the leader clapping me on the shoulder as he went by, and yelling—actually in the Sri tongue, though with atrocious accent—for the wagon master.

Gyest, Jebbo, and Ossif emerged, and handed him a crock of meal and a jar of koois. The bandit demanded nothing else, seemed pleased, nodded and bowed repeatedly, and shook Gyest's hand. Ossif's white dog, well trained, barked and wagged its tail. Then Jebbo's woman's daughter came up with fresh firewood for the morning hearth.

Here's trouble, I thought, for the girl was the child of the wagons, a lissome fourteen, and deer eyed to boot. Sure enough the bandit leader trotted over to her—they appeared hardly ever to get off their horses, save to obey nature in one way or another—lifted her one armed, and was about to nuzzle her, when the girl smilingly produced a little green snake from the fellow's mouth. I had already learned that Sri women were also adept conjurers, and the little snake was none other than the girl's pet, but it took the bandit by surprise. He shouted with uneasy laughter, and put her gingerly on the ground. When she slipped the snake between her breasts, his face was a study. The Wilder-men fear serpents, and have never discovered which kinds do no harm. He ordered his men to carry her wood for her, bowed and smiled to Gyest, and soon all six rode off again.

After this, visitations came regularly, with variations.

On the eighth day, ten bandit men took another jar of koois and some dried meat and a bronze chain, which they would melt and re-forge as a spear-head. When they had gone, Jebbo's woman found two of her bracelets missing. She went off muttering, and that night I saw a green fire burning behind their wagon. Next day one of the bandits caught up to us and returned the bracelets, saying that his comrade, not he naturally, had stolen them, and begging us to release him from the spell that had given him such nightmares. Jebbo's woman looked smug, though if it was her sending or just the bandit's superstition I was unsure.

On the nineteenth day, the right foremost wheel of the sister wagon came loose. We made an early camp at one of the rare watering places of the desert. Before dusk, another group of bandits had arrived, exacted their little tribute, bartered new rivets for the wheel, helped fix it, then stayed to share supper, even providing most of their own nourishment from a fat pony-skin of tasteless gummy drink. This horrible substance, which they ferment from rock grasses and probably less happy ingredients, is highly potent. Since they were generous in passing it around, Ossif and Jebbo were soon as drunk as they were, while I, who swallowed a couple of mouthfuls, felt somewhat better than I had. In the end the bandits rolled back on their horses, having taken no advantage of the celebration, and I, for my part, somehow ended in a copse of fig trees, lying over Jebbo's woman's daughter. The pleasure brought no burden, not being spoken of after either for good or ill. She was knowing for her years, that I remember, but later on we had to find the snake, which had slipped away during our dialogue. When she got it back she covered it with feverish kisses, presumably so I should be cognizant of my place in her world.

Our guests that night had questioned if we would seek the camp of Darg Sih. This miscreant, apparently a robber-overlord of the region hereabouts, had organized, in the grand manner, a tiger hunt to catch a beast that had been eating his horses—thieved in the first instance. In fact, Sri do not hunt as other men. They mesmerize their prey, as the serpent often does, by means of gesture and a curious vocal whining, then kill quickly while the animal is tranced. I have never seen it done, and speak from hearsay among bandits and Sri alike. Also they eat meat rarely, for their creed resists slaughter of any kind except when unavoidable. Still, I never once saw a man of them set out for game and come back empty-handed, and my own offers of hunting for the pot they politely put aside.

In the morning, Gyest told me we should be stopping a night or so at Darg Sih's camp, not to slay tigers, but to ask use of his smithy, the best in the Wilderness. The bandit clans have become canny at smithing, and can turn anything to anything from long practice. I had already seen a couple of murky but credible alcum knives brewed up from their forges.

I did not inquire, however, what Gyest wanted with a forge, considering it his own business.

Darg Sih obviously had Masrian blood. He towered over his men, ruddy brown of skin, shaved bald on the scalp and heavily bearded below, and with a pair of skew eyes, only one of which looked at you, while the other went about its own affairs.

We got to his camp, using some invisible track quite plain to the Sri, and arrived at sunset. The place was crowded with extra thieves, most yet mounted. They had been hunting the tiger with a couple of mares as bait, and a pack of dogs as prone to growl, snap, and fight as were their masters. Nevertheless, they had got the beast, an old one, that had no doubt reckoned a corral of horses as good as a banqueting table laid out for aged tigers. It had died cleanly, a spear-head lodged between its round ears, but by now the dog pack had savaged it, and some of the bravos had tapped its vitals, believing tiger blood a magic draft strengthening to heart and muscles. Remembering the beautiful slinking shape of a tiger seen days back at dusk, heading its prints away across the dunes, this rent and pilfered corpse stirred me to a confused, half-felt pity. How many aeons ago it seemed when I had been fourteen and stood above the two shot deer in the winter valley, pitying their death because I had grown aware of my own mortality.

Darg Sih, still astride his pony, bowed almost to his own belly before Gyest, and accepted koois and a bag of silver cash.

"You are welcome to me as my own life, Gyest. We have need of magicians."

As they spoke, courteous bandits relieved the Sri of their cleaver-blade weapons. As far as I could see, they never had recourse to them in any case, and now made no objection. There was a lot of bowing and shaking of hands, and the gummy drink offered around, and even a cup of tiger's blood (refused).

"What need of magicians do you have, Darg Sih?" Ossif asked,

"A man mauled by the old cat there. It has fine teeth before it dies, though no longer, for the women steal them for necklets." Darg Sih laughed. "You will come and work heal-magic? The men of the Red Camp tell me you wish the forge. That will be payment, yes? To heal my man?"

Gyest said he would look at the man and see what could be done. Darg Sih's straight eye, meanwhile, had run up my uncovered face while the other gazed at my boots.

"Who is this one? Not Sri, not Hesk, not Seema-boy. Nor Masrian, I think. Who?"

"A northerner," Gyest said.

"North—what is north?" demanded Darg. "And has the scut no tongue?"

"Tongue and teeth," said Gyest, sounding amused, though probably this was a precaution. Insults and threats flew about in the bandit camps; if everyone kept smiling, they could be supposed friendly, but to ask for water with a solemn face might invite wrath.

"But I long to hear the voice of him," said Darg. He leaned precariously, poked me in the chest, and grinned and said, "Eh, boy, thrill me with your speech."

A year back this would have put me in a rage. Now I

bowed low, and said, smiling of course, "The thrill of my voice to you, oh master, would not compare to my delight at hearing yours."

Both his eyes popped, one on me, one on my belt. Plunging from the saddle with a bellow, Darg Sih embraced me, punching me in the back and roaring. I had spoken inadvertently in his own polyglot bandit language, heard as I came in the camp. He thought me a bandit now, regardless of racial characteristics and garb. He was pressing koois on me, the gum drink, tiger's blood, and inviting me to couple with his women and his sons.

It was me he bowleggedly led, crowing, toward the tent of the mauled man, telling me the while of Gyest's cleverness as healer. Gyest and the brothers followed, their women clustered close, returning bandit grabs, where they had to, with productions of snakes, phosphorescent lights, and careful laughter.

The camp lived in a diversity of dwellings—in huts of piled stones, in grubby tents, in wicker-work bothies. At its center a spring of white water opened in the rock, and made a pool where wizened fruit trees grew, and here, in a cave, lay an unconscious man, with most of his right arm chewed away. A boy wept at his feet. Darg swept him up and kissed him noisily, trumpeting that the magicians had come and all should be well.

Gyest and Ossif bent to examine the man. There were broad claw-marks on his breast, too, but they were clean and would close. The arm was useless. A city physician would long since have had it off and bound up the stump before a gangrene set in.

"It is his mare, you see, offered for bait," Darg explained. "This one, he runs and leaps the tiger. *Chunk!* The tiger's teeth meet in his wrist. He thinks it an appetizer, the old brown one."

The boy wept in the doorway.

"I doubt he can keep his arm, Darg Sih," Gyest said.

"His *right arm*!" Darg roared. "Consider, his *knife hand*—you must save it." He tapped his smiling jaw with a playful finger. "Save, or no forge."

Gyest straightened, came over to me, and said in accurate if slightly halting Masrian, "I can only salvage, and then he may still die. The bandits of Ost Wilderness don't understand that our magic is mostly illusion. We are not great healers. There's only one here who can actually heal."

"No," I said.

"You renounce the good Power with the bad, then? You have learned nothing?"

"I swore I'd never play sorcerer again, Gyest. I meant it."

"You are long-lived," he said. "How often will you force this denial from yourself in all the years before you?"

The man began to rouse, and started to cry out in weak stutterings of pain. The boy ran to him, and took his sound hand.

"It doesn't move me," I said to Gyest, as if this were some show he had ordered them to put on in order that I be impressed.

"But, Vazkor," Gyest said, "when has human suffering ever moved you?" I had not expected that. It went through me like the distant cast of a spear, like hurt in a scar long sealed. "You have no compassion," he said quietly, without anger, merely telling me a fact. "You survive all human ills. How can you expect to feel compassion? You must see that the sympathy any man feels for the plight of another is, at its core, simply a realization and fear that he, too, might suffer the same plight. We grow cold in the loins and about the heart when we confront disease, wounds, death, because we know they are also our heritage. But you, Vazkor, who have overcome any and all these devils of the flesh, how shall you tremble and ache for us?"

My mind slid back, as if he had directed it, to the shot deer at the pool, my fourteen-year-old pity sprung from my own terror at the aspect of death. I thought, too, of how I had worked among the victims of the yellow plague, trying to ease their wretchedness, as if thereby I would ease my own that I knew would come to me. It was exact, every word he spoke. Yet I should never have fathomed it without Gyest.

"Don't chide yourself," he said now. "Expect only what you can give. Which is pity, rarely, accidentally, some trigger sprung by nostalgia or regret. True sympathy you will never give. Yet how much more you are able to give. Ask the dying man if he would rather you wept for him or healed him."

Darg's hand fell on my arm.

"What's this? Masrian you speak and my soldier howling like the she-wolf. Come, Gyest. Heal! Heal!"

My voice sounded rough as a boy's when I said, "Gyest, get all of them out. If I must do it, I want no witnesses, no shouts of sorcery."

The place was cleared; he spun them some yarn of me,

that I had been tutored by a doctor-sage in Bar-Ibithni the Golden, and so on. Even the youth was taken away, sobbing, which left me the writhing, moaning man.

I healed him. No wonder now, no hubris, no surge of pleasure or contempt, not even my own questioning that I felt nothing. Just healing. The absolute, as I had finally been shown, does not need the accompaniment of pipes and drums.

He came to himself shortly. By then I had bound his arm with a strip of rag lying on the ground, to conceal its wholeness.

He fixed me with blazing eyes, and told me the pain was gone and he could flex the fingers and wrist. I told him he could expect total recovery, providing he did not remove the bandage for seven days nor look at the wound. He gawked, and began to argue that he could feel no wound, that I was a magician. I leaned very near, and promised him if ever he called me that again, to my face or at my back, I would send a ghoul to gnaw on his liver.

We parted in unfriendly silence, my patient and I.

I sat on a rock, some way above the camp. Smoke, firelight, and a yapping of hounds and men filled up the space below. The space above had changed from carmine to indigo, and the brass dust-moon of the Wilderness had just risen. Somewhere the dog-rats of the waste were twittering, barely audible, out of a vast hollow quiet. It is a phenomenon of such spots that any noise is encapsulated in this ringing stillness, and made strangely tiny, however loud. The shouts of bandits and the squeaks of fauna sound as if confined in bubbles, a symbol of their impermanence. Only the desert endures.

I sat a long while there. Now and then I noticed the glare of the smithy fire burst up, and thought, *Well, I have won Gyest his forge*. But mainly my mind went wandering. I was digesting my life. To say I was at peace would not be honest, but to say peace showed itself to me, brushed me with its cool breath, yes. There is, too, a sort of relief in admitting defeat. Struggling to drag a mountain from my path, acknowledging at last the mountain would remain, lying down beneath the mountain, thankful for the shade of it.

About five hours must have folded themselves away into the night. The moon had touched the roof of the sky and turned her sail to the west.

I was gazing down into the fire-blur of the camp, gathering myself to return there. All at once I glimpsed a man dismounting from a black horse. It caught my eye, for the horse was finer than anything I had seen of the bandit mounts this far. Then the man turned. His hair was curling, cropped rather shorter than mine, and he was gaudily dressed, yet he had a look of me. A second after, I saw a woman on a mule; he had moved to converse with her. They were speaking trivial words, yet I could sense something between them, like a current of heat or energy. The woman was dressed in black and the black shireen of the tribes. Her hair poured around her like unseasonable snow.

It was gone as suddenly as it came. It did not dismay me; it was like a dream.

Gyest was standing beside me. He said softly, "What were you seeing?"

"My mother," I said. "My mother, and some man not my father."

"So," he said, "and there is no anger now."

"No anger. Yet I swore a vow to some dark thing once, some remnant of my father's despair, that I would kill her."

He seated himself, asking me if he might, on the rock nearby.

"You know you can never rest until you find her," he said.

"Oh, I can rest. As much as I shall ever rest, perhaps."

"Once," he said, "you sought within my brain. One adept, read by another, also reads. You learned something of me, and I something of you. Did you appreciate this?"

"Lellih scoured my brain as she would scour a cookpot with a knife," I said. "Yes, gift for gift. What do you know of me?"

"Enough to show you the way," he said.

A snake moved inside my belly. I was waking up. Visions, truths, reverie, leading me back to consciousness and feeling, to involvement, to life, where, perhaps, I was reluctant to go.

"Gyest," I said, "we had this through before. If I seek her, I shall kill her. This I believe. I have no hate left, but he has cause to hate her, and it is his genius, his will, that created me. Ah, Gyest, if only I had known my father!"

"The shining dark," Gyest said, "the reflection of the flame upon the wall: Shadowfire. Vazkor, you are too much of his, too much of hers. You can't escape this road. You must confront them both in order to resume yourself. Now. Suppose that you seek her, how shall you do it?"

"The Power of my will, the very thing I don't mean to use again. Very well, I will heal, but not this other. Not again."

"A focus, then," he said. "As the Sri use it. Small power, much concentration. To trace a man, you take something that has belonged to him, a garment or an ornament, preferably something worn often. If he has not left you such a thing, then you fashion one in the semblance, as near as may be. There is an image in your brain when you think of her. You're accustomed to the form and have mislaid it. Uast the cat, the white lynx. Look."

He opened his cloak, and put before me on the rock the silver mask I had dug for in Ettook's treasure chest, the mask Demizdor had worn about the krarl, the mask Tathra had shunned, the mask the Eshkiri slave had brought. The mask of my mother, Uastis, Karraket, the witch. The face of a silver lynx with open black eye-holes, the yellow strings pendant from its back like sunrays on the rock, each ending in a flower of amber.

I cursed aloud. The blood shot to my heart in a pang I had forgotten could take me.

Gyest went on calmly, extending this calm to me.

"The silver is debased, and the flowers are only yellow glass, but the illusion is as perfect as I could get it. The mold Omrah made at my direction, the rest is the skill of Darg Sih's clever smith who at one time, before he slew a man and fled here, constructed jewelry in Bar-Ibithni."

"Why have you done this?"

"To aid you."

"Why aid me?"

"God has moved me to help you. Or, if you prefer, it was my reasonless inclination to do so."

I reached out, and took up the mask. I half anticipated the shock to go through my palm when I touched it, as it had when I first drew it from the treasure chest. But this was not the same. It weighed heavier in the hand, and the gems more lightly. It was a focus, as he had said. If I stared down into the blank eye-holes of it, what witch-eyes should I behold staring back at me across lands and seas and time itself?

"No," I said, "I am done with this."

"It's not done with you," he answered.

No, truly it was not. She had sat her mule in the camp below, her white hair around her shoulders. No, it was not done.

I got to my feet, the mask in my hand. I walked into the

Wilderness just far enough to put the small lights and sounds of men behind me.

About a quarter of a mile from the camp I halted by a narrow towering fretwork stack, like a pillared temple carved by the wind. It was the very wind I could hear blowing now, through the empty bell of the desert. The dust stirred like smoke underfoot. The brown moon lay on the horizon's edge.

I held the mask between my hands, and let my Power drip slowly down on it, like my soul's blood.

I woke in the dawn. The plains of the Wilderness were exploding into light. It was the first hour of day, one of the two most beautiful hours of the desert, where sunrise and sunset are the queen and king. I kept where I was and watched till the mystery ended. Then I got up and went back into the camp of Darg Sih.

It seemed to me I had slept. I recalled no dream, no revelation, nothing. Yet I knew the way. I knew the way to find her. I must do what only madmen do, turn aside before the Seema-Saminnyo, travel to the brink of the southwestern ocean, bribe some ship's captain to take me south and west again to that unknown featurless land—I had not seen it, knew it only as one knows some object one has touched in the dark, through gloves—and there she would be. Sea-girt, summer gone with the birds from that anchorage, maybe even snow there now, and near to a place of snow. It was apt for her, my snow-haired dam.

It recurred, the image Hessek had shown to me: The sorceress was sinewy and raddled, with her claws of fire and her cat's head. My fear was dead, yet still she seemed an inspiration for fear, of all the world's fear if not of mine. An elemental? A witch? What would she do indeed, when I walked up to her on some western street, or in some icy garden there, under the pale winter sun? *I am your son, Uastis of Ezlann, whom you abandoned to the stinking krarl of savages, and trusted never to meet again. I am the son of Vazkor, your husband, by whose shadow I have sworn to slay you, Uastis, and let dogs destroy your healing bones and fire your healing flesh so never from that wreck can you remake yourself. There shall be no part or portion left, Uastis, that can heal itself; not a grain, not a hair. True death for a daughter of the Old Race, and I bring it.*

Of course, my preparations for her death had undergone a change. There had been before no precautions of fire, a total destruction that nothing might return. Remembering the Eshkorek legend of her, that she had risen from a grave once or maybe twice, and having the proof of this oddity in myself, aware it might happen, my plans were half unconsciously altering and reshaping themselves. From that conclusion rose an unassailable revelation.

Since the beginning of it, rejecting or reveling in my Powers, I had claimed them from my father, who had been a sorcerer before me. But my father had died. Though his body had never been found in the ruined tower, yet it lay there, or somewhere. If he had lived, there would have been news of him in twenty years, some tale, some battle, some fresh striving would have revealed his life. No, he was dead; my whole argument sprang from his death. She it was who could not die. She, and I. It was *her* blood that made me more than human.

The bandits, their dogs and women, snored in the camp. The corpse of the tiger lay where they had left it, already vile smelling, with ten black desert birds circling above, afraid to come down to feast with so many live things about.

Then, under the stunted palm that grew above the spring, I observed Darg Sih sitting with Gyest, playing one of the southern checker games in the dust, with elegant, certainly stolen, counters of red soapstone and green jade.

Caught by the incongruity of this, I paused to let the bandit chief make his move. He pulled his moustaches and grunted, and rapped with the green counter on his teeth, as if they might supply the answer.

Shortly, the counter slapped down. Darg Sih had won the game. He roared for koois, and from a tent nearby a boy ran and gave him the flask Gyest had brought. Darg gestured me over with flailing motions of his arms, embraced me, and offered me the rum. We drank, and Gyest, lifting the red veil, also drank. Darg watched this with childish fascination, digging me in the ribs. No iota of countenance came visible as Gyest drank. Presently he handed back the flask.

"You go south, then, bandit brother, take ship? Bad, bad," Darg said to me.

"Does Darg also read minds?"

"Gyest tells me," he mumbled. "Why go to the poxy stinking port? Stay and hunt tigers with Darg, eh, brother?"

"He must seek his kindred," Gyest said.

"Ah," Darg said. "Kin. Not scutty Sri ways, no man knowing his father, eh?"

"How did you decide my road?" I asked Gyest.

"Not I. Long ago you foresaw a ship would take you there."

"That time I was in error."

"Not this time."

"No," I said, "not this."

We drank more koois, and the boy brought a plate of cold meat and figs. He had gold earrings. I could not work it out if he were Darg's son or his leman.

"If you need a ship, then you must reach Semsam port. Ships there." Darg skewered his meat with the knife that a few days back, probably, had been slitting some merchant's throat. "If you go to Semsam, I will give you a pony and send three—no—four men with you. No trouble in the Ost, then"—he beamed at us, using the Sri word to better our understanding—"and no trouble in Semsan either, where they are dogs who cut up their babes for supper."

I thanked him for his generosity.

When we rode out an hour later, the Sri wagons and my guard of four bandits, Darg Sih wept copiously, and swore he would offer prayers to his gods on my behalf. I think I never inspired such instantaneous and fulsome approval in my whole life, before or since.

My parting from Gyest six mornings after was more constrained. I assumed I should not see him again. Each farewell in my life had been final, and men's days were short. It is extraordinary. I had not known him long, nor intimately beyond those psychic interchanges on which ground we met as fellow magicians, and I the greater of the two. Neither did I ever see his face, or learn anything of note concerning his history or his aims (if aims he had; I think he was content to *be*). I never had the father with whom most men expect nature to equip them. I had instead the hatred of a red pig, and a shadowy myth given me by enemies and strangers. Even if my father had been Gyest, among the Sri I could not have been sure of it. Still, he was the closest I got, maybe. Or maybe I let sentiment influence me. Say then only this: I shall regret always the loss of his good friendship, his unpretentious wisdom, and his half-amused quietness under the hand of his god.

Every one of the four Sri women kissed me good-bye, and the white dog licked my hand. They gave me food for the journey, and Ossif handed me a copper charm from his wagon. These charms they acknowledge as toys, their god cares for them anyway, but man in his weakness likes visible proof of caring. It is a joke between them and the Infinite.

The four hairy bandits seemed pleased rather than otherwise at being my escort. I wondered if they meant to try to kill me, or sell me on the way or in the port itself. What would I do then? Power, or the knife I had bartered for in Darg's stronghold? As it turned out, they had no tricks in mind, and were simply enjoying scenery different from that of the camp.

The track to the southwest shows clearly an old road of Hessek make with a decrepit shrine to some Hessek spirit at its beginning. The deity is not Shaythun for sure; he has chipped wings and a tiger's head. An iron bell without a clapper rusts in the dirt nearby. There must have been a priest to tend him once, but he was gone, and the hermitage returned to the dust of the plain.

It would need sixteen days, a little less with hard riding, to get to the coast.

Gyest and I had not spoken again of where I was headed, my destination nor my goal. I had ceased quarreling with it, and he had ceased showing me my way. Destiny or gods or fortune—whatever one is pleased or innocent enough to call them—they seal men to their decree. There comes an hour when batle ends and one put's one's neck beneath the yoke.

I forget most of what was said. A platitude or two, probably, wishes for safe journeying, kind weather. The best men fall back on them when wit no longer answers.

When I was mounted, I thanked him without specifying my thanks.

"You have time. Go slowly," he said.

I knew what he meant, and I said, "Still, I swore it to him. I mean to do it. I can kill as well without anger as in a rage. Better."

He said quietly, "I see a jackal running. His name is *I Remember.*"

A slow shiver went down my spine. I had thought myself past such things. But I raised my arm to him and bade him good-bye, then rode off along the Hessek road to Semsam, the four bandits whooping after me.

3

Semsam glowed muddily in the rain. It was a place of ramshackle itinerant bivouacs and worming alleys crowded by makeshift hovels, which had somehow, against all odds, endured. Near the shore, decayed mansions of Ancient Hessek balanced on marble stilts, like terrible old dying birds. The rain, which had started three days back on the shore road, looked fair set to wash this slimy disaster of a port away. There were no walls, no watch. It was a center of robbers and reavers, and of certain illicit trades of Tinsen from the west, and various outer islands to the south. In dock, the canoes of the black jungle men lay alongside the tall slavers and the single-deck galleys of Seemase pirates.

A Hessek palace three stories high, five before the top two floors collapsed, had been reborn as the Inn of the Dancing Tamarisk. Here, traces of weird Hessek splendor remained, an antique silver cage of crickets chirping just inside the door, round-bellied lanterns of red glass, a costly, threadbare pornographic carpet on the wall. Painted Thei-boys sat primly in a row on a low gallery, peering through latticed fans, waiting to be picked by the customers. Meantime, the rain hustled down the cracked panes of green crystal, and plopped through the ceiling.

My four bandits were good insurance. Modest Darg had not told me Semsam paid him tribute. As the friend and "blood-brother" of a bandit lord, and a Sri magician into the bargain, I was fed and accommodated at no expense, and promised a ship to wherever I wished to journey. Probably they reckoned me a fugitive from justice. Many such, I imagine, dashed in and out of Semsam.

Presently we donned oiled sharkskins, and walked down to the dock.

The sea, pebbled and scythed by the deluge, blended into an auburn distance. Westward, beyond the points and spits of rocky bays, the sun was lowering itself on the silver wires of the rain. My guide, a crippled Hessek cutthroat missing a selection of items from his anatomy, indicated the shipping with a portion of finger.

"There, Lauw-yess. The *Tiger* or the *Southern White Rose* both trade with the outer islands."

"Master wants to go farther south than islands," rapped one of my bandits in inventive Hessek.

The retired cutthroat marveled at me, and rubbed his broken nose with his left hand, from which all members but the thumb were missing.

"The Lauw-yess wishes to go south and west, then, to the big land there, the land with the white mountaintops? That's a journey of many months, lord, or more. Gold there, and gems they say. Only one ship ever went there and came back rich."

"What ship is that?" I asked him.

"Dead ship now," he said, "and the crew—" He made a gesture that meant "Prison" or "the rope," in other words the law of the Masrians. "Yet," he added, "Lanko might risk the voyage. He's had bad dealings with Masrian patrols, and could do with ocean between them and him. If you can pay—"

"Pay?" demanded the talkative bandit. "The blood-brother of Darg Sih to pay?"

In fact, I had come from my tomb with some money in my belt; not that I had thought to provide for myself, it had merely been there. When I attempted to pay for my keep among the Sri, I had found the coins put back, with the finesse of a slit-purse, in my pocket the next day, and the next, and at length I had given in to their generosity. However, if I had sufficient to reimburse a pirate captain for a many-month excursion into the unknown remained to be proved.

"Take me to Lanko and we'll argue it out."

My guide said he would rather I went without him, Lanko being a man of uncertain mood. His vessel lay around the nearer point, in a cove, obviously hiding from Masrian lookouts.

In the driving rain, therefore, my escort and I picked our way around the point, over black and white sands, and up a narrow by-water, which assured me at least that Lanko's navigator knew his trade.

There was a break in the cliff; the ship stood against the silver brownness of the sky, black on the rain light, great sailed, as if he were primed to be off again, asleep with one eye open. If I had needed a portent to tell me, here it was. This was the ship as I had foreseen it on Peyuan's island, exact in every detail, as the *Vineyard* had not been. The ship that would lead me to Uastis.

It was two masted, like the *Vineyard*, but with only one bank of oars, built tall, nevertheless, tall and knife-slender, a greyhound of a ship ready to run.

A man challenged us as we went along the bank.

The bandits grew vociferous; it appeared Lanko disclaimed fealty to any other than himself. I dissuaded them from brawling, and we got aboard.

A number of sailors, Seemase from their look, stood and stared at me and at Darg's ranting soldiers. I noted some of the watchers had that unmistakable top-heavy build of the oarsman, though none were shackled and did not seem to be slaves.

The man returned, and told me Lanko would see me alone. The bandits roared and snorted with the false but lethal, hastily conjured fury of professional villains. Finally, I got into the midships cabin, and the door was shut.

None of Charpon's luxury here. Plain furnishings, a deal jug of liquor of the kind with stoppered mouthpieces from which to drink. Lanko himself was a tall Seemase, Conqueror blood somewhere, with a lard face and canny eyes.

He glanced me over, and said, "Sri, eh? Bit of a way from your wagon, eh, conjurer?"

I thought, *I killed Charpon for a ship I never had to use. That crime sticks in my throat because it was futile, as much as anything. And here is a new Charpon. His ship I must have, but I won't kill him, not I, nor any other I send as a deputy of my cowardice.*

I said, in the Seemase tongue Lyo had inadvertently taught me, "I want transport on your vessel, Lanko. How much?"

"Huh! You speak Seemase, do you, boy? Not money, though, I think. I carry no passengers."

"One passenger," I said.

"Where to, Sri-man?"

"South and west."

"No land there," he said.

"Three or four months out, there's land."

"You're speaking of the continent where the gold grows in apples on the trees, and the whales swim alongside and lay down their bones for you on the deck, and in winter the girls sit up on floating pillars of ice in the water and show you their goodies." He unstoppered the jug, drank, and stoppered it. "More ships go that way than come back. Plenty of stories come, but no men."

"One ship got rich there."

"Rich, and the Masrians had it from them."

"I heard," I said, "that you'd be glad to put some sea between yourself and the Bar-Ibithni patrols."

"So I would," he said. "You clever lad."

He had a knife and he was going to instruct me with it. I felt this from him like a sudden heat in the cabin. I had wondered what I should do in this sort of situation, and now I found out. As the knife ripped upward toward my face, I caught and spun it from his grasp, untilizing the energy of my will more quickly than ever I could have acted with my body.

He snatched himself away from me, and his chair went over. His cunning eyes showed calculation rather than alarm.

"I said you were clever," he said. "Now magic a mouse out of my ear."

"I'm not a showman, neither your enemy," I said. "State your price, or let me work my passage. If you won't go westward, take me as far as some isle where I can find another ship that will."

He picked his knife up from the floor and stuck it in the table. There were marks there where he had done it before. He did not bother with the fallen chair.

"Why do you want to go west to a land four months from Semsam?"

"That's my affair."

He smiled at the knife. I thought, in a desultory, pointless way, *I could dispense with all this, bind him to my service, hold him to it, and kill him if he failed me.* Somewhere a voice answered: *Charpon, Long-Eye, Lyo, Lellih. Malmiranet.*

"You're set on going anyway, to evade the Masrian patrol. Why not pick up some gold while you're about it? By the time you get back, they'll be through hunting your ship. If they have not, you can buy them off with your riches."

"You have it worked out for me, do you not, Sri-man?" he said. He looked at me smiling, then, "Can you row?"

It was like fate catching hold of my arm.

"I can row. But not as a slave."

"None of my rowers are slaves. This is a free ship. I'm one man short since the stenchful soldiers chased us. That's my offer, then. You for the oar, and I'll carry you for your usefulness. When we reach the isles, we'll see."

"Very well,"I said.

"Very well," he parroted. He dislodged the knife and pointed it at me. "What else can you do, wizard? Charm fair weather for us? Call breakfast fish from the sea?"

I thought, *I could walk it. Three months stroll over the azure ocean, fly up and lie on a cloud when I grew weary, couple with mermaidens when I itched.* My Power seemed abruptly preposterous, funny. It had never seemed so previously.

"You employ me as oarsman. Nothing else."

On deck, I read the name of the ship, written along the inside of the bulwarks as well as without: *Gull.* At long last, a ship named for the sea.

It was still raining in the hour before sunup when *Gull* edged from the cove.

His sails (he, too, was a male ship) were the dull gray-green of open autumn water, a camouflage. I was below, and did not see the headlands slick away into the rain, nor the sun come up at length on the larboard side.

I had pulled this oar, or the forerunner of this oar, part of a day aboard the *Hyacinth Vineyard*, Charpon's ship, that the portent of this. But no shackles now, and no Comforters with their eager flails. These were free men, though no doubt escaped galley slaves off other vessels, putting their compulsory education to use.

I recalled how I had played a game, waiting, Power like a trick in my sleeve, on Charpon's ship. I had rowed then for the sake of the game, amusing myself because I knew that when I chose I could resume instantly my superior role of god-magician. Now I rowed with no hope of this transformation scene to exhalt me. My chained lion of Power. I would unfetter him to heal, to defend myself—indeed, that much had been instinctive. But to unleash my abilities to master others simply because it was convenient to me, because it saved me coins or labor, that I would no longer do. If I feared anything anymore, I think I feared that I might break my own resolve.

The grinding of the oars jarred my flesh against my bones. I had got soft in Bar-Ibithni. This bitter medicine would do me good.

We were leaving one Wilderness for another, for the sea is

also a desert. Besides, there are deserts of the soul more arid than any bone-bleached waste of the world. I was yet in a Wilderness, would stay in it till the questions of my life had been answered, if they ever were. A great sweep of mental landscape, empty of comfort save for the brief watering-places of human companionship, liking, love, where now the wells had run dry. Before me, across the waste, was a faceless goal of white stone: the place of the sorceress, but whether at the desert's end, or simply at the horizon with another wilderness beyond, I would not see till I had come there.

4

The dream of western gold had tempted Lanko, as I had known it would. For thirteen days of warm, sullen, blowy weather, *Gull* ran between the outer islands, here coming to dock for taverns, sex, barter, or robbery, now and then fleeing like a scalded cat before the prophecy of Masrian shipping. The isles were broad rocky chunks protruding from the swirl of the ocean, their inland hills bearded with forest where wild sheep galloped. Mostly the men there lived by fishing, and were of the Old Blood. Great pyres were lighted on the uplands, smoking as the ship went by. It was a festival of Ancient Hessek, "Burning the Summer," to propitiate winter, which brought storm winds, rains, and riotous seas.

Shifts at the oars were split in two sections of six hours each, with two hours between. At night the ship made do with his four tall sails and the shark's fin at his bow. When in port, the rowers also went ashore to carouse and let loose trouble where they pleased. They shared any booty with the crew, had a ration of salt-meat, fruit, biscuit and wine, and koois after a hard forced shift—when pursued by Masrians, or themselves pursuing some hapless craft. I discovered myself rowing *Gull* on such a course of sack one night, having been roused from sleep along with others. I thought at first we were escaping the patrols, till the grunted felicitations of the wretches about me set me right. A small merchantman, strayed off course from Tinsen and at anchor by some island, had been spotted by Lanko's predatory watch.

The Drummer beat like a madman, grinning and yelling

encouragement the while, and we burst our arms from the sockets. Presently we must have rammed the luckless merchantman. A crash of timbers and men falling from the benches followed, next a berserk scrambling aloft to participate in the prize.

I came out on the deck, and saw the trader-ship leaning in the water, holed in the starboard flank, upper deck ablaze with torches. It was not a Masrian vessel but a Tinsen galley, black as pitch, with a single red and black sail. An iron grappler provided a dangerous causeway for Lanko's men, who struggled over it and then returned with sacks and casks. The Tinsenese had offered no opposition but cowered in the torchlight, imploring their ancient gods, promising Lanko's vessel a vengeance plague such as had fallen on Bar-Ibithni the Beloved of Masri.

When we were clear and cruising off down the night, leaving the bright-lit, howling Tinsen trader behind, the crew of the *Gull* waxed joyous with koois, showing each other ropes of black pearls and figurines of milky jade. The query arose: What need to go to the west now?

I leaned by the rail, watching all this. I knew this ship was my means of passage, yet I did not intend to force Lanko to do anything. The riddle was resolved by Lanko himself, who appeared in a filthy red velvet Masrian kilt and shirt.

"We'll sail to the westlands, because I have decided it, and because this gentleman, this half-naked Sri gentleman stripped for helping our oars along, promises gold there. Rivers of it, lakes of it, and gemstones growing on the bushes. Don't you?" he added to me. I said nothing. Lanko looked around and said, "We all remember hanged Jari's ship that he brought back from there, so low in the water from riches he near sunk?" Getting drunk on their easy piracy and the koois, Lanko's dogs barked for him, and for me. They began to call my advent beneficial, declaring the Tinsen galley was due to my good fortune rubbed off on them. Lanko, little eyes sharp, offered me a piece of the loot. I declined. He said, "Come, Sri, you don't travel so light. What of that silver cat's face in your pack?"

I knew someone had been fumbling there, not he, but they had told him.

I still said nothing. He smiled at my silence, and looked me over.

"Never been in a fight?" he said. Stripped to my breeches as I was, he could see the absence of scars.

"Not in any fight I lost," I said.

I could perceive he recalled how I took his knife.

Smiling, he went away.

They caught a big fish on the fourteenth day. Its flesh was saccharine and I did not care for it, but Lanko's men were delighted, savoring it as a delicacy, and telling me this, too, was lucky.

They had begun to consider themselves now not merely pirates on the run from justice, nor reavers getting out to pillage, but doughty adventurers sailing to uncharted realms. Their talk was all tales and myths, and the recountings of Jari's men before the law mounted them on ropes. Huge white sharks gamboled in the western seas, that would play with men rather than devour them, and girls with fishtails still conveniently equipped with organs of pleasure. South of west lay cold lands, where ships constructed of ice made war upon each other, ramming and clashing under the huge stars. Northwestward the sea was warmer, yet the mountaintops were capped with snow. One dusk, as the fellow rowers of my shift gnawed and champed their supper on the upper deck, I caught the name "Karrakess." It was sufficiently like the other to stir me. I asked the man of whom he spoke.

"Oh, some god-lady," the man said. "She's worshiped along the coast there."

"What is she like?"

"Oh"—he made round eyes at me—"ten feet tall, with snake-headed breasts and a vulture's head." He burst out in guffaws at my guileless childish interest in goddesses. It was only some name he had picked up from Jari's crew; he knew nothing.

On the fifteenth day we saw the final island melting behind us under a pall of rain, but the ocean ahead was clear, sparkling like smashed green glass.

I wondered after if in some way, not meaning to, I had yet influenced them psychically. They had grown to such enthusiasm and determination to proceed, even at the year's turning, when weather was uncertain and inclined to violence, and their wild baying of stories had none of that superstitious glowering under the eyes common to Seemase, Hessek, and mix sailors. And, most peculiar, there was this strange, sudden eulogizing of myself. A fresh wind—then I had sent it. A sunny day—my work. On one occasion the watch spotted a trading ship to the north of us. They were about to abandon their course to appropriate this bounty, but a squall blew up and they lost sight of it. Then it was, "The Sri magician's god has directed us away, for the ship had no treasure aboard."

Presently, the inevitable occurred. A man with a festering sore in his foot came to me to heal it. I had already put an end to these miracles once, and resumed at Gyest's prompting. He had shown me that the burden, which the suffering of men would lay on me if I refused them help, was eventually unsupportable. So, I healed the sailor, trying the trick with the bandage as I had with the man in Darg's camp. Naturally, this one did not obey me, investigated his sore, and found it gone. Soon, I had the whole of the ship's invalids to attend to. My days, and nights, grew leprous with rotten teeth, galls, skin cancers, and similar honey. My reputation burgeoned, to my disquiet and boredom, and my black shame. It is a common, not illogical supposition on the part of the cured to reckon you have done it out of love for him and for humanity in general. This naïve and stupid trust, coupled to my unliking heart, sent me running like a sick and angry cur into some kennel-yard at the bottom of my soul.

On the twentieth day, we had seen the last of any land for some while. *Gull* was stocked below with kegs of water and wine, salt meat and dried fruits. The air of adventuring and excitement continued. My best hours had become those twelve when I could bury myself with the pole of the ironwood oar, mindlessly turning in the dark toward the unknown faceless thing on the horizon of my wilderness.

It would take three Masrian months to achieve the western shores, four or five months of the Hessek calendar, some seventy-six days in all, discounting the time we had already used up getting through the southern islands.

Open sea. Featureless some days, on others alive with the life beneath, with leaping fish, striped as tigers or spotted like cats, with birds above going landward to the north. In the sky vast cloud lines, armies of cumulus on the march, at sunset scarlet galleys rowing there with green and silver sails, or the storm warning, that dark chimney with the head of an ax, a screaming vent of wind. We had three or four storms but weathered them. None was as bad as that hurricane I myself had mastered.

Events marked each day from another.

Some with rain, some with wind, some with the fall sun and the calm of the turquoise water-meadows beneath us.

Some with fights and brawls. One noon two men were hung to whine on the foremast, a punishment; brought to me to be healed with black lips and crying eyes after, so they would be fit for evening duties. Nights were marked with random sodomy, heard and glimpsed in the dark, not always willing.

Sometimes there was a sight of a distant fleck of land spotted at sunup; later, one or two minuscule islands where fresh water was gathered, and a big crab, the size of a small dog, might provide dinner for Lanko and his favorites, which had not been its intention. Incidents. A rower, tough as bull-hide, starting to weep because he had dreamed of a boy lover of his youth, a mixie boy sent to be a whore in Bar-Ibithni; a man drowned in a sudden storm, which had caught him obeying nature at the bow; another vanishing, having spit in the eye of Lanko's second. After forty days at sea, some of the biscuit went to mildew, and they shouted at me to say a spell and make it good. It was not my plan anymore to revive the dead; even this food-death, absurd though maybe the comparison was, sent me weak in the legs, images of Lellih swimming up in my brain, and that other necromancy. When I refused, there was bad feeling. I told them I would miss my own rations two days out of every four; I ate little in any event, but the spectacular gesture drew off their wrath. The magician was contrary. They let him alone.

Each day differing. Yet each day the same.

I came to know the oar, to understand its physical person as one would come physically to understand a woman one lies with forty, fifty nights. My iron-wood wife, with her blue blade combing the water and her slim hard body in my arms, across my breast and thighs. Six hours of copulation, then another six. A demanding lady. Yet she left my mind free. How many hours of how many days of how many months the shadows and the fires crossed my brain as I sat in that black ill-smelling hole, while the oar opened my palms on their own blood, no protective scars to armor me, and the faint pink light of dawn at the hatches faded into gray and into pink once more at the day's decline. The climate had cooled, the skies, when not obscured by cloud, had a purer, thinner look to them; by night the stars shone large and brilliant. On the winds that blew down from the west came an aroma of winter, like the old winter of the northlands, biting bitch gale, lash of sleet, marble weather with a thick snow down.

On the fifty-first day there was a fog. The ship sailed into it, and a chill silence settled on everything. The sea below was gray with a staring blue beneath; the masts scaled over with rime. Lanko's men cursed and put on their jackets and cloaks. The sun showed as a lemon-metal ring. Nobody looked for naked witch-girls riding on pillars of ice.

Through this soundless blanket we rode, the oars making a sucking, muffled noise. The southerners did not care for the fog, neither this particular penetrating clarity of cold. The winters of Seema, Tinsen, and Bar-Ibithni are not positively cold, cold simply by contrast with the blaze of summer; dust winds blow and rains descend; hail and thunder and black clouds. But snow never falls on the golden lands of the south and east, and only on two or three high mountains of the archipelago do they find it, and then they bring it down in clever sealed flasks to cool the drinks of lords, that, obviously, being its only purpose.

I at my oar, deep in waking, blind-eyed dreams (of Tathra, of Demizdor, of Eshkorek and the black krarl, of the Crimson Palace, of Malmiranet, of a silver mask), suddenly heard the cry around me, men with labor-sweating faces leaning from their stations.

"The magician brought us here, promised us gold. Let him lift the freezing fog."

I looked about at them and they fell quiet. Their faces were hostile. I was no longer lucky.

"Well," the man on the other side of me demanded. He was a felon from some southern town, a mix with no ears. "Well, can't you do it, *mighty* sorcerer?"

"The fog is a natural thing and will pass. You need not fear it."

The mix laughed, showing me off to the others about him, as we all, without a break, bent and straightened with the pull of the oars.

"I am thinking the Sri magician is also a natural thing, and will pass."

I thought, *I could lift the fog, shut up their din. Easy. Why not?* But that was how it had begun; why not walk on water, why not fly through the air, why not raise the dead: I thought, *I can suffer this. God knows it's little enough.*

They chaffered and bawled at me a while.

I paid no heed. How I had altered.

A couple of hours later we rowed out of the fog, straight on our western course.

By the seventieth day they had begun to fret for land. Rations were low, mainly due to the greed of Lanko and his second officer—I honor him with the title—and the lack of organization aboard. Thieves by trade, they stole also from each other. Hardly a night now without someone caught in the hold with his fingers in the stores. Lanko devised an extravagant execution; a man apprehended drinking koois was held head down in the koois jar and drowned. Lanko then offered the jar to any who wished to drink. Lanko's own private stores, kept separate from the crew, were never raided.

They had had one old brown map, pinned by a lady's brooch to the table in Lanko's cabin. This scrap indicated the west land, a vague melted shape with no bays or harborage marked in, more guesswork than charting. According to this map, however, the land should by now have revealed itself. Yet the sea, blue-green and cold, was featureless.

They were like men waking from opium. Their adventurous spirit had guttered out; they seemed to come to and discover themselves, like sleepwalkers, miles from home. What were they doing here in this chilly water-desert, with its scents of snow and emptiness?

Some ice went floating by, miles off to the south, like sails of rusty glass. Muffled in oddments of clothing, skins and pelts and furs subtracted from the cargoes of merchant ships, the sailors pointed to the ice with fear. They had told stories about it, but somehow they had not expected to see it. At least, in the stories, it had been warmer.

Suddenly an image of the sea demon of Old Hessek, Hessu, was set up in the prow. Apparently Seema acknowledged him, too. There he sat, astride his lion-fish, lightnings in hand. His copper was all green, and the enamel wings of the fish had lost their luster. They rubbed him over and began to offer to him libations of wine, the odd inedible sea-thing dragged up on the lines at the bulwarks. Gods indigenous to Seema were mentioned, too; even an occasional grudging scared dawn prayer was offered Masrimas.

On the seventy-fourth day, when I was due my abbreviated rations, none were forthcoming. I did not need to ask why. Their mutterings, the shifting near me in the night, once waking to behold a man at my pack, who scuttled away when he noted me stirring—these had tutored me. I went to where Lanko's second was engaged in doling out pieces of gray biscuit and strips of salted gristle. He winked at me, and smiled about.

"None for you."

I reached across and picked up the ewer of wine and water and drank from it, then selected a segment of the brick-dust biscuit, which I ate. He did not try to stop me, but when I was finished—it did not take long—he produced his knife and showed it to me.

"See this, lovely boy? Lanko says you are to starve, and so that's what I say, too. If you come up here again I'll make a pattern on you so nice you'll never tire of looking at it."

Conversation being pointless, I turned my back on him and started to walk away. He did not like that, and threw his knife at me. It would have hit me under the left shoulder and gone through into the heart; he meant business. Every defense of mine leaped. In the splinter of a second I was aware of the knife, next moment I experienced a surge of energy rising and thrusting from me, at my direction, yet so fast it seemed almost to move of its own instinctive volition. The knife sizzled and spun away as if it had hit an electric shield, and the clustered watching men groaned and backed off. They had anticipated magic and were not amazed, only disheartened. They had wanted to see their bad luck killed.

Their bad luck did not bother to glance around. I went below to take up my oar again, noticing the sinking tingle of the shield as it retreated into me. It seemed this Power, which mostly I would not use, was stronger now than it had ever been.

Word got about.

A man crawled up to me in the rowers' station, begging me to say if we should ever reach a shore.

I knew we were near to land, sensed it with certainty. In two days or less we would make it out from the opaline greeness of the ocean.

The next day a flock of gulls went over, white gulls with black-barred breasts and red eyes; some perched on the masts of the ship, screaming and beating with their wings, as the gulls in my fever had beat in the vitals of Lyo's corpse. The sailors grew more cheerful, drank wine. One brought me his frostbitten fingers to heal, like a gift.

Then on the seventy-sixth day out from the islands, the ninety-sixth day out from Semsam, they saw what they believed I had sent them to.

5

The land rose from a flat platinum sea. A broken paving of thin ice glittered on the ocean's surface, under a gray sun; it was bitter cold. The land itself was an irregular pinnacled whiteness. Nothing moved there. No inlet gave access to the interior. The cliffs were sheer.

It was plain to me we had come, after all, too far southward. Lanko's instruments were doubtless faulty, and the clever navigator, though he would boast he could thread a ship through the eye of a bone needle, had no genius for direction.

Winter arrives swift and absolute at the southwestern tip of this continent, and we had sailed to meet it.

Men gathered at the rail, their breath blue, and acid with fear. Lanko strode from his cabin wrapped in red Tinsenese bear furs, the second at his heels. They made straight for me.

"Where's the gold, Sri-boy? Eh?"

The second observed me narrowly. He said, "He doesn't feel the chill like a normal man. His dirty magic keeps him warm."

It was a fact that I had come above in just my tunic and breeches, having no other clothing to get into against the weather. Though, in truth, it seemed I could now control my body heat—involuntarily, almost without thinking, as I had deflected the murderous knife. I did not notice the cold more than as a mild discomfort, and now the second put his hand on my arm.

"He boils like the copper!" he shouted, and snatched his hand away again.

"Come," said Lanko, "he won't hurt you. Will you, eh, my darling? He's good for all sorts of tricks, but he's no stomach for a fight. Ah, I know, his sprite-familiar pushed off your knife. *I* say it was your pox-mucky bad aim."

The second remonstrated. Lanko shut him up with a look.

Lanko put his arm over my shoulders.

"Well, now, I was asking, where's the gold? Not up those snow cliffs."

"You've brought your ship too far south," I said to him.

Not that I imagined he could really be reasoned with. "Set *Gull* for the north, keeping this coast on the left hand. Seven or eight days of oars, even without a following wind, should see a milder climate."

"You swear this for a certainty?"

"I reckon it to be so, yes."

"And how would you know, my fine boy? The same way you knew I should get rich here?"

The second broke in, in a flinty scared voice trying to be menacing, "I'd say, Lanko, that he's a devil who led us here to get vengeance. Maybe some Masrian wizard set a curse on us and this is his instrument, eh, Lanko?" He laughed, attempting now to make a joke in case he became the joke instead. "A nasty devil-sending to lure us to our deaths."

Lanko said to me, "Our stores are nearly gone, magician. Care to magic some up for us, see us over these eight or nine or ten or a hundred days of sailing up the coast?"

"Lanko," I said gently, "need only open his private store to feed the whole ship."

He smiled. Even the sharp little eyes smiled. He liked me for enabling him to despise me.

"And you," he said, "won't ask for further rations till we reach landfall. Will you?"

"Since there is so little, I will agree to that."

"Ah," he said. He bowed, took my hand and kissed it. "Now get below, you bloody Sri bastard. Get to your oar."

There was no guilt in me at their fate. They were at best robbers, and most a deal worse than robbers, and besides, I never imagined they would perish here. I was not the angel of their deaths, contrary to popular opinion aboard, nor their bad luck. What I said to them I knew was exact—the winter was less severe northward. Somewhere a river opened into the land, part frozen at its mouth. The cliffs were the fortress walls; we had only to search out a door.

Still, I had grown aware of what was due.

I was sleeping in the below-deck at the end of my second shift, though at my bench, while some were yet rowing in response to Lanko's hurry to leave the cold behind.

I woke without alarm to find men binding me with thick cords. I lay quiet, and let them do what it reassured them to do. My use for the ship was ended. I sensed something before me, some test, some knowledge I must achieve, that waited for my solitude. I was not afraid, nor angry.

They finished with the rope, whispering. I opened my eyes

and let them discover I was alert. They stumbled back, cursing with fright. When I did not struggle, thinking me restrained, they became more courageous, and one kicked me in the side, another wrenched my head up by the beard and dropped it back so I should see diamonds flash in my brain. I did not defend myself with Power. I said, "Be careful," and they trampled over each other getting away from me.

Then someone shouted from the hatch, Lanko's second. The braver men hoisted me, and presently I was out on the deck under the dome of polished jet that passed for a winter sky.

The sea roared softly around us. The wind was getting up, and the great sails spread to it lovingly, and aft the windcatcher creaked as it was drawn over.

They were burning incense before the Hessu god; I could smell the cloy of it. I could not see Lanko about; maybe he was sleeping off his fat ration of wine, missing the resurrection of these ancient customs. For I was to be the scapegoat, the sacrifice. The sea did not care for me, was peeved at my presence; as a mark of her displeasure she had misled the ship, rotted the rations, hidden the green and gold of the land behind hard white armor. So they would give me to the sea to eat, drown their bad luck, and fortune would beam on them once more. They did not even keep my pack, nor anything in it, but threw the bundle with me; bad luck was bad luck.

I did not confuse the transparency of their belief with protestations, threats, or unnecessary miracles.

Not till they flung me, with a hilarious shout, over the rail did I cause my bonds to part like frayed wool. Not till my feet touched the water did I stay my fall, and catch my bundle neatly as I stood on the sea.

I had come to Charpon's vessel walking on the ocean. I went from Lanko's galley in the same way. It had a certain ludicrous aptness. After all, I could not swim. It was wiser to walk than submerge myself in icy fluid in order to reassure a band of brigands, and keep my inflamed conscience peaceful.

Again, no wonder. No pride, no disdain. It was useful; I was glad I had the art of it. They screamed behind me. How often, in my wake, those cries as the magician passed.

It is, after all, a very small thing to be a lord of men, men and their lords being what they are.

I came ashore.

That place. It might have been waiting for me. In moments of foolishness and delirium that followed, sometimes I supposed it had been. Philosophy had replaced human terror for me, for I must employ my brain in some fashion while I endured. Occasionally, I reckoned the winter ice-fields of the southwest lands were figments of my mind. Or of some vaster and more astonishing mind, that thought in continents, dreamed in worlds.

Certainly, I was better equipped than most to face the rigors of the glacial open, which would have killed the strongest man in a few days, or less. My body continued to meet the cold unflinchingly. My skin dried, but did not corrode or flake itself raw; my eyes stayed clear though the lids swelled; and after sunshine, for about an hour once the light went, a temporary snow-blindness would haunt my sight with white gauzes. Even ice burns vanished from my hands in moments. I was not comfortable, but I was not in pain or distress. It was an extraordinary magnitude of self-preservation, never before at my disposal. As a child learns intuitively to make sounds, to organize its limbs, to recognize symbols, so I had learned, just as intuitively and with no conscious effort, these abilities, and activated them spontaneously.

I had determined to walk northward, sunrise and set being my guides. I say "walk" and walk I mean. I did not spring into the air. To levitate—or fly, as Tuvek might have termed it in his tribal days—is as wearying at last as to rely on the natural means known as legs. I had even been able to scale the cliffs above the shore without recourse to sorcery.

All this was simple. I had my goal, I had my healing and self-protective flesh. I had my indifference to doubt.

I had no food.

Throughout my life, I had been able to make do with little. Here and there, due to circumstances, I had made do with very little indeed, going days without nourishment. This was now the case. It did not impair my strength to begin with; actually, I took small note of it. I was convinced I should shortly come on some sign of habitation, or, failing that, game of a wintry sort I could bring down, if I must, with a bolt of energy. I had also snow everywhere to melt in my mouth for drink.

Six days passed, then twelve. My last meal had been a bit of biscuit I had consumed on the ship. Oddly, I had felt no hunger since, appetite gradually stifled by the low rations before. Suddenly, on that twelfth day in the cold lands, hunger returned to me like a howling ravenous dog. The pack on my shoulders changed to lead. My guts knotted with vipers, a black light freckled my eyes; like a savage out of some prehistoric nightmare, I tumbled on all fours and crammed the fiery clots of snow between my lips, swallowing and gulping and scratching at the frozen ground with my knife for more. This makeshift dinner did me no good. I presently vomited, and lay afterward facedown in the broken snow, till the dim flaring of a magenta cloud told me the sun was going undercover for the night, and I had best stir myself to do likewise.

The land had been rising some while, and it was hard to make out toward what, for most days there was ice mist or thin snowfall to obscure the view. Once or twice I had seen loomings that might be mountains, or only further banks of fog. Once I had traversed a dismal wood, most of its branches lopped by the weight of the snow, and reduced to a forest of gray pylons with the sun running above and speared systematically on each. When it grew dark, I took shelter in a diversity of rocky outcroppings, in caves or on platforms, mainly to avoid the wild beasts I had hoped to encounter by day. I had even made a fire (for show I believe, as I did not absolutely need it then), using my Sri tinderbox rather than Power, and scraps of dry growths found fossilizing within the rock crevices.

On the evening of my hunger, I pulled myself up and staggered over a rise and into a narrow valley. It was exceptionally clear weather, and I could make out the darkening terrain. It seemed I had been already ascending the flanks of a mountain for a time, and had not been cognizant of the fact.

The valley was high, surrounded by uplands and peaks. A group of these seemed ominously to smoke, as if some dank furnace were going to their chimneys. The sun went, and the valley and the mountains were suspended in a silver twilight.

I found a cave. By the opening, a slender pillar of fluted glass stretched from the overhang above to a basin of greenish mirror below: a frozen waterfall. Sometimes, on its east side, it would warm at sunrise, the ice there would crack, and for a couple of hours smashed shards and water would splash down onto the unreceptive pool.

The cave was shallow and dark. In one angle lay a white bone. This bone became important to me, since it signified earlier occupancy, a link with the races of men and beasts.

I had seldom been alone for very long. Alone in my brain and my soul, yes, but who is not? But physically unaccompanied. Crowds, bystanders, women to lie on, men to fight, enemies to be outwitted. Here there was only silence. The sounds and shapes I heard and saw were products of the landscape. No bird flew, no wolf cried; when a shadow flicked like a wing on the mountainside, it was a cloud passing.

The first night, I scraped up dirt and woody growths to make a fire in the cave. I chipped off a piece of the static waterfall and sucked this tasteless burning confectionery. I had begun to feel the cold in a strange, dislocated way, and my hands trembled from hunger. I fell asleep, and dreamed, as in stories they say the hungry man does, of roasts and mounds of bread and the fancy concoctions of cities. In the dreams I gorged and stuffed myself, and was never filled. Near dawn I woke with a groan, shivering, and with the snakes redoubled in my vitals. It reminded me of the plague, and presently I lapsed off once more, and dreamed of that.

I came to about noon, too weak to move, except that shortly I had to crawl into a corner to relieve myself, and thereafter often. My bowels were loose as if I had been eating rotten fruit and my bladder scalded, and several times I threw up, though I was hollow as a scraped gourd.

The day smoked out into night.

I lay on my back, with my Sri cloak rolled under my head, staring out across the blackened ash of my fire at the huge gems of the stars, of which some were bluish and some faintly green or pink. My head was quite clear. I was not even afraid. I knew I would not die, though I had begun to wonder what would become of me. Maybe, by use of my Power, I could draw sustenance to me, an animal from its winter burrow, a man who would help me. Yet when I tried to concentrate my will, I was aware only of the blank emptiness of an untenanted world. Not a whisper of life. Eastward the coast ran. In front of me, northward, another inlet of the sea, but how far away, hundreds of miles, days of traveling. . . . My mind began to cloud as I thought of it, and the weakness flooded through me. My Power was at a low ebb, after all, smothered like a flame. My hands were wooden and white, frozen now. I should lose fingers if this kept up, and would they grow again?

I had sensed a test before me, a knowledge I must achieve. Was this, then, the test, the knowledge: starvation, the reduction of my physical self to a puking, helpless frostbitten baby on the floor of a cave with a bone in it?

Eventually the pain went away. I had no strength, but could just pull myself to the opening and look out upon the white valley, the pale thunder colors of the mountains, smoking earnestly as caldrons, volcanoes perhaps, trapped by an age of ice. I began to examine the bone, for I had stopped wondering now about my future or the actualities of my trouble, and had commenced reflection in the form of those huge symbols of infinity, or the invisible symbols of the nadir.

By constant touching of the bone and meditating upon it, I came to know its history, an insignificant and ghastly one, and from this reverie passed into others that dealt with earth and sky, surcease and eternity, men and gods. I grew very calm, a calm I had never known before and which left me afterward, for truly, I do not believe a man could retain this serenity, this strange content, and dwell in the places of humankind. It seemed to me I had fathomed the innermost secrets of myself and of everything, and maybe indeed I had; it was the fee I paid to life and living that when I began again to live I must forget them. In the tales of many lands, the prophet goes forth into the wilderness, the waste of sand or snow, or aloft on the barren black mountain, and when he returns to the people his eyes are great and luminous, his face is altered; he tells them he has seen God. I will suppose that God, if He is anywhere, is to be found in men, the nugget of gold buried inside the mud. I will suppose, too, that the wilderness washes off for a moment, or forever, the mud and the clay. Perhaps, then, the returning prophet should not say, "I have seen God"; but rather, "I have seen *myself.*"

If I were to total up the time I spent in the cave, I think, all in all, it would be near enough fifty days, but I shall never be sure, as I will never be sure of the mysteries I learned there, and forgot.

The end of the rite was very ordinary.

I appeared to wake from a pleasant dreamless sleep. The sun was rising and the pillar of waterfall splintering on its east side and the bright drops spinning down to the pool. I felt neither hunger nor thirst, nor sick nor weak. In fact, I felt quite normal, strong and able, my brain lucid and my body ready for any action I might require of it. This was patently absurd, and I knew it to be absurd. The visionary mood had sloughed off, I was entirely a man again, and reasoned like a man. Still, there seemed no harm in trying. I stood up, stretched, and my arteries responded with a singing healthy flow of circulation. I was not cold, and no part of me had suffered from lying invalid here, immobile in the ice. After a minute, so taken with it as I was, I ran out of the cave and across the valley and back.

I had never been more fit. I think I cavorted in the snow like a clown, till I remembered something and sobered up. I remembered the Old Race.

The Old Race did not eat. I could recall very easily Demizdor's mutterings, the Sarvra Lforn with its jeweled fruits, the nonexistent latrine . . . yes, neither eat, nor dispose of the by-products of eating—two tyrannies of nature dispensed with. Recall, too, my shame in that place of theirs because I had not been free of such essentials. And now. Now I was one with them. Blood told. My mother's blood, for she, the white phantom, was so palpably a descendant of that Lost People of winter hair and white metal eyes.

I returned slowly to the cave, sat down there, and opened my pack. I removed the counterfeit silver mask, which Lanko's scum, in their terror, had left me, and I looked in its blind gaze a long while.

Probably it had all come from her, all my Powers, from her race, their heredity in me. Perhaps there was nothing in me of my father after all, beyond a physical resemblance, a few memories of his retained in the cells of my brain, a brief flaring of his ambition, which I had at the last foregone. Apart from that, my abilities seemed of her alone. Even that time upon the fortress-rock near Eshkorek, when I had thought his shade or his will was guiding me, when I had grasped an alien language as if it were my own, even then, maybe, it had simply been my legacy of Power passed down from her, breaking in me because it was the season for it, because I had a need of it.

It seemed the memory of my father Vazkor was leaving me.

Three days later, breathing deep of the cold air, and needing no other substance to sustain me, I was making north across the ridges of the caldron mountains. Five days later, striding down their backs, the weather mellowed somewhat, and no snow fell.

I came to a river, frozen save at its center, where there was a gap narrow enough for a strong man to leap. Seven days beyond the river, I came on a forest of pines and next of black oaks, green with ivy. From a high terrace, I saw a loop of the sea below and the land curving off about it to west and north. I went that way and discovered a village down on the shore, before evening.

Blue seals were bathing about half a mile out in the sunset water, and men—they looked in the distance much as men do everywhere—sat mending nets by a great fire, and I could smell the frying fish, which no longer stirred my belly, and see the yellow lamps lighting.

I did not go there, having no necessity, also, I believe, out of the way of mixing gregariously.

I was journeying, because it must be, toward that habitation I had sensed to be Uastis' own. I wanted questions answered, and maybe still I wanted her death. Yet love of life is a curious thing, and comes like wine fumes in the heart and head at certain seasons.

Gazing down at that village on the shore—the playing seals, the western flash of the low sun—I needed no more than simply to exist, in order that I should be thankful for my birth.

Part II

White Mountain

I

I continued northward, parallel to the sea on my right hand. The quality of the winter, and of the terrain, had changed. Inland, forests folded away into round-topped hills; I saw a distant town with walls and towers, and birds flying overhead. I saw pasturage, and even the stacked steps of vineyards, everything under the snow now, in stasis before spring should powder the earth with other colors. A couple of times I found myself on a road, and passed men there. Wagons with roofs of painted hide drawn by shaggy horses, a fellow in an open chariot, driving wildly, as if he had some fury to get rid of, cursing me from his way. The chariot had a noble clumsiness, big-wheeled and breast-high in front, and clanking with plaques of bronze. The man had a head of peppery blond hair, lopped at the nape of his neck. He looked for all the world to me like a Moi tribesman got up in Eshkorek city clothes, though the fashion was somewhat different, the voluminous cloak of scarlet wool looped and pleated about him, caught back over the right arm on a shoulder boss, to show the striped gray fur that lined it. A day or so after this encounter, a woman went by in a litter draped with white bearskin, and she herself muffled up in other white furs. She, too, was fair haired, though more darkly fair than a Moi. She made her bearers and the three outriders stop and one ride after me to take me back to her. She wanted to know who I was, where I was going, if she might help me in any way. It appeared that wherever I went I should find women much the same.

I said I was a stranger. She said she could see as much. The language we used reminded me, in an odd way, too, of the city tongue of Eshkorek, though it was, in its essentials, different. She told me she was the daughter of a lord across the next hill; the road had turned inland about a mile back toward a pink-towered mansion, no doubt his. She entreated me to break my journey there. When I courteously refused her, she laughed. Since I had not given my name, she began playfully to call me "Zervarn," which in this tongue meant something like "Dark Acquaintance." From that I gathered black hair to be uncommon.

Finally, she put her white-gloved fingers on my arm and said, "Let me guess. You're going over the river to Kainium, to ask for the goddess. Ah!" she added, triumphant. "He blanches! So. I am right."

Whether I lost my color, I hardly know; I think I must have done. Expecting it all this while, the shock of finding it jolted me.

"Kainium," I said. "Which goddess is goddess there?"

She smiled, taking on her, strangely, a kind of occult air by proxy.

"I don't know for sure, Zervarn my darling. They call her Karrakaz."

My heart hit my ribs. I said, "That might be she I seek."

"Go then, chase your goddess. It is some two hundred miles away, and then you must cross the river. Better to remain with me."

I told her I should never forget her kindness in directing me. She kissed me, and we parted.

Two hundred miles, a river, a name: Kainium. I foresaw a little farther than that: a breadth of sea, and from the sea, lifting, a shoulder of alabaster. A white mountain rising from the ocean, face to face with a scatter of a city on the shore.

I had bad dreams that night, lying in a ruinous watchtower above the coast where the steel-blue sea ran in and out among the ice floes. Malmiranet was carried dead to her death box, and the outer air gushed in to waken me in mine; Demizdor was swinging from a silken rope, her neck broken like a bird's; Tathra lay between my hands with her unblinking eyes. . . . It all returned to me, and more.

Then, near dawn, this: Noon on a cold slope, white snow down, white sky above, at back the smoke-stained wall of a city. Between the slender penciled shapes of winter trees, a woman and two men riding. Light lost in black garments, bright as arrows on metallic masks. The men wore the Phoenix of the cities, though not like the designs that I had seen in Eshkorek, cast in silver. The woman wore the face of a cat, cast from warm yellow gold, with green gems about the eyes, emeralds dangling from the pointed ears, and golden plaits behind, mingling with her white hair.

They came into a miserable scramble of huts. It was a steading of the Dark People, Long-Eye's multitudinous slave folk. I saw the gray-olive wooden faces, the rank blue-black weeds of hair. A crone came up; the woman dismounted from her horse and went away with her into a hovel.

So much I had seen from a distance. Now something drew me close, into the door. I saw women's things: blood, pain, vileness, through the smoke. The crone bent to her task like a black toad. What she did sickened me, yet I could not look away.

Uastis the goddess groaned only once. She was brave as she tried to get rid of me in the healer's hut.

The day washed out in night, the night into a predawn gray.

The white-haired woman stirred. She whispered, "Is it finished?" Her voice was very young (she had been a girl then, hard to remember it), very young and tired, worn out with hurting.

The black toad crouched there and said, "No." Uastis said, "What now, then?" She braced herself for what would be next, the way a man will when he's told the probe must go deeper yet to free the spear-head from his flesh.

The toad woman said, "Nothing now. A loving child. He will not be parted from you." And Uastis sighed, only that.

Yet her desperate denial, locked up in her brain, rent me, burned me. I withered in it. She would have cut her womb from her with a knife if she could have cut me from her with it.

I woke in a sweat, and some of the salt in my eyes was more than sweat or the sea, for the habit of tears, once learned, is facile. I thought, *Well, but I knew this all along, that she hated me. Though I did not know she set bone instruments to dig me out, yet I might have reasoned it. Well, but I live, I live, and she's near and shall answer.*

I felt a depression like a black cloak smothering me.

I got up, and started out on the two-hundred-mile walk to the river, and Kainium.

It was nearer to the spring in that direction, still winter but more yielding.

I passed through several towns, something in them of that northeastern style I recollected from the ruins of my warrior youth. White arcades, tall towers that no longer looked so tall to me, roofs of colored tile. Westward and inland there was a form of government, some prince or other sitting on his backside ordering this or that. Here, along the coast, was a shore province, far-flung and considered feral. Such gems of information I picked up from gossip as I went through. I was more interested in other news.

I heard a deal of her, of Karrakaz the goddess. The closer I got to the river estuary, the more I heard. Kainium was a rough, haphazard area, less lawful than this provincial coast. It was where one went to get ensorceled. If one came back, one came back with goat's ears, or in the form of a warm-water seal. For the home of the goddess, that was a mountain of crystal out in the ocean. Sometimes there would be a road on the water that one could cross over by, sometimes the sea would cover it, and sweep the unlucky into the depths. If one were sick, one might risk the journey. Men in the last months of terminal disease had reputedly returned whole and well—unless they had got goat's ears, or been changed into a seal, presumably.

Within ten miles of the estuary the towns had given way to villages. Here they spoke a different dialect, and had a new name for Kainium that meant "The Lost Children." That took some fathoming, and they had not bothered to fathom it. An old fisherman declared to me that it meant babies were sacrificed, to appease the goddess in the sea. I thought to myself, *Only one, and he is here.*

The land rises above the estuary. An ancient track, once paved, now broken and all over snow and weeds, led me to the brow of the rise. Winter woods ran down to the river, which was soft red with evening light, the sun setting across the curve of the water into the farther curving of the shadowy shore. The estuary was about three miles across, broadening into a sea like a plate of rosy lead beyond. One ultimate small village crouched below, in the lee of the wood.

I had not meant to enter the village; I had no need of it, no need of food or particular shelter, and I had got used to roughing it. It was what I had been bred to, indeed, in my tribal days. But a man came by, driving six curly tabby goats, assumed I was making for the village, and volubly bore me along with him. It turned out there was a makeshift inn there, and the goathered was the innkeeper's brother.

2

The inn was a poor place, catering to liquor-liking peasants, and the odd ship that swung this way into the estuary, making for the towns upriver. The walls were checkered with red and brown squares, and beans and shallots hung from the rafters, and fish above the hearth to smoke, and dogs ran about the floor in the industrious, urgent way of dogs.

I had no money, and ended by bartering my Sri cloak, muddy but serviceable, for bread and beer I did not require and subsequently ignored, and a rickety bed upstairs.

In such a spot, a strange face will always cause a stir. To this flaxen people, my coloring alone was of interest. Darker men apparently came from the inland regions. Their prince had raven's feathers like mine, they said. I told them I hailed from some town I had heard of farther south, of which they knew nothing. With their altered speech, even my new adopted name passed unchallenged. It was the cognomen the girl had gifted me with from her litter. "Dark Acquaintance," Zervarn. The idea of entering the witch's stronghold garbed in my father's name had begun to unnerve me. I had no right to steal that after all she had stolen from him, and maybe I had no right to anything of his. I would go to her a stranger.

They were friendly people in the village, not thick-witted as such outlanders often are, but swift and curious. They had concluded I was going over the river, and said not a word about it, except for a man who offered to row me to the shallow water in his fishing boat, but no farther. Could I wade the rest? I thanked him, said I could, and asked him what he feared.

"What you do not, clearly," he said, "or you wouldn't be going there."

"Savage territory," I said. "A city of lost children; an island in the sea with a magic road out to it. A witch-goddess."

"Lost children," he said. "Yes."

A quiet had come on them. The serving girl who all evening had been edging my uneaten food toward me, I then edging it away, said, "One from here, one time. I was three.

My mother's sister's little boy. He had white hair. My mother's sister, she says, 'The lady has marked him.' She put him in his wicker cot and went over the river, and walked to Kainium, and left him there. She had ten children in the house, eight of them sons; it was no loss."

"Do you mean," I said, "that the goddess claims albino babies as her own?"

"This wench has no business to chatter," said the man with the boat.

"It does no harm," said the girl. "Who'll hear me?"

The inn door opened behind her, letting in a draft of vicious night air. What came out of the night turned me colder.

He was almost my height, built like a warrior, too, though fine made as any silver statue of Bar-Ibithni. He stepped into the light of the oil-wick lamps, and his young face was clean-shaven, arrogant, and handsome; he looked like some prince of Eshkorek. All but the ice-white skin, and hair that grew to below his shoulders that was like a shining cloth of rare white silk, the eyes that were no color but the color of polished diamonds.

The serving girl screamed at this too-perfect answer on her cue.

He, turning elegant as a panther, said quietly to her, "Don't be afraid. I shall harm none of you."

Then he looked right at me.

Something moved in the back of those uncanny eyes. It was like staring through crystal at white fire; I could find no floor to his glance, and no veil or screen across it either. Eyes to deflect searchers, sorcerer's eyes.

He had spoken the village dialect perfectly, like a native, which I part supposed him. Now he flung abruptly at me, in an accent no less perfect, "Sla, et di."

It was the tongue the cities had used, which I had spoken in Eshkorek, but somehow older, in an original form. He had said, roughly, "As I deduced, you're here." It took me a moment to understand him, for I was dumbfounded, like the rest of the room, by the unpleasant suitability of his arrival.

"Et so," I said eventually. ("I am here.")

The villagers, sniffing danger from him like a scent, relapsed abruptly into a flawless display of normality. The fisherman at my side nodded to me and went off. At adjoining tables, dice commenced rolling and talk started up. Only the serving girl ran among the pots and pans to hide.

The white man came and sat facing me. He was well dressed; his shirt looked like velvet. His clothes were all white.

"Well," he said, in the familiar yet unfamiliar tongue, "you speak languages cleverly. But you haven't eaten the supper these worthy people have left you." I said nothing, watching him. "Come," he said. "The beer is good, they tell me."

"If it's so good, my friend," I said, "you drink it. You've my leave."

His face was almost too beautiful, it could have been a woman's; yet not really, there was overmuch steel in it for that. There was no scar, no blemish on his albino hide.

"I am past beer and bread," he told me. "I live on god-food. The air."

Something caught the light, above and between his white eyes. A little green triangle, some jewel fantastically inserted just under the thin topmost skin; naturally, this bizarre operation had left no mark on his healing flesh.

"Did she birth you?" I said slowly. My hands would have begun to shake if I had let them, thinking I might be opposite my half-brother, one son she had kept by her.

"She?" he said laconically. "Who is *she*?"

"Karrakaz."

"No," he said. "She is my Javhetrix. I am merely the captain of her guard. I am named Mazlek, for another who once guarded her to the extinction of his life. As I should do."

"But you can't die," I said. "Can you, Mazlek, captain of the Bitch's Guard?"

His eyes grew hot, white hot, then he smiled. He was a spoiled brat, but a strong spoiled brat, a brat with Power.

"Don't insult her. If it upsets you to think me immortal, I can assure you I'm not. Not quite. Not as she is. She breeds fine herds, but we haven't her blood. Only one man has that."

"She sent you, then," I said. "She anticipated me by sorcery, and let out the dog."

"What do you want," he said, "to fight me?"

He was younger than I was, maybe three or four years younger. When I had been at the age at which he had learned to work miracles, I had been thrashing around in Ettook's battles, rutting and roaring among the tents. But then, this Mazlek had had expert guidance.

"I don't want to fight you," I said. "I mean to go upstairs and sleep. What will you do about that?"

He said, "Go upstairs and sleep, and see."

When I turned my back on him, I wondered if he would move, but he did not. He was intending to play the game my way. About the inn, they studiously ignored our foreign conversation and our parting.

I went up, through the leather curtain that served as a door, into a dark little room with an oil-wick lamp on the broad windowsill, a wooden slab with rugs (the bed), and a chamberpot in a corner. The chamberpot amused me. I set it just where he would stumble over it on coming in. Then I lay down, and trusting to my senses, which had become so magical, I sank asleep.

I should have known better. He crept in like the white cat he was. He had a knife lifted over my heart before I came awake, bursting up through an ocean of blackness and fire. The Power in me reacted quicker than I. I was barely sensible, but the blow shot from me in a pale explosion, sending the knife upward with such force that it stuck in the rafter, knocking my assailant flying till he hit the wall.

I got off the bed and went and stood over him. At the risk of reminding myself of Lellih, I said, "If you have Power, why use a knife?"

"I thought that to use Power would wake you," he said.

It was not the truth. I realized he was not quite as much the Mage as he would have had me imagine.

He picked himself up, and looked me in the face and said calmly enough, "No, I'm no match for you. Kill me if you like. I've failed her."

"She sent you to execute me, then?"

"No. She didn't know I was coming here. She will be angry. Her anger could be terrible, but you can't fear what you love, can you, Zervarn?"

He must have got my name from below. He did not question it either, though, with his grasp of tongues, he would surely notice it was mask rather than name.

"You love her."

"Not in the way you mean," he said. He laughed amiably. "Not *that* way."

I recalled Peyuan, the black chief, the man who had been with her by that other sea, how he had said he had not desired her, only loved her. *This is how she binds them, then,* I thought, *not by the phallus, which you can forget when the act is done, but soul and mind.*

"You'll have guessed," I said, "that I mean to see her."

"Yes. She guesses it, too."

"How many more attempts will you fruitlessly make on my life?"

He shrugged. Now I was recalling Sorem. Sorem had had Power, but not sufficient; it had been simple to forget he was part magician. Still, if I needed proof that Power might be there in all men, and not limited to gods, he had been that proof. She knew, my mother. As her Mazlek said, she bred fine herds.

The light caught him as he turned. It looked unreal, all that whiteness.

"I'll swear truce," he said. "Will my lord Zervarn?"

"Very well," I said. "But you'd better return to your Javhetrix; tell her how near I am."

"She is aware of that. I think I should guide you to her."

"You're a fool," I said, "If you suppose you can hinder me."

He went to the doorway and bowed to me.

"Tomorrow," he said. "Sunup on the bank below. Gentle dreams, Zervarn."

Long before the village was rousing, or perhaps while the village kept purposely dormant, I met him on the pebbled, snow-mottled strand of the estuary. Eastward, out over the sea, a lavender sheen promised the dawn. Everything else was wrapped in a clear deep blue, even the snow, even the white hair of what strolled to meet me. He had been skimming flat stones, making them bounce on the water, remembering he was seventeen; now he was solemn, proud, indicating the scatter of fishing boats and the broad river.

"No boat is needed, is it, Zervarn?"

"I would prefer to travel in a boat. Where's the craft you came in?"

"*I?*" He raised his brows.

Now he reminded me of Orek and Zrenn, both Demizdor's kin rolled in one. Was this his major talent, to call up the characters of one's past? He said even that she had named him for some guard who had died for her.

But now he was done with debating. He walked down the strand and onto the ice that fringed the river's margin.Then onto the water of the river.

He was nonchalant, the bastard. Sauntering, damn him.

Presently he turned and faced me, his feet balanced on the mild tidal shift of the estuary.

"This is how I crossed last night," he said reproachfully. "Don't try to pretend you can't do the same."

"She trained you well," I said.

"When we were just weaned we went to her," he called back. "To the Frightful Unknown, the Terror of Kainium." He sprang around, agile as a snake, and began to run over the river away from me.

I glanced about like a fool, looking for my friend of yesterday with the fishing boat, but of course he had kept out of the way. The inn had been very merry last night, and very silent later. I had lain awake listening to it.

He was lengthening the gap between us. I had no choice, unless I stole a boat. It seemed pedantic, suddenly, my reserve.

I, too, stepped out onto the river, and went after him.

I had gone half a mile before he looked back and took note of me. He stopped once more then, balancing, and I saw him laughing; either that, or he was doubled in pain. Seventeen, and a magician. Well, he had something to make him cheerful, I supposed.

That should have been me, out there on the hyacinth water. Able to laugh, able to remain a boy for the duration of my boyhood, to become a man without going through the pit of hell to get there. That should have been me.

He began to flag after a couple of miles. I suspect he must have used a boat part of the way before; he had not quite the psychic strength, the full rein of Power to keep him up. Sweat broke on his fine pale forehead; his booted feet began to slop under the water. The far shore, dim with a fine morning mist, was coming closer, not quite close enough. I had drawn level with him. He stumbled and caught hold of my shoulder.

"Oh, Zervarn. I shan't make it. Will you let me drown? There's a girl from White Mountain, one of my Jahvetrix's people; she'll weep if I die. And, Zervarn, I *shall* die, believe it."

I looked at him. His arrogance and fierce pride were mainly his youth. His laughter was his youth, too, and even now, he was half laughing, ashamed of himself. I perceived he had been strutting to impress me. I did not hate him, had no cause. So, she had favored him. It was not his fault she bound him with love. Even my father had been prey to love of her.

Which was a curious thought. Somehow I had never imagined love between them, at least, no love on my father's side for a witch he had married as adjunct to his kingdom.

"Keep your hand on my shoulder. It will prevent your sinking."

"I know it." We walked on, he with his boots clear of the water now. After a while, he said, "It's most of a day's journey to Kainium."

The sun was rising, shining white on the blue estuary, blue on the black and misty land. We came ashore. A dog was barking, back over the river, sharp as flints in the frosty air. It was a very rational noise. I thought, *I am leaving the rational world of men behind me.* Just then I was aware of Mazlek attempting to read my thought. I had blocked his questing instinctively; now I turned and looked at him. I was all of twenty-one, but he made me feel like seventy.

"Are they every one of them like you, this bred herd of the goddess?"

"Every one," he said. "But you will master us. You're better."

3

We did not overly converse on the journey. It was rough, snowy, uphill going, and thickly wooded farther on. At noon we paused by a frozen stream. He lay on his belly across the ice, staring down, saying to me he could see blue fish swimming far beneath. Another time he reached his hand into a tree and drew out a small sleeping rodent, admired it, and put it back without disturbing its slumbers.

We had gone inland somewhat from the coast; in the afternoon we angled back. The day was clear, and coming from the woodshore I saw the gray sweep of ocean on my right hand stretching into a far green horizon. Between the shore and the horizon, about a mile out and some way ahead of us to the north, a pointing ghostly shape rose up from the water.

"White Mountain?" I asked him.

"White Mountain," he said. "It looks a chilly rock, but in spring and summer the island's like a mosaic for colors. You'll see."

I doubted that, but then I had not thought ahead. Where should I be in the spring and summer, the deed accomplished, the crisis passed?

An hour later the mountain in the sea looked no nearer, but I had begun to make out something below, in a fold of the coastline.

Kainium.

Not a live city, but a dead one. Old as the shore itself it seemed, maybe older in some incomprehensible way. I could hardly tell it from the snow save that, like the bones and teeth of any dead thing, it was slightly yellower. White mantled cypresses led down a broad paved road toward it, with a great arch on pillars fifty feet high straddling the thoroughfare about a mile off.

I had seen and dreamed enough to know the place for a metropolis of the Old Race. I would not even have needed that tutoring to smell it for something ancient and curious. It had a secretive brooding aspect under the snow. I wondered how much wickedness and magic had gone on there to leave this feel after so many centuries. And I wondered if she had deliberately selected this spot, and if she reveled in its proximity.

We went down the road, Mazlek and I, under the blue shadow of the pillared arch. The sea clawed at the icy beaches with a tearing, desolate noise, but no gulls cried, and there was no clamor of men or beasts.

Then I saw smoke mundanely rising to the left of the road, from a stand of trees, and next a building came in sight with a chimney-vent above.

"A hospice," Mazlek said, "prepared to receive all who wish shelter. Mainly, the backlands folk who seek Karrakaz are afraid to enter a city of the Lost Race, and shun the hostel. But you naturally, lord, will welcome the luxuries of civilization."

"Will I?"

He smiled.

"No trick, lord. Did you not save my life on the river?"

To say I did not trust him would be overcourteous, yet I was pained to admit I was glad of a diversion from my path. I should meet her before another sunrise, which was all at once too soon. An hour with hot water, a razor, and some thought would not be amiss. I had been bathing in fistfuls of snow and the smashed glass of pools, and for my beard and hair I looked like a wild man escaped from some carnival.

Truly, I would rather not go to her like this. Not out of vanity—it was that she had left me to struggle up a savage, and I would not be one for her. I meant her to see, despite the odds, that the wolf's cub reared among hogs was yet a wolf, and fit to match her.

There were two flaxen attendants in the hostel, men who did not, presumably, fear the ruin or the witch. One shaved me and trimmed my hair as I lay soaking in a green sunken pit brimmed with the scalding water from the hypocaust. I asked him what he did there. He said his village lay over the hills to the west, that he had been a leper, but through the goddess of the mountain he had been cured. Then his service here was in payment for the cure? Not so. He liked the locality, the mystical aura of Power hereabouts stimulated him—mage-craft he called it. He was inclined to chatter, so I questioned him. I asked him what his goddess was like. It turned out no one had seen her, saving, of course, her own people, those she elected to take because they were white, as she was. She never left the island, and none ventured there without her express invitation. Those who met her, met her veiled, almost invisible, in some dim sanctuary. Generally they did not need to dare such a thing, for her selected companions (the attendant called them specifically *Lectorra*, "Chosen") could heal in her name, even the very sick.

Yes, he said, the Lectorra came now and again to Kainium and the villages. You could not miss them. Like my guide Mazlek, they were notable for their albino looks, their pride, their enormous attraction. Young men and girls beautiful enough for gods. Which, he said, they could safely be accepted as. Yes, yes, he had seen them walk on water, fly, change base metal to gold, vanish into air, take on the form of beasts, call up rain in a dry season, calm storms so the boats farther up the coast could fish the ocean. Also they had strange teachings, for example: that the earth was round instead of flat, a ball floating in a void; the sun a similar ball, all fires, about which the earth circled warily. And the moon ran about the earth like a round white mouse, pulling the tides with it.

The attendant, like Long-Eye, was not afraid of the everyday actuality of his gods.

Presently his fellow brought me a suit of clothing, such being kept here apparently for the use of ragged travelers. (I had been many things in my time, now I was a ragged traveler.) However, the new clothes were a good woolen weave dyed dark blue, the calf-length tunic with a border of red. It would not humble me to wear them.

Emerging from the bath chamber, I did not search for Mazlek. He would have slunk off as soon as I gave him the chance, and by now would have taken boat, or boot, or that pebbled sea pathway I had heard mentioned, and got to the mountain. She would want to be informed of every detail: my appearance, my mood, my capabilities. However, it was no huge matter, for she had seemed to know plenty in any event.

The attendants brought me lastly my bandit knife, having cleaned and polished it to the high gloss only a non-fighting man would coax from a blade. The irony of this symbol amused me somewhat. That knife, returned so freely. She did not fear me at all, it appeared. Or else, she would have me suppose she did not.

Thus, I walked down the broad ancient road into the cadaver of Kainium. My reflections were dour. I believed myself stoical. I might anticipate every manner of happening now, yet I was equipped to meet it. Before the sun sank, I should probably have met her, too. Whatever fate would spring from it would be fulfilled. A lifetime of question and doubt answered. The book closed.

The streets were straight as good spears. My footsteps echoed off walls, along colonnades, as if another strode near. Bits of crystal sparkled in windows. It did not have exactly a bad feel after all, the city. Just age, death, the resentful cold lament of something forever finished.

I walked north. The big mountain-island showed between the shapes of the ruin, still ghostlike over the mirror of the water.

The sun was westering already, painting streaks of thin red color on the whiteness of the avenues, washing the features from distant roofs and platforms, and hiding their decay. In silhouette I could have sworn those heights were habitable, save there were no lamps. Then lights came from another quarter, northward and below, on the shore. A greenish fever of torches between the city and the sea.

I halted and watched these lights a moment. It would require no more than a third of an hour to reach them; by then the sunset would be crushing out the day. But they looked like an ominous greeting, a beacon to summon me, torches to light me to the feast.

Just then something brushed my brain, soft as a finger brushing the neck. There, in the portico of a tumbled mansion, poised and quiet as if it were evening in some market town and she stepped out to view the traffic from her porch, was a girl in a green mantle. Her hair was white, all looped and curled like a court woman's, and on her shoulder sat a white kitten, stony still. It was an apparition to make any hesitate, and as I took in her face, I beheld what I can only describe as an almost unnatural loveliness, perfect enough that I never reckoned to see better. Truly, as my barber had declared, one could not miss the Lectorra of the goddess.

She had not tried to probe my mind. The signal had been communication merely, and she did not aim at more. She spoke.

"You are Zervarn," she said. It appeared that Mazlek had dallied to spread news here, too. (The cat yawned. Its eyes were nearly as pink as its narrow tongue. The girl's eyes were white; she had the same green gem in her forehead as Mazlek had had. No doubt it was some unnecessary extra mark of their order, which they all affected; Lectorra uniform.) "Welcome to Kainium, Zervarn."

"My thanks for your welcome."

"My thanks for your thanks," she said. She pointed past me, downward to the beaches. "That is the way to what you seek."

"What do I seek?"

"Karrakaz, or so you have frequently been saying."

"So I have. And are you to guide me now?"

"You need no guide. Follow this straight street to the terrace of steps, and descend. An old garden leads toward the beach. The torches burn at the end of the garden, where the shore confronts the mountain in the sea."

She made no move to come closer, so I turned and obeyed her directions. It had an atmosphere of theater, all this, which I assumed deliberate and infantile on the part of the one who had planned it. Yet it fitted excellently the aura of the city and the day's ending.

There were some two-hundred-odd steps twisting down between the broken columns; at one point a dry fountain on a marble plinth depicted a girl wrapped with an enormous serpent, a pornographic, beautiful thing to rouse the blood, despite the ice frozen cold on their ardor.

The garden spilled from the steps and folded away toward the beach and the sea, audible but no longer visible, for the eastern vistas were closed now with tall trees. The sky was reddening, reddening the snow. To the southeast several towers rose at intervals from the pines and cedars of the garden. I had not glimpsed them before, but I soon stopped to regard them better, for they had that unmistakable seal of unreality I had come on in the Sarvra Lforn of Eshkorek. The two nearest towers thrust only their summits from the trees. One was shaped like the head of a horse, basalt black with a glittering eye like green sugar; to the east of it, the other was the mask of a lion with a mane of gilded brazen spokes. Farther south statically bloomed the cup of a giant orchard, whose gold-tassled stamens, rising from the layered cervix, I gauged as the turrets of four inner steeples. Where there was a break in the pines, one complete tower revealed itself as a rearing snake with a lizard's head, the scintillant eye a window, on its throat a collar that must surely be a balcony. From the green glow of it, it might be jade, vast plaques of jade set on in scales. The low sun caught the blink of gold and jewels on all of them, these monstrous toys.

As I stared, out of the tree shadows before me came strolling two white people, boy and girl. They were about fifteen, adolescent, yet not like their age. The boy said to the girl, "This must be the man Zervarn."

The girl laughed and said, "How he gazes! We are not ghosts, Zervarn." But in their whiteness, the sun blushing on them, making them look part transparent, the dark around, the fantastic carved gem-towers beyond, they were stranger than any ghost I had ever trusted did not exist. "He is examining the tombs," the girl said, "the tombs of the Lost Race."

"Should you like to enter one?" the boy asked. "We will show you."

Tombs—I had believed the Old Race did not die. Yet the dead city itself belied that. Something could kill them, certainly, and white bones lay for sure in the lizard towers and orchid towers, amid the jewels burning, and probably with treasure heaped on the floor. A prosaic piece of reasoning occurred to me, the yarns of Jári and Lanko's kind of the gold that grew on trees. No doubt that was some memory of this very tomb garden, and others like it, maybe. But I wondered how many pirates had dared pilfer from the Lost People of Kainium.

"Tombs are for the dead," I said to the surreal children in front of me. "See, I am alive."

"The Lost did not die as men die," the boy said. "Each lived for centuries. And then, after more centuries of sleep, sometimes they would wake, rise from their tombs, and return."

"She told you that," I said, "Karrakaz. Fount of wisdom."

I thought, as I had thought with every one of these beings I met, *Is this her seed, half kin to me, a son or daughter got from her lying with some albino buck, some child she kept?*

Suddenly, hand in hand, like a cabalistic painting on the wall of a magician's house, the two of them rose upward in the air and drifted away, grinning back at me, among the trees.

Hot and cold chased over my spine. Though I could perform the selfsame act, now I witnessed it for what it was: The mirror of my Power held up for me to see.

I told myself I had begun to understand her plan now, if plan it was.

I found a glimmering brown skull in the snow. I could not tell if it was mortal or god, and there seemed a sobering moral in that. I took it up and snow fell from the eye sockets. I set it back beneath a white-clad cypress, and its black glare watched me away.

This dreamlike wonder-working, the extra-normal surroundings, were meant to rob me of any human values, and any human rage or vengeance I should have left.

The sun sank into the depths of Kainium as I emerged on the beach a few minutes after, a beach broad and white with ice between the city and the water. Beyond the ice, silver mud flats ran out into the surf, and the sea was like cold silk flung shining there toward the advancing eastern night. And against that night, garishly lighted by the last sun ray, the huge mountain in the ocean, directly opposite this shore and finally immediate, was a shock of cinnabar.

About forty yards off the torches burned, still greenish in the dusk, and a crowd was moving there on the light, men and beasts, and farther on a bonfire splashing up at the dark, showing the humps of wagons, carts, and the other traveling impedimenta of humanity.

What this was I did not know. Yet I had only to pause, to use my wits, to guess.

Lectorra, the goddess's chosen, roamed the mainland, and a crowd of people gathered here facing the mountain-island itself. It was to be a time of healing, when these uncanny adoptive progeny of Karrakaz laid their restorative hands on mortals. *She* did not come. She never left her island, I had been told, but her Lectorra could work her magic, having been taught by her, and I had seen as much.

The torches were not a beacon for me, after all, except in as much as they should demonstrate to me that my Powers were far from unique in Kainium. Healer, magician, in all things the tribe of the goddess were there before me.

I went slowly to the light, slowly out of a kind of bitter savoring of events, these last drafts of wine to be tasted.

Men, their women and offspring, packed close together about the fire and the resin brands, singing, which I heard over the breakers as I came to them along the beach, some parochial ballad of their villages. All this to keep the night at bay, the phantom city from exercising its spell, while they waited for gods to arrive.

On the outskirts of the group, a boy feeding a shaggy horse before a wagon caught my footfall and froze, nervously eyeing me. But I was a black-haired man, not white. His alarm changed to simple curiosity. I must be an Inlander and obviously sick, or I would not be here where invalids came seeking aid: nothing to fear.

I could see sick ones now, lying about on litters, some of them unable to move, a few alert with desperate attention. A small stir as I passed through. A woman made room for me on a rug spread near the fire. A man, unspeaking as she, offered me a mug of hot beer they had been mulling to warm themselves. This mute kindness touched me, the compassion of human beings pulled together in harmony by the peculiarity of their mission.

I had not decided whether to play my part and remain to watch with them, or to make on, when their singing broke off, and two or three pointed along the shore, southward.

The Lectorra had appeared abruptly, apparitions evolving from the crimson dusk like slender twinkling white lights. They were not walking but gliding this way, their feet some inches off the ground. It would have been nicer, if they had flown through the air; this was the calculated unostentatious ostentation of a cruel mocking and insensitive youth. Decidedly, Gyest had had the right of it. Sympathy is the sister of fear. These creatures had nothing left to fear, and fear in others was a game to sport with.

The human crowd made no sound. Somewhere a single dog whimpered, but fell quiet of its own accord.

The Lectorra alighted a couple of yards from us, just where the torchlight would make marble of them. There were five, the girl and the boy I had intercepted in the tomb garden, another two boys about sixteen years old, and a girl the same age. All were garbed in white, as Mazlek had been, white on white. All had that green speck between and above their eyes. All were beautiful with a beauty that knotted the guts and stifled the breath. Not a beauty to be restful with, unless one was inclined to worship them. Which I was not.

I had no necessity to puzzle what they would do next, for they kept none of us in doubt for long.

"Ressaven is not here," said one of the older boys.

"She should have come," the elder girl said. "See how many there are." She glanced over the people. She smiled contemptuously and said, "How ignorant and rough they are. What point in saving them?"

"They should offer us homage," the youngest boy, he I had met in the garden, remarked, "but they only gawk. They think we're the circus show come to amuse them, perhaps."

"I don't want their homage, but they should bring us gifts," the elder girl said. "They should bring us their gold if they have any. Or perfume, or good leather for harness, or horses. Anything. But they expect all for nothing. I do not think I wish to touch their smelly brown bodies with my hands."

"Nor I," said the younger girl. She slid her arms about her male companion's ribs and murmured, "I will touch only you, Sironn."

They had been speaking all this while, of course, in the city tongue, or that more antique version of it Mazlek had used. I alone understood their simpering banalities, the crowd merely waited, in unknowing meek patience, for the noble gods to begin their miracles.

Whether the Lectorra had noticed me among the throng I was not certain. Perhaps not, for a form of inner silence had steeled on me that seemed to shut me from everything.

The gods had fallen now to noncommittal staring.

The people, unsure, stared abjectly in return.

Presently a man near me, mistaking the immobile stance of the Lectorra for invitation, or else unable to support further inactivity, stumbled out of the crowd and up to them, and kneeled down on the ice before them.

"Lordly ones," he stammered.

The Lectorra gazed at him with delighted distaste.

"What does he require?" the boy Sironn asked of the sea.

"Mighty ones," whispered the man, "I am blind in my left eye."

The elder girl it was who fixed him with a white frown. Very carefully and clearly, in the village tongue, she said, "Be thankful, then, that the right eye is yet healthy."

Her companions, diverted, laughed, the fiendish silly laughter of imbeciles.

The man at their feet, obviously thinking his comprehension, or his speech, at fault, explained again. "I am blind in my eye. I can see nothing."

"Oh, there is litle to see in any case, I would suppose, in your wretched hovel," said the oldest boy, who had spoken before.

The younger girl bent to the man, and sweetly instructed: "Take a fire-charred stick at midnight and put out the eyes of all the other clods in the village. Then you can master them with just one eye. They will make you king."

The man, kneeling on the icy beach, put his hands up to his face. His expression had altered to terrified confusion, and still he reckoned it was his own fault, that he had not made himself lucid to them. He stretched out to the elder girl, instinctively begging sympathy from her superior years and what he imagined to be the qualities of her womanhood. His fingers brushed her mantle, and she wheeled to him with a dazzle of fury in her colorless eyes, and lifted her own hand. From her palm sprang a thin dagger of light that struck him in the brow.

The energy of that blow was weak, not from her choice, I thought, but because, being young, she had not come to her full Power. Lucky for him. I believe she would have slain him for touching her, otherwise.

Again the mirror. This hubris. An infant unlearned and unlessoned. But if I felt anything, it was not anger. I made my way through the floundering voiceless anguish of the crowd, and came up behind the man, who had fallen backward. I leaned over him, touched him, and healed him.

He rolled over on his face, clutching his eyes, then rolled again and sat up. He had good reason to be bewildered. He could bring himself to his repaired vision only in stages. The crowd was uncertain of what went on, but looking at them, I perceived the Lectorra knew well enough.

I have seen a lair of wild dogs react much the same, physically bunching together before the spears, their eyes gleaming and their mouths open to bite.

Shortly, one of the dogs snarled, as one always will.

"You," Sironn grated, "you're only a man. What are you doing?"

Then the pack bayed freely.

"A trick!"

"The goddess warned Ressaven of him."

"He cannot withstand us."

The blind fellow, no longer blind, leaped to his feet behind us. From his yelling, we became aware that he supposed the bitch's lightning shaft had healed his eye. It was she who denied it, by slinging a twin shaft at me.

I knocked her feeble Power aside easily. There was a crackle in the air, energy deflected upon energy. The crowd of humans behind me made their first cry.

I observed what the Lectorra were at, a collective attack upon me gathering in their unhuman faces, their vital brains. But they were only children, spiteful because the scourge had never harmed them, because they knew the world was round and they the lords of it.

I had made vows and to spare, but the present cannot be ruled forever by the past. I used my Power for this small enterprise, because it was the time for it.

The Lectorra, all five, I forcibly levitated some feet up in the air, like kicking dolls yanked on strings. I held them like that, with a grim exactness.

They squalled in a panic, and attempted to release themselves, and found they could not. They could not equal, let alone disarm me. They tried and the bolts and flares of energy they cast at me began a fetching firework display upon the beach. I heard, from their bawling, how Sironn, the youngest boy, had a voice not yet broken. The little girl—I had lain with younger than she, yet her fifteen years seemed slight to me then—engaged my pity, for she began to weep. The older ones blustered, meaning to kill me, exhausting themselves with their futile thrusts of Power till the sweat beaded and the fine hands trembled. They had never had such a thrashing, and in public, too. At length I let them down, like eggs, upon the snow.

The moment I turned away, one final levin bolt smashed uselessly at my back. I guessed it was the elder girl, who had taken her medicine hardest. I said, not looking about, "Let it go, sweeting. I've surprised you sufficiently. Don't entreat for more."

There was peace after that.

As for the village folk, they had shied from me in horror. I had shattered their legends for them, and their faces were resentful and unwilling. The man with the cured eye was at the fire and pouring beer into himself, and ignoring me the way the feasters are said to ignore Death who sits down among them in the Masrian story.

Then, when I raised my hand, a number flinched and shouted, imagining more violence to be unleashed now on them.

I said, "If you will stay, I will heal you."

It needed a woman to call, and from the rear of the crowd, "Are you hers—the Chosen of the goddess?"

"No, madam," I said, "nor do I laugh at the blind."

"Well, then," she said, "I've my sick boy here. Shall I bring him to you?"

"You bring him," I said.

They let the woman experiment for them. She brought me a boy with a disease of the lungs. He was coughing red phlegm and had to be carried. I made him well in a moment and, after that, seeing I had earned my salt, the others came to me.

Behind, on the dark night just behind the torches, the Lectorra stood motionless, like five white trees rooted in the silver mud.

I thought, the sores and maladies vanishing under my hands, *Here I am again at this rusty gate*. Yet I was glad of it. I think, all told, I shall rarely be eager to heal, but it is a marvelous thing, and in truth I am thankful for it at last, aware of what has risen in me from the seeds of indifference and mockery.

And then, at length lifting my head, I found the crowd had slid aside, and some ten paces off another waited, though not for healing.

A sixth Lectorra, a girl, and alone.

Her mantle was bluish black as the sky and the sea had grown, but a white hand held it, a white hand with a narrow wrist ringed by a bracelet of green polished stone. Her hair was white as the moon's white rising, and her face was beautiful enough to strike through my loins, my joints, the ribs of me, like a note of music sounded in the depth of sleep.

I beheld her distinctly. She looked a year or so older than

the others, about nineteen. Yet her eyes were swords; they pierced me, then pierced into the white children who lingered there at my back.

"Ressaven," I heard the oldest boy call to her. "Ressaven, you were not here, and he—"

"I saw what he did. I saw what went before." Her eyes returned to me. Though she was young, younger than I, yet her eyes were clever in their knowledge. It seemed she could have read me like a magic crystal if she willed it. "You are Zervarn," she said.

"I am Zervarn. Did she tell you to expect me?"

"She?" This Ressaven questioned as Mazlek had questioned me.

"Your goddess Karrakaz."

"She is not a goddess, but only a woman possessed of Power," the girl said. "Your Powers, too, are to be reckoned with."

"So I believe."

"Oh, you may believe it," she said.

She began to walk toward me, and my blood turned like the tide. To stare at her was as if I leaned above a chasm of lights. *Of the whole tribe of Lectorra, she is the nearest one to the old lady*, I thought. *It shines on her like phosphorus, that closeness of Power.* The torchlight burned in her hair, and as she moved, I could see the line of her apple breasts through the dark mantle, the dancer's narrow waist, and strong, slender limbs. The green Lectorra gem was between her eyes, also. She put back her head to look at me.

"You have sought Karrakaz a good while," she said.

"And you, Ressaven," I said, "shall take me to her."

"Perhaps it would be less harmful to you if you left well alone."

"Does she threaten me, then, the old hag on the mountain?"

"No. She wishes no ill to you."

"That's generous of her. I cannot promise the same."

Her breath carried the scent of flowers, and her mouth was the color of a winter sunrise in that winter face. Lashes, like dark silver blades, did not play about with her straight glances; those terrible young witch's eyes poured out their naked and uncompromising verity upon me. She had no lies to bandage up the cheats and inadequacies of others. Here was a plain where no quarter was given, or accepted. I tried, for one instant, to conjure in her place the ivory of Demizdor, the amber of Malmiranet. But the beauty of all the beautiful women I had known was guttering out like lamps.

To test myself, I put my hand on this one's shoulder.

A shock of electricity went through me at the contact, like Power itself, and obviously through her also, so that for a moment the alcum of her eyes was clouded.

I thought myself then a fool to have searched for kinship among the others. Here was my half-blood, my half-kin. A daughter of Karrakaz. Ressaven was my sister.

4

I had come searching for wormwood. I put my hand into the pit of vipers and found instead flowers grew there, and wine cooled in a silver chalice and the sun rose in the black window.

Then I thought, *This is another enchantment, one more ploy to throw me from the trail. The hound forgets the scent of the bear when he catches instead the tang of a she-wolf in the spring. She will have me riding her white mare, and unremembering all the rest.*

Ressaven. My sister.

I could recall, if I wished, Peyuan's daughter, black, blue-eyed Hwenit, her overfond liking for her brother, and my portentous verbiage upon the matter. And here was I in the same case, lusting for my sibling, and the morality of it, the incest—damned and inappropriate word—slid off me with the ease of smoke. I needed no argument to fortify myself. Confronted with the fact, no ethic restrained me, nor seemed to have a right to.

Maybe she noted the passage of this through my eyes, for her own became suddenly extraordinarily still, almost opaque, as if she heard some word inside her mind that frightened her.

Karrakaz had sent her to me, yet not warned her of the outcome. Then again, perhaps even this was part of the drama, the dream, meant to ensnare me. The mortal crowd had melted back toward its wagons, and the Lectorra came slinking up to Ressaven now. They apparently held her in some awe; no doubt, being the first among the first, Karrakaz had made her their mentor, the intermediary between them and the goddess.

She turned from me and said to them, "You have the blood of the Lost, and you become like them. Always I have been with you before on the days of healing. This one time you have shown me how it is with you."

The talkative oldest boy gazed at her defiantly, revealing his unease.

"You tell us the Lost Race perished because of their pride, but they had a right to be proud, and besides, Karrakaz lives and she is of their race, and, as you say, we are descended from their seed, which they spilled in women's loins centuries ago for amusement. That is why she chose us, since we bear their likeness. So they are not dead, Ressaven. See—here they are."

"Yes," she said. Her face was grave, and her voice, though it had no anger, was like steel. "They are here, in you. Humanity's curse, which found them out, may find you also. Think of that." Then she observed that the younger girl was crying again, and she went to her and stroked her hair gently, and said, "It is hard, I know it. It is very hard."

Presently, like the children they were, she sent them home to the island. The tide shifted about this hour, leaving bare an old causeway that began in the sea a quarter of a mile out from shore. The quarter of a mile, needless to relate, they ran over, and the village people moved from their fire and their wagons to watch that white flitting of specters walking on the ocean. For me, the villagers had few glances. I was the unknown factor, I did not fit into their scheme either of normalcy or the supernatural, and was best ignored.

"You were lenient with her brats," I said to Ressaven.

"And you were harsh," she said. "You have encountered the fire that burns and fines; you have come through it. They have no fires, no ordeals, no yardstick."

"You are Lectorra, too. How is it Ressaven is not like the others?"

"I have had my fires," she said simply. "Not all of us can avoid them."

"Also," I said, "you are nearer to the lady on the mountain, are you not? A deal nearer."

She looked very long at me. You could tell little from her face, only this youth, this loveliness, and this stunning clarity.

"You are the son of Vazkor. Truly."

"Truly I am," I said. After what I had thought in the valley, of his memory going from me, it was strange she should say this to me. The surf made its noises pulling from the beach. The mountain had faded from red to gray. "She told you everything, did she?" I said. "How she would have skewered me forth from her, and when she could not, and had murdered him, she left me to become a boar-pig among the tents. I might have been a king, but for her meddling." But when I said it, I tasted how stale it had become, my eternal accusation, with so much use.

As if she knew that, she said, part smiling, "You are a mighty sorcerer and a mighty man, and could carve a kingdom, if you wanted, from any portion of the world you chose. No one made you a king, Zervarn. You have made yourself what you are. Be glad of it, for it is better."

"How am I to judge that?" I said. "I never had a chance at the other."

"When she bore you, Karrakaz had no birthright to offer you. For herself she hoped for less than nothing."

"She has been feeding you these lies since first you lay on her knee," I said; "that is why you credit them."

"You hate her, then," she said, and her wide eyes widened further, as if to see me more clearly.

"I am past hating her. She is the riddle of my life that must be answered, that is all. Will you take me to her now? I can seek her alone, if I must, and discover her. I have got this far."

"Indeed you have," she said. "Come, then. Her dwelling is some hour's journey across the island."

We walked up the shore some way, beyond the fires, to a place where we could cross over the ocean unseen. Neither consulted the other in this, but it did not surprise me to note we were of like mind. I asked her how long the causeway kept above water, for the tide was already swelling in once more. She told me that path would be gone before we reached the island. She did not ask if it would trouble my Powers to make the whole crossing in the sorcerous way.

The sky was black, and the sea, both gemmed with stars.

I said to her, "I grew among men who thought those lights to be the eyes of gods or the lamps of spirits or the souls of dead warriors shining with their valor after death. Now I gather that the stars are only circular worlds or spheres of flame like the sun. It is a great disappointment to me." She laughed. It was a pleasing laughter, like bright fish flashing up from a shadowy deep pool where one did not think they would be. "And where did you learn such stuff?" I said.

"Karrakaz was once the guest of men who knew these things to be true. That the earth is round, that it spins, and that the sun does not move."

"No doubt she was shown the proof," I said.

"No doubt she was."

"Well," I said, "she has filled your head with fine stories."

"Think, Zervarn," she said softly. "The sea glides under our feet; we tread on the backs of waves. You believe *that*, yet you cannot believe the world is round?"

A cold wind blew from the farther shore, from the jaws of a tall silver cloud above the mountain. It blew her hair like a fire behind her. I swear I never witnessed anything more beautiful than she was, stepping over that dark ocean, darker than the sea and paler than the stars, with those wings of her hair spread upon the wind.

"If you believe it," I said, "I will believe it."

"Will you believe what I said of Karrakaz?"

"I will believe that you believe it, honestly. But for me, I must have her excuses from her own mouth." After I had said that, Ressaven was silent. I wanted her to speak to me, for somehow her being there with me was hard for me to accept unless she spoke in a woman's voice. She looked unreal, or worse, more real than anything else, rather as the fabulous ruin of the city had looked more real, as if it had stood in space before the sea or the coast or the sky were made. I did not like this effect she had on me. I had the mistress of the house yet to face, I could not afford to kneel before the slave. I said, "Inform me, at least, Ressaven, how she came here and began this breeding stock of hers."

So, as we walked over the water, and presently up onto the long strand of the island, she talked to me of White Mountain, and of my mother. Despite myself, I hung on the words, hungry for news I had waited twenty-one years to get.

Yet I was struck immediately by the tone in which Ressaven now uttered the name of Karrakaz, with a curious kind of tenderness, and regret. It seemed the child became the mother during the narrative. Manifestly, Ressaven marveled at her witch-dam, and simultaneously she pitied her. It made me wonder suddenly to what estate the sorceress had descended, if she were failing or debilitated, or what; and if I, the questioner and the avenger, had arrived too late to snap at a crumbled bone.

Karrakaz, lost daughter of the Lost Race, had survived, by a prodigy, a kind of prolonged catalepsy, the death that overtook her nation. She had, thereafter, journeyed through a diversity of delusions, and several hells—Ressaven was not specific—to reach a treaty with herself. During that era of struggle she had wandered the northlands; later she came to the south, and there, perhaps near Bar-Ibithni, or in Seema, she had been brought a sailor's rumor of the western shores, their ruins, their treasure, and their fair-haired races who bore, with some frequency, albino children. It was too close an omen for her to avoid. Some forerunner of Jari, a pirate adventurer, had brought her west. Probably her voyage had been better managed than my own.

She reached the wreck of Kainium. She had seen its like before and recognized it as the building of her forebears. Once, she had experienced a terror of such spots, for she had feared the Lost and the strain of their blood in her; that hubris she had finally sloughed. With her demons conquered, she no longer feared either her race or their ruin. In a bizarre fashion she even felt a tug of nostalgia, pleasant homesickness sweep her, pacing that decay of majesty, all that remained of the places of her infancy.

The villages about stirred gradually to an awareness of her. Intuitively they sought her for healing. Shortly, she came upon a white-haired child wanted by no one. (I interrupted to ask Ressaven if this oldest and initial Lectorra were she; I was trying to catch her out. But she smiled and said, "No." She looked almost playful for an instant, the way a girl will, veiling her origin in mystery, but, continuing, her face resumed its solemnity.) She said that from my own trouble I would understand the loneliness Karrakaz had felt, one woman, and extraneous to the clans of humanity. I refrained just then from answering with the obvious, that she had borne a son, and need not have been alone. As for the loneliness, it was no stranger to me, that gap of isolation. Karrakaz, apparently, had mastered her solitude, but, meeting the albino baby, plainly atavistic blood of her own Lost Race, she visualized irresistibly that the child would resemble her, and could be trained, if the strain of Power was accessible in it, to a similar ability. It was the last temptation, and she had succumbed.

The island of the mountain was rich then with summer. It was a garden of slender waterfalls, fields of wild flowers, wild bees, and wild vines, with everywhere the sea folding blue as sapphire about it. It was like the paradise of some mythus, where gods should live; unconsciously, I think, she had not been immune to her deification, though she disdained its associations. She picked, from some village, a nurse for the children, for she had been brought another child swiftly, word of her interest having flown. The nurse was a woman with a talent for babies, a peasant with no inhibitions and no offspring of her own, barren, and sore with unsatisfied maternity. Karrakaz selected others like her in the years that followed to attend the physical care of these charges. She herself, as the children grew, free as all the other wild things on the island, began to uncover in them those magic Powers that had descended to them, with their whiteness, from the Lost.

Karrakaz was not a lover of children, I had reason to know. She had few dealings with their extreme youth. But this she saw to: that they should be untrammeled by the dogma and the codes that society, in whatever form, barbaric or civilized, imposes on its creatures; that no query of theirs should be ignored; that no injustice should overcome them. She could read their minds, and did so. Frustration was a dog that never bit them. Anything that might have clogged their psychic heritage was kept at bay. Love of life, celebration of mind and flesh, the purity of unstigmatized sex and fearless meditation, this was the cornucopia she poured upon them. She gave them everything that inadvertently she had denied to me. They should have turned out better than they did.

Yet, venturing from the mountain, this free, this perfect, this brilliant, to observe the unfree, imperfect, dull and fettered world; she had not planned for that, nor the chemistry that would begin to work on them. Before, they had been only happy; now, reflected back from the gritty glass of contrast, they noticed they were gods.

Hearing Ressaven speak of it, I could only conclude that she had also followed this mirage and endured its dissolution with her demon-mother, and that she perceptively shared in the guilt of Karrakaz, her ominous sorrow and regret.

Of Ressaven herself, no hint was given in the history. I supposed she kept from me that she was also the child of the sorceress, because she was persuaded I would become hostile. It seemed she might reason I should not stumble on the truth, since we were so unalike in appearance. I considered the notion of her father, pondering if my sister had ever known him, and if she had despised him ever, as a mortal. She had mentioned a purging of fires, but not where she had found them in this cushioned life.

That she had been appointed guardian to the Lectorra was apparent. I recalled the tale that Karrakaz never left her mountain.

We had reached the island shore by now, a long skirt of crystalline ice that fanned out into a pleated palisade of cliffs above, all bathed in the transparent black of night. The silver cumulus had sunk upon the mountaintop. It was how the Masrians would paint a holy mountain in a picture, its summit girdled with a band of cloud. Surely, this was a mysterious place, apt for its role.

I stood on the beach, and said to Ressaven, "What does Karrakaz avoid on the mainland? Why is she so afraid to leave this citadel, that she sends you in her stead?"

"What does she avoid? Simply her own legend, what she has become for men, despite her efforts to avert it. She did not mean to be a goddess of the western lands, nor to recreate a race of gods. But, as you see, she is a goddess and the Lectorra are gods. In the villages, here and there, they have begun to worship her and her white brood. So now she withdraws the legend, keeps herself aloof."

Then she told me something that surprised me indeed: That Karrakaz no longer communicated directly either with the shore-folk, or with her Lectorra. A handful of them, her first chosen, still dealt with her face to face; my guide, Mazlek, was one of these few. For the rest, none of them had seen her or heard her voice in some years.

"She is deliberately making herself an enigma," Ressaven said, "because she intends to ease herself from their minds, and ultimately, Zervarn, because she intends to leave this mountain, to abandon her Chosen to their hubris and the harsh lessons of the world. For how else are they to learn? How else is she ever to be free?" She stared at the ocean with her wide cool eyes. She said, "What was begun was foolish. She understands that now. To continue the foolishness would be a wickedness. To ignore the wickedness would be worse than wickedness. The enterprise that Karrakaz began here, out of her loneliness and her own unthinking dream, might bring back the very horror that her race engendered, and perished by. The Lost were evil, vile, debased. They could not help it, they had no fire, no measure of the soul, only this endless possibility of Power. And the Lectorra are the same. Throughout these years of her hiding and her silence, she has permitted no more albino children to be brought to White Mountain. Presently she will leave those that remain. They must work out their own destiny. She has harmed them enough by her nearness; now only her desertion of them is feasible."

"Yes," I said. "She is clever at that."

Ressaven turned to me. "Bitter words," she said, "yet you have come from it very well. Do you suppose these poor little gods you held in the air, blustering and weeping, will grow as heroically as you, or as strong?"

"She disgusts me," I said. "Her schemes, her vacillations, her mistakes. Everything fits. Disorder and cruelty. Haphazard misery. That is her."

Then I saw her anger. I had not anticipated it; her serenity misled me. Niether had I ever imagined the rage of a woman could unnerve me, but she was like no other.

"You are no longer a barbarian among the tents, Zervarn," she said. "Do not mock a bloody sword; you carry too many in your belt."

I mastered myself. She was only a girl, though it was hard to remember it.

"You and she," I said. "Either you lie together in a bed, or she birthed you."

That threw her, as I intended. She frowned, with that stasis coagulating in her eyes again. Then she said, rather low, as if she, too, must take herself in hand to speak, "We are losing time here." She moved away from me, and on ahead, to where a narrow path opened in the cliff.

It was as I had guessed. My beautiful sister, who had not wished that I discover it.

On the rocky way I noticed for the first time that her feet were bare as they met the frozen cliff, except for twin anklets of gold, which shone down on the snow.

As we climbed, the sharpness of the breakers softened below, to a sound like the distant running of horses. It was so quiet then that I heard my breathing, and hers, and the muted chink of those gold anklets, which sometimes struck together.

5

Inland, the cliffs poured over into a valley bowl of black and white woods, with the mountain rising from them at the island's center.

The path, which led us upward and over the rampart of the cliff wall, slid downward to this interior valley country, which seemed hidden, as if by intent, from the beach, the sea, and the mainland. The only flowers there now were snow flowers and the ferns of ice patterned over winter pools, yet from the shapes and skins of trees beneath their flaking bark, I made out hawthorns, wild cherry, rhododendron, and countless others which with the thaw would fire into white and violet, blue, carmine, and purple. It would be a maze then, this secret plain, starred and powdered with lights and shades, and the winding canals curdled with shattered blossom. I wondered what birds would come there, and what fish dart in the streams, and if they would be good to eat—and then recalled I had no need of the death of their pink flesh. In any event, I should be long gone from White Mountain when the spring entered its gate.

But Ressaven. What would she be doing here in spring? Flowers in her hair no doubt, as a girl would have, and her arms and shoulders bare and spangled with the green and lavender cannonade of sunlight shot through blossom. Probably she would open her thighs for some white-haired boy-man among the grasses. Or maybe she would be far from this haven, out in the unfree, imperfect, dull and fettered world, with me.

Half a mile from the cliff, something pale shone in fragments through the weave of the trees. The path looped in and out, and there against a glint of frozen water like an oval coin was an extraordinary tall house, three terraced stories, spear ranked with pillars, with windows of multicolored glass: a miniature mansion of the Lost Race straight from Kainium, but not a wreck.

"What's this?" I said. "Do you bring humans here after all to labor for you?"

"No," she said. "There are several such small palaces on

the island, and a marble town on the mountain slopes. They were in ruins, but the Lectorra rebuilt and repaired them."

"I don't visualize you, lady, neither your fellow gods, toiling about the masonry with mallets, scaffolding, and pulleys."

There were pebbles lying between the villa wall and the brink of the pool. Suddenly six or seven of these flew up like startled pigeons, skimmed across the congealed surface, and plummeted down with a crack of breaking glass upon the ice. She said, "The Power of the mind and the energy of Power that can fling pebbles can also raise a marble block, shape a column, and lift it upright on its base. True, men from the mainland advised us—at least, spoke with Karrakaz some years since, to advise her. But we employed no hirelings and forced no slaves. What help we asked we paid for, sometimes in gold, to which we are able to gain access in the city, sometimes in humble barter, wild honey, fruits, and the milk-cheese of our goats."

"Now I am to picture you at the milking?"

"Yes. I have milked a goat," she said. "And I have learned how to charm the bees so they do not sting me when I must steal some of their harvest from them."

"A homely milkmaid witch." I did not believe her story, or not all of it. The white villa-mansion would have required vast strength to set it to rights by mind alone, a mental strength I had not observed among the Lectorra. Those pillars—I might have raised them, if my brain had been turned to mason's games. But those here could not, save for Karrakaz herself perhaps, and this one, the daughter.

I said, "I have had much traveling and little rest. Is your palace equipped for us to break the journey in for an hour?"

"Yes," she said. She smiled, and I wondered if she knew what I was really at, suggesting we pause here, and if it meant she complied.

The bare blossom-trees grew about the porch. The double doors were oak wood, and gave at a twist of the iron ring. The house was as it must have been centuries before, or near enough, an irony of Karrakaz's or Lectorra whim.

The anteroom was flanked by red pillars. The pillars in the hall beyond were green and slender, carved to resemble the stems of great flowers, the flower-heads opening scarlet against the flat roof, which was the clear blue of a summer sky, and painted so cunningly with clouds I part expected them to move. Screens of fashioned ivory stood before the red marble walls, with one huge window set in the chamber's farther end. Its leaded mosaic panes—red, blue, green, and purple—would admit a fantastic daylight. A staircase went up to one side; the balustrade was ivory enhanced with gold, the shallow steps, white marble. In an urn of green jade at the room's center grew an orange tree in a full double bloom of flowers and tan fruit, some freak fancy of the Lectorra, doubtless, to outwit the season. Its scent filled the hall, which was unnaturally temperate. I thought of the system of hot pipes in Eshkorek, and realized a similar construction must be in use in the villa, though with no slaves to tend it, if her protestations were to be credited. (I was coming to credit them. I felt a casually expansive yet controlled and sensitive use of Power here, something I envied, being still uneasy with my own. In fact, to reveal these riches, Ressaven had set fire to the ranks of candles on their silver and golden stands by single intent glances of her eyes. It disquieted me still, to see these arts exercised thus unselfconsciously by another.)

There was a couch in the form of an ebony lioness and ivory chairs in the form of her crouching cubs, all snowed over with furs and rugs, as was the heated floor.

"You must go trapping often," I said.

"Never," she said. "We take only the pelts of beasts that die in the course of nature, or the woven fleece of living animals." She looked at me, a strange look, and said, "But you have been hunting often, and would not understand such measures. Now, shall I bring you food and wine?"

The dwelling, which must be hers, seemed well supplied for visitors, its hypercaust going, candles ready, larder stocked. For whom did they keep food? Could it be, despite Mazlek's boast at the inn, that some of the Lectorra still needed to cram their bellies?

"No wine or food for me, lady," I said. "I live on air, as they say, as any magician should."

"So I was told," she said.

The candles blazed bright. I put my pack down, with the mask hidden in it, on a lion-cub chair. She stared at me, and abruptly her face sharpened into desolate hunger, as if she had glimpsed some distant sanctuary she could never reach. I thought, *She is nineteen, yet maybe she has never been with a man, never come on one she desired, and they dared not force her*. Though I could not, even then, be sure of her, if it was to lie with me she wanted, or some deeper unknown thing, some ancient wish or fear in her heart. For she looked afraid, too.

I went near to her, and put my hands on the fastening of her dark mantle. She did not stay me, only went on staring into my face. For myself, I kept my eyes on the lacing, and spoke trivia for safety.

"This splendid palace would have been only a humble rustic outhouse to them, I suppose, your Lost Kainium fold. I saw an underground road of theirs once, clothed with gems and metal and high as the sky, which they had named Worm's Way. And this, possibly, they would call the Dove Cote or the Hut. Fitting mansion for a witch who milks goats and gathers fruit in her white hands." At that I took up her hand. I anticipated the tactile electricity to sear between us again, as it had the first time, but now we were primed to it. There was only a dazzle of nerves in my skin that touched on hers, which ran straight through me like silver wire.

"Well," I said.

The mantle slipped off. She wore a blue dress under it, blue as the ceiling, with her whiteness gleaming under. Her body looked like a fire, trying to burn through that gown to reach me.

But she drew her hand away.

"Zervarn," she said, "son of Vazkor—"

"No names," I said. "No more names, Ressa. You led me here, and I followed most willingly."

"I did not mean and I did not think—"

"Think now, and of me."

"Karrakaz," she said.

"Let her wait. That's for tomorrow. I've forgotten her, as she expediently forgot me."

"But—" she said.

"Be still," I said.

Her eyes swam, her mouth, even now trying to speak to me, merged into mine before it could form words, forming instead to welcome me, and draw me in. Her body stretched to me. Her shoulders came free of the blue water of the dress, her breasts rose from the cloth into my hands, each with its central star of fire that became the axis of my palms. She turned her head and cried out softly that this must not be, and yet her arms wound on my back and clung to me as if the world tumbled and only I remained to hold her safe.

I folded her aside and against me and had us down among the mounded furs. Wherever our bodies met, a fresh conflagration stirred our flesh. *This is new,* I thought, but the thought burned from my skull. The dress had been expressly designed for me to loose it; the fastenings melted. Her limbs were cool and smooth, but a warmth within. The silver fleece on her loins did not look human, nor any part of her spread out before me like a flaring snow in the candle-shine, and jeweled with the smoky flush of mouth, the two pink stars upon her breasts, the rose cave into the ice. She was not virgin, and yet, like some goddess-maiden in a legend, her innocence seemed renewed especially for me. But she was knowing, too.

Her head fell back. She surrendered herself to me with a silent, savage delight, no longer denying anything.

The unpainted lids of her eyes were like fine platinum. I put my lips there, and tasted salt. I asked her why she wept.

"Because this should not have been between us."

Many a woman has said that, a tedious lament, but with her it was not the same.

"It was bound to be," I said. "We are like and like, you and I, Ressa."

"Yes," she said.

"And can it be that is your objection? Because we came from the same door, brother and sister? No matter. The fathers were different. Besides, it is a tribal way of seeing things, to balk at this little incest. Come, am I to suppose you educated in a tent? I thought a Javhetrix schooled you."

Her tears were dry. Her eyes, which I had seen blinded by pleasure a minute before, were now once more those large opaque disks, unreadable, but reading everything.

"Then again," I said, "who will know, since we shall be leaving this magic mountain of your birth?"

"No," she said. "You must leave. But I remain."

"You will come with me," I said. "You know you won't let me travel alone."

"I will let you."

"I will ask the old lady for you," I said, attempting to lighten this shade across her face like the first shadow of night. "I will kneel to your Karrakaz—"

"No," she broke in, and her strong, slender fingers dug into my arms. "Never go to her now."

She is afraid, I thought. *She reckons she has betrayed the sorceress by lying with me, and will be punished. So much for our loving mother.*

"She shan't harm you when I am near," I said.

Ressaven's eyes flamed up. And I saw it was anger.

"You are not a fool," she said. "Do not act one. This I give you is a prophecy, a warning. Abandon the island and make your life elsewhere. Forget this coupling, and forget your search for Karrakaz." Her anger faded, and she said gently, "Now, let me go."

"I am not done with you," I said.

"But I am done with you, Zervarn. Yes, it is half my blame that we are here. And yes, you are my conqueror and I yield to you. But now it is over. Do not make me battle. You are not accustomed to the women of this mountain."

The argument had made me lust for her again. She did not struggle after all, and when I stirred within her, she moaned. The curve where her shoulder met her throat held a scent of strange flowers, clearer than the orange blossom. It was the last perfume I breathed for some while. My head was full of light one second, then full of black, a painless blow struck from within that ended our couching as surely as a knife in my heart.

I had the last dream of my father that night.

I did not properly grasp its import then; it was only another jagged blade picked up in the cold dawn that woke me alone in that place.

How well do I remember it, as if it were reality, a memory, which maybe it might have been; or in some other life where circumstances are other than in this, perhaps it has been, *is*.

I was a child once more, in the dream, possibly five years of age. He had taken me to a high window to look down upon a marching of troops in the streets. It was winter there also, snow white on the ground, the men and the horses clattering black against it. He was black, too: black clothing, black prince's hair, the dark skin and the black jewels on it. Gazing up at him more often than at his troops below, I saw, with the alarming foreshortened image that the child generally has, a leaning pillar of dark with the blank face above it. But when he said, "Look below," I obeyed him at once. I was five years, yet I knew, I had learned: he was to be obeyed. "You must remind yourself at all times," he said, "that you accede to this, strive for this, train your body and your brain for this. I will not have you mewling in the hall with a puppy like any peasant's brat in some steading. You were born my son so that you shall become as I am. Do you understand me?" I said that I did. He turned eyes on me that were like dead coals. He moved me about and away from him with his impersonal fingers. I was aware that I hated and feared him, that this was the bond between us, fright and a child's loathing that one day would be a man's. Then I should kill him as efficiently as he had killed my dog. Or he would kill me.

When I glimpsed my mother in the doorway, I walked to her—he had persuaded me not to run many months ago. Her face was masked in gold and green gems; I had never seen it unmasked. Yet, despite herself, she was my safe harbor, and I hers, for such a thing one may know at five years of age, for all one could not voice it, nor set it down.

The lights of the mansion window roused me, and the caress of her hands in the dream, which had seemed like the touch of Ressaven.

Part III

The Sorceress

1

One morning hour saw me across the wooded valley and at the roots of the mountain, the villa hidden far behind in trees. It was a tranquil day, to be sure, the sky clear as glass. A long-necked bird rose from a glow of water as I passed, its wings beating their own winds. It had been drinking there at the brink of the broken ice, not a care in the world, no feuds or aspirations to plague it.

She had left me no footsteps in the snow to follow, no stamp of those agile and beautiful bare feet. She had levitated in order to deceive me, as she had deceived me in the warm candlelight with that little sound of hers that made me forget she was witch before woman. I had not been ready for the onslaught of her Power with which she had stunned me. It was her dread that made her betray me, yet it set my teeth on edge that she had not trusted me, put my strength at least beside the strength of Karrakaz.

Still, she would come to learn. I did not have to depend on footsteps for my guide. I had recollected the marble town on the mountain slope, which she had told me of so incidentally. The moment I pictured it, I knew with the force of divination that the town was the sanctum of the sorceress.

I kept to the ground, to the cloak of the trees. I did nothing to stir up alarms. Only the bird's flight could have marked me, and then, not for sure. I was still woodsman enough to make, otherwise, a quiet road to the mountain. I had a conviction she might be watching for me.

I had left my pack in the villa, opened, with the mask staring up for any to discover—my signature, perhaps, upon what had happened there.

By now the dream had returned to my mind, that picture of

my father I had never before constructed. Yet, not so strange. Not one man or woman I had encountered who knew his name had had a good word to spare for him. They held him in awe, and they hated him; I had had evidence in Eshkorek of that awe and hate they would have eased on me only because I was his seed. This much poison cannot pour in one's ears without it will leave some trace. I would have been strange indeed if somewhere in me I had not begun to wonder. Would he have been to me the princely father I had imagined, or as I had finally seen him in the dream? The impetus of his despair had left me. I had almost imperceptibly ceased to reckon him the pivot of my life. I had vowed murder to him, yet it was no longer a passion in me to achieve it, and I felt no driving force rebuke my flagging vengeance. Had these issues perished with my youth in Bar-Ibithni, destroyed by plague and terror and resurrection? Or merely because I had begun to reason him less than I had at first supposed?

Then again, I pondered if the dream were some witchcraft worked on me.

I myself had conjured false images of him—the shadow that rose from the fire, the unreal guide in the Eshkirian fortress, and the force that pushed me to the slaughter of Ettook—all overflowings simply of my own thought, not a momentous ghost but spillage from a cup. And in Bit-Hessee, in the circle of beasts, others had conjured him inadvertently from my brain with their rampant spell.

Traversing that valley, I began to go over the rest, seeking for Vazkor of Ezlann inside myself. And he was not there, not anymore. Certain of his mental fires had remained in me to deceive me once, and now they also were dead. I recalled the cave that night I tracked the Eshkiri raiders, and that death-vision of water and the teeth of knives, and waking to say, "I will kill her." It was the last thought he had had, futile, floundering, impotent. That had been his legacy to me, a sword he could not take up, and which I had no right to draw for him. Whomever I slew or spared in my days on the earth, it must be my quarrel, not another's. It is unlucky to weep at sea for, they would tell you, the ocean is salt enough. For sure, we have enough griefs of our own that we should not assume the burden of others.

Sending or otherwise, the dream of my iron father had brought me to the truth.

I met no one on my journey. Once I noted the tracks of a she-fox in the snow. Where the trees gave way to the bald white upsurge of the mountain, I found a girl's silver bangle hanging on a bush, like a signal of derision, but maybe it was innocent.

There was a path up this side of the mountain; I was inclined to follow it, for it seemed worn naturally by the passage of many feet, and would no doubt lead straight to the witch's sanctuary.

A few trees grew about the path, stands of holly and bold briars. I climbed doggedly for near on an hour up this smooth slope and along another, between the trees, over the worn path. At last I realized I had been clambering there too long, and the landscape had not radically altered.

There was sorcery even here. I halted and cleared my mind of its inner thoughts and gazed around me keenly. I was still at the mountain's foot. I had gone about twenty yards and stridden in a circle, or up and down, I know not which, for it was all one. Like any peasant or yokel they had wanted to mislead, they had confounded me because I had been too sure and too unthinking. No more. I would be careful now.

I did not take the path after that, but trod the rocky way. In a few minutes I was clear of the woods and on the upland. Looking back, I glimpsed valley, cliff-line, the shining pallor of the sea, and the silver clouds boiling up from it like curled steam from a caldron.

I kept my senses outward, my instincts ready. Once I noted a symbol carved in the snow by a stick, some wizardly item meant to confuse the brain. I kicked it into a slush before I went on.

Finally there was a wall of slaty stone, and a tall door in it of iron inlaid with semiprecious gems. It looked incongruous enough so that I took it for a spell, but it was not. Just another fancy of the Old Race for spectacle. Above, the far peak gored the ether, its whiteness changed to blue steel on the white sky. The door of iron had no bolt, no bar, no ring or knob to grasp.

Had Ressaven come this way, escaping me?

I saw in my mind's eye that white hand of hers with its jade bracelet—that hand, one of a pair which had clung to me—laid on a panel of quartz in the iron door. When I guided my own fingers there, the door slid aside into the wall of rock.

A black pine stood beyond the door. Beyond the pine, the mountain town of the goddess.

For a moment, I was shown a waste, fallen pillar drums, smashed tiles, the empty courts of a ruin. But I grimly put the illusion aside from me, and the mirage drifted off like dust, leaving reality behind.

There was one central street forty feet broad, straight as a rule, that ran for half a mile right up the slant of the mountain. It had a bizarre aspect, this road, being laid with alternate square paving stones of green and black, from which the snow had been scoured or on which the snow had never been permitted to alight. It pointed into the distance, a perfect toy of mathematical perspective, and at its peak rested a building of steps and columns and many roofs piled one above the other. In a Masrian play, a drumbeat would have thudded as I set eyes on it: Here was the citadel of Karrakaz.

On either side the street of jade and black paving, the royal mansions mounted or declined at pleasing angles on the slopes. Every vista was aesthetic, everything arranged in relation to its neighbor, like the model of a city made for a king's child to play with.

It was silent as a model, too. Another would have thought it dead as Kainium, but I felt their presence there, the Lectorra, I felt their stealth, their curiosity, and a hint of something more, a nebulous and unadmitted fright.

A dry fountain stood a couple of feet along the road, a roaring dragon with open jaws. As I stepped on the paving, the dragon's muzzle of ice cracked off with a loud noise, and green water gushed out. Next second, the water changed color to the appearance of blood. It seemed they had not given over their games. I went by and up the street without another glance, for it had the spoor of Lectorra all over it, that oldest trick of liquid into blood.

There were serpents crawling about on the stones farther on, a pool of fire, and an impassable broken area with the guts of the mountain yawning under it miles below. All these elegant illusions I trampled over, without even a bow to them for their ingenuity and the accuracy of the portrayal. Though, when an eagle shot down from a tower straight for my eyes, I own I ducked. Then I remarked, as I dissolved the beating pinions and the rending beak in midair, "A single hit for you, my children."

Midway along the road, a lion padded from one of the palace porches, a snow lion with a gray mossy body and black mane and eyes like summer heat stored up in him against the cold. He was real, a genuine inhabitant of this locus, though probably some whimsical import of the Lost Race rather than native to the western lands. After a century or two of roaming in a changeable climate he had developed a winter coat, like any fox or weasel.

It was odd for me to confront him. I had no need of his flesh to feed me or his pelt to clothe me, and no need to beware his moods. Any attack of his would slide harmless from my invisible armor and he go toppling all the valiant, lean length of him. In my krarl youth I would have counted him a prize, hunted him with skill and hot excitement, to prove myself his better, driving my spear or knife into his brain, wearing his hide on mine. Now, needs, defenses, contests no longer meaningful, I took the time to run my eye over him, liking him for what he was in himself, rather than what he could be to me.

His tail went this way and that, his nostrils and his glands telling him I was neither enemy nor easy prey. But as I drew level, he put his forefoot out in my path, as if to stay me. I turned and met his gaze and he moved the foot aside. It looked weighty enough to have staved in a man's skull, but the claws were scarcely visible. He lay down like a huge cat. Somewhere there would be a lioness, and his sons and daughters, the pride.

He reclined by the road and stared after me a minute, then I glanced over my shoulder and he was gone.

There were no further illusions or beasts.

The last palace loomed on my horizon. The pillars were circled with brazen bands and as I got closer I saw a rose tree growing in a bowl of earth before the steps, and it was in bloom, crimson flowers and dark green thorn daggers out of time, like the orange fruits and blossom in that room where I had lain with Ressaven.

Ressaven, who fled me in terror of the sorceress, who thought me so feeble in Power I could not protect her from one bitch's wrath.

Well, we would find out, the three of us.

There were three others first. I had not seen them for a moment on the steps. That white on white, marble, flesh, hair, and white velvet garments. But I caught the sudden glint of swords.

Mazlek was the nearest, my guide to Kainium, who had crossed over the wide river with his hand on my shoulder.

Two others behind, a young man about eighteen and a girl in male tunic, trousers, and boots, and with a man's sword ready, competent as a man. A white kitten had climbed into the bowl of earth and began to nibble at the roses, waking my memory. This girl was she I had met in the old city, the kitten on her shoulder. She seemed as calm now, and she called to me, "Go back, Zervarn. Was the lion in your way not presage enough for you?"

Mazlek moved down the steps onto the paving. He held the sword negligently, and said, "The blade is only a symbol. But we will use whatever we must to drive you off, Denarl, Sollor and I."

"Of course," I said. "You are the goddess's guard."

"Oh," he said, "self-elected, I confess. She has no actual requirement for us, but it was a fashion among us since we were very young—as we adopted the fashion of the jade in the forehead from her, which in turn the younger chicks of the brood copy from us. How else could we show we honored a goddess who refused to be honored? To mimic her guard seemed good to us, to offer ourselves as a weapon, however flimsy. And we have named ourselves from three captains of Ezlann who once served her, the older versions of their names, as her own people would have used them."

"Was one of that guard also a woman?"

"No, to be sure. But Sollor, trust my word, is our equal. Don't underrate her."

I said, "I could kill the three of you in three seconds."

He raised his brows. "It would take you so long?"

"You have a nice humor," I said. "Live to enjoy it. Get from my path."

But the girl Sollor called again, "Kill us, then. Do it now."

She was beautiful. Not as Ressaven was beautiful, but enough. I recollected how, staring at this face in the ruined city, I had not supposed I should see one lovelier.

I did not want to slay or harm them. They knew it.

Mazlek said, "We are only symbols, like these swords of ours, like the lion. Suffice it to say, Karrakaz begs you to return from here. To leave her in peace. And yourself."

"*Begs* me? That's a new song, I have not heard it before. Karrakaz begs, the sorceress, the goddess-Javhetrix. On her knees, perhaps. Let her come out and kneel to me, then, where I can watch her do it, and be sure."

A blue cloud had lifted itself over the mountain, raising an awning of shadow above the street.

I went toward Mazlek, and abruptly his sword swung up and a lightning burst from its tip. There was a ripping of the air about me as the white vein struck on that psychic shield of mine, which now I did not even have to bother with but which answered for me instantly.

Mazlek leaped back, his sword slashing bright arcs of metal and energy. He did not aim another cut at me, nor look afraid, nor even amazed. He had known he could not match me, which made this foolhardy barricade an idiotic puzzle.

I understood I should not get by him, however, while he was upright, nor by the other two. Even the maid had devilry ready; I could see it in the flex of her wrist and her intent mouth. I was not obliged to butcher them, merely quell.

I sent a shaft at Mazlek that spun him about and dropped him on his back. Dual bars of light sprang from the other two, but I set them aside, and laid the protagonists down. The kitten looked up from its feast of rose petals to spit at me, but the girl Sollor had suffered no great hurt. All three appeared sleeping rather than fallen warriors. Then I imagined I had her reasoning, the reasoning of the witch. She had sent them to test me, how vast my grievance should be. That I had incapacitated but not slain would reassure her. Wrongly.

I raised my eyes, and there on the steps above me was Ressaven.

She wore male garb, like the kitten girl, but of black wool, and there was no blade in her hand.

She regarded me steadily, as if there had never been a word, let alone a coupling, between us.

"Only I separate you and Karrakaz now," she said.

"A dangerous separation," I said. I did not accept her stance; it was too exact. *She remembers everything,* I thought, *and to spare.*

"No," she said. "I am here to prevent you, and I mean to do it. I am more gifted than the others."

"How she values you, that stinking hag," I said, "to send you out against me."

For that last instant she was my Ressaven. Then she blazed up like a candle. The fire of the Power left her like a flight of burning birds. It burst through my shield, and hit me.

I had not expected this strength from her, despite her trick, despite the very appearance of her, which might have warned me.

The blow was enough to stagger me, and the atmosphere crackled from the charge. Swiftly the thought went through my head that the lady meant business, and that she might master me if I did not settle her first. But I did not like to strike back at her. Though neither she nor I, the descendants of Karrakaz, could receive death, and each must be aware of that.

A second fire sizzled from her; I blocked it as best I could, and sent my own bolt flying, running after it up the staircase toward her. As her Power impaired mine, mine must lessen hers. The daylight seemed to detonate about her. That she felt the impact I never doubted, and in its aftermath I seized her and held her pinned against me. Though her psychic force rivaled my own, physically she was not at all my match. I searched her eyes, in which the Power flicked and surged.

"Ressaven," I said. "Know me, Ressaven. Cease fighting me."

"And you, cease fighting me," she answered, her voice the coldest thing I ever heard, and the most desolate.

"You could not kill me," I said, "nor I kill you. Even if both of us willed it. And would you see me dead, even for an hour, and rejoice? Do it, then."

"As you say, I could not. But I ask you—"

"I will go up to her," I said, "and no threat or plea of yours will stop me."

She smiled and said, as one other woman once said to me, "I am so little to you."

"You are world's end to me, and the heart of my life. But this has been before me since I was begun in her womb."

She eased herself from me.

"There is the door, then," she said to me. "If I cannot keep you from it, I cannot."

I turned from her and stared up the steps to the wide-open porch under the pillars. Her resistance had seeped suddenly from her as occasionally it will in any hard battle where the cause is already lost. I thought no more of it.

I had not lied; I loved her and had determined to have her, but for now, only that stairway and that door had meaning. The slow thudding in my side reminded me of disquiet, and the ice of the winter had pierced through into my vitals.

"Ressaven," I said, though I recall I did not look at her, only at the door ahead of me. "If there is anything in this you must forgive me for, I hope you will forgive me. And have faith in me, too."

She did not reply, and I did not glance again at her, but went up the stairs in long strides to keep pace with the pounding in my chest, beneath the porch and through the portal.

The discarded whimperings and sweats of childhood and the sick fears of a man had found me out. I swam through a heavy sea of horror, but nothing could push me from it.

The hall was lofty, sculptured with gloom. I grasped not much of it, its size or shape or furnishing. Only one rich chair of ivory and jade, placed to confront any who dragged himself through that door as I had done.

I stopped and faced the chair, and ached with my fear to the roots of my bones and the beds of my teeth, like a whipped boy of three or four who is hauled to the priest of the tribe for a further striping. Then everything went from me, and there was just a blank immobility and a silence in me, like death.

For sitting in the ivory seat, veiled and unmoving and as immediate as the ground, or the air, or my own future, was the sorceress. Was Karrakaz, my mother.

2

I could not make out her face.

I had come this far and through this much, and yet I could not see her.

I stood there, stuck to the spot, and gaped at what I could not see. She spoke to me.

"A last favor, Zervarn. Come no closer."

"I owe you no favor," I said. I swallowed and got it out, "No favor, my mother."

Her voice was like a mist. It floated about in my head rather than in the room, where my own rang and roused echoes.

"What do you want from me?" she said.

I laughed, or I believe I did, some stupid noise that meant nothing.

"Yes, I suppose I must want something, or I should not be

here. Are you alarmed, Mother, to find me here? Your son you imagined safely stowed in the northlands, in the tent of Ettook."

"You wanted at one time to kill me," she said, "but you have become aware, I would hazard, that you cannot kill me. What else is there? There is no love between us, no claim."

All true. I could not kill her, could not avenge my father, no longer meant to try. What questions could I ask her that she would not turn aside with lies? What could I demand from her even? I had grown into my Power, and wealth and kingship I could take, as Ressaven had said. And for Ressaven, I could attempt to make her go with me, and if she would not both of us would lose some part of ourselves, but I could not force her after all. She was not a woman I could simply take. She was as much as I. Thus, in the end, what did I want here before the witch-goddess? Yet I did not turn about to leave.

"I request you to tell me," I said, "what passed between you and my father. I would get it clear, you understand."

"I am willing to show you, in your mind, what passed between Vazkor and Karrakaz. But you will not credit what I show you as being accurate."

"Probably not. But do it. I can judge you, lady; even the falsehoods will reveal events to me you strive to hide."

I knew it meant I must let her further in my brain, but that, of all things, did not trouble me, nor the contact seem distasteful. Let her come in and observe how cunning the apartment was, the glints and fires of a magician's cleverness, that could withstand her, now that I was ready and alert. Let her notice I had done well without her.

She came there. She gave me her history, her time with Vazkor, which had not been long, not even a year, although she bore the scar of it, his cicatrix that he had scored in her emotions as he marked it on the bodies of others.

Despite my own reassessment, it was bitter for me to face the actuality of Vazkor. Most surely not my god or guide. The antithesis of myself. No fervor in him, no greed for life, only his ruthless craving to possess, which took no pleasure in possession. He would have mocked my method of existence; he would have warped me from myself if he could. She did not lie to me, I grasped that in an instant. It was full of the turmoil of her woman's pain, that story, and its rawness proved its authenticity. Yet, he was a man, an emperor, a mage. His genius stirred me then, and to this hour. I wish I could go back across the years to him to find him out. I pity him, my father, who began me in a single spasm of calculated sex. I pity and I revere him.

He had risen from obscurity, the Black Wolf of Ezlann, some city noble's bastard got on a girl of the Dark People, and inveigled his way into the proud ranks of the Gold Masks by means of treachery, violence, and sorcery. He was a magician, self-taught, and he meant to build an empire worthy of his stature. He removed what came in his path. When Karrakaz came there, he used her to create a goddess-figurehead, the curtain that concealed his power-lust and made it possible. He taught her misery, cynicism, and hubris. She would have given him her service from love, if he had asked it, but he left her at length no option but dislike. He had scourged her spirit in his efforts to crush her ego. At the end he had destroyed any of humankind who were dear to her, not to influence her then, but merely because it was expedient. All cloth must be cut to his fit. Me, he put in her like a beast in a stall, both to chain her and to ensure his kingdom. When she would be a warrior he reduced her to a womb, and when she would be a lover he showed her she was a garment hung on the wall for his occasional wearing. Some women are such things, but not Karrakaz. He overreached himself with her, as in all else. Presently his luck turned, his empire tottered, his armies deserted him and the jackals howled about his stronghold. Then came a day when he dealt one final blow to her she would not brook. In her desperation, she found she could outmatch him. Thus, she killed him with Power, as sometime one with Power must have done, as I should have, I believe, if I had lived as his son and he had set such lashes on me as he set on every other. Yes, I should have slain Vazkor, as I had slain Ettook. Indeed, I should have hated Vazkor with a hatred beyond any hate I ever experienced. If she had bowed herself beneath such a yoke as his forever, she could not have been the vessel that fashioned me.

Her magic left her at his death; she did not think she would regain it. She bore me in the tent on Snake's Road, glad to be rid of the last fetter of Vazkor. But she had no enduring gladness; her demons belled at her heels. She had nothing to give any other, even if she had wanted me. So I was her gift to Tathra, which saved my mother (I cannot call her otherwise) from disgrace, ousting, perhaps, a blacker wage. I had been the sword that kept off Ettook's injustice from Tathra for nineteen years. Only her gods know if there was any joy in them for her, but I will hope that there was. She would not have had them if she had not been given the status of a living son.

When I raised my head, my eyes burning and my mind tender from the beating it had got, there was a desert in me, as if the cities of my character had crumbled. For the truths I had sketched for myself so glibly were riveted now upon the wall.

"My thanks for your account," I said to the veiled figure who sat quiet as a stone before me. "I will decide some other day how I am to swallow it. But I admit that if you have wronged me, you also have been wronged. There is an emptiness between us, lady. That is the sum of it."

"Then you will leave here without rancor. And without profitless delay."

"If you wish. But, lady, have you never been curious about me? Did you imagine me dead, or what?"

"For some while I sensed you approach to this place, your search for me. I never realized you would achieve such Power. You are all any mother would desire of her son, a prince among men. And for a sorceress, what better son than a master-sorcerer? But it is too late for kinship."

Her un-voice was melancholy in my skull. I understood she had not spoken with her lips at any time.

I said aloud, "But I have never seen your face. Even in those psychic visions of your past, I never saw it."

"Lellih showed you a face," she said. Then she had read my brain, though I had not essayed hers. No matter. I felt no menace from her, no seeking to undermine me.

"A cat's face, a hag's face. Not yours, surely. Lady," I said, and my throat dried so I mumbled like an old man, "Let me look at you once, and I will leave you."

She did not answer. I waited. She did not answer still.

It was not the fury of a god or the petulance of the child whose parent denies him, it was my tribal upbringing, which would not let me be cheated of my bargain.

She was the goddess Karrakaz, but she was not in that moment quick enough for me. I sent my Power like a gust of winter wind to lift her veiling off her body and her face and cast it aside.

Karrakaz had sat as immobile as a stone, and small surprise. She was a stone. The image of a seated woman made of a pale polished marble, dressed in woman's garments, veiled and fixed in the ivory chair. I had all this while been entreating from a statue. What had hoaxed the mainland folk had made a clod also of me.

What went through me I can hardly say. I was angry, but not hot or from my wits. For the mind-voice of Karrakaz, which could not be any other's but her own, had come from somewhere near.

I did not take a step either way, but I filled my lungs and I shouted, "Where is she? Let her come out. I am done with jokes. There will be death and hell let loose on this mountain if there is one more game played against me. Where is the sorceress?"

"She is here," a woman said at my back. The voice was flesh and blood. It said, "I did not mean to lay this heaviness on you, Zervarn. I intended only to fathom what you were, to draw you, if I could, to an acceptance of me, not as a myth and a vileness, but as a living creature. I loved you from the first; how could I not? You are Vazkor's image, Vazkor that I loved, and very like another, too, a man I knew as Darak. . . . In some strange fashion you also resembled him, as if his seed had lingered in me to help form you. More than these, in you I beheld myself, not the albino Lectorra of the westlands, but a full-fledged magician, a man of my own race born again through me. I did not recognize what the rest should be, but it was some fate on us. And you have lived sufficiently as a mortal and by mortal codes that this will trouble you and make you afraid. I tried, how hard I tried, you remember, deceit on deceit, to keep you from this knowledge. If only you had been obedient in a single thing, you could have gone from here without a weight upon your shoulders."

I recognized the voice and had no necessity to turn, but turn I did, and found her there close enough to take once more in my arms.

"I used my mother's name, in the beginning, to deceive you. The younger Lectorra know me only by that name, and the shore people, for long since I expunged my physical memory from their brains, so they should not cry after me as the goddess I was not. Mazlek, Sollor, Denarl, they know me and who I am, and would have saved you this, as I would."

I went on staring down at her, but I had grown sightless.

I should have reasoned other things before. That the self-renewing flesh of the Lost Ones, which defied blemish or scar, would neither age nor wither. That forty years or more would not therefore mar her skin or body, that she could look nineteen, and did. I should have read her eyes, the likeness between us, her holding off from, her weeping.

My Ressaven. Not my sister. This woman I had loved, this woman I had lain with, was Karrakaz. My mother.

She predicted for me accurately. I had been too long with men to forswear their codes. A sister half my blood was a minor thing to this. In the kiln that had formed me, I had stayed my own appetite. The serpent gnawed upon its own tail.

My manhood shriveled. It seemed to me then that never again could I lie on a woman without the ghost of this speaking its clammy incantation in my loins to make a eunuch of me. It seemed, too, that never again could I walk among the clans of men but that the brand would glare from my forehead. Maybe I had been marked for this from the beginning, for it had come to me suddenly how Chula had railed against me that I lay on Tathra, that perhaps Chula's dirty mouth had been, in that moment, an instrument of prognostication.

This, then, was the gift the sorceress had laid by for me, this atrocity. She had not meant it, no, but she had foreseen. I had wandered in ignorance into the trap.

I left her, and her mountain in the sea. I said no word to her, could not bring myself to exchange words. I ran from that place with no pride, and no capacity for anything.

I did not walk over the ocean to the shore, but attempted to swim and partially drowned myself, and crawled on the land to spew up salt water, trying to spew up my anguish with it.

In these fevered actions I strove to bury the most terrible despair of all. For many months I strove to bury it. She had never been mother to me, would never be. Tathra was my mother, and Karrakaz my enemy once. And now, only a woman. A beautiful woman, world's end, life's heart, those phrases one brings out that never touch the burning certainty within that has no use for phrases. I loved her yet. That was the rock on my back, the felon's mark on my brow. I loved her, my sin and my shame.

3

I went inland and traveled about the towns and cities of the west. Sometimes I healed the sick, but privately. I accumulated no tags of god or wizard; what I did I did from pity, to relieve my guilt, as Gyest had prophesied I would. I could have been thankful for Gyest to talk with in those red-roofed cities. I do not recollect any meetings of note. I had a woman in some town there, who ran after me up the road for three miles. I was still man enough for that sort of trouble after all, despite the burden of my incest.

I never had a single dream of Vazkor. That dark shadow had entirely gone from my side. Shadowfire, the reflection of the flames upon the wall; how little I had anticipated the fire itself.

Of her I never thought. My mind was closed to her. My musings were only of the dark venture we had shared. Here was the strangest part of it, for while the sense of the sin nauseated me, yet I could not, even now, equate her with the sin.

It was the abstract nature of the world that brought her back to me. The sound of waves breaking on a clear cold shore, the moon coming up through a cloud of trees, the silver bird that cries for dawn, the spring, which was flowing over the land at last.

Eventually the tide of the spring had reached the headland where I had slunk to gnaw on nothing. The wild fruit trees in the valley beyond the ruined cot that housed me became surfed with white and green, as they would have become by now in the valleys of the mountain island, and I could not go on with this death of mine that called itself life.

I sought for counsel, which only she could give me, for purpose, which was with her. She and I, the gods knew, if gods knew anything, how long we should continue to exist on this earth. Seasons and empires and centuries might go by, and we remain. She on her island or wherever she might wander, and I who had no race, no home, no country, and no kin, wandering some other road, not hers. Dear God, she was my mother by blood, but I never suckled at her breast, I never grew in her sight. She trained me to nothing; she never knew me, save as a lover returned to her.

I have seen the result of breeding, parent with child, in certain backward sties of villages. They say it makes for imbeciles, for any weakness in such a close relationship is amplified. But she and I had no weakness; if we bred it would be strength adhering to strength. My sons should be also my brothers, but what sons, with Power to ride the skies and run across the seas. Her race begun again, with two to guide it, two without hubris, who had come through the fires and understood their lessoning.

I had never even dreamed a dream of her to bring me comfort.

Five months had sloughed from me, and I had not changed. Only the shame had sunk away. It seemed not to concern me. I had done with it. That onerous millstone on my neck had lost its weight. The incest of Hwenit and Qwef had seemed little in the face of death. And ours, in the face of eternity, how much more little.

I retraced my way to the White Mountain, and saw its peak in the ocean with that awareness of homecoming I never felt before in my days among the tents and towers of humanity. Then, like a child, I thought she would be gone, abandoning her Lectorra brood already, and the ill memory of me, to journey in some disguise even my Power could not unravel.

At that, I understood for sure I must not lose her, for the earth is not the earth without some light to see it by, and she was mine.

Then, looking up, I glimpsed her on the path of the cliff above me, and I can argue no more with what must be.

I need explain nothing to her; she guesses it all. Her wisdom, which her eyes revealed to me in their brilliance, is a calm that stops the mouthing of excuses or falsehoods. Where she stands—the blue sky, the blue mountaintop behind her, the blue mantle about her that leaves bare her white girl's shoulders and the slim, strong arms of her youth—where she stands is the end of this chaos, the horizon of the wilderness, which opens on another land.

I will be judged by none but she. No other knows my life, nor how I have been constrained to live it, nor what I have gleaned, nor what I am entitled to. At the end she is mine, and she will not deny me now, for I am no longer ignorant of the fate that binds us. Seeing her there before me, the final gem in the circlet, I half suppose this road was mapped for both of us, before even we were born.

Worship or deny them, we are all, perhaps, in the hands of the gods.